Leaving Walloon

by

Cheri L. R. Taylor

For Barbara,
 A brilliant writer and one of "the red dress gals"!
 I'm really looking forward to what we create together.
   Love,
   Cheri L. R. Taylor
   Lost Woods Lodge
   Lincoln, MI
       June 7, 2015

copyright (c) 2013
Cheri L. R. Taylor

Cover Art by Fred Tovich
Beach Glass Necklace Courtesy of Holly L'Hommedieu
HL Sea & Beach Glass Jewelry LLC

For RT, thank you for more than 30 years of encouragement, love, support, and so much laughter. You make all the tough things easier.

Acknowledgements:

Writing this book has been a labor of love that was sometimes exhausting beyond words, sometimes a battle and often a sheer wonderment. I want to thank the following people for their support, love and encouragement. You have all contributed to me in ways you may never know, but which have uplifted my heart and made me believe that all dreams are possible:

Randy Roberts, my son, the brightest comet ever to hit this atmosphere, and whose dedication to his own art is a constant inspiration. T. Andrew Caddick, whose questions moved me to publish this book at last, and whose love is the steadying hand whenever I have wavered. Melissa Wilson, Lynne Fiscelli, Michelle James, Lori Volante, the bestest besties a girl could ever have, your love is a constant life jacket. Patti Balint and Stephen E. Gork, for sending me to Walloon, where this book was waiting for me to write it. My grandmother, Irene Roseberry, who taught me the meaning of courage. My brothers, Matthew Hilts and Greg Geisler who know what only we siblings can know. My first writing mentor, Stellasue Lee, who taught me the value of showing up to the page with honesty, even when it takes every ounce of courage I have.

Finally, I want to thank my mother and father for making me who I am.

I have realized that the past and future are real illusions, that they exist in the present, which is what there is and all there is.

—*Alan Watts*

Chapter 1

I was 16 when I fell in love on the soft leafy bank of Walloon Lake. I can remember the exact moment that it happened. Angel Manotti and I were wading in the lapping blue edges of the water, still cold from springtime's passing. We had our blue jeans rolled up as high as they would go, exposing our winter whitened calves. He squatted down, toad-like, to pluck a sparkling piece of beach glass from the shallow place near the big oak tree that stood guardian at the edge of the lake. I'd wandered over to see what he was after and he looked up at me, holding out the treasure in his hand. His rich coffee eyes turned up at the edges in excitement, a smile pressing the dimple in his left cheek, the summer wind giving his hair an affectionate tousle.

The moment hung suspended in my eyes, and though I moved and squatted down beside him and lifted the softly polished glass from his gritty wet palm, all I could see, all my vision could comprehend was that look; the glowing half-boy expression showing on his young-man face.

He kissed me that day. It was the first kiss I'd ever had in my young life. It was 1978 and if my mother had seen it, or known about it, I'd have never had another. Mother didn't approve of Angelo Manotti, his shortened name "Angel" had offended her, his dark Italian looks frightened her. She'd warned me not to be alone with him.

"Men," she told me for the seven hundredth time, "are only after one thing Susannah Suffolk , only one thing, and don't you forget it!" Hearing it in my head, I could practically feel the sting of her hand across my mouth as he leaned in toward it.

But it didn't seem to me that Angel was after anything, and anyway, I didn't care. All I knew was that I felt things when I was with Angel that I felt at no other time and with no other person.

And so, clutching a rounded piece of azure beach glass tightly in my fist, I leaned against the oak tree for support and I let Angel get close to me. He rested a hand on my shoulder, his palm warm on my skin. He ran the palm gently down the length of my arm and tangled his slender fingers in my own.

I shifted nervously when his nose brushed the side of mine. My cheek stung with Mother's imagined blow.

"It's okay Susie-Q." he said so softly that only the oak and I could hear.

His lips were still in the process of a smile when they actually touched mine. I felt his front tooth on my upper lip, smooth, wet, and then his mouth found the kiss.

I closed my eyes.

He tasted sweet, like the cantaloupe juice that ran down my arm in the yard every summer, each supple mouthful sweeter than the last. His kisses were the same, each one a bit longer, a bit wetter, a bit deeper. He held the back of my head in his palm, and I could feel the beach glass getting wet with sweat in my hand. He pushed one leg gently between mine, his knee pressing against the oak, his chest pushing into mine, the length of his body to mine, an unfamiliar hardness against my hip.

It was ten kisses, maybe twelve until we were startled by the sound of a boat across the lake.

I had never before seen a man's eyes filled with that sweet dopey arousal. The kind of eyes that stay half closed even when they stare. I wondered suddenly what my eyes looked like, and the thought made me look away from him, for fear that he could see what was happening to me. Something seemed to be blossoming between my legs, it was a strange swollen feeling, almost like a fat lip, but infinitely nicer. That I liked it was the most frightening feeling of all.

Without looking up, I gently pulled my fingers free and rested my palm on his chest. He leaned in and kissed me on the cheek before stepping away.

I remember clinging to the oak, my head, heart, body spinning and dancing in ways I never knew existed. He held out his hand to me and we walked the entire circle of the lake holding the beach glass between our tightly clasped palms…

As I think of it, that very day was the first of what I came to call Mother's "inspections". I don't think I'd ever fully realized how fearful she was of my sexuality until that moment. I was so lost in my own ecstasy that day, I'd forgotten to be cautious about how I looked. It was always best to come in and head straight for my room, head down, eyes averted. That day, she'd cornered me in the bathroom.

"Take off your clothes Susannah." she said.

"What?"

Her slap across my mouth was so quick I didn't have time to prepare at all.

"Take off your clothes." she demanded again, and then pulled the metal slotted spoon from behind her back.

When Mother was being forceful she had a tendency to stand too close. She'd push her body up against mine, as if to enforce how much bigger than me she was. Today was no exception. She pushed against me with her breasts. I could smell her perfume and hairspray, I could see how she'd smeared the mascara she tried to put on that morning.

I didn't dare ask why, I didn't dare speak at all. I took a small step back, just enough to give me room and stripped everything off, grateful I'd already emptied my bladder.

I held my hands in front of my breasts, in front of my privates. I had no idea what might come next.

"Put your hands down! What are you trying to hide? Where did he touch you?!" She struck out with the spoon at my thigh. The sting was tremendous, and I yelped and dropped my hands. Now I understood, Mother believed she could tell if I had been touched by a boy.

"Turn!" she said and I did, tears now stinging my eyes worse than the welt from the spoon on my thigh. She put her face close to my body, so close that I could feel her breathing on my skin. She'd poke me every now and then with the spoon to get me to turn. She lifted each of my arms above my head, she pushed a heavy hand on my back when she turned me away from her and made me bend over as she examined my bottom.

I imagined myself turning into particles, disintegrating and falling through the tiles in the floor, nothing more than dust.

"If he touches you, I'll know." she jerked me around, her face millimeters from mine. With a final shake, she released me and walked out, leaving the bathroom door open, to make her point that there was nothing I could hold private.

I didn't speak, I knew better, I just gathered up my clothes and shut the bathroom door behind her as gently as I could. If I'd have slammed it, or acted as if I were the least bit angry, she'd have been back for me. She'd have beaten my legs raw with that spoon while I closed my eyes tight and tried to imagine I was somewhere else. I would cover my face and wait it out, imagining my body floating in the water of the lake, imagining that it was the next day, that it was over, that I was already healed.

I'm thinking a lot about Walloon today, and I realize this with a turn of disgust in my stomach. These are thoughts I don't often allow myself. Thoughts of those long rolling Michigan summers spent in the grass there and on Lake Charlevoix at Grand's, and the winters when there was nowhere to be but inside the house. I know that I have to pick up the phone and call Grand now and tell her, but it seems to be more than I can manage to move my hand to the phone.

My assistant, Michelle walks in and sets a cup of coffee on my desk. I am startled, but I have long ago learned to control those kinds of impulses and my body does not move.

"Can I do anything?" she says, the way that people say those words when someone has died.

"Yes, actually" I say to her, "you could get me something hideously sweet to go with this coffee."

She smiles, Michelle my friend, knows of my sweet tooth under pressure.

In another second she is gone and I wish I hadn't sent her anywhere. I pick up the phone and wait for Grand to answer. A sudden tension springs into my chest.

I fight the urge to turn my head, and look behind me, my instinct to begin some kind of apology, to announce some kind of eternal grief to the ether and drop to my knees.

I take a slow deep breath and give in to the urge to turn my head. I am flooded with relief at the sight of the window behind my desk. Below, Woodward Avenue teems with cars. I can smell the faint hint of garlic from the pizza place on the corner.

"Leave me alone." I say aloud, and turn my attention back to the phone.

"What?" Grand's voice says in my ear.

"Grand, it's Susie." and after that my voice fails me. My throat goes tight as if there are fingers clenched tightly around it.

"Susie, what is it?"

My head swims. I force air down my throat.

"Mother is dead." I blurt and hate myself for not being strong enough to break it to her in some gentle way.

"Well…" Grand says and I wish I were there with her, to hold her and set her gently on the sofa. Why in hell hadn't I sent Father Satine over to sit with her first?

"How… how do you know?" she asks and I explain the call from the county office.

"They say it was a heart attack."

" Oh… dear.." she whispers, and then Grand is silent, too silent and I know she is crying.

"I'll be up tomorrow, Grand, I'm so sorry…" my own voice trails away and we cry together. I hate my own helplessness. I hate my own mouth for speaking the words that have hurt her, and I hate Mother for causing her even more pain.

Grand tells me she loves me before she hangs up, making kiss-kiss noises even though she is sniffling and her throat is hitching.

Quick as I can hang up the phone, I call the church. I am vaguely comforted at the thought that there will soon be a veritable battalion of little white-haired church ladies standing on Grand's porch, casseroles and tea cakes in hand.

I dab my eyes and feel another pang of guilt. My tears are for Grand, not for Mother. It has to be the worst of all possible experiences to lose a child. I cannot even let myself imagine what she is feeling. I trace the flower-gilded edge of the frame around Matthew's smiling face with my finger. My son, my only child, I shudder and kiss the picture just for the comfort it brings me.

I had already called Matthew. He had taken the news well, as I expected he would and he was coming home from college to be with us at Walloon. He'd be driving from Ann Arbor in a day or so, and the more that I stare at his picture, the more I wish he were here now.

The skin on my inner arms aches at the thought of him. I can almost feel his infant body in my arms. I can smell the scent of his head. Almost twenty years ago and still it rests around me in memory so vivid, it's as if I can feel my breasts leaking milk.

My chest begins to hitch. There is another call I want to make, a voice I want to hear. I pull out my cell phone and search my contacts to "M". I find the name, and the phone rings in my hand.

I answer, knowing that Michelle is still out hunting me something of the refined sugar species.

"Susannah Suffolk." I say in my best lawyer voice, fighting the shards that are stuck in my throat.

"Hey there Beautiful, how're you doin'?"

At the sound of my brother's voice I begin to weep. He hushes and shushes me, and when all else fails him, he makes me laugh.

"Geeze, I'm glad it makes you so happy to hear from me, Sis.." he says and I can feel his wry side-winding smile through the phone.

"When are you coming up, Rob?" I say, wanting him to tell me that he is already on the road.

"I'm already on the road." he says, and I laugh out loud, and confess my thoughts.

"It's okay, Susie, really…I mean…I think it's for the best what with …everything…you know?" he says this, not wanting to say aloud the things that we are both thinking: That it's good that she is dead. That she was only getting worse, that she was making all our lives miserable and had been ever since we could remember. That she was headed for an institution and was spared it by dying.

I fiddle nervously with my necklace, twisting the gold chain with my fingers and feeling the smooth cool pendant with my thumb.

Susannah, you will RESPECT ME! --mother's voice suddenly rings in my ears.

"How long before you get there?' I ask, hoping he will be there before me. The drive from Ohio would take him 12 hours, he says he is about six hours away and I am happy. It will be bad enough to go back there, but it would have been worse to have to go there alone.

He tells me that he is going straight to Grand's and that he will call her next so she'll expect him. I picture her changing the sheets in the guest room and baking her Walnut Oatmeal Delights, Rob's favorites. She will be making her Infamous Apple Cake in the morning for me. It's good she'll have something to busy her head and her hands until we get there.

Rob says he loves me and I love him too and then he hangs up and I linger listening to the soft fuzzing sound on the phone. And because I'd rather not be here, or thinking of what I have to do next, I let it remind me of the sound of the lake and another day with Angel.

It had been just a day or two after that first dangerous kiss and Angel borrowed his brothers row boat to take me out on the water. I wore my favorite cut off, blue jean shorts, the ones with the fluttering fringe of ragged denim on the edges, the ones that showed just a touch of bottom. They barely passed Mother's inspection, as did my tube top and white button down shirt tied at the waist.

"Stay away from those boys at that rental cabin down the lake!" she'd warned that day, "You know what a gang of boys will do with a young girl if they get her alone!"

I left the house without a word, weary of her sexually assaulting warnings. It was ironic looking back now that she was already giving me the education she so feared they would. I don't know which was worse really, the times when she was vicious and hateful or those rare times when she would sit down with me at the table and look at me with teary, terrified eyes. Those times when droplets of sanity would make her aware of her illness and she would reach out to me, a child, who could only sit there and stare back. I remember my legs going numb from sitting so very still, hoping that I could make the moment stay, but knowing it never would.

Angel met me on the far side of the lake that day, at the peer under the awning of Mrs. Jablet's boat rental booth. He took my hand, excited, full of his manhood as the breeze blew in off the lake with the same kind of gentle swooshing as the empty phone line. He was taking me out on a boat; me the damsel and he the shining knight. I was to sit in comfort as he rowed and sweated in the high sun.

The boat was small and dented and dingy, but we didn't care. We saw nothing that day but each other. We talked. He had dreams, big ones, and he shared them with me, unafraid. He was so different from the men in my family, those uptight, crane-like men with their stiff necks and stuck tongues. I saw them only a few times in my childhood. Only a few holidays before we never went to any more. They spoke of "manly" things; of business, of sports, and when they thought I couldn't hear them, of sex. It was all "tits and the f-word" and I only listened in hopes of learning something about this mystery that my mother so feared and that men so adored. I never did learn anything from them, except maybe that they were not the kind of men I wanted to be around. I wanted a man like Angel.

Angel wanted to build a house. It was a house like nothing I had ever heard of. It was round, as he described it, but the roundness came from an intersecting of straight lines, of triangles.

"Triangles? How can a round house be made out of triangles?" I said, and laughed, thinking he was teasing me.

"It's called a geodesic dome. It's kind of like if you took a round ball and started cutting little triangles off each side." His face went very serious, he stopped rowing and gestured with his hands. He chewed is bottom lip between explanations and his dimple showed every time he started to talk again. I thought my heart would explode.

I'd never heard a boy my age talk about anything like this before. The guys at school wanted to make stupid dirty jokes or ask me what size my bra cups were. Or worse, they wanted to know if I was crazy like my mother. Angel never talked like that.

"Do you see what I mean?" he said, and I didn't and I loved that I didn't, because the more he could see that I could not get a picture of it in my mind, the more passionate his description became. He wanted to share this vision with me, he wanted me to see his dream as clearly as he did.

"I picture it on the east side of the lake, see, over there?" and he pointed to a beautiful spot that had yet to be developed. It had a kind of natural bluff around one side and the adults spoke often of how they'd like to put something on that piece of land.

"If you look, the living room could have a row of windows, right there on the side and you'd get the sunrise over the lake. And in the bedroom there'd be a skylight right over the bed. You'd wake up to the sky every morning and fall asleep to the moon and the stars every night. Wouldn't that be cool?"

I could barely answer. I was too busy imagining what it would be like to wake up every morning in a bed with Angel, and to fall asleep again with him every night. I wondered if I would even see the sky. At that moment I couldn't imagine looking away from him.

After twenty minutes of rowing and talking, Angel looked winded and we steered the tiny boat to the side of the lake, next to the big cabin owned by the wealthy family from Lansing. Grand would shake her head and say what a shame it was that such a beautiful cabin sat empty for so much of the year. She was right of course, because it was expansive and the front porch alone took up yards and yards. It was big enough to hold parties on, which they did during the two or three weeks a year that they actually made it up there.

We pulled the boat onto the sandy embankment and we ran up along the side of the big cabin. Angel had a spark in his eye and he pulled my reluctant hand all the way to the front door. I was squirming, pulling with all my might and laughing, trying to get off the porch of the rich people!! What if their butler came out and saw us here?! To my further horror, he shushed me and reached into the potted plant on the porch and produced a gold colored key.

"Angel!" I cried, "No!"

"It's okay," he said, "I water their plants for them, they pay me fifty bucks every summer since I was twelve!"

He led me inside the most beautiful home I had ever seen. The great room was tall, the ceiling seemed like sky, and our footsteps echoed up into it like ascending geese. The floors were polished to a glaze and the whole place smelled of cedar and some sharp smelling kind of spice. Small carpets tossed about were fluffy white and pristine. An overstuffed sofa sat beneath a window covered with an amber curtain. The sunlight through it cast a pink glow into the room. A fireplace big enough to contain our living room sofa, sprawled across the far wall, stuffed deer heads stared blankly out from the space above.

Angel took me through the entire house. It all struck me as being so soft, and comfortable. So this was what having money meant. It was white carpets instead of fading braided toss rugs. It was a refrigerator stocked with food that no one would eat, a case of soda in the bottom, a dining table that could seat a convention, a hammock strung in a room full of books, a pink room full of toys for a little girl who would only play with them for three weeks a year, and then outgrow them before her next visit.

It was the biggest four poster bed I had ever seen, with a hand made quilt that I knew the woman who owned this house did not make with her hands.

As we neared the bedroom it seemed like our footsteps became louder. The floor began to groan beneath our feet.

We stood awkwardly, looking at the serene paintings, the dresser top full of expensive perfumes, the armoire in the corner.

He shuffled to the edge of the bed and sat down tentatively.

"Come on, sit with me." he said and showed me his dimple.

Men, Susannah Suffolk are only after one thing!

It was as if Mother was in the room with us, standing just behind me, glaring at Angel over my shoulder.

I hesitated, clinging to the wall, backing against it just a little, and wishing it were the oak. This room seemed smaller all of a sudden, the walls seemed to have stepped in.

"Susie..." he said

I went to him slowly. I took small deliberate steps, hearing mother in my head.

One Thing!!! she was shouting over and over again. I pictured myself naked in the bathroom, Mother swinging the spoon. . .

Angel held his hand out to me. He gathered me to him as soon as he could reach me, wrapping his eager arms around me, his biceps emerging from beneath the sleeves of his t-shirt. He sat me on the bed beside him and with one arm around my waist he started to kiss me. He lingered with his lips just millimeters from mine. I breathed in as he exhaled, breathing his breath, tasting it. He licked his lips and I licked mine in imitation. My chest began to feel tight. Why was he waiting? I didn't understand. All I knew was that with every second that he hovered there with his lips so close to me, I was feeling more and more swollen between my legs. Soon, I started to go cold in my chest, anticipation and fear and arousal stealing the air from my lungs and tripping my heart into fast, unpatterned beats.

When he finally pressed in to me, I startled with the feeling of it, the open loose feel of his upper lip finally contacting my mouth made something in my stomach twist in on itself. I felt a kind of shiver that traveled from that swollen place into my chest. It somehow stole my regular voice and I made a high pitched kind of sound. The sound I made, and the fact that I was starting to shake seemed to move him and he lifted me by my hips and laid me on my back. He lowered himself onto me quickly, kissing me faster and harder.

I couldn't breathe, I couldn't see. I didn't want to. The world had tossed itself inside of Angel's mouth and I went with it.

I felt him relax the muscles in his legs. He had been over me and on me, but tense, and now I felt the full pressure of his weight on my body, the hard spot pushing into my thigh this time.

Suddenly, between Angel's lips, between my teeth, I felt a warm, wetter sensation. For a startled moment, I couldn't figure out what it was. It swirled inside my mouth, soft and wet, exploring me, rushing across my lower teeth, sliding between my lip and my upper teeth and finally it seemed to be hunting for something. It was then that I knew, it was Angel's tongue, the one he had shared his dreams with me upon, and now that I knew what it was, I wanted it.

I took a feeble poke, and Angel held his tongue still and let me. I ventured again, this time sliding it over and under his just slightly and hearing a sound come from his throat. I lapped at him, danced my tongue in and around and over his, I enticed him further into my mouth with it. I felt the sudden, new, heady rush of sexual power as the spot on my thigh was pressed even harder and as Angel's arms began to shake. My tongue seemed to have freed my hands as well and I found that they were pulling at him, running over and inside his sleeves, down his arms, over his head, into his hair, that thick, wavy, jet-black hair that my fingers could disappear into.

Angel's hands became free as well, and they ran down my neck and over my shoulders and finally, he stopped and pulled his mouth from mine. I cried out in protest, I felt as if he had severed my line to the top of the ocean. I reached for him, and saw something in his eyes that had not been there two days before. That altered, sleepy arousal was joined by a fire, a hungry dilated pupil. It frightened me in the most delicious way.

It was the same feeling that I got at the top of the snow covered hills at Boyne; that moment, just before I went plunging down on borrowed skis, the feeling that I could be hurt or die, the anticipation of impending speed, of snow snapping at my face, the rush of trees flying dangerously past.

"I want you, Susannah." he said to me, " I love you and I want you. I want to touch you."

I gulped air in to my throat sufficient enough to give me voice.

"I'm not ready…" I said.

He hung his head a moment, composing himself.

"It's okay," he said, "but can I just touch you? I'll stop any time you say, I promise, Susie. I really want to touch you, please let me touch you—and I want you touch me."

His voice, it was different than I'd ever heard it. He wasn't "just after one thing", Angel was after everything, all of me, and I knew it in that moment. I knew when he rested himself on his hip and ran his fingers through my hair, over my forehead, my cheek, his thumb brushing over my lower lip. He continued down my neck, tipping his head to the side, studying me, following his hand as it met my shoulder and finally as it rested upon my breast.

"Oh, God, Susie.." he said, "You're so beautiful…"

His hand rested there, cupping me, holding my breast in his hand as if to comfort me. He began to caress it, and he kissed me again, and his tongue pushed into my mouth again, searching me, and I slid my hand under his t-shirt and across the prickly hairs on his stomach, I felt myself becoming braver and braver with each caress, running my hand lower and lower toward his waistband, the hair getting thicker and denser as I did. In a minute he had unbuttoned my blouse and pulled my arms out of it, leaving my midriff bare, the tube top showing my nipples underneath, hard as rubies. He ran his hand over both of them, caressing them, lingering at the nipples and even holding them between his thumb and forefinger through the elastic top. He began to tug at the fluted part on the top, pulling it downward. I caught his hand, but only for a second as he stopped and looked into my eyes, seeking permission. I became drunk with sexual power, drunk with sexual arousal and I propped myself on my elbows, reaching over with my hands on either side and pulling the top down myself.

"Uuuunnngh" went Angel, and we both watched as he reached out to touch my breasts, his dark hands a stark contrast against the cameo white of my breasts and the rosy pink nipples. He caressed, he cupped and finally he kissed. He kissed me on my breasts, both of them, all the way around my nipples, all the way around each one. I had never imagined a man kissing me on my breasts. I never knew a man would do such a thing. I arched my back with the feeling and he laid me down again. He kissed closer and closer and finally he took the nipple in his mouth. His tongue stroked it, he opened his mouth and licked it outright, and the swelling between my legs seemed to burst into the rest of my body, I shook with it, not realizing that he had placed his hand there, right there at the swollen part and he had been rubbing me. I felt the rubbing now and I pushed against it and rocked my hips in rhythm with it, and I found Angel's swollen place and I rubbed it, and Angel sucked hard on my nipple as we came together.

The world turned in again and again upon us, it disappeared and reappeared and the sun sped around it and burst out from me into Angel's mouth and out from his swollen place leaving us both panting and breathless and wet. Angel's dark hair glistened with sweat as he rested his head on my chest, between my breasts as we clung to each other. We kissed and kissed until we noticed that the sun had returned to the sky, and the earth had righted itself and evening was about to fall.

That night, as Mother inspected me in the living room, I didn't care. As I swallowed the embarrassment, I realized that while I was touching Angel, I didn't think of Mother, that this life and this house melted away to nothing when Angel pushed his tongue inside my mouth.

I can't think of Walloon without thinking of Angel. Mother is always there, but Angel was all the sunny places in the rainstorm of my younger years. If I had happy childhood memories, they did not begin until Angel came into my life.

Michelle dashes suddenly through the doorway and places a box of Krispy Kreme donuts on my desk. I decide at this moment that she is getting a raise, and she winks at me and nods as she snitches one from the box and then leaves me alone with my racing head. I lift a pillowy round donut and take the biggest bite I can manage. The sweet pastry fills my entire mouth, practically choking me, practically encumbering me from chewing entirely. I let it melt there a moment, feeling the saliva pool around it. I sigh heavily and decide that I am putting Mr. "Krispy Kreme" whoever he is, in my will.

When the taste of it has begun to satiate me, I pull three bulging file folders from my brief case, holding the donut in my mouth, and spread the first one open on my desk. These are my three current cases, which would all have to be put on hold for three or four days while I get my family business in order. I try to be happy to be getting a break from the law for a few days, but it isn't easy kidding myself. I would much rather stay here, let the county coroner's office cremate Mother's remains and then bury them deep somewhere far away from me where I would never have to think of them again. I can hear her ranting in my head just at the thought of it.

Susannah, you will respect me, I am your Mother!

She always said it as if it were some kind of deity, like the word "Mother" gave her some kind of all-knowing all-seeing all-important power. I shake her voice from my head and sigh again with something like relief as the pastry continues to melt on my tongue.

I shuffle through paper work and I make phone calls to my clients. They are kind and amiable and they all offer condolences and words of comfort. Powdered sugar dusts the files as I make notes of my conversations with them. I thank them and assure them that I am fine and that flowers are not necessary, but if they would like to make a contribution to the charity of their choice in the name of my Grandmother, that would be lovely. I give them Grand's name, not Mother's. I will not have her remembered by an act of kindness.

I hear Michelle's voice in the next room. She is accepting a delivery and I will the feeling of anxiousness from my head. Overhearing things was never good at Walloon. Too many nights I sat outside the closed door of Rob's bedroom as Mother read him endless Bible verses until all hours of the night. It was a sickening sound, Mother droning endlessly, and knowing the smack of the belt was waking Rob each time he drifted off. I remember walking to the bus stop with him one summer morning, a bright red belt mark across his neck where she'd swung and missed his arm. Fury fills me at the memory, my hands begin to shake. Awash with shame, I find myself hoping her death was painful. I try to smile and shake it off as Michelle comes in and places a Fed Ex envelope on my desk. She hesitates and frowns at me.

"You look really pale." she says and puts her hands to her chest.

"I'm okay."

I hear the words coming from my mouth just like they always did, just like Rob always did. No matter what injuries we sported, when we were asked, the answer was, " I'm okay."

We got very good at : "I fell down."and "walked into the door wall." as well.

"Do you want me to hang out in here while you finish up?"

"No thanks." I manage another weak smile."I'm fine, really.. I'll be okay."

"Well, you know where to find me!" I notice she leaves the door open a crack behind her.

It is then that I come to the Williams file. My stomach tightens. This case has had me in varying states of fury and helplessness since it began. As I stare at her name on the file, I picture Hannah Williams, 9 years old, clinging to her aunt in the child protection office as if her life depended on it. Sadly, it did.

Emmett Walker down at Child Protective Services had called me that day. He knew I'd take the case. I did a lot of pro-bono work for CPS.

"Susannah, we need you." he'd said in such a leaden tone, that my heart sank, " Nine year old girl. She's beat up, she's terrified, but she's beggin' to go home."

"Is there family willing to take her?" Please, let there be family.

"An aunt, but—"

When his voice trailed off, I knew the rest of the story. The aunt would be young, in her twenties I'd guess, likely living with a boyfriend and not making much money. She'd not have any other kids and she'd have had past problems with drugs or alcohol—or a record.

"Dammit." I said "I'll be there in an hour."

When I arrived at CPS that day the workers had that look in their eyes. There was something Emmett hadn't told me. I could almost guess.

"What is it?" I said before I could even sit down in his office.

"There was a sibling." He said.

"Was?"

Alex looked down at his desk and shook his head. He handed me the report. Ten years ago, Hannah had a brother. I was looking at a coroners report. It was a blunt head trauma to a three year old boy. CPS had suspected the mother, Alice, but there was no evidence. The story she gave was credible, the boy had slipped on ice and hit his head, and the father corroborated the story. But the boy had other bruises, old bruises, and the x-rays had shown broken bones never set and healed over.

At the hearing, Alice Williams had ringing endorsements from family members, and even a few local celebrities. It swung the jury and she was acquitted. Apparently, it didn't take Alice long to have another baby, and poor Hannah was born into the cycle. There was nothing to stop abusers from having more children.

"Can I see her?" I asked, and Emmett nodded. My chest went alternately cold and hot as I went up the hallway to the Quiet Room. These children were always a shock. I'd been down this hallway hundreds of times by then, but the children were simply always harder to look at than I anticipated. Every time I met one, I felt the urge to apologize for the hand that life had so cruelly dealt them. I felt as if I somehow should've been there to stop it from happening, to hold them in my arms, to make sure that the adults in their lives knew what treasures they were. Children were not toys, they were not status symbols, they were not a means by which to get more money from the welfare system. I couldn't see how any adult did not understand these things. I couldn't see how my own mother never understood these things.

When I opened the door, Hannah startled and jumped to cling to her aunt's arm. I had to keep myself from gasping at the sight of her. I clasped my hands in front of me to keep them from shaking. Hannah's eyes were both blackened, her lip was swollen and looked as if would bleed again if she spoke. There were scratches on her forearms and marks that looked like they could've been burns. I swallowed a hot lump down my throat and took off my shoes and jacket before I stepped in. I didn't want to frighten her even a little bit.

The aunt held out her hand.

"I'm Amy Braken, Hannah's aunt, are you the attorney?"

I told her I was and introduced myself. Then I knelt down, not too close, to introduce myself to Hannah.

"Hello, Hannah" I said "I'm Susannah. I'm here to help you."

She looked at me with cautious eyes. I recognized those eyes; they were mine. She sized me up and then she said, "If you don't take me home, my momma will be mad."

I fought tears, fought my urge to lift her into my arms and run off with her.

"Does your momma get mad a lot?" I said.

She stared at me.

"Well, my Mom used to get mad a lot and sometimes, she'd get so mad that she lost her temper. I know she didn't mean to, but there was no one to help her with her temper, so sometimes I got hurt. Is that what happened to you?"

"How did you get hurt?" she asked, and I could feel those steely little eyes sizing me up still.

This girl was no fool. She'd know an authentic story. I looked into her she was way too old behind those eyes.

"Well," I said and settled myself into a cross-legged position on the floor, "sometimes she hit me with a big metal spoon from the kitchen. Sometimes she threw things, sometimes they hit me, too."

I felt tears welling in my eyes and I tried hard to stop them. It was as if I was in confession. I had to look away from Hannah for fear she'd see. This wasn't the first time I'd spoken to the children about my own experience, but there was something about this girl. Maybe it was her age, maybe that her hair was cut so much like mine was at 9. I swallowed a couple of times and tried to continue.

"Sometimes I didn't get to eat lunch or dinner. Sometimes she'd make a lot of noise banging things in the kitchen and then she'd pull me in there and—"

Suddenly, Hannah Williams stepped forward and put her arms around my neck. Her little hand patted my back, and I felt the entire world come down on my shoulders. This little wounded creature, taken from her home, beaten and bled, unsure of what her life would be for even the next five minutes, this child who likely has never known comfort, was comforting me.

I felt a sob escape before I pulled myself back into lawyer mode. I held her and rocked her back and forth and when she leaned back to look at my face, I promised her that no one would ever hurt her again.

"Hannah, how would you like to live with your Aunt Amy?"

Of course, now that I had promised her protection from her mother, I had to find a way to make that happen which did not involve Hannah being shuffled from children's centers or foster homes for the rest of her childhood.

Aunt Amy's story was just as I'd thought. She was 23, living with her boyfriend, an out of work construction worker/bass player named Roofus, and she had two DUI's on her record. Worst of all, she worked at a place called The Landing Strip, where the waitresses served topless. Upon hearing that news I had laid my head on Emmett's desk

"Ohhhh Emmett, this is bad."

"Yep, sure is." he said and I heard him open his desk drawer, the one he kept the scotch in. Emmett only poured scotch when things were very grim.

"We'll have to get her another job." I said into the desk.

"And prove that Hannah did not jump out of the family car as it was pulling out of the drive way." Emmett said and screwed the cap back on the bottle.

"Oh GAWD, that's the story?!" I felt my heart sink. It was a good story, a believable story, a story that could result in any number of injuries.

"Well, lets get her x-rayed and have the psychologists talk to her and—"

"The usual." Emmett said, and smiled at me.

I have a tendency to talk the process out loud when I'm overwhelmed. Emmett has come to know this. I could see it in his eyes when he passed me the glass. He had nice eyes, kind gray eyes with large expressive pupils.

"The boyfriend might have to move out." Emmett said.

"I'll file the protective order and the injunction for temporary custody tomorrow. Has she had dinner?" It was a ridiculous question. Of course she'd had dinner. CPS had seen to it that she was fed and clothed and they'd even managed a room for her to stay in with Aunt Amy at their group home.

"Susannah. . ." Emmett said softly, and I swallowed down another lump with a mouthful of scotch.

Three months had since passed. We'd managed to keep Hannah in her Aunt Amy's temporary custody, but we were still pushing the judge to keep it that way. No matter the evidence, there still seems such reluctance to take a child away. To our favor, Hannah's x-ray's show healed over broken bones, just as her brother's did, and we have a teacher from her school wiling to testify. Still, Alice Williams is an upstanding citizen, a vice president at Alltoll Bank and a member of dozens of community clubs and programs. The family lives in Bloomfield Hills. They drive a BMW. The father is a voiceless businessman who runs his own brokerage firm. These people have it all, and an attitude of impunity. They threw money at their problems and those problems had a tendency to disappear.

These are the kind of parents I despise the most; the one's that put up such a perfect face. The barely-twenty-year-old crack addicted mothers from Detroit at least had their own problems to deal with, the forty year old divorcee on welfare in the Ypsilanti trailer park had her own desperation pushing her, the hopelessness of her own life bearing down into her hands as she rose the belt into the air. I'm not saying the privileged don't have pressures of their own, it's just they always fight the hardest for the illusion. It takes hours of questioning and days of trial to get them to crack and sometimes they never do. It's amazing how self-righteous a few dollars can make a person.

I pick up the phone and dial Emmett.

"Emmett Walker."

"Emmett, it's Susannah, I have to tell you something, but I don't want you to say any of the things that people say when someone tells them this thing that I have to tell you." I hear myself say this, and I cringe.

"Uh…okay…" he says.

"My mother died. I'm going to have to go up north and make arrangements and clean out the house and have her buried. I am putting my cases on hold except for Hannah's and I want you to keep me posted while I'm away."

There is a pause on the other end of the phone.

"Well," he says at length "justice at last."

I am stunned into a momentary silence. I feel the back of my throat tightening again, my eyes getting hot.

"God, Emmett," I finally manage "thank you."

"It's not the greatest time for you to be away. I know you have to, but Judge Hartaway is getting really antsy to wrap this up. I got a call from her clerk yesterday asking me if we were ready to submit the papers on Aunt Amy."

"Dammit! Did she find another job yet?"

"Oddly enough, topless waitress experience doesn't seem to be a real winner on a resume. She's had six interviews, five turn downs and one proposal—and not for marriage."

My head spins. I know I have resources for such things, but my mind seems anchored to some blank place that won't let me produce the necessary information.

"Stall Hartaway's office. Tell them Amy's birth certificate was lost in transit and we can't get copies 'til Monday. I'll see if I can think of something between now and then."

"Right. I'll call Joan over at the unemployment office and ask her to grab me some unpublished postings." he says.

"Great Emmett, thanks." I hesitate.

"Finish it up for yourself, Susannah. Go up there and finish it. It's time." he says and my breath catches in my chest.

"You have my cell, right?" I manage after far too long a minute.

"And you have mine." And I know he means for more than just the case, if need be.

After the last phone call is made and the rest of my paperwork signed and ready, I pop the last bite of a chocolate donut into my mouth, and begin packing up my bags to take home. I always seem to have several bags with me wherever I go. Legal forms, files, books, my make-up case, wallet, check book, business cards, aspirins, a brush, a bottle of water, a protein bar, dental floss…it just never all seems to fit in one bag. I keep buying bigger ones, and I keep outgrowing them.

I wonder if this says something about my mental state, this insistence upon bringing my home with me wherever I go.

Michelle's voice buzzes into the air from the intercom.

"Are you taking client calls?" she asks, already knowing the answer.

"No, and you don't have to keep checking up on me Sweetie, I'm fine." I say, feeling my heart swell a little. It's nice to be in the presence of someone who cares for me.

I hear her laugh and then the snap of the intercom disconnecting. I look around at my office with the odd feeling that I am somehow leaving it forever; the gray painted walls, the recessed shelf lit from beneath, the pottery pieces I bought in Mexico. I pause in front of my favorite painting, swirling with color and activity. I run my palm over the backs of the round, sleek chairs and the sparse looking table, it's concrete slab and metal legs. I feel as if I am saying goodbye. I don't want to leave this room so far away from Walloon and Mother and all the quicksand of that former life. I heave out another sigh, I know I am stalling and that I should be going home to pack.

I lift my bags and heft them into the outer office. Michelle takes one from me in spite of my objections and walks me to the car. She hugs me as I am about to get in, and I feel myself going stiff. It makes me feel awkward and outside my own skin. I don't like to be touched by women. I do my best to hug her back and I even close my eyes for a second and let her hold me, and I manage to let myself to feel comforted by it until she says, "I love you, let me know if you need anything."

    I pull away from her a little too abruptly and thank her and pat her arm as I dive into my car and shut the door. "Thank goodness she knows me well, and thank goodness she loves me." I think to myself, as I watch her disappear in the rearview, waving and dabbing at her eyes with a piece of tissue, her smile never fading.

The shadow is what we think of it; the tree is the real thing.
   --Abraham Lincoln

Chapter 2

I love the city. I love to feel the blast of cars flying past me on the streets, the busy hustle of shoppers and foot commuters and bicycles, its constant and ever changing activity, the life all around me. A million faces, a million bodies, the infinite possibilities. I love the buildings; glass and chrome dignitaries, reigning benevolently above the city, sheltering the business makers, peering beyond the skyline. I love Saks and Neiman Marcus and Nordstrom's, the gleaming counters filled with delightful scent and over priced make-up, tended by sales girls who look down their noses at me and deign to attend me if they have nothing better to do. I love the lights at night. The shining, beckoning lights that call to me, begging me to come out and play, to dance, to drink, to be in the middle of the pulse of what makes people feel alive.

I am getting a dose of my city as I walk from the parking structure to my apartment. A woman walking two tiny dogs on two tiny leashes walks past me. Her watchband matches the leashes and collars, her lipstick is the exact same shade. I can smell cappuccino drifting toward me from Starbucks, just a few doors down. The sales girl of the moment at the boutique across the street is out front, leaning apathetically against the glass and smoking. Two small rumpled men with canes walk side by side stopping to comment loudly in Yiddish about the prices in the windows. I soak in every sight and sound and take them inside with me.

It had taken me a while to find an apartment here in Birmingham, Michigan. Much like my office, it is a space uniquely mine. Each piece of furniture, each painting, chair, and rug of my very own liking and for no one else. I dance through the front door and close it behind me, my bastion against the beckoning north, the trip to come.

The clock says 3:30, and Chipmunk rushes me as I drop my bags. She is purring madly and rubbing my legs with her face over and over again, her white and brown dappled tail fanning proudly behind her. I fight a funny lump in my throat upon seeing her.

"Baby…" I say, and bend down to stroke her, gratified as she "talks" back to me.

We make our snuggling way to the kitchen and I feed her some tuna and get myself a glass of wine. Falling into the sofa, I pull the clip from my hair, letting it pour over the arm behind me. There is silence in the room and I cherish it. There was never silence at Walloon.

My skin begins to prickle at the thought of it. When mother wasn't raging or smashing the flowerpots, beating a pan on the counter, or weeping, there was the lake. The sound of the lake itself wouldn't have been so bad, but it would forever be a talisman of Mother. If I could hear the lake from my bedroom window, trouble was about to happen. Something awful would be in the air, and it would be coming for me. Mother was only quiet when she was planning something.

I close my eyes and I can hear her coming toward my bedroom door, calling my name sweetly. I remember feeling as if my heart were getting larger in my chest with every beat. She called me again, her voice so gentle, it made the hair on my arms stand up. I stepped toward the door, knowing I should go out the window instead, knowing in my deepest heart of hearts that I shouldn't. I cracked it open the tiniest bit, and jumped back just in time to get out of its way as it flew back toward my face. She stood on the other side for only a second before she lunged for my hair, yanking great handfuls of it and pulling me down the hallway to Rob's bedroom. It felt as if it would all come out in bloody chunks.

"Do you see what you've made your brother do?!" she shouted at me, pulling the magazines out from under Rob's mattress and waving them under my nose, a big breasted model looking at me demurely from the open pages.

"What?!?" I cried, feeling the searing pain of hairs being pulled at the back of my head as she held me there like a cat, by the scruff of my neck, "I didn't do anything!" I shouted.

"Well, what do you think it does to a young man to have a half naked girl running around the house all the time, hmmm?!" she said, throwing me onto the bed.

I was 14, and I didn't understand any of it. I knew that Rob, at 17, had magazines under his mattress and I knew he looked at them and I had a vague idea of what they were but I certainly never thought it had anything to do with me.

Rob dashed into the room just then and stood in front of me. He snatched the magazine from Mother's hand.

"It's not your fault, Robert." she said to him, at once eerily calm. "She's a slut, a whore and it influences you. You're a man, you can't help it, you're sick," she said and she stroked his face with her hand and walked serenely out of the room, counting the beads on the rosary she kept always around her neck.

Rob sat down beside me on the bed and I numbly righted myself, pulling my Hardy Boy's t-shirt down to cover my exposed belly, and running my hand over the back of my stinging head.

By 14 I rarely cried any more. Rob and I did not speak. The lake rushed in and out of our ears through the open window, and when I could find my legs again, I stood uneasily upon them and walked to the doorway.

"Suse.." Rob called to me.

I turned to look at him, pale and disgusted.

"You're not a whore," he said.

I sit up from the sofa a little too abruptly and knock over my wine glass onto my beige carpet.

"Dammit!!" I yell and dash for the kitchen. I snatch a tea towel from the rack and run back to the carpet to blot the stain up. I am mesmerized by the way the red of the wine seeps up into the wicks of terry cloth. I feel suddenly sick, remembering again, more.

The day Rob turned 16, Mother had decided he was a man. She'd called him from bed that morning yelling the words "Get up, Man." until we both stumbled out of our bed rooms bleary eyed, hoping we were hearing her wrong.

"A man doesn't sleep late on weekends," she said and slapped him hard before he even had a chance to really get his eyes open.

Rob had gotten good at blocking even Mother's quickest shots, so it had been a long time since he'd gotten one full force in the face.

I put my hands over my mouth to stop from gasping. It was one of those moments when something changes. A moment when the air becomes charged with a kind of energy, and there is never anything that can turn it back the other way. Rob had had enough; he turned as if he were going to head back to his room and then, just as suddenly, he turned back around.

Before I could stop him, he lunged forward and grabbed both Mother's hands by the wrists.

"You know something, you're right," he said into her horrified face. "I am a man now, and there is something you should know."

I shook my head no, no, no at him from across the room, but he didn't stop. I thought my heart would pop out from beneath my pajamas.

Rob held Mother's wrists up high, higher than her shoulders. He was taller than her by almost a full foot by now, and he'd become more vocal about her attacks. In essence, Rob had started fighting back.

"I am stronger than you are now. Bigger and stronger, and you better start thinking of that whenever you decide that you are going to start with me, Mother, because from now on if you hit me, I am going to hit you back."

He punctuated the words with a jerk of her hands and shove. He pushed her away from him. It was a good hard push and Mother toppled backward into the hallway wall. It hadn't hurt her, just set her off balance and with that, Rob went back into his room and closed the door.

Mother stood against the wall looking as if she had seen Satan himself. She stared at Rob's closed bedroom door until I couldn't stand another minute and moved as silently as I could into my own room.

A few hours later Rob and I both emerged again only to find Mother in her bedroom. I peeked in. She was on her knees by her bedside saying rosaries.

We didn't speak, knowing as we did that Mother was safest was when she was praying. The day passed. Rob and I walked to Grand's, where we had birthday cake, and Grand and I gave Rob his presents. We came home to quiet, and we went to bed that night thanking our lucky stars that the day had passed. Special occasions tended to make Mother worse, tended to push her beyond previous limits. Somehow, we both surmised, Rob's assertion of power had taken her down, pushed her off her power. I went to bed actually thinking that this could be the start of a real change. Perhaps if Mother were just slightly afraid of Rob, she'd think twice before doing those things she did.

It was a sickening sound that woke me that night; a cross between a clang and a thud and Rob's voice, something like a scream and a sob all at once.

I was out of my bed and into Rob's room in what felt like one step. A ringing "clannng" stopped me, and I threw my hands over my head out of instinct. I opened my eyes to see Mother swinging a shovel over her head, whacking the head board of Robs bed, swing after swing. The first one had got him in his sleep. His head was bleeding badly, and she swung again, catching his hand between the edge of the shovel and the bed. Rob cried out again and I knew it was my turn to do something.

"Mother! STOP!" I screamed as hard as I could with no effect. "Mother, STOP IT!"

I pulled at her arms, tried to tug her around the waist, but I was small at 13, and simply did not have the strength. Finally, I did the only thing left. I dashed in between them. It was the first of what would become many times.

She swung for him again, and then looked startled into my face.

"Mother" I said as quietly and gently as I could, "you need to stop that now."

"Don't you tell me—" she said, and I saw my error quickly.

"Mother, would you like to read us some verses? We've been sinning, Mother, we have, and if you read us some verses, we'll be saved. You want to save us don't you, Mother. Mom? Momma?"

Her expression fell. She looked at me as if she had never seen me before in her life. I took the momentary pause to cover Rob even more fully. I stepped up on to the bed where Rob was now in the fetal position against the headboard. I stood dead in front of him, my calves backed up against the heat of his body.

"Mother, we'd really like to hear some Bible verses. Would you read us some verses, Mama, please?" I said as softly as I could manage while my chest was pounding.

She looked at me blankly. Then she dropped the shovel and wandered off into the living room to pull her Bible from the shelf.

I dove down to Rob who seemed momentarily unable to uncurl himself enough to even let me see his wounds. I don't think I've ever seen that much blood. The bed was soaked with it, Robs face was covered, his hand looked mangled. Blood ran down to his wrist in deep red rivulets, a purple lump had swollen up on the back of his arm.

I pulled the pillowcase off and pressed it against the wound on Rob's head. It was a gash, about four inches long and I couldn't tell how deep.

Rob lurched forward suddenly and shoved me out of the way. He bent his body over the side of his bed and threw up. He wretched over and over while I tried to keep the pillowcase pressed to his head.

When he finally stopped, he sat back against the pillow and looked at me. His eyes seemed to disappear and reappear and his breathing was more like panting.

Mother's voice startled us both. She had chosen a verse and begun reading from her chair in the living room.

I took the opportunity to lift Rob's hand to the pillowcase and press it down and then to dash for the phone. I had to be quiet, I knew I had to be. Fast and quiet, cause if she heard, she'd beat me to a pulp before anyone could even pick up at the other end.

I called Grand. My heart wanted the EMS, I knew it was what he needed, but it was an unwritten law. Mother had warned us of the dangers of "taken away children", how they wound up raped and prostituted, how they woke in foreign sweat shops and white slavery rings.

It took what seemed a long time for Grand to answer. Being that it was roughly 2 a.m., I knew she'd be startled awake and have to take a moment to right herself before she got to the phone.

"Hello?!" her voice, at last, the best sound the universe had ever created.

"Grand, help. It's Rob, it's bad, he has to go to the hospital."

It was all I could get out before Mother stopped reading. She'd heard. I hung up the phone as quietly as I could and grabbed a bag of frozen peas from the fridge and a towel from the counter to take back into Rob. It's funny how much a child learns about treating wounds when there's been no one around to treat them.

Just those few minutes away and he'd passed out. His hand had fallen from the pillowcase and now his face was obscured by the rush of blood. I sobbed out loud, one single sob that was all I could allow myself in case Mother heard.

I dashed back to his side and pressed the towel to the wound. I placed the peas on top of it and held my breath. It would take Grand 15 minutes at the very least.

"Rob. Rob wake up." I said, as loudly as I could without disturbing Mother.

Her voice rang into the room.

"Thou shalt not steal, thou shalt not murder. . ."

I felt my stomach coming up and fought it back. Rob's hand was bleeding badly too and I hadn't brought anything to help it. I grabbed the sheet and folded as much of it as I could with one hand and pressed it down beneath my knee. Two hands on his head, my knee on his hand, pressing with all I had. Keep the blood in. It was all I could think. Keep the blood in.

"Please, Rob, please wake up." My whole body was taken with heat. What if he died? "What if you die, Rob? Please don't die, Rob, please. . ."

His head had lolled over to one side and his face had gone the palest shade of human flesh I'd ever seen.

Mother read on through the commandments as I waited and strained to hear the sound of Grand's car in the driveway.

It seemed hours. Rob would twitch and moan every once in a while and try to open his eyes but he never fully came to. The first time he did it, I started to cry so hard, I couldn't breathe. It meant he was alive. He was alive. Mother couldn't take him from me. He'd moan, and thrash now and then and when Rob would make sound, Mother would get louder in her reading.

Finally Grand was at the back door, she let herself in and we bundled Rob in the quilt and between the two of us, we managed to get him out to her car. Mother just kept reading, reading... louder and louder.

On the way out of the bedroom, I glanced back at the vomit on the floor. I couldn't stop staring at it. It was bright blue, the same color as the frosting on Rob's birthday cake.

I sit up from the sofa and wipe mascara from my face with the back of my hand. I sit for just a moment before I turn on the television. I like sitcoms. I tape them and save them for when I am in need of non-interactive company. It allows me great freedom, and there is laughter. There is life and tragedy, but always laughter. I slide in my favorite and let the characters chatter as I pull my suitcase out of the closet. It hits the floor with a thud that makes me jump. I try to shake off the jitter and listen to the television as I place underwear and jeans and tops into the suitcase, watching my own hands complete the tasks as if I am watching them on the tv instead.

 I wander to the bedroom and throw open the doors to look for a dress to wear to her funeral, the funeral that Rob & I will be expected to orchestrate. I pull out a staid black skirt suit, the one I wear when I am talking to my stuffiest clients. It will do. I lay it on the bed and root around for a blouse, my hands running with pleasure over the fabrics. These too are signature items in my life. I feel such a need to separate myself from her, from who she was and what she liked. My hand finds the tiny beads of a fire engine red party dress that I discovered at Macy's one afternoon and I am filled to the bone with sudden pleasure.

 I was pleasure shopping, the kind of shopping a person does when they need absolutely nothing, and there in the Misses department was the dress of my dreams. It was short, slinky, beaded on the edges and bright red. It had straps the size of spaghetti noodles and it showed far too much cleavage. I bought it and I ran with it out the door, delighted. It was an act of rebellion at 39, and even though I knew that, it didn't change my utter joy in having done it. I am surprised to find the tag still attached; I could've sworn I'd worn it at least once.

 I picture myself strolling into St. David's Church on the hill, the same church she dragged me to Sunday after Sunday for hours and hours of mass. I picture myself marching in, wearing that red dress! I saunter over to her body and give her a coy wave of my hand and then I tip up the wine glass I am drinking from and shout, "The blood of Christ!" to the horrified crowd just before slamming the coffin lid and lounging across it, legs akimbo, sparkling red, and jamming a spiked heel into the wood. . .

 I take the dress out of the closet and put it in my clothing bag, shutting out my head to the sound of Mother's voice trying to ring inside my ears. Just bringing it along would have to suffice. Somehow, I have a murmuring idea that if there is a God, who or whatever that may be, would understand.

 After a while I have everything packed and I find myself pacing the floor. I feel caged, knowing that I am going to be trapped in that house, going through her things, making up niceties for someone to say in eulogy of her, choosing Bible verses and hymns, picking out flowers. My stomach lurches.

I pick up the phone and dial.

"Charlse Franses," a voice says to me.

"Hi Charlie." I say, so soothed by his voice that I feel my knees wobble and I have to sit down on the coffee table.

"Q-Sie!" he chirps, delight in his voice.

"Um…" I respond, feeling a lump protruding in my throat.

"What is it?"

"My mother died this morning." I say it flatly, feeling the lump burn down into my belly.

"Oh, My God, Susie…well, do we laugh or cry?!" he says, and I am reminded why I love him so.

"I think we dance," I reply and am greeted by laughter.

"When do I pick you up, Sweetness?" I tell him that 8 is fine and rejoice in my wisdom in choosing Charlie as the best friend of my life.

I shower and dress in dancing clothes. Tonight it will be my long Hawaiian dress that glows under the black lights at the bar and clings to me in all the right places. I sit in front of my vanity table and put on too much make up. I line my eyes with a brilliant blue that matches the shadow I have already applied. I brush on a purple tinged blush and shocking pink/purple lipstick.

I have dried my hair by the handful so that it hangs in bunches of wild curls and I rat it up in the back and put clips in on the side to hold it high on the back of my head. I glance at the clock. It's five to eight and I begin to shake. It occurs to me that I have eaten pretty much nothing but a stream of Krispy Kremes and I rush into the kitchen and begin rifling the fridge. Cottage cheese, yogurt, half a sandwich I had left from yesterday. Nothing seems terribly promising until I notice the box of donuts I'd brought home on the counter, three left in the box. What the hell, I snatch two out of the box. The first one makes it down my throat in three easy bites. I feel my lipstick smearing but I don't care. The next is Bavarian crème and I bite into the center until the crème starts to fall out. If I tip my head back, I can catch it all, and I do. I glance at the clock again licking my fingers. Two minutes to eight. Two donuts in three minutes--must be a record.

I freshen my nail polish and pour myself another glass of wine just as I hear Charlie knocking at my door.

I let him in and he spins in the living room ala' John Travolta, looking handsome all in black, his chest bulging under a tight black turtleneck, his gorgeous, thick red hair combed back.

He let's out a long slow whistle and spins me around appreciatively, his crystalline blue eyes twinkling at me.

"So are we going to one of yours or one of mine?" he asks, and winks at me.

"Mine," I say, and he is only a little disappointed.

"Well, I just think it's a shame that the guys at La Doll won't get to look at me tonight, that's all I'm saying," I shake my head gravely, in agreement.

I have turned to pick up my purse when I feel him step toward me. I turn back to him and he wraps his arms around me and holds me. He doesn't say a word, and he doesn't let go when I try to step away.

"Stop it, Charlie," I say, feeling my heart thumping.

He shakes a no and places a hand on the back of my head, stroking my hair. Another minute, another ignored objection, and then I am sobbing.

I met Charlie when I first moved "down state" to go to school at The University of Michigan in Ann Arbor. I was at the registration desk, trying to manage a stack of books for which I needed a wheelbarrow, and Charlie had bent down to tie his shoe, when in a spectacular demonstration of idiocy, I fell over him, books and bags and legs flying everywhere. My torte book fell in an unfortunate but amazingly precise manner, and gave him a black eye. I nursed him apologetically on the sofa of the medical office for the next several hours during which we became fast friends. It was instant love between us, and I so needed a friend.

Mother had been dead set against me going to school. It wasn't "a woman's place" as she put it, and women who entered the business world only got anywhere… by spreading their legs, Susannah! Mark my words, young lady, you'll be every boss's leavings!.

Angel had insisted. I'd earned the scholarship, it was mine and she couldn't take it away from me. He must've said those words to me a thousand times before I heard them and knew he was right, and yet I spent my first six months at college in full white-knuckled expectation of Professors with come-on's and invites to orgies disguised as keggers. Charlie would literally drag me to parties, often giving up after I'd had one glass of soda and begged him to take me back. He started calling me "the youngest old lady on campus".

Charlie lived in the dorm, one floor directly below me and we used to talk through the heat vents, yelling television stations to each other and watching the shows "together". He teased me about never going out and I teased him about going out with every guy on the campus. We both moved to the "burbs" after graduation and we never lost our instant love. Many nights we still watch TV "together" on the phone.

Charlie keeps his arms tightly about me as I sob so hard I think I will never breathe again. It is the most agonizing pain and dizzying relief I have ever experienced, all at the same time. My head feels as if it is stuck inside some kind of pressurized tunnel. My legs begin to buckle and Charlie walks me to the sofa, snatching the kleenex off the counter on the way. He sits with his arms around me and we lean back. He wipes a torrent of tears from my face and he rocks me gently back and forth, stroking my arm rhythmically. A long time passes before I can speak.

"Why should I cry for her?" I choke out the words, angry.

"Because she was your mother, Sweetness," he dabs the tissue at my cheek again.

"You knew her, Charlie. You know…" I say, shaking my head and fighting hard to stop another wave of weeping.

"You've earned this grief in every way. If you deny it now, this will be the thing that kills you. You survived it, all of it. Now, you get to let it go." I am stunned by his wisdom, by how well he knows me, by how much he loves me.

I cry and cry until I feel that one more sob will render me unconscious. Charlie wipes away the last of my tears, makes me laugh by calling me Nora Desmond as my make up is running like mad, and then takes me back to my vanity mirror to repair myself. He pours us both a fresh glass of wine and then busies himself going through my ipod while I re-apply with a shaking hand. And so, to the tune of "Shake Your Booty", I reline my eyes and drink my wine until my nose looks a bit less like a piece of red cauliflower.

Charlie and I hold hands and rush into the elevator, giggling like children and singing, "Shake, shake, shake…shake, shake, shake…" all the way down to the first floor and out into the night.

My favorite place to dance is called Have a Nice Day Café. It's in Pontiac, downtown, along a strip of several blocks that is home to dance club after dance club. Top 40, house, salsa, Caribbean, pretty much anything a person is looking to dance to, can be found on the strip.

Have a Nice Day plays music from the '70's, the music that played when I was not allowed to dance to it, when all I could do was stand by the sidelines and pray for morning while a generation was dancing their butts off. I watched. I waited…

Tonight the place is on the empty side, just the way Charlie and I like it. The light up disco dance floor is empty, the mirror ball turning it's lonely way along with no one to follow. We order drinks, claim our usual table and hit the dance floor with a vengeance. It is Earth Wind and Fire and Rick

James and A Taste of Honey. I dance at first in freedom, my arms sailing out before me, reaching out into the air, I spin and spin and we laugh.

Suddenly, I feel something rising in my stomach. I don't recognize it. Maybe it's the donuts, I think and ignore it, downing another vodka and a glass of water and jumping back out onto the floor. The alcohol is making me feel a little dizzy, but I can't stop. The ceiling begins to swirl, the floor is moving under my feet and I am feeling crazy; free and crazy and wild.

I am a wild thing, a creature borne new this night, an animal, untamed and untamable, vicious, stalking and feral to the bone. I dance dirty. I move my hips, I bump and grind and gyrate. Charlie follows suit, always ready to play whatever game suits me. We are entwined on the floor, perpetual motion, perpetual grind. I feel Charlie's pelvis against my leg, against my hip. He runs his hands down my body, starting with my arms, which are straight up in the air over my head. He follows down over my elbows and then over the sides of my breasts on both sides and my hips to the tops of my thighs. He brings his hands back up to my hips and rests them there, dancing me, moving me. We know we are being watched, putting on a show.

Whatever other people are in the room, they think we are lovers, or people who have just met and are soon to be. It's one of our favorite games and we play it to the max. I run my hand down his chest and grab the silver belt buckle on his pants and pull him toward me. He raises his arms this time and I actually lean in and kiss his neck, just on the side.

By all rights, I should be totally turned on-- I'm not. This is not about sex, this is rebellion, the same burning feeling that had me secreting a red dress into my car, into my closet, and upon the news of my mother's death, into my luggage.

Sweat pours down my face, I can feel it running down my back and my legs and I don't care. I am free; finally, at long last, freedom…freedom! I let out a scream, a wail. She is gone, really truly gone. Not gone like 3 hours away or gone like in the nursing center , but gone, gone forever, gone for good.

I dance hard and drink harder. It's 4 drinks and 5 and then I lose count. It occurs to me that the only reason I am not on the floor is that I am dancing so hard that I must be sweating some portion of the alcohol off. I have blisters that are peeling, leaving semi-circles of pink flesh glowing on my heels and the soles of my feet. I don't care, I don't feel pain, I don 't feel anything but the music.

After several hours, literally hours of stopping only long enough to down another drink and a glass of water, we sit down at the table and take a rest, panting and fanning ourselves with bright yellow cocktail napkins.

Charlie excuses himself to the restroom and I nod, poking my nose purposefully into my drink.

Charlie is not gone a minute when I sense a presence behind me. I look over my shoulder and meet eyes with a young man. He is burly, college aged, and from the look of his pinpoint red eyes, he has had a lot to drink.

"Y'havin' a good time?" he says and smiles enthusiastically.

I nod and turn away, I am not in the mood for this tonight; the bait and fish game, the hunters, the gropers. He taps me on the shoulder and I turn sharply, he is not allowed to touch me, especially from behind.

"C'mon let's dance!" he says wetly, pointing to the dance floor with his beer bottle. This is a phenomenon that has always fascinated me. That a young man will expect a girl to compete with his beer on the dance floor is a thing beyond my comprehension.

"No thank you," I say, and I even smile. I am trying to be nice.

There is a moment's pause as I give him my back again.

Another touch on my shoulder and I feel him come around to my side, leaning with his back against the railing that surrounds the elevated platform which holds the tables. My entire body is tense from the instant his fingers touch my shoulder.

"C'mon, I saw you dancin' with that guy. He looks like a fag. Dance with me, I got what you need Baby!" he slurrs, and looks at me as if I am to perceive him as a "naughty" and "cute" little boy, evidently trapped in the body of an ass!

Fueled by alcohol and heady with my newfound singularity, I turn to face him on my high stool. He leans in a little, vulture-like with his head, his shoulders placed against the barrier, arms stretched out cockily to the sides, his back leaning circularly forward, one foot tipped casually over the other.

I stare into his pissy eyes and begin to slide my skirt up. I smolder at him, sliding it inch by inch by inch, exposing calf, then knee then slow thigh.

"Ohhh, Baaby..." he says, staring alternately at my thighs, my cleavage and my eyes.

I pause a minute, letting the moment sink in and then, with visions of a thousand Rockettes in my head, I cross one leg over the other, my knee pointing high into the air, my skirt hovering dangerously close to exposing my panties. He laughs, smirks, focuses... and then in one move, as fast and sharp as I can muster it, I pin him to the railing with my platform shoe directly in his crotch! He jumps, drops his beer, spreads his legs dumbly as if the four inches of heel that are digging into his (so called) manhood will fall through suddenly to the other side. Instead, I use it as an opportunity to brace my foot, dropping my heel so that it falls between his legs and contacts the railing, the ball of my foot pinning him still.

"Crazy Bitch!!" he screams, and stares at me in shock, unable to move for fear of tearing off something he thinks he will some day need.

I feel ice cold and numb inside. I feel fury.

"Don't ever use that word…fag," I say deeply, through gritted teeth, "and don't ever presume that you have what any woman wants." I say it with more menace and intent than I have ever said anything in my life. If he moves, I know in my bones, I will kill him. I can have his blood.

I picture what his stricken, puffy, pink face would look like with four deep scratch wounds in it. I like it, a lot.

He swears at me and reaches for my hair just in time to have his wrists caught by two python-armed bouncers, who happily escort him to the door, him spitting and shouting obscenities all the way.

Charlie returns to the table applauding slowly. He had seen, he had called the bouncers over, and now he pays the tab and gets me my coat.

"I think we've had about enough fun for one night, don't you, Crusher?" I bend over laughing.

In the taxi on the way home I am beginning to feel a little dizzy. It's not the euphoric, dance floor dizzy I had going just a few scant minutes before. This is different. This is taking over my entire body, making it hard for me to sit up, to move my head, to see. I slide down on the seat and rest my head in Charlie's lap. He strokes my hair and calls me Sweetness. The only thing that I am sure of as the cigarette smoke infused taxi rattles block after block toward home, is that Charlie is there.

I see Mother. She's in the kitchen cooking Sunday dinner. My stomach lurches and I wretch a little. I hear Charlie's voice in the background asking the cabby to let down the back window. Mother begins to dance. She is on the dance floor at Have A Nice Day, spinning with a pot in her hand. She bangs the pot on the edge of the railing, keeping up with the beat. I laugh a little, watching her face. She seems so happy. It's almost as if she is relieved about something. But her lips are turning a funny color--bluish, and her eyes are starting to sink into her head. Her hair starts falling out in clumps around her on the light up dance floor. When she opens her mouth to smile her teeth have turned brown, and the hand holding the pot begins to shrivel. She drops the pot, and falls to her knees. I see her closer and closer, as if I am on wheels and someone is pushing me in. I am only inches from her fallen down body. I want to move back, but I can't. Her face is disgusting, the skin is shrinking and shriveling in front of my eyes. I want to run, but I'm riveted, something holds my arms at my sides, something holds my feet in place. I want to run! Please, let me run! I am close enough to see three of her eyelashes fall off, like a tree losing its leaves. Suddenly her shriveled fingers reach up and snatch a shock of my hair! Her lids open wide and she smiles her brown smile, a murderous fire glows in her sunken eyes.

I scream and begin to flail and fight her. I feel Charlie's arms shaking me, pushing my head toward the air from the window until the lights of the dance floor begin to dissolve into passing streetlights, until I can feel the cold side of the cab with my palm and I begin to see the streets of Pontiac, the streets of now, whizzing by.

"Jesus H, Suze!", he says and rubs my back as I rest my head in the open window.

Inside, he helps me to the bathroom where I remove my dress, take off my shoes and promptly throw up. Charlie raps at the door and asks if I want him to hold my hair back. I tell him no thank you as best I can, and I am vaguely aware of him rattling the tea kettle in my kitchen. I wretch repeatedly. My stomach rejects and rejects until there is nothing more coming up, until I am entirely empty inside, a thing I have often feared happening to me for good.

Finally, I stand on quivering legs and look at myself in the mirror. My ratted hair is matted and crushed on one side, the other side hangs limply toward my face. My eyes run with rivulets of blue that flow to my nose and then to the side of my mouth. Black mascara has smeared the entire circumference of my eyes and there is a smudge of it across my cheek. My lipstick has traveled left, migrating toward my ear. I stare at myself in shock, in disgust and horror. She'd been dead less than a day and I had become what she had always said I was. I was a whore, a woman who gave herself to a man on the dance floor… a man who didn't even want her. I was one of those women that she always talked about. One of those women, like the one that stole away my father, the ones that who sex, who seek it. The ones who cry out in porno movies, and yelp and beg and plead for it. The ones who do it for money, but secretly enjoy it. There I was looking just like one of them, and as mother always said, "If it looks like a duck and quacks like a duck and walks like a duck…" "…and dances like a duck and drinks like a duck..." I think to myself.

I am still staring at myself and hearing her voice berating me in my head when there is a gentle rapping on the door. When I don't respond, Charlie opens it slowly and peeks around at me.

"C'mon, Boo-boo Kitty," he says, "Let's wash that beautiful face.."

He gets out a thick white wash cloth, one of my good ones, one of the ones I save for company, the Egyptian cotton ones that I paid far too much for at Nordstroms; the ones I never use just for me. He lathers it with my facial wash, and he sits me on the closed toilet, ignoring the fact that I am only wearing my bra and panties and hose. He tips my chin up with one hand, the way one does for a small child and he begins to wash away the horror from my face. He brushes the cloth gently over my cheeks, clearing off my mother's judgments, redeeming me with every pass of the cloth, absolution in soap and friendship. I close my eyes and let him care for me. I let him mother me. He is so good at it.

After my face feels as if it should be glowing, he kisses me on the tip of my nose, gets my pajamas and robe from the bedroom and then starts the shower for me. He stands me up, turns me to face it and then unhooks my bra from the back.

"The rest is up to you, Q..." he calls over his shoulder and closes the door behind him.

The second the water hits me I am weeping. I weep with the falling of the water and it weeps with me. I cry for myself, for my piteous, pathetic self. I cry for a 41 year old woman who has to kick a kid in the crotch because her mother bullied her all of her life. Because she let her mother bully her. I cry because I am sick and half drunk. I cry because in the morning I have to drive to a beautiful place that I should be able to love, but have to hate because of what my life was like when I lived there. I cry because I have to go there to make a memorial for a woman I want to forget, and I cry because I am orphaned. I lean against the cool tiles and brace my hands against them. For a minute I don't feel anything at all and then the water begins to soothe me. It is warm on my shoulders, warm on my back and I stretch and let it pour over my head, rinsing away the sweat and hairspray and humiliation. I shampoo my hair and rub my scalp hard, rubbing in my own consciousness, and lather myself with vanilla scented body wash. I use twice what I need and surround myself in the luxury of the sweet foam. I put lavender conditioner on my hair. Perhaps I will survive, perhaps over the years, I have gotten good at mothering me too.

I towel myself off and rub lotion into my sore feet and my legs and all over. I bandage my blisters, put on my pajamas and robe and step into the slippers Charlie must've snuck back in with while I was lost in the shower. I wipe a spot clear on the mirror and comb my hair back from my face. After I brush my teeth, I feel almost human, and my last look in the mirror feels almost satisfying.

I venture out into the kitchen where Charlie is wearing his boxers and my oversized Winnie the Pooh T-shirt. He is making eggs and he has a cup of tea all ready for me, with milk and sugar in it, just the way I like it.

"Marry me…" I sigh, sitting down at the table and then choking a little at the clock that says 2:30 am.

"Sorry Sweetie, I can't be caged," he says and winks at me as he sets a plate of scrambled eggs and toast in front of me.

My stomach screams at me, suddenly I am starving. He sits down across from me with his own plate and his own tea and we eat for a moment in the most comfortable silence I have ever felt, the errant scraping of a fork or the crunch of a bite of toast, the most personable of conversations.

"Thanks for letting me go nuts," I say finally, sipping my tea.

He shrugs at me and says around a mouthful of eggs, "That's what I'm here for." He winks at me again.

I say a small prayer in my head. It is the first spontaneous prayer I can ever remember saying, to a God I'm not sure exists.

"Thank you for Charlie."

The eggs have been eaten, and the teacups emptied, and Charlie and I crawl into my bed. We had done this a hundred times in college, but it has been years. That it still feels so natural is a delight and a miracle. We curl up tightly together like week old kittens. His arms feel better than anything I have felt in so very long, and I revel in it, even fighting exhaustion just to listen to his gentle snoring, not so far off from a purr, the damp spot from his kiss on my forehead not entirely dry.

Boldness, be my friend.
　　　　　　--William Shakespeare

Chapter 3

An uncounted number of short hours later, I am being shaken by someone who evidently, does not value his own life very much. I am not a happy person in the morning, have never been an early riser, and I pretty much would still sleep until noon every single day if I could. I am shaken again and I swat out blindly, refusing to open my eyes and I groan my best threatening morning groan.

"That won't work on me, Missy…c'mon, move those buns…" Charlie's voice says.

I want to clock Charlie in the head.

I roll over, pull the covers up, and pull a pillow over my face. A few moments pass, and then I smell something. The heavens have opened up and let down a scent. It's rich and beckoning. I move the pillow and crack open one eye just enough to let in a sliver of sight. I see a steaming coffee mug, and Charlie's thumb at the rim.

I reach out for it only to see it move away from me. I reach further and it jumps again.

"Uh-uh…if you want this you have to come to the table," Charlie's voice says, and I still want to clock him in the head.

I try to ignore it and go back to sleep, but the aroma has infiltrated my senses and I can taste it on my tongue. I sit up and the pillow falls off my face and onto the floor. I sliver both eyes and can just make out the kitchen table through the doorway. A bright yellow coffee mug sits dead center, steaming away.

I put my feet on the floor and stagger in to the table. I stand there in front of it, not quite able to find the coordination necessary to bend over the table and lift the mug into my hands. Charlie appears and hands it to me, chirping, "Good Girl!" and turning me toward the sofa where I sink in and bury my face in the wonderful, life giving steam.

I take a sip and eyeball him. He is showered and dressed and somehow smells wonderful with some scent I know I don't own.

"Nazi…" I grumble at him, taking another sip of the coffee and feel it seep into my very bones.

He giggles and kisses me on the top of my bed-head hair.

"I have to go to work and pretend that they pay me to actually do something," he says, "I want you to call me when you get there, and then

I want you to call me when you know the day and time of the funeral, because you know I will be there. Now, there is to be no crawling back into bed, and there is to be no falling asleep on the sofa. I will be calling from the cell phone in fifteen minutes to make sure. Don't forget to pack your Xanax, and take a box of tissues and a bag of M&M's in the car. Clear?"

    I nod at him and smile through my sleep addled sub-consciousness. I peck him on the lips and thank him and he leaves me feeling full and satisfied.

    I drink my coffee slowly, admiring Matt Lauer on the morning news show. He always looks so sweet and so friendly. I wonder why 'ol Matt doesn't move to Michigan. Half a cup down, I am beginning to remember my own name and why I am up at 7a.m. on a day that I am not going in to the office. I wish I were going into the office. I notice that Matt's tie is just slightly askew and I imagine myself as his co-host, reaching over to adjust it.

    Three quarters of a cup down and Matt is cooking with a really large man in a chef's hat. He wears an apron. His tie is still askew. I wonder what Matt would cook for me. One last swallow and Matt is sitting comfortably on that sofa in front of the window where the crowd is gathered around outside, peering in like the only kids not invited into the tree fort. He smiles, straightens his tie and sends the show into a commercial and I know that now, I have to move.

    Charlie calls from the cell phone and I assure him that I am indeed conscious and moving. I shower and dress and before I know it, I have kissed Chipmunk goodbye and dropped off my spare key to the super who has promised to feed her and I am in my car with a clothing bag swinging wildly by the window in the back seat each time I make a turn. I stop at Starbucks and get myself the biggest cappuccino they make, and just across the street at the Jewish bakery where God has blessed their efforts and things are sweeter and richer and fluffier than anywhere else on the planet. I lay in a boxful and then a bagful of supplies. It's a long trip, four and a half hours at least, and I know I will need it all, every morsel.

    8:30 am in the city and traffic is at a snarl on I-75. It comes to an agonizing stop and I resign myself. There's no sense in being upset, it will move when it's ready and not a second before, and besides, I have to admit that I am not really in such a big hurry today. I'm happy to sit here sipping my cappuccino, feeling the rich bitter espresso, gritty on my tongue and the frothy milk. I love the feel of the whipped milk, light and smooth on my lips. I bite into a piece of apple strudel and chew it methodically, feeling each plump piece of cinnamon laden apple pop between my teeth, the gooey filling still warm from the oven and heavenly. I turn on the radio and listen to the morning people talk. They laugh and they make jokes and they play a song every now and then.

It occurs to me that I could just stay right where I am at this minute. Just sit here and eat my morning treasure and feel the autumn sun on my shoulders and look across the freeway to where the leaves on the trees are turning and bright. It's a lovely fantasy.

Too soon, the traffic begins to move and I must follow. I drive on until the radio station has begun to get blurry in my ears and I pop in a CD. James Taylor sings in his woody, earthy voice, "Long ago a young man sits and plays his waiting game...", and I see Angel in my mind, sitting outside on the stoop the way he would, just out of sight of the living room window so Mother wouldn't see, waiting for me to come out. It was almost better when we were forbidden to each other. At least then we knew what the game was, we could get a feel for the rules. She was at her worst when only she knew, when all the rest of us were playing something else and thought she was too. I remember all too clearly when Mother found out about Angel and me.

The rental cabin down the lake was always rowdy. Each year it was rented for weeks at a time by various groups of college students or business men on hunting holidays. That summer it was a group of boys from Ann Arbor. There had to be 15 or more, they must've been sleeping on the floors and in the chairs, but they didn't seem to care. There was always a party going on. Long after midnight I would hear shouts and music and laughing coming from the other end of the lake. Mother warned me repeatedly about the rental cabin that summer and all those "dirty boys" who were renting it.

They fascinated me, those dirty boys. They were so full of life and so unashamed. They were loud and drunken and often could be seen skinny dipping in the lake.

It was the hottest day of the summer when I decided to get a closer look. Angel was up town with his mother that day and wouldn't be back until afternoon. I don't suppose I would've ever gone over there, but I was lead by someone evidently as curious as myself.

Paige Warren was the daughter of a man who owned ten rental properties on the lake. She was tall and blonde and always tan. She wore mini skirts without stockings and high heeled Candies shoes and she tied a white button down shirt just beneath her breasts, which were full for her age, for my age. I spotted Paige tip toeing, sneaking along the edge of the lake, out of sight of her parents, toward the rental cabin. She crept closer, and I followed.

I loved and hated Paige. She had everything. I wanted to be her, and yet she was so superior, such a snotty little thing that I couldn't actually like her. I envied her. I envied her tall slender mother who called her into dinner every night at six on the dot and her tall and handsome father with the soft voice who wore suits and ties and called her "Punkin' and bear hugged her in the yard. I hated Paige for having everything and being too stupid to know it, and I loved her for being my ideal in bright red Candies shoes.

Paige was hiding behind a tree, watching as the boys roughhoused and drank by the edge of the lake. They wrestled and fell into the water. They took punches at each other and then grabbed each other around the neck and hit with knuckles on the tops of each other's heads. They drank beer from a shining silver keg. I could smell it on the breeze, with just a hint of Paige's Love's Baby Soft perfume. I stayed back farther than Paige. Even in rebellion she was better than me.

One of the boys, a wide, sweaty one with brown hair and a patch of black hair in the center of his bare chest staggered away from the group and toward Paige. I could see her startle. She jumped, a small quivering movement, but she held her feet still, too clever to give herself away. The boy moved closer and closer until he stood at the front of the tree that page stood behind. He opened his shorts and grasped hold of himself and peed. He peed long and he took his time, and Paige began to get nervous. I could see her breathing heavy, afraid. I could see her trying to keep herself still, her arms twitching, her fingers moving wildly. Sweat began running down my back, I knew it was running down Paige's.

The boy finished peeing and leaned back against the tree to zip his shorts. He hopped twice, hit a soft patch of grass and finally he fell against the tree with a thud. At the thump of his back Paige jumped and yelped like a puppy and fell down in the grass.

"Whoa! Hey!" the boy said, and then shouted to his friends, "Hey, shitheads, c'mere!!!"

Something about the way he was looking at her made my throat go tight. I wanted to yell, "Run Paige!! Run away, right now!! Run!!" but I knew if I did, they would see me too, and I did not want them to see me.

Paige seemed to be paralyzed. She kept looking sideways with her eyes as if she were trying to get her body to move in that direction, but it wouldn't go. She stood and stared back at the boy, her fingers still moving madly as if she were making some kind of signals.

Another boy wandered into view and then two more and then three more until there were nine or ten of them. They circled her. Somebody let out a low whistle.

"Looks like fresh meat!", a redheaded boy said.

"You a virgin, girlie?" the dark haired boy asked, leaning in close to her face.

"She don't feel like talkin' to you Carl!" a taller boy said and they all laughed. I didn't like the way they laughed. Suddenly, it didn't sound so festive, or so free. And I could smell alcohol on them. They'd been drinking a lot. An awful lot.

One of the boys took her by the arm and they dragged her into the clearing by the lake where the keg was, where the rest of the boys were. They gathered all around her in a circle again. At first I could still see slivers of her between them, standing in the center of the circle, spinning around and around looking for a place to run and crying. Then I couldn't see her any more and some of the boys were bent over where she had been. I could hear her screaming and crying. I was terrified and angry at the same time. They were making my mother right. I didn't want Mother to be right, and I didn't want Paige to be hurt.

I didn't know what else to do, so I ran up slowly to where Paige had been standing. I could see much more clearly now and I felt ice in my chest. Two boys were holding Paige's arms down on the ground, spread out to the sides as if she were about to make a snow angel. Another two boys held her legs in the same way. Still another boy, the one who had discovered her was pulling open her blouse. Paige tried to kick, tried to punch, tried to move, but she couldn't. She writhed and wriggled as best she could, her now bare breasts jiggling and bouncing with each jerk of her torso. The boy bent down and sucked her nipples and she screamed and shrieked. It could barely be heard above the roar of the boys laughing and cheering. One or two at the edges of the group didn't look so sure. They honestly looked like they wanted to run away, but they didn't. They didn't do anything to help Paige, either.

I started to run to her a hundred times, but fear muddied my feet and held me still. I didn't want to be the girl in the dirt with her chest bare. Another boy came up and pushed Paige's skirt up, she had on bright red panties with a cartoon of a kitten on the front.

"Hey! Nice Pussy!!" one of the boys shouted and they laughed and cheered and called out for him to take off her panties. He did, and he stood back as the boys holding her legs spread them further and further apart. I thought she would split like a wish bone at Thanksgiving, and maybe I would get my wish. That all of this was just a nightmare and I was about to wake up with sweat on my forehead and crawl into Rob's bed because I had been scared and it had been awful. But I never got my wish.

One of the boys began touching her between her legs and I stomped my foot in fury. It was a mistake. I was noticed.

"Look, look, it's another one!!!" a blonde boy with a red nose and pocked face had been lingering outside the edges of the circle, he'd found a spot where the ground was a little higher and he had been standing there so he could see. He was closer to me than all the rest. He shouted and ran for me. I found my feet fast and took off between the trees, dodging and ducking as quick and as sharp as I could, running for my life. It was a low branch that tripped me, and I fell face first into the dirt, gouging my forehead and then spinning on my heels to kick at the pock faced boy who had a hold of my leg and had begun dragging me back toward the circle. I screamed with all I had inside me, with every ounce of energy with every bit of power in my lungs.

The circle turned and looked at me, and as the pocked boy threw me into the center, I could see Paige, her legs still held apart, a different boy at her chest and one pushing a beer bottle inside her. I screamed and screamed and lashed at them and shouted and swore and kicked and scratched. I drew blood more than once and was rewarded with a slap across my face each time. They were trying to lay me next to Paige, to pin me to the ground so they could torture me too, and I decided in that moment that it would be better to die.

I kicked the pocked faced boy hard in the ribs, in the crotch, I even got him once in the face. He slapped me each time but I felt nothing. I bit at other hands, I spit, I scratched, but soon I found myself pinned neatly to the dirt next to Paige. She turned her head to look at me, her eyes wild and unseeing, her mouth shaping a scream that had no sound. I felt my shirt tearing, I felt hands at the zipper of my jeans. I writhed and fought, I got my leg loose and kicked another boy square in the nose, his blood spurting into my face. They slapped me harder that time, and I could taste blood of my own. Paige found her voice again and shrieked.

My bra was torn off me and rough hands came down on me when there was a cracking, splitting sound. It seemed to rake the air in two and an unreal silence followed. All motion was suspended, every voice quieted. And again it came, a crack, a boom, sharp decisive, explosive.

The boys stood and backed slowly away from us. My arms and legs were suddenly free and the circle opened to reveal Angel and Rob and Paige's Dad and Angel's Uncle Tony. Tony and Paige's Dad had shot guns, Angel and Rob had their baseball bats. Sheriff's Department cars came screaming in behind them.

Angel pounced at the pock faced boy and swung the bat hard at his throat, Rob took hold of another, Paige's Dad still another and Tony one more. Paige and I clung to each other in the dirt, gathering the shreds of our clothing about us as best we could and sobbing, listening to the sounds of fists hitting flesh, the cracking of teeth, choking and spitting noises, the dull thump and high crack of the bats. Eight men from the Sheriff's Dept. cars all stood and watched a minute, then gathered the other boys into rows and made them stand still. Then they turned their backs and spoke softly among themselves as Angel, and Rob and Tony and Paige's Dad gave each boy a beating; a bad one.

A lady deputy arrived and wrapped Paige and me in blankets. I had lost track of exactly what they had done to Paige, but I had noticed that she was bleeding from between her legs. The lady helped us into to the ambulance that arrived next. The EMS men spoke to us softly, they examined Paige gently and gave her a sedative. She had not stopped sobbing. I sat on the gurney, silent, seething, noticing with pleasure that some of the boys needed medical attention themselves. They sat crumpled and bruised and beaten, bleeding and sobbing like babies. They would travel roughly to the jail house, it would be hours before their wounds were tended.

The EMS man put an ice pack on my eye, and one on my jaw. It was broken, but I didn't know it. They weren't slapping me, they had been using their fists, but in the panic, I just hadn't been able to feel it. I had gouges across my breasts from where they had ripped off my clothes. I was bruised everywhere, but for one thing I was grateful. My jeans had been unzipped, but they were still on me when rescue came.

They let Angel ride with me in the ambulance. He held me close and rocked me. He cried and apologized for not being there sooner. To this day I don't know how he came to be there at all. I never asked, and he never offered. All I know is that Angel and my brother saved my life that day. If those boys had done to me what they did to Paige I surely would've died. Mother would have tortured me until I did, she never would've tolerated a gang-raped whore living under her roof.

Mother had burst into the hospital demanding to see me. I was terrified. I didn't know if I was in for another beating, or maybe worse, a verbal bashing. The choruses of "slut and whore" would surely be epic. And even worse than the college boys, Angel was there and the truth was soon out.

She came into the room slowly. Angel sat beside me on the gurney, his arm tight around me. She stepped over to me silent and staring, her hands were shaking as they ran across the rosary beads. Her eyes took me in. they took in Angel. She lowered herself into a chair across from us.

"Have you been ruined?" she asked quietly.

"No. They tore off my top, and they touched my chest, but that's all." I felt as if I were in confession, "Bless me Mother for I have sinned…"

"And you, Angelo, you called Robert and the Sheriff?"

"Yes Ma'am." he said, "And I helped give those guys a beating."

Mother looked at the rosary in her hands. She stroked the silver cross with her thumb.

"Are you a Christian, young man?" she asked, cocking her head and looking him in the eye

"Yes Ma'am." He squeezed me tighter.

"I love your daughter," he blurted and we braced ourselves for the implosion.

There was silence in the room; a thorny, fearful thing. I kept holding my breath until I felt faint and then taking a little gasp to right myself.

"I can see that." She said it so gently, that I had to look again to be sure it was actually Mother saying the words.

She stood and came over to me and she lifted my chin and then ever so slightly, she stroked my bruised cheek. Tears sprung into my eyes as if someone had flipped a switch. She turned away abruptly and dabbed at her nose with a tissue.

"You'll come for dinner on Sunday, young man," she said, and Angel nodded as I felt the pain of attempting a smile.

She stopped at the doorway and turned back, a different, more familiar look in her eye, "I told you not to go near that cabin, Susannah. Just what were you looking for?" She looked me in the eye and glared for just a moment before disappearing behind the doorway.

I wipe tears from my face with napkins from Starbucks and turn James up just a little in hopes of shutting out the memory of how I felt that day. Mother's immediate return to her cold, accusatory self had left me worse off than the physical beating. There it was, after all, my fault…

all of it. I rode home with Angel so sick at my stomach he'd had to pull over four times before we got home.

    I reach into the box and pull out a bear claw, deep fried and crisp, looking as if it had been dipped in glass; a thick layer of sugary glaze clinging to every bump and crevice. I bite into it; one of those gigantic, mouth filling, soul filling bites, the kind of bite that pushes everything else out of consciousness. It's nothing but sweetness, nothing but soft. A sigh catches in my chest as the sugar-love engulfs me.

    After about an hour and a half, I notice city giving way to long stretches of untouched woods. The trees are on fire with color—-red, yellow, gold, brown, green, a patchwork of light and movement and shape. The sun dances along on each leaf, the breeze plays them. The trees sway along in time to the song of the wind, the song of freedom.

    I try hard to enjoy them. But they look like guardians to me. I remember a movie I saw once in childhood where trees sang low and menacing, "This is the forest of no return!" as two small children wept in fear. This beautiful place, to me, this is the forest of no return, and I have just entered it.

    As they fly past, I look into the bushes where I almost expect to see the shape of Angel and me huddled down together, waiting for one of mother's rages to stop.

    She had allowed Angel to come "court" me, as she said. He would come and knock at the door and there was a ritual. Mother would open the door and invite him in. It had to be her inviting him, not me. She would ask him to sit at the table or in the living room and she would bring him a cold soda from the refrigerator. She would sit across from him and smooth out her dress and begin talking to him. It was the oddest strained pleasantry I have ever witnessed. Her hands frantically counted the rosary beads as she asked Angel banal questions about his father's building company or his mother's summer canning. Her voice was low and calm, but her eyes—I saw it, the angry pupils, the seething heat beneath. I twisted my fingers into knots waiting for it to be over each time. Angel was always respectful, and though we almost never saw the first 5 minutes of a movie together, he tolerated this ridiculous presentation every time he came to see me. It always ended with an invitation to come to church with us on Sunday, which Angel always accepted.

    I was horrified the first time she lapsed into one of her fits in front of Angel. It was a Sunday dinner, and we had all just sat down to eat. The first ten minutes of a meal were always the most nervous time. If she was going to go off it was always then. I've never known why. Rob and I had gotten into the habit of stuffing down as much food as we could in that first ten minutes. We ate quickly, knowing that any second the meal could be over, we could be watching our plates sail out the window like little flying saucers covered in roast beef and green beans, gravy trailing off behind them like exhaust.

That Sunday, we had reached nine minutes. I was just about to relax and looking sideways at Angel next to me. He was scooping macaroni and cheese into his mouth, looking more like a boy than a man again, with a smear of bright orange cheese across his cheek. I had just reached over to touch it off his face with my napkin when I heard the crash. This was how it always began. I never seemed to see it first. It was always when my thoughts had traveled just the tiniest bit from the idea that it was about to happen, just when I'd let my feet down.

And it was always a crash.

She had thrown her water tumbler into the sink where it shattered and sprayed glass over the counter. A piece or two came tinkling onto the table, across her still empty plate. There was a silence as all movement came to a stop, and my heart sunk in a way I will never forget. It was as if my chest had become a cavity and my breath had drained off down some kind of drain inside me. She glowered across the table.

"Who the hell do you think you are young man?!" she said to Angel, who dropped his fork and stood.

"I said who the hell do you think you are coming around here panting like a dog over my daughter!!? Sniffing around like you smell her!! Pig, you can't have her!!" She began in full shout then and lifted her plate to throw it at Angel.

"You can't have her!!! She won't be your whore!!! You can't have her!!"

He moved just in time and took hold of my hand as we duck-walked as quickly as we could from the kitchen to the doorway, bits of glass and ceramic raining down on us as it hit the wall above our heads. Rob was right behind us out the door, and we all three ran as fast and hard as we could out into the woods, the sound of her banging the counter and shouting scripture still ringing in our ears.

Angel had held me as I cried and apologized over and over again. I clutched at Angel's shirt as Rob sat staring across the lake.

"I'm so sorry, I should have warned you." I sobbed into his chest, feeling his arms come tight around me, the best, most glorious thing I'd ever felt in my life. I remember pulling back just as quickly to search into his eyes for the lie, the one I'd been told over and over again, the one about me being loved.

"It's not your fault," he said, "she's sick."

"But I should've told you not to come, I should've said—"

Angel put both his hands on my face.

"Susie, did you think I didn't know about your mother?"

I couldn't think of what to say in response. Of course, of course oh, of course he had known. Angel and I had been in the same schools since we were 12. Of course Angel knew, everyone knew, and I hadn't until that moment.

"Shit, Suze, what are you a moron?!" Rob said, kicking at a mound of sand before he dashed off into the trees.

I collapsed against Angel and cried. It was the first time I'd ever let anyone really comfort me about Mother. Angel held me and rocked me back and forth and stroked my hair. He kissed the top of my head and rested his cheek against it.

I couldn't stop; it felt as if I hadn't cried ever in my whole life, like I'd been filling up with it inside since I was born, and now I was drowning in it. He did everything he could to calm me, but nothing worked. A lot of time passed, it could have been hours. Suddenly, Angel whispered in my ear.

"Once upon a time. . ." he said.

I held my breath.

". . . there was a quiet place, the quietest kingdom in the whole world. In this place everyone wore slippers on their feet and no one was allowed to make any noise louder than a whisper."

My chest hitched up and down as if it were connected to electrodes.

"No one shouted, and no one stomped and no doors were slammed, and at the end of the day every day, when anyone came home, it was the rule that they had to sit quietly together on the sofa for ten minutes before speaking."

Angel's voice was a whisper. The lake shushed in and out behind him, the wind brushed across the trees in a hush.

"All the streets were covered in pillows, and all the windows were made of felt. Telephones only blinked small white lights instead of ringing, and there were no radios or tv sets. People spent all their free time making marshmallow sculptures to show to their neighbors, and at night, when the sun set, every house wrapped up in their special sunset blankets and they all fell asleep together to the sound of their hearts beating, and growing bigger and bigger inside. . ."

If I closed my eyes, I could see it. I could feel the blanket around me and when I stopped sniffling, I could hear Angel's heartbeat. I began to believe in this world. I began to believe that Angel's arms could make it real. It was the day I found only the second-ever safe place of my life, it was the day I truly found Angel's arms.

To this day I can remember details of Angel's Quiet Kingdom Stories. Angel would do a lot of whispering to me in the days and years that followed.

The long stretches of highway before me sprawl out sleepily along, and even though I am going about eighty miles per hour, it feels slow. I am getting anxious, anxious to be there, to endure the shock of seeing the place, anxious to see Grand and Rob and Matt. I decide to head straight to Grand's as Rob will be there, and we can go back over to the old house together.

Visions of Grand's house come gently to me. I loved being at Grand's. It was my first-ever safe place. I spent a lot of time there.

Grand's house is a little log cabin at the edge of Lake Charlevoix, just a mile or two from our place if you knew how to go. My grandfather had died when I was very young so it was just Grand and Lollipop, the little terrier she doted on. There had actually been three or four Lollipops over the years. When one would pass on, she'd get a new puppy. Lollipop was a perpetual reincarnation.

Grand's living room was the warmest, most inviting and quiet place. She had an old gold sofa that sat very near the fireplace with a quilt that she had made from bits and pieces of cloth she had collected over the years. When I was small, she'd hold me in her lap and we would cover up with the quilt and she would tell me where each square came from.

"This was your mother's graduation dress…and this was Robert's christening gown…oh, and this was your baby blanket …" she'd say, and we would run our fingers over each piece, and I would try to imagine what it looked like before it was cut into a square or a triangle and sewn up. Sometimes Grand's hands would pass over mine on the fabric, her warm gentle hands that never yanked hair or twisted arms or threw meals into laps. She'd rock me and read to me and listen as I read to her. It was the safest of safe places, to be with Grand on that sofa.

Sometimes, I would stay over night with her. She'd give me extra socks to put on, big wooly ones that used to belong to my grandfather and hung off my feet and flapped within minutes. I'd wear one of her flannel night gowns with sleeves rolled up and the skirt dragging the floor and we would brush our teeth together and then we'd snuggle under the covers listening to the warm wonderful snapping and crackling of the fire place and Lollie's steady, stuffy snoring as we drifted off to sleep with everything right in the world.

Early, early in the morning she'd wake me rattling around in the kitchen. She'd call me out by 6:45 and she'd wrap me in the quilt and settle me in on the floor in front of the television. I'd watch Captain Kangaroo and eat Rice Krispies from a bowl so full that I could barely get the spoon in and out without toppling a few onto the floor. A tablespoon or two of sugar crusted the top, damp with milk and I can remember licking it off my lips, grainy and sweet after each bite. Warm buttery toast and juice went with it. She brought it all to me, I never had to move. She seemed to delight in seeing to it that I was warm, happy, comfortable. Soon, she'd have her coffee mug and she would sit in the rocking chair behind me and watch with me, the persistent rhythmic squeaking of the chair reassuring me that she was there.

I am uplifted by the sweet memory of Grand's house, and now the urgency to arrive there seems more pressing than ever. I am getting a headache, and my stomach is hurting. I know it is the revenge of the pastry, and I know I need something more substantial in my stomach, but I just cannot bring myself to stop. After all, Grand will have a smorgasbord waiting when I arrive and I am only about an hour and a half away by now.

My coffee has gone cold, but I drink it anyway and I wonder what it will feel like to walk into the old house now that Mother is gone. I had only gone back there a time or two over the years, learning my lesson early that going "home" meant going away from that house. It was three or four holidays after leaving for college that I decided not to go back any more. I'd leave school relatively confident and settled and come back weeping and shaken and unsure, memories of hot food being thrown in my face or lap, memories of being yanked by the hair into the yard, of Rob sitting where he thought we couldn't see him, crying so hard that his entire body shook, and making sounds I've never heard from a man.

The cell phone rings. It's Rob, and he wants to know how far away I am. It's about an hour I tell him, and I can hear Grand fussing around in the background, and the sizzling sound of something cooking on the stove. He says to hurry but be careful and I promise him I will. I hang up and am slightly light headed. Maybe from the sugar rushes and declines of the morning, maybe from the caffeine and drive, and just maybe from Rob being in this place and the sound of wellness still being in his voice.

Do what you can, with what you have, where you are.
　　　　　　　　　　　　　　　　　---Theodore Roosevelt

Chapter 4

There is nothing like the warmth of Grand's arms around me and I hold her and we rock each other back and forth. She still has the same smell as when I was little, that combination of rose perfume and clothing stored in mothballs. It is the sweetest scent I've ever known. She kisses me on both my cheeks and holds my face in her hands as she stands back to get a look at me. She laughs and pronounces me beautiful.

Rob wanders out of the house eating a plateful of something and gives me a wet, food-laden kiss on the cheek. I gross out dutifully and Rob is very satisfied in his big brotherness.

Grand's house is unchanged and the current Lollie jumps on me excitedly as I try to move about the living room. There is a strange feeling as I walk through, a haunting notion that we should not all be so happy at this moment, but we don't fight it. This family has learned to make the most of its happy moments.

In the kitchen, Grand has cooked more food than three people could eat in a week. She had occupied herself well in the last 24 hours, undoubtedly a mechanism for dealing with her grief. The table is set with her favorite blue stoneware dishes and steaming platters and bowls leave little room for the plates. Turkey, mashed potatoes and gravy, green bean casserole, coleslaw, rolls, potato salad, a relish plate with cheese and olives and pickles, the apple cake, cookies, brownies; the table is a vision.

My stomach is knotted and hungry. I sit, and she and Rob settle in across from me. We heap our plates and talk with our mouths full. Rob tells of his business and his latest girlfriend and Grand and I exchange little hopeful glances when he says he really likes this one, and her name is Karen. She's even coming up for the funeral once we decide when that will be. I tell them that Matt is due to arrive some time today, and I talk about work, and Grand talks about her garden and Lollie's asthma.

My cell phone rings. It's Emmett, and at the sound of his voice, I feel my stomach tighten.

In the living room, I listen as Emmett delivers less than happy news.

"The boyfriend just got picked up for possession," he says. His voice is angry.

"You've got to be kidding me?!" I am beginning to wonder if poor Hannah might not just be better off with a foster family.

"Wish I was kid, coke and ex," he says and I hear the clink of the whisky bottle hitting the rim of his glass. "And that ain't all, the lease on the apartment is in his name. Aunt Amy lied. It's not her apartment. We gotta' move her. There's no way we'll get an approval to put Hannah in a druggies apartment, it's a dicey part of town as it is."

I feel as if I may weep.

"Oh my God. . . now what?" I say, trying to make my head function. I am suddenly seized with fear. What if I can't help Hannah because Mother has died and I can't think? What if I can't help Hannah because of *Mother?!* The thought makes me furious, it kicks my brain back into gear.

"Alright look, my friend Charlie's ex-boyfriend is an apartment complex manager in Southfield. I'm going to call Charlie and see if I can sweet talk him into helping us get Amy an apartment. Think you can pull some grant money to get her a first and last and deposit?"

Emmett groans.

"Come on, Emmett, you have no idea the size of the favor I'm calling in," I say, knowing as I do that Charlie's ex, Richard Mills, manager of Cherry Peak apartments is still in love with him. Charlie is going to have a conniption.

"Oh, Christ, Susannah, I'll try."

I hear the bottle clink again.

"Go easy on that stuff, Em," I say this knowing it will make him laugh. Emmett pours teaspoon-sized drinks. One bottle lasts him for years.

He rewards me with the laughter I'm looking for and we say goodbye, promising to let each other know what happens as soon as possible.

I head back to the table deciding to call Charlie after I have some food in my stomach. I re-fill my plate liberally, piling it high with every good thing Grand has put on the table. I am so hungry, it feels as if I can't get the food into my mouth fast enough.

As I eat, I am finding it hard to breathe. I am taking huge bites of the food, and swallowing way too much at a time. I know I am doing it, but I can't seem to stop. I have to take a big drink of my soda to push down a lump of food. There seems to be some kind of magnetic pull between myself and the mashed potatoes. I take a breath and another drink of my soda and try to slow down with the next bite. I consciously make it smaller and try to chew it more slowly, feeling a bit more settled. I push around the rest of what is on my plate with the fork.

"Aren't you hungry, Dear?" Grand looks concerned and I feel my heart swell.

"I'm just about full." I watch as she raises her eyebrow at the remainders on my plate.

Grand often fed us as children. Sometimes, after several days of interrupted meals we'd make the walk to Grand's just to get something in our stomachs. She'd sit at the table and watch us eat like animals, covering her nose with a tissue, claiming her "allergies" were acting up again.

I assure Grand that I am fine and then head out to the porch to call Charlie. I pick at my cuticles as I wait for him to answer.

"Charles Franses, how may I help you?"

"How much do you love me?" I say.

"Oh, God protect us from faux suede, what is it?"

"Charlie, I've got this case—", I tell him the story, emphasizing Hannah's liquid eyes and the deep purple bruises on her pale skin.

"Geezus H!" he says.

"Charlie the aunt's boyfriend got picked up for possession. We have to get them an apartment of their own, and I mean I was hoping. . . well, you know since Richard—"

"Oh Fuck Me Runnin'!" Charlie's voice pierces my ear.

"Please, Charlie? I know it's so awful and I know you never wanted to talk to him again, but please, Charlie—" my voice begins to break. I'm losing it.

"Q, don't cry, for God's sake," he says.

"I'm sorry Charlie, really, I know that's not fair, I didn't mean to . . ." my voice breaks again and I hate myself. "We've only got three days to get it all done and I'm trapped up here for this fiasco of a funeral instead of home where I want to be." I take a breath and stop for a moment.

"Ohhh Suze."

"I know, I know. The thing is, Charlie, by Monday 9 a.m. we have to have a signed lease, not to mention that we have to find her job."

"Baby, you owe me big on this one," he says.

"Oh myyyyyy, Nah don't tell me you'll be taken' advantayage of poah' li'l me! Not that again Captain sah!" I say in my best bad Southern Belle accent.

"Frankly, Scarlett I want to borrow your red shoes," he says in a smarmy, gay Rhett Butler.

We laugh. It is the best, most reviving medication there is, laughing with Charlie.

"Alright, let me get on the phone to Mr. Dick and get back to you."

We laugh together again, though I hear the nervous tone to Charlie's voice.

"Goodbye Miss Scarlett."

"Charlie," I say.

"Yeah?"

"Thank you."

"I love you, Q. Hang tight."

With that the phone goes quiet and I miss him so much that my chest aches.

After the dishes are cleaned up, we collapse into the soft furniture in the living room. I choose the gold couch, worn and velvety and wonderful. My fingers playing again at my necklace, I slip off my shoes and tuck my feet up beneath me. Rob sits on the floor, his back against the sofa, and Grand is squeaking away in her rocking chair. For a moment we sit in silence. We know we have plans to make, difficult things to do and say, we know we have a lot ahead of us, but for now, we just sit in warm silence and listen to the sound of our liberation. We three are veterans of the same battle, the wearying war of my mother, Camille.

Grand had told me that she had always been a difficult child, headstrong and set on having her way, but there hadn't been any signs that anything was really wrong until after Rob was born. My father had gone to see her in the hospital and she had thrown a soiled bed pan at him. The doctors shook their heads and told Grand and my father that sometimes a woman's just not right after birthing, that she needed time to get over it, to get better. And she did, according to Grand, she got better, and she was better for a long time. Until I was 10. Until my father left. At least, Grand said, she didn't see it until then, but she thought that it may have been one of the reasons he did what he did. She thought it happened in private, when we kids were sleeping, when they were alone. She said she thought there must have been a lot we didn't know.

I am certain that Grand actually spoke to my father and he told her those things, but she would never say so. It would have been considered a terrible betrayal and Mother would've gone on the war path.

By the time I was a teenager, a doctor had actually diagnosed her. The word Schizophrenic was never to be spoken in our household after that day, and no matter how sick or injured we were, Mother would never take us to a doctor herself. If it came down to absolute necessity, Grand would come and take us, or a neighbor would offer. Our tiny community became very aware of Camille Suffolk, and the way she behaved.

    Neighbors to the left of us would come to the back door and slip Rob and I away when she was rampaging, throwing dishes and glass and banging the counter over and over again with an aluminum pot. When things were quiet after hearing her screaming, and seeing our dinners being tossed out the back door, neighbors to the right would tap on my window and bring over sandwiches and slices of pie that Rob and I ate in silence behind the closed door of my bedroom. Sometimes it was after midnight. I am grateful for the things they did, and angry that they never did what they should have. I can only remember once that the Sheriff's Department actually came out to the house.

    It was one of those hot kinds of summer days when everything is covered with a humid sticky wetness, one of those days when just drawing a breath was almost more effort than a person could manage. She'd had that look in her eye at breakfast. That look that said that I should leave the house and not come back until dinner time. I had dressed and was just combing out my hair when she burst into my bedroom. She slammed the door open so hard that the knob punched a hole in the wall on the other side. She stood there a moment and then charged at me. She was going for my hair again. She always went after my hair. She insisted that I keep it long and I always understood it was so that I would maintain that vulnerability.

    I don't know what made me do it that day, maybe it was the aggravating heat, maybe it was having Angel in my life, feeling like somewhere on the horizon there was another life waiting for me if I just survived this one, but for the first time ever, I stood up and deflected her snatching hand.

    I shouted at her. I shouted one word.

    "NO!"

    She stopped in shock. I never fought back, never spoke, I always had just let her rage and bully me until she was done, but not this day.

    I pushed past her out the door of my bedroom and ran to the one place I thought she would never follow, since she never had. I rushed up the narrow stairs to the attic. The attic was small and as airless as a tomb. Heat hung palpably in the dusty space as I sat and listened. To my utter shock, what I heard was the sound of her heavy steps on the stairs.

Mother was big, she had always been big. She'd had a weight problem as long as I could remember and at the time she had to have weighed over 400 lbs., and I never thought she would climb those stairs! She did, and more quickly than I ever would have thought she could.

When she reached the top I could see that she had chosen a weapon. It was the slotted metal spoon this time, no doubt because she had noticed that I was wearing shorts and she would get me at the tops of my thighs again.

Anger burst up in me like nothing I had ever felt before in my life. It was red and burning, hotter and more stifling than the attic, and as she stood there at the top of those stairs, I suddenly had a vision. I saw the end to my problems, the end to these life draining rages, an end to it all.

One push.

That's all it would take; brace myself with my right leg, take one step forward, level my hands at her shoulders and just--push. I could feel my body getting ready to do it. My leg moved behind me, my arms began to reach out, I could envision her expression of shock and then the sight of her tumbling backward down those stairs. She would surely break her neck. It was so simple and it was within my power. My power. I could stop this. I could make it stop forever.

Sweat came from every millimeter of my body, I was wet with it in an instant. She braced herself triumphantly in the doorway, brandishing the spoon in front of her, waving it madly in the air and smiling at me. She thought I was beat. She thought she'd have me crouched on the floor, up against the wall as she had so many times while she hit me again and again with that damned spoon, leaving bloody welts on my arms and legs, and bruises on my head.

"Not this time. Not today," was all I could think. I was 17 and I had had enough.

I took a step toward her and I got ready to push. As I got closer, I wanted even more than an ending. I don't know if it was revenge exactly, but something surged up in my chest, it was hot and bitter, something like the taste of blood. I snatched the spoon from her hand and I bent it in two in front of her eyes, as close to her face as I could get it without touching her. I wanted her to see my murderous intent, to feel just a glimmer of the fear and uncertainty that I had endured for so long.

I opened my mouth to speak and again, only one word came out. "NO!"

She lunged toward me and I side stepped, throwing the spoon as hard as I could at the attic window, listening with pleasure and something beyond excitement as the glass shattered. As she stood with her hands dangling at her sides, mouth gaping at the window, at my action, I took the opportunity to force past her, and dash down the steps.

I honestly don't know why I didn't push her that day. I wanted to, really truly I did, more than anything I'd ever wanted in my life. It was as if my own hands betrayed me.

I locked myself in my bedroom and put all of my clothes into garbage bags as I listened to her in the kitchen banging that damnable pot on the counter. I tossed the bags out the window, climbed out myself and loaded everything into Rob's old red wagon. Then I started the two mile walk to Grand's.

I was not going to live with her any more. I was old and weary at only 17 and I needed a place to retire for a while, to live in relative quiet. I was tired of the war and feeling so shell shocked that I was certain I would never think clearly again.

The Sheriff's car pulled along beside me just as I was leaving. I wasn't even half a mile away, my hair still wet, my eyes red and puffy, I was sniffling as I walked along.

"You all right, Susie?" The officer's name was Stan, and I remember him being kind and funny. He had a pink face and blue eyes and he was drinking a Pepsi to ward off the heat.

I shook my head yes.

"Where you goin'?" he asked, and it was then that I knew why he was there. Mother had called.

"To my grandmother's house," I said, and looked into his eyes and then I did something that I tried hard never to do.

I let my eyes show him my pain.

He hesitated just a moment and then he got out of the car and stepped toward me. I thought he was going to grab me and take me back to her. I saw my freedom dissolve like an Alka Seltzer, and fizzle off into the air.

I stood icy still and watched as he lifted each bag out of the wagon and put them in the trunk of the long white car. He opened the back door and loaded the wagon in next and then held the front passenger door for me.

"C'mon, Sweetheart," he said and looked at his shoes, "Lemme' give ya' a ride."

And so it was that I had a police escort the day I ran away from home. He left me there at Grand's, sitting on the porch, waiting for her to come back from town, three garbage bags and a red wagon beside me, drinking a Pepsi.

I don't know what the Sheriff's department told Mother, or if they called her at all. All I knew was that I was not going back there. He'd have had to shoot me to get me to go.

Suddenly the front door flies open and my Aunt Jenna steps in, fresh off a flight from California. Almost fifty years old and wearing hip huggers, she looks a little like a well oiled leather catcher's mitt, her brown skin glistening, a sliver of it showing at her belly button. All legs and attitude, she strides in and tosses a Louis Vuitton suitcase into the center of the room. She flips her newly blonde hair dramatically over her shoulder and folds into Grand like a sobbing slide-rule. There is a faint hint of coconut in the air as Rob and I raise our eyebrows at each other and stand to hug Jenna.

"She was too young, just too young...," Jenna sobs and now I understand why she is crying. The one thing Jenna fears is aging. This is the final wrinkle, the fatal one, stronger than Botox and more powerful than the plastic surgeon.

I wipe Jenna's mascara from my cheek, and watch as she wraps herself around Rob who nearly topples into the sofa.

Finally somewhat composed, Jenna seats herself and starts talking. Jenna talks in questions which she answers herself and then becomes angry when she feels you are not "investing" in the conversation.

"Well, I suppose we have to plan a funeral don't we? My God it's just too soon to be planning a funeral for my sister. Should we ask Father Satine to do the ceremony? Of course we should, he was her favorite. He's still there isn't he? Oh of course he is. It's just so awful, so very awful, she was just too young, too young wasn't she? My God you're all just sitting there like zombies, don't you have anything to say?! This is all so exhausting, isn't it? Susannah and Rob, you must be just devastated. You're devastated aren't you? Oh, it's just awful…"

We nod and try to edge in a word here and there. It is Jenna who brings up the topic of clearing out the old house, and before I know it, Rob and I are holding hands in the back seat of a bright red Mercedes that Jenna has rented for her sister's funeral. Have I mentioned that I love Jenna?

We turn the last curve before the house and I feel a wave of nausea overtake me. I crack the window and rest my head against it, listening to Jenna talk to herself about the season change, and how she had gotten so used to the palms and sun in California that she had forgotten how beautiful the fall was in Michigan.

"Isn't it just beautiful?"

Rob is rubbing my shoulder as the house comes into view and we both feel suspended for a moment. His hand is still on my shoulder but I can't feel it. Jenna is still talking, but I can't hear her. Grand sighs in the seat in front of me and it sounds like the wind on the lake.

We get out of the car and just stand staring at the place for a while. It is so unchanged that I feel as if I have stepped backward twenty years.

There is still tape on the attic window. The back door hinge is still broken. The back porch steps are still slanted and uneven. The same peeling white paint ruffles in the wind. Rob takes ahold of my hand as we walk through the back door.

My stomach twists in on me instantly as we enter the kitchen and I have to run to the bathroom and throw up. So much for my satisfying lunch.

The kitchen is in a state of post-rage shambles. Broken glass is everywhere, the refrigerator door is open and the food inside has been dumped upside down and spilled in the floor. The cupboards are open and the few remaining dishes are sitting askew and tumbled. She had actually raged herself to death. The Coroner's Office had said it was a heart attack, and now we knew why.

By the time I exit the bathroom, wiping my face with a cold cloth, Jenna is already sweeping and Grand is collecting the dishes from the cupboard and putting them very slowly into a box. She is crying in that way that she does, that quiet way that she thinks hides it from us. I leave her to her grief, she has earned it.

Rob is in the living room where he has begun packing up books; the stacks and stacks of religious books that would glare at us from the shelves in the living room whenever she was lecturing us on our sinfulness. He seems to be dropping them into the boxes with a bit more gusto than is necessary and he gives me a tight faced smile as I walk past. I go to Mother's bedroom and drag a box in from the hallway. I can't bring myself to go into my old room. I am not yet ready for all my child-ghosts to come from the woodwork.

Mother's bed is made and her crucifix is laid upon the pillow the way she always did. I never quite understood what it meant. Was she hoping that Christ would come to claim it and be found sitting on her bed when she arrived, the ultimate blessing awaiting her?

I open the top drawer of her dresser and dump it's contents into the box. I have no desire to touch her things, to look at them, to remember her by them. This is an unpleasantry that must be tolerated and nothing more. The second drawer is the same and I dump it into the box and I am not shocked when three brand new rosaries, still in their plastic wrapping come bouncing out on top of the pile. I empty the third drawer and finally the fourth, but the fourth is heavy and I can't lift it. I scoop up a great armful of clothes and drop them into the box, disgusted. Something square and dark is stashed at the bottom and I clear off the rest of the clothes to reveal a black box, the lid taped shut, wrapped around and around with tape.

I get a knife from the kitchen and sit on the bed as I slice it open. Inside are two dozen video tapes. I lift them each and look at them. Each one is a romance movie. Casablanca, Gone With the Wind, Love Story, a few I don't recognize and a few that I am surprised by, more recent movies. On each video tape is a note taped to the back in her handwriting, listing scenes with kissing or sexual content. Each list is detailed.

"Casablanca:
Kissing, 20 minutes into the movie, lasts 5 minutes.
Kissing 30 minutes into the movie, lasts 3 minutes.
LM 45 minutes into the movie, lasts 4 minutes."

I interpret LM, it's "love making" and it strikes me that this was mother's collection of pornography. I feel my own hand clap over my mouth. In her restricted mind, these films were dirty, and she loved them. I can tell she did by their obvious wear and tear. Some of the covers are nearly falling apart and some of the tapes are so worn, and rattle so when I take them out that I am certain they will not even play any more. There are layers and layers of tape on the box, where it had been cut open and re-taped; Mother's struggle against her own flesh.

I place them all back inside the box and tape it up again. I know that I could drag it into the living room and expose her to the rest of the family, and the temptation is certainly there, but I decide that it could hurt Grand and so I set it aside the rest of the contents of her dresser and tape the bigger box shut. I keep thinking that there should be some satisfaction in this discovery. It only makes my head hurt.

My cell phone rings and I answer it feeling grateful for the distraction. I do not want to contemplate Mother's sexual obsessions.

"Mom." A voice says into my ear and tears spring immediately into my eyes.

"Matthew!" I say and try hard not to let him hear that I am crying.

"Are you alright?"

What a question. On my best day, I couldn't answer it.

"Sure. Where are you?"

"Close. Are you at Grandmother's?" he says and I am struck by the formal way he speaks of her. Not only did she put me through hell, she cheated him out of a grandparent, just as my father did.

"Yes, we've started cleaning it out."

"Okay, well I'll head that direction, I uh. . ."

There is a pause.

"Matthew?" it's not like him to mince words. Matthew is a straight shooter if ever one were born. It is one of the things I admire most about him.

"Is Uncle Rob there?" he says.

"Yeah he got here a bit before me."

"Who else is there?"

"Aunt Jenna and Grand are here with us. Is something wrong, Honey?"

"Uhhh, nothing," he says a little too quickly, "I'll just see you soon."

We hang up and my stomach surges again. He wanted to tell me something. What could it be? God, if her death has hurt him in some way I can't anticipate. . .

Unable to avoid it any longer, I turn back to Mother's things. I pick up the tape encrusted box and hold it in my lap.

I don't want to, but I can't help but think about what this means. Mother seemed to be able to find the sexual danger in every situation. My dating Angel was treated like such a constant 911 sexual emergency that I was insistent that Angel and I wait until we were married for the actual "consummation" of our relationship. Mother had pounded it all into me so thoroughly that I really believed it. It had become my own conviction, and if Mother had known how many times I had come close to the act and resisted, she would never have needed mention it to me again.

Angel and I took every opportunity to be alone, to kiss, to touch. There were times when I wanted to make love to him so badly that my body hurt. Once, on a beautifully warm summer night, I kissed Grand on the cheek and told her I would see her in the morning. She understood and only warned me to be careful and to make sure that I kept true to my own heart. It was the perfect thing to say.

Angel was waiting for me outside and we took a blanket and a basket of dinner down to the lake. We ate sandwiches and talked for hours, and it was midnight when we decided to take a swim. Angel stripped off his shirt and I mine. It was suddenly a duel. He took off his shoes and socks and I did the same. Next came his blue jeans and mine were off too. He took off the gold cross he wore around his neck, and I my bra. Finally, he stepped out of his underwear and I tossed my panties beside them.

We stared at each other for a minute. I had never seen a man naked before. I let my eyes follow down to the furry place just below his belly. I wasn't quite expecting what I saw, because Angel had an erection, and it seemed implausible that what he had could fit inside of what I had.

I suppose I looked startled, because Angel took me by the hand and said, "C'mon…it's ok, let's have a swim!"

We ran together like children to the water and jumped in splashing each other madly and screaming and squealing. The water lapped in such freedom on my naked skin. We swam and ducked under the water and grabbed hold of each other. Angel pulled me to him and lifted me in the air and tossed me back into the water. We played like sea otters, floating on our backs and twirling and spinning together. My awkwardness at being naked in front of him was suddenly, and forever gone. It was the most natural thing in the world. He pulled me to him again, and this time our bodies connected. I felt all of his skin to mine, the water soothing us both, licking waves at our backs. He wrapped his warm arms around me and kissed me deeply, lake water and saliva mixing in our mouths.

We kissed and kissed, the moonlight glinting on the water, the lake whispering, until Angel lifted me and carried me out of the water. He put me gently me on my back on the blanket and dropped down beside me. We pulled the blanket around us for shelter from the chilling breeze.
I reached for him, I ran my hands over his damp skin, the hair on his body wet beneath my fingers. I kissed him hard, and I pulled him on top of me. I felt as if I couldn't get close enough to him. Our skin was a barrier, it held us millimeters apart. It was almost unbearable.

Angel's tongue searched my mouth and I searched back. I had gotten good at meeting him, at giving and receiving in this love play. I pulled my mouth from him and kissed his neck, sucking off the droplets of lake water and suddenly feeling the urge to bite. I did, taking folds of his skin between my teeth and nipping him on the neck, on the chest, on the belly.

    He took both my breasts in his hands and kissed them. He placed his thumb beneath one of my nipples and took it in his mouth, directing it with his thumb and tongue, playing them both in his mouth, he slid his hands down my body, pulling my legs around him on either side. He ran his right hand over my thigh, up, up toward my bottom, grasping it and squeezing hard as he kissed me again. I found his bottom as well and did the same, his erection pressing into my belly. His hand wandered between my legs and I held my breath. With an open palm he cupped me in his hand and then he stroked me. I was swollen and suddenly wet with something other than the lake. He parted me gently and with one finger he found the source of the swelling and caressed it. I'd never felt anything like it. Mother's continual warnings had kept me from even exploring myself. I had no idea.

    Angels fingers were playing me and I wanted his swollen spot to feel the same. I took my hand to him, touched him gently with my fingers finding the head and then the shaft and seeing how it fit into the palm of my hand. He reared backward once I had a hold and I understood how he wanted me to move it and I did. I pulled back and forth and Angel rocked with me and I spread my legs farther than I ever thought I could, welcoming Angels fingers as they began to alternately play the swollen spot and push up inside me. I wanted them deeper it seemed than they would go, I began to rock with him as well and soon we were lost in it, this dance of our own creation and the blanket was tossed aside and the breeze mingled with the heat of our skin and left us with goose flesh.

    Suddenly Angel tossed his head back and there was a wetness in my hand and on my stomach and a spasm took my swollen place and I wrapped my legs tight around Angel and came hard against his leg.

    We washed each other in the lake and wrapped ourselves in the blanket where we slept deeply, and I knew that Angel was my peace on earth.

    I woke only once that night, startled from a dream in which Mother discovered us there on the lake and chopped off Angel's hands with a shovel. To discover that I was in Angel's arms when I woke was a shock and a comfort all at once. I wondered if I'd ever find a place where Mother would not intrude. Angel was as close as I had found.

    As the walls of Mother's room return to me, I am staring into the eyes of a tiny woman. The top of Mother's dresser is a shrine to St. Mary.

A figurine of the Blessed Mother stares up pitifully with raised hands, candles on either side, a white embroidered cloth beneath. A rosary the same color as Mary's red robes rests perfectly in front of it.

"Where were the saints and the Holy Sprit when this woman was beating her children with metal spoons and rolling pins?", I wonder as I ponder it's pristine, dustless state.

I charge a little too quickly into the living room to get another box. Rob gives me a raised eyebrow as I dump out the few things he's put into it already and march back with it to Mother's room. I swipe the shrine off the dresser with my arm, feeling it bang and clatter into the box. With satisfaction I toss in her Bible and reading glasses, her crucifix and the four pictures of Jesus and the last supper from the walls. I tape it up and kick it into the hallway; the last vestiges of her reign.

Rob pokes his head around the corner and looks at me. He nods toward the kitchen where Grand is still slowly filling boxes with glassware, and I get it. He's telling me to knock it off. I nod back at him and take a moment to try to collect myself.

The room is in semi-darkness. She always kept the shades pulled and the curtains drawn. Mother was always certain that men were trying to peer in upon her when she was undressed. I walk to the window and throw open the curtains and let the shade up. I open the window as wide as it will go, and do the same for the window on the other side of the room. Sunlight pours in and for a moment I can't see. The walls are looking relieved, as is the dresser top and it has a bit of the same affect on me. It has been far too long since any light was shed upon the inside of this house.

The brightest light in the house was always after a hard snow. We had a lot of snow on the lake. Winters were the worst, bleakest times of my childhood. Snow days, those days when they closed the school, were not the celebratory things that my schoolmates loved so. Rob and I dreaded snow days. It meant we were trapped indoors with Mother. The feeling of entrapment seemed to make her condition worse.

Once, after 3 feet of snow fell, Mother decided to put salt on the walkway, only she felt it had to be sifted first so she went out and kept shaking the sifter over the snow. The salt was way too big to fit through the sifter, and the result was a bent sifter and Mother screaming outside on the walkway for two hours straight. One of the neighbors had come by later and salted the walkways and shoveled the drive while we were asleep. When Mother woke the next morning, she told us that St. Mary had come during the night to bless her with salt. And to thank her, we had to each drink a glass of salt water and do a hundred Hail Mary's. My chest hitches, picturing Rob throwing up the salt water from his empty stomach. We'd had no dinner the night before and no breakfast before she'd forced the water on us.

I walk to her dressing table and begin loading cosmetics into a bag. They are used, I reason and no one can use them. They are garbage. In my haste to throw away her most personal items, I knock over a bottle of ancient Chanel perfume, the only scent she ever wore. It shatters on the edge of the dressing table and the scent immediately engulfs the room.

I am suddenly dizzy. I can't breathe, I can't see. The smell of it is choking me and blinding me. I back away and fall over the boxes, tumbling on my hands and walking crab-like, back, back into the doorway.

Everything feels blurry. The smell is in my nose, it's on my tongue. Dear God, she's here! I smell her! I know she's coming up the hall. It's all been a big trick and she's here! She was hiding, just watching what we'd do with her things, waiting to see if she'd get the respect she always felt so strongly she deserved!

I back away farther and farther from the scent, my hands and elbows scraping the floor. I can't seem to move fast enough, can't make myself turn and run for fear she'll come at me from behind. Suddenly there are hands on my shoulders. I scream, a horror-filled, blood chilling scream until Rob turns me around to face him.

"Hey, hey…," he says "it's okay, it's just me…c'mon."

I turn and fall into his arms and breathe in the scent of him, pulling wads of his shirt to cover my nose and mouth, the smell of her pooling in my nose.

Rob takes me outside while Grand and Jenna clean up the perfume and open the other windows. Rob sprays Lysol, an obscene amount, into the room and finally I can stop pacing in the yard and come back inside.

My hands are shaking now as I pull the blankets and sheets and pillows from the bed and fold them all a little too neatly, and set them into another box.

Together, Rob and I heft the big mattress and box spring out into the yard. It should've been replaced years ago, something for the junk yard, her place of rest, now upheaved and tossed into the dirt. We both push and toss with gusto and watch as the mattresses and the pieces of the bed frame fall in a satisfying heap. We stand a moment and stare at it, both of us breathing heavy at the effort.

Back inside, the room is so empty, I feel it echo in my stomach. Being inside the house is really getting to me. I feel myself shrinking with every moment inside. Whatever had been taken from me in my childhood, she was taking again. This house knew imprisonment, knew how to close off the sun in summer, how to capture an airless winter.

"Toss that box of books out," Rob calls from the open window.

I push it through and watch its escape into Rob's arms and the bright fresh air of the yard.

And though the hour grew later and later,
*   I would hold on for one more heartbeat.*

--James Taylor

Chapter 5

The next several hours blur. I am tired, beyond tired, and yet I want this job done and behind me. I am unaware of just exactly how much time has passed until I hear a commotion in the kitchen and I emerge to find Matthew standing there, looking so grown up that I almost don't recognize the young man smiling and holding his arms out to me. He is tall and handsome, dark like his father, but with sharp blue eyes, a gift from mine, and a bit more blondness. He flashes a smile at me so charming that my heart flutters.

"Hi, Mom!" he says, and he picks me up a little with his hug.

"Oh!" is all I can manage, and then, "I am so glad you're here."

"Me too," he says "are you okay?"

I realize suddenly that I must look terrible. Between losing my lunch and sweating my way through Mother's bedroom and half of the living room contents, I must be more than a mess.

"Y-yeah.." I splutter, "I'm just tired, you know from all the…work…" I am searching for words and fussing with my hair and fidgeting when I realize that there is someone else in the room.

Standing just behind Matthew, looking slightly unsure but smiling, is a girl. She is blonde and breathtaking, with waist length hair parted down the middle, warm chocolate colored eyes and a rose bud for a mouth. She has her hands in curvaceous blue jeaned pockets and one hip cocked slightly, one foot pigeoned just in front of the other.

"Oh!, Uh, Mom, this is Marie," Matthew says and puts his arm around her, scooting her forward.

I am speechless at the implications of her presence, and I turn to look at Grand and Rob who are having the same experience, Rob smiling broadly. Jenna has her hand over her mouth. I am grateful.

"Well," I finally manage, "Hello Marie…welcome, it's very nice to meet you, Sweetheart."

I hold out my hand to shake hers, but something about the action seems wrong and instead we hug each other, her instincts meeting mine, and our eyes meet with a commonality that surprises me entirely. We instantly have something wonderful in common; Matthew.

She steps back beside him and looks up at him smiling, he tightens his arm around her shoulder and smiles back at her. I am so taken by the sight of them that I find myself staring. It isn't that it never occurred to me that Matthew has girlfriends at college, but he only talks to me about them sparingly and for one to be with him now, well it means that she is more than someone to go to the movies with. It means she is someone important. And if she is important to Matthew, she is important to me.

As Marie and I continue to beam at each other, the decision is made to go and get some dinner. I excuse myself and take my purse into the bathroom where I excitedly refresh a bit of make up on my face and smooth my sweat laden hair.

We make the 20 minute drive into town, Matthew talking almost nonstop about school and the latest adventures of his unfortunate friend Albert who seems to forever be in trouble. We laugh, and as Grand and Jenna follow along behind us in the red Mercedes, it seems impossible that we have gathered for a funeral. It would seem entirely disrespectful if a person didn't know, as we all do, how very much her death is a gift.

It crosses my mind as we pass the school and the post office that even she, in her lucid moments would prefer this. I can see her sitting across the table from me, pouring tea with a quivering hand and passing me the cup.

"I don't know what came over me…," she said that day, surveying the shambles she had left in the kitchen, and the red mark on my face where she had slapped me.

"Susannah" she said, "you know that I …" her voice seemed to tremble off into nothing for a moment, "that I don't mean to…how sorry I am.."

I wept with her that day and I even went to the other side of the table and hugged her. I let her hold me and stroke my hair and rock me back and forth so much like Grand always did. It was the best and worst feeling I'd ever had. The best, because for a single warm moment, I had a mother who loved me, and the worst because I knew it would not last, because I knew that I couldn't really have it. Those sentient moments were few and far between for Mother. By the time I was sixteen, I don't remember her having them at all.

I am brought back to the present by catching a glimpse of Matthew's eyes in the rear view mirror. They are whole and full of joy, so different from the uncertainty I always saw in my own at his age. And they are so like his father's, though they differ in color.

Matthew has Angel's heart in his eyes.

We pull in to the one restaurant in town, a rustic, yet somehow elegant place called The Embers. The decor is log cabin, but with linen table cloths and real silver on the tables. We sit near the fireplace and we talk and laugh like a family; like a real family. It occurs to me with an almost startling clarity that I am happy and satisfied in this moment. Wellness is not a feeling I am familiar with. It seems to rest upon my shoulders uneasily, as if it is afraid of putting its feet down. I do my best to lure it in, however and watching Matthew and Marie from across the table seems to be helping me.

I find it so odd that seeing him with someone dear to him is having such an effect. I feel as if I should be doing something more "parental" in the situation. I should be eyeing her suspiciously and asking what their intentions are. I should be grilling him about propriety and at the very least we should be talking about "safe sex" and the consequences of the opposite. But I see in him a mature young man, one that I trust, one that is in command of his own existence, including his own sexuality and I am satisfied and even proud, if a bit unsure of my role as Mother of An Adult.

He smiles at me, and a dimple presses into his cheek and I suddenly have a lump in my throat. Angel and I were just a few years older than he is now when we were married. I had graduated only a few weeks before and things were so hysterical. The wedding had Mother in an absolute state of one fit connected to another.

The day of my wedding shower I was a nervous wreck. Grand had assured me over and over again that people "understood" the situation and that if Mother should begin to act up, surely they would take it in stride. Angel's mother was going to be there, his aunts, his sisters. I was horrified at the thought that their first real glimpse of the inner workings of my family would be in the form of one of Mother's rages. Maybe, if God was indeed watching, just maybe, she would be having a lucid day. Could I dare ask for that? I asked. I decided it meant enough to me to set aside my anger, get down on my knees and make the most formal prayer I had ever made in my life.

" Please, Lord," I begged, "let her have a normal day, just one day when she isn't so crazy. I'm not asking for you to cure her forever, just give me one day, that's all…"

When mother arrived at the banquet room, the decorations were up, the food was ready and Angel's family was already there. Angel's mother fussed over me in the most embarrassingly wonderful way. She held my face in both her hands and said things in Italian that I didn't understand, but knew were wonderful. She turned me around and patted my belly and told me I was "A-too skinn!" and urged me to "eat eat eat!!" A thing she still does to this day.

Mrs. Manotti was sitting next to me, running her hands through the back of my hair and talking about what a beautiful bride I would be when Mother walked over. She sat on the opposite side of me and did not speak. She stared silently ahead of her and said nothing. A trancelike look upon her face made my heart stop.

"Mother?" I looked into her eyes.

"Oh, hello," she said, and looked at me blankly.

Mrs. Manotti watched with her head cocked to the side. Angel's two sisters watched in the same position. They looked like figurines, still and perfect and staring.

"She's a-nerves...she's a-nerves." Mrs. M. said, patting me on the back and then touching Mother gently on the shoulder.

"I'll get you some tea, Mother." She nodded absently and stared into space.

I rushed over to the beverage table and with shaking hands fixed her a cup of tea. When I returned, Mrs. M. had slid one chair over and was next to Mother with her arm around her shoulders.

"You only daughta', and she leaves you! You just a-nerves. . .ok…ok…" Mrs. M. was saying and rocking Mother gently back and forth.

I handed over Mother's tea and sat on the other side of her. She had an entirely and completely blank expression. I stared and stared at her as the room filled with Mother's church friends, my few friends, more Manotti's and other people I didn't recognize.

Charlie's entrance was spectacular, bursting through the double doors and announcing that the party could now begin followed by a full chorus of "Here comes the Bride" as he carried in a gigantic, beautifully wrapped box.

He leaned over the table and kissed me and shot a quizzical look at Mother and then back to me. I shrugged and went back to being mesmerized by her. It wasn't until Jenna arrived that I began to get a clue as to Mother's current state.

Jenna was already hitting the bar at 10 a.m. I watched as she looked about herself surreptitiously, and then took two full shots of Vodka, one after the other and gazed woefully in the direction of Mother.

"Jenna, may I speak to you in private, please?" I said standing and calling to her from the table.

Jenna looked at me like a toddler with her hand in the cookie jar and once out in the hallway, immediately confessed.

"It's Valium," she said flatly, downing another Vodka.

"What!?"

"It's Valium, ok!? She was already starting, Susannah!! She threw her shoes at me when we were getting dressed. I told her they were aspirins for her headache and she took two of them!"

"Oh, Dear God…," I said, and held my stomach. I had no idea what this drug would do to her. Her illness caused her to react differently to many medications. On Librium she thought she could fly and had tried to climb up onto the kitchen table.

"I'm sorry Crumb Cake, I did it for you!" she called to my back as I rushed back inside.

Mother remained unchanged. She stared quietly ahead of her and did not even speak. Angel's sisters began the festivities, and pinned corsages on me and Mother and Grand. Grand stayed dutifully by Mother's side, spotted now and again by Charlie or Jenna.

I finally decided that I would relax a little, and I actually began to enjoy myself. We played the obligatory games, we ate, and finally I was opening my gifts. I was holding a large casserole dish above my head for all to see, when I heard a thump. The entire room looked in the direction of Mother who was laying face down on the table.

"Ohh!!! Ohhh!!" Mrs. M. was shouting, and a chorus of "Oh My God! and Oh No!" seemed to follow.

I rushed to her, dropping the casserole, which shattered loudly on the floor. The EMS was summoned and the shower was over.

Mother was fine, she had simply passed out sleeping from the Valium. She slept for a day and a half, and I supposed that what it all really meant was that I should be careful of what I ask for.

There would be no engagement dinner, as mother had been in one of her states just minutes before we were to leave. We called the Manotti's and told them that I had a migraine and we were terribly sorry. Mrs. M. had taken the phone from Angel and when I said hello, she said to me, "The Lord only give us what he know we can a-handle, child. You call Mama and I come to you, eh?"

"Yes,…" I managed, "thank you." I hung up the phone and cried myself to sleep. Did people really grow up with mothers who said that sort of thing? It was a wonder to me and my heart ached just at the thought.

I was terrified of what would happen at the wedding. The only solace I had was that the wedding would be at the church which seemed to be the one place in which Mother could keep herself from flying off the deepest end. She would lose her patience, sometimes say outrageous things, but usually, she could keep from an out an out rage. The closest she had ever come was in the parking lot just once, and Grand and I had managed to get her into the car by singing one of the hymns softly to her and coaxing her into the car to join in.

The day of the wedding, I was so nervous that she would ruin the ceremony that I was physically sick. She had spent the better part of the morning praying loudly in the church hall, counting off her rosary beads and wailing from time to time, Jenna fluttering about her and trying to keep her volume down. I paced about in my dress, checking my watch and taking antacid tablets.

20 minutes before it was to begin, there was a knock at the door of the bride's room. I opened the door to see Angel's smiling face. He kissed me softly and told me that I was a vision in my dress, and then he shussed me and pulled me by the hand down a back hallway in the church. There, in a small room, lit by the sun shining in through a round, stained glass window, were the groomsmen and bride's maids. They stood in a semi-circle with the Father in the center. Grand and Rob, Charlie and Angel's family stood on either side. Angel left me just inside the doorway and hurriedly took his place, Rob walked me the five steps from the door to the make-shift alter and he kissed my cheek.

"You deserve for this to be perfect." he said, and we both began to cry.

Angel took my hand and the Father performed a beautiful, quiet ceremony. I looked into Angel's eyes and told the world and God that I wanted to be his wife forever. He looked into mine and pledged "til death" to love me.

It was ten quick minutes of my life, sheltered away from even the chance of Mother stealing away some of my joy. We were married in intimate, loving, romantic perfection 5 minutes before our ceremony in the great church hall. The photographer took a few pictures and we were off.

No one even noticed that Angel wasn't really putting a ring on my finger out there, he just went through the motion and beamed at me as mother knocked over a candelabra and dropped to her knees to pray loudly. It didn't matter, I didn't care. I'd already had my wedding and it had been blissfully whole and perfect.

Discussion at the table suddenly turns to business at hand. Over coffee and chocolate cake we plan the funeral. We will ask Mother's church friend, Mrs. Yates to offer a eulogy. We will have a mass, we will sing mother's favorite two hymns, we will have a reception in the church social hall afterward, which the church's women's association will cater. We discuss flowers.

"Oh, Darling, I'm sure you will want to make the pall flowers won't you?" Jenna says and I am horrified. "Oh, of course you will. The ones you made for Great Aunt Beau were just stunning! Besides, it will save a little money and you know how practical Camille was...oh, Dear!?" Jenna dissolves into Matthew's shoulder. He places an arm around her and looks sincerely into my eyes. Unfortunately, I have made all the family pall flower arrangements, my artistic outlet since childhood a penchant for floral design.

"You don't have to if you don't want to, Mom," he says.

Marie looks at me and I feel pressured. I know I shouldn't but I don't want her to think badly of us, of me.

"No, I want to," I say, lying just as my cell rings. I excuse myself from the table and take the call in the bathroom. It is the perfect excuse for a small escape.

"You owe me big time Q!" It is Charlie, with good news.

"Richard says he'll help, but I have to meet him for coffee tomorrow. If this hadn't been for a beat up little girl, Suze, I'm telling you—"

"Oh Charlie, that is the first good news I've had in two days! Thank you so much!! I love you I love you I love you!"

"Yeah, yeah, I'm superman," he says, "but it's going to mean I'll be later getting up there tomorrow than I had thought."

"That is totally fine, I understand. God, Charlie, thank you so much!"

"Oh, and there is the matter of $1550.00 for first and last month's rent and security deposit. She has to have it the day she comes in, no exceptions. Dickey says the management is really sticky about it."

"I'm working on that part. Okay, I'll call Emmett and have him take her over there tomorrow. God, thank you Charlie."

"Prepare to massage my tootsies when you see me," he says.

"Got your oil warming even as we speak." He laughs.

"Well in that case..."

"See you tomorrow Charlie, you're a miracle."

"They parted the red sea when I was born, Baby!"

I call Emmett and he is less enthusiastic than I would like.

"$1550?! Goddammit, Susannah!"

"I know you can do it, Em. C'mon, we'll have signed lease papers for the Judge on Monday!"

"Susannah, does it occur to you that we are setting this woman up in an apartment that costs $600.00 a month, with a little girl to care for and she doesn't have a job?!"

My head hurts. My dinner is not going down well, I took too many big bites at the start and my stomach is cramping. I know I should keep my reactions under control, but somehow it's more than I can manage.

"Well dammit Emmett, no that has not occurred to me! Gee, thanks for pointing that out.!"

"Oh.. God.." Emmett's voice grumbles disgustedly at the other end of the line.

"Emmett, I am doing everything I can from here. I will make some calls to a couple agencies tomorrow, but for now we have to take whatever damned piece of the puzzle we can get!"

"There's more, Susannah."

My head reels, how could there be anything else?!

"She got a new attorney. The mother. It's that scum sucker Franken."

My heart stops. Geoffrey Franken is a big shot attorney who has won a very public, very controversial case that involved a state senator and about ten pounds of cocaine. To put it in a nutshell, even though the drugs had been found in his car and he was high as a kite at the time he was arrested, the "good" Senator did not go to jail. Since that time, Franken has done his best to get a hold of every news-making case in the state. His face was as common on the five o'clock news as the weatherman's.

"Why the hell would Geoffrey Franken be interested in this case?"

"Alltoll Bank would make him lots of money if he scored all their legal cases. He's takin' care o' business."

I rarely feel outmatched in court. It is the one place that is so far removed from Walloon and Mother and the dredges of who I used to be, that it makes me someone strong and capable and whole, the one place that I am not Camille Suffolk's beaten daughter. But now, picturing the spectre of Geoffrey Franken opposing me, I feel myself shrinking again, feel the house around me. I swear I can smell Mother's perfume.

"Any chance he wants a continuance?" I rub my nose to make the smell go away.

If Franken wanted some time to catch up on the details, Tuesday's hearing would be put off. We'd have more time to get Aunt Amy a job.

"Oh hell no. He's smarter than that, Susannah. He's raring to go. In fact, he was on the news a little while ago saying that the government has no right to harass—"

I interrupt him.

"Please, don't tell me." I know that Franken is very good at putting pressure on local politicians by pushing his cases in the media.

"Listen, I have to go. My family is waiting for me. I will call you tomorrow and please keep me posted. If you see Hannah, tell her..."

"I'll tell her we're doing our very best," he says, and now I know how bad it really is.

I take a moment to splash my face with water and I have a moment of realization. *I could leave.* I could go home and just do my job. Grand would be upset, but it's for a little girl and she'd understand.

Eventually, she'd understand.

For a moment, I feel a rush of relief and liberation. It's a valid reason. This is important, and now with Franken's involvement, it means the stakes have ratcheted up even higher. Protective Services could lose credibility. This could effect all kinds of cases if Franken makes them all look like a bunch of over-reactive power mongers. I have all the children in the system to think of.

I emerge from the bathroom and manage to catch Rob's eye. I motion him over and start telling him about the case.

"What are you getting at Susannah?" he says.

"I think I have to leave."

I am anticipating Rob's soft eyes, his gentle voice telling me to do what I need to do, his supportive words.

"Fuck you, Susannah," he says.

"What?!"

"None of us wants to be here. Do you think I wanted to drag my ass all the way up here and do this? Do you think for a minute that my life is easy to put on hold? Do you think that I like having everything I'm doing interrupted for this bullshit?"

"Of course not, I wasn't implying—"

"No, you don't have to imply it Susannah, you say it, you come right out and say it all the time. You're an attorney, you managed to "make it" in spite of everything and what the hell is wrong with your brother the goddamned factory rat, right?"

"What? Rob, no, I never said—"

"I'm the man, right? I shoulda' been the one to get my act together. I shoulda' been able to help you more, shoulda' stopped her, right? I'm the oldest so I can just stay here and take care of everything 'cause I deserve it, right?!" Rob is raising his voice and now Matthew stands and comes over.

"Uncle Rob," he says popping Rob on the back.

Rob swings on him a little too sharply and Matthew grabs him by the shoulders.

"Whoah! Uncle Rob, it's me. Let's take a walk." Matthew's voice is firm and his eyes level at Rob's. My chest goes cold as I stare at him. He is handling the situation like a man.

My heart is in my throat as I watch Rob's shoulders start to slump forward. Matthew leads him outside after calling over his shoulder to the table that everything his fine and I rush back into the bathroom and splash my face with more water. I am crying so hard that I can't stand up straight. My chest hurts. My stomach hurts, my head pounds.

How is it that I am so blind to what my brother thinks of me? Or more accurately, what he perceives I think of him. While I have been busy dealing with my fear, Rob has been dealing with his manhood. Mother left him forever scarred there. He will never feel fully powerful, fully whole. She emasculated him and my being a woman, and a successful one, apparently rakes across his scars. My head spills over with hatred and regret. Have I missed opportunities to tell my brother how proud I am of him? Have I told him how many times I know he saved me?

Now I am swept away in memory worse than the pain of the moment. I was 12 and Rob was 15. Mother had spent the morning dying Easter eggs. It was odd how she could occupy herself quietly for so many hours and then suddenly emerge with such fury. I had come in and passed by her at the table. She didn't seem to even notice me. She had Easter baskets set out on the table. There were three, which was her usual number. One for me one for Rob and one that she left on the doorstep. We never understood the reason for that and never asked. Mother did not like to be questioned, she took it as disrespect.

Even as we watched her putting them together, we never counted on actually getting them. Mother could just as easily wind up throwing their contents all over the house or stuffing it down the garbage disposal or tossing them into the lake.

When I closed the door to my room that day, I knew it made a sound. Mother didn't like closed doors. We closed them anyway, but we tried hard never to make a sound. When the door flew back open and hit the wall, I knew for certain. Mother had heard.

"What are you hiding in here?" she said.

"Nothing, Mother." I said as quietly as I could, my throat going tight.

"Don't you lie to me!" she said and charged for my hair. She grabbed a great handful and pulled me into the kitchen. It seared when she pulled and she held me on it as if it were a great whip, tossing me forward by yanking again and again.

She pushed me to the sink and forced my head under the sudden stream of ice cold water.

"Wash the lies out!" she shouted.

"Mother I didn't lie!" I said, trying not to cry, trying not to shout, and hoping to keep my breath under the water.

Her body had me pinned so tightly to the edge of the sink that I was finding it hard to breathe. My chest was compressed against the counter. I gasped and took in a mouthful of water. I choked until it came back out my nose.

Mother pressed harder against me. I couldn't take a breath. I couldn't get my chest to expand. The water rushed over my nose and mouth again and with horror, I saw that mother had also plugged the sink. It was filling fast.

"Mother I didn't lie!"

I choked out the words as best I could.

"Wash the lies out!! Holy water! Holy water!" she chanted over and over, each time punctuating it with a push of my head and the press of her body against mine. She dunked my face into the water in the sink and held my head under. She pulled it up again and just as I opened my mouth to take a breath, she pushed it down so the water went into my my lungs. I coughed, choked. I could feel the air being pressed out of me by her body, the water up my nose, in my mouth, in my chest.

Suddenly, as I began to feel dizzy. The room spun, Mother's voice echoed. The water came over my face again and again. I was fading out, slipping off somewhere when I felt Mother's body move away. I stood up too quickly, staggered and as my head was swimming, and the room seemed tipped to one side, I could barely make out what looked like Rob standing behind Mother. He'd heard the commotion and come in. Somehow, he had pulled her back away from me.

"Stop it, Mother," he said.

She whirled on him and slapped him hard in the face.

"I said STOP IT."

Mother stood very still for a moment. She walked calmly to the other side of the table.

"Robert, your sister is a filthy liar. If we do not stop this, Robert, she will become a common street walker and burn in hell. Do you want your sister to burn in hell, Robert?"

Rob knew as I did that there was no talking to her, there was nothing like reasoning with her.

Rob slid sideways and took hold of my arm. He pulled me away from the sink and toward the bathroom. He held on tight to my arm as he ducked in and grabbed a towel. His movements were liquid, hypnotic and slow. Mother stood and watched while it seemed like all air drained from the room. A hesitation hung in it like a movie stuck on the screen.

We would have to pass by mother to get out the door.

Rob began to move us in that direction. He was fluid, slow perfect movement and I did my best in my somewhat addled state to mimic him.

Mother watched us. Her eyes moved as her body stayed as still as a statue. We made it halfway, we made it almost to the door. We turned our backs to go out and that was when Mother chose her weapon.

A beaker, heavy glass on the bottom and she threw it with amazing accuracy at the back of Rob's head where it shattered.

Rob stumbled forward a moment. He braced himself in the doorway, keeping from falling onto me. I steadied both hands against his chest to keep him from falling forward out the door.

Mother began banging her pot on the counter and shouting .

"Wash the lies out, wash the lies out, holy water holy water!!!"

It took Rob only a moment to regain himself and then we fled out the door. By the time we'd reached Grand's that day, Rob had a full blown goose-egg on the back of his head. I'd had to stop twice on the way to choke up the water inside me, but we'd made it. Grand nursed Rob with ice and gave me warm soup to soothe my stomach. I remember looking over at Rob, laying on the sofa with the ice on his head. He looked so tired, and yet to me, he looked so strong. He'd challenged Mother and made her stop. He saved my life.

Rob was my first hero, and he never knew. I never told him.

How could I have never told him?

My thoughts of escape vanish and I am ashamed of myself for even having them. It is my love for Rob and Grand that keeps me here, not respect for Mother. Somehow making the distinction makes it at least a little easier.

I push my hair behind my ears and blot my face off, determined to remember what shreds of my family are left as I leave the bathroom.

Rob is standing so close outside the door that I nearly run into him. I fall into his arms and we cry together in the sheltered hallway outside the bathrooms.

"You were my hero." I say to him and hear him sob.

"I should have taken you away from there," he says, and I see now that in his very young manhood, he was faced with the notion adopting his own sister.

"Rob, you couldn't. Where would we have gone? How would we have survived?"

"Anything would have been better than that."

"You were always there for me." I say it and I mean it. "And I am sorry that I never told you how proud I am of you, and how much I love you. You saved me, Rob. You saved me all the time. You still do."

He hugs me tight.

"Shut up, Stinky," he says, and I crack up and sock him playfully on the arm.

"You shut up, Butthead!"

He smiles at me and paws tears off his cheeks.

"Will you go sit down?!" he says and pushes me jokingly toward the table. "God, you're always making a sceeeene!"

I sock him again playfully, and we head back, watching all the heads turn to see us coming.

When we smile, they all look relieved.

Soon it is established that the funeral will be on Saturday, which gives us another day to prepare, to call family and friends, to put an obituary in the paper. It gives me a day to make a pall arrangement that I have no idea how to begin.

We travel back to the old house, and Matthew and Marie roll up their sleeves and dig in to the project. I find myself packing up towels and linens with Marie.

"Mrs. Manotti," she says to me. I laugh a little and tell her to call me Susannah.

She smiles and twists an amethyst ring round and round on her finger.

"I hope it's okay that I came with Matt. I mean, I wouldn't want to intrude, and I know you really didn't know that I was coming and all…" I tell her that I'm glad she came and that I know Matt wanted her to come very much.

"Matt hasn't told me too much about his grandmother, but I get the feeling that sometimes, she was a little difficult." She says this as she folds a sheet set and places it in the box.

"Well, that's quite an understatement," I say, "she was pretty sick, emotionally, mentally. She wasn't easy to be around."

"You must have missed her."

She says this in an almost absent way, and I am stunned by the insight of the comment.

"Yes, I suppose I did."

She nods gravely. I hand her a blanket to place in the box.

"It's like looking at something through a store window. It's just inches in front of your nose, but you can't have it," she says looking into the box.

I feel tears welling in my eyes and I stare at her dumbly. She looks up at me from the floor with tears in her own eyes.

"When I was 16 my father was in a car accident. He had a closed head injury and he never really recovered. He's there, but he just…isn't." I see a girl aged beyond her years. I see myself in her liquid brown eyes.

I hold out my arms and bend toward her and she raises up on her knees to meet me. I hug her, and it doesn't feel strange, and I feel a kinship to her like nothing I have ever felt. We fit together like those Russian dolls that nest one inside the other, the same shape of the larger engulfing the smaller. I hold her for a minute and then I rest my hand on her dampened cheek.

"I'm so glad you're here," I say, and she smiles a ray of light into the room.

By 11:00 we are all exhausted and we travel en mass back to Grand's house. We are bedded down everywhere. Three of us girls are in Grand's bed and Matt and Rob are on the sofa and the recliner in the living room. Jenna is in the guest room alone. Before long, Grand is snoring and I can hear the gentle rhythm of Marie asleep in the center. Every bone in my body is aching with fatigue, but my head is awake. I cannot sleep. I try a few different positions, I do some deep breathing—nothing.

Finally, I can take no more and I slide out of the bed and put on my sweater, I slip out the side door and stand peering over the edge of the lake. I sit beneath a tree and think of how much time I've spent hiding in them. I run my fingers over my forearm and feel the delicate edges of a scar, and suddenly, it is happening again in front of my eyes.

I was 10, long before I'd thought of boys myself, but not too young to have Mother suspecting me of some kind of sexual misconduct. I'd come home from school with a book that one of my classmates had lent me. It was a Tuesday and mother was boiling water for pasta on the stove. I left the book on the table with my notebook and Mother picked it up while I was in the bathroom.

'What is this that you've brought into my house, young lady?" she said when I came back to pick up my books and take them to my room.

"It's a novel. My friend Allison—" I was cut off by the quick snap of Mother's hand across my mouth before I could finish. She hit hard this time, I tasted blood.

"How dare you bring that smut into my home?" she said, her eyes narrowing, her hands twitching at her sides.

"I didn't know it was smut." I said, and she slapped me again.

"You know full well what you are doing. Don't you give me some pathetic excuse, I didn't raise you to be a whore!"

She was shouting so loud and her face had gone so red that I was actually afraid she was going to choke and fall over, or maybe I was just hoping she would.

"You were going to take this in your room and touch yourself!" she screamed at me. "My daughter will not be some whore!"

She grabbed hold of my hand before I could get far enough away. She started pulling me and I couldn't understand where she was trying to take me until I realized she was yanking me toward the stove. She held my hand over the pot of boiling water. The heat from the steam was enough to burn and I shouted and tried to pull away.

"This is how we'll clean your dirty hands!!" she said and pulled my hand closer toward the pot.

The steam almost obscured her face, but I could see her eyes, her lips grim in determination, her teeth set hard. She was going to do it. I would have to fight if I was not going to have my hand plunged into boiling water. I pulled against her as hard as I could. I braced my foot against the side of the stove and pushed hard with my leg.

"Mother, I didn't DO anything!" I shouted, too terrified to cry.

"Don't you tell me what you did or didn't do!" she said and she yanked hard, and I fell forward, my forearm slamming down onto the edge of the pot, the metal searing into the tender skin, and I screamed as the hot water splashed up over my arm.

The water splashed Mother too, and she suddenly let go of me as if she'd awakened from a dream. Her eyes were wild and panicked, and she stood shaking and threw the pot into the sink. I sunk to the floor sobbing and clutching my burning arm to my body.

Rob came running when he heard me scream. He'd been down by the lake and when he saw what had happened, he grabbed an ice tray from the freezer and scooped me up off the floor. He took me away from the house to the edge of the lake.

I couldn't stop crying, the pain was terrible. He'd wrapped the ice in his t-shirt and made a pack for my arm, but he was scared, I could tell and so was I. It didn't look right, the skin was bubbled and peeled away, there was a kind of rut where the edge of the pot had burned into my arm, the skin was purple.

As we sat trying to calm our minds enough to figure out what do to, we could hear mother in the kitchen beating the pot on the counter and wailing.

Rob looked at my arm. The second the ice pack was removed, I cried out in pain again.

"C'mon.." he said, and with his face set in the most determined frown I'd ever seen, he walked me to the neighbors house.

I remember feeling as if I were sinking, standing out on that porch, my 13 year old brother without his shirt on, me with no shoes. Rob knocked on the door and the neighbor lady opened it. Her eyes looked frightened as she took us in.

"Um, our mother is um… sick and she can't take my sister to the Dr. or anything, but she got hurt. She was trying to cook some spaghetti and …"

I lifted the ice pack to show her the burn and she clasped a hand over her mouth and flung open the screen door.

In a few minutes we were in her car, traveling to the hospital. She had called Grand who was meeting us there. I remember looking at my feet in the slippers she'd lent me, and feeling the edge of her husband's shirt as Rob sat next to me in the back seat with his arm around me.

At the hospital, Grand held me as the Dr. treated the burn and the nurse took Rob down to the cafeteria to feed him some dinner.

I hated the look in the nurse's eyes. It was the same look the neighbor lady had when she'd turn her head to look at us in the back seat of her car. I came to recognize that look very quickly, it was the look that would forever remind me that I was not "normal", the look that told me I was pitiable, handicapped, marked forever by Mother.

We stayed at Grand's for a week that time, and only went back because Mother threatened to have Grand brought up on charges. Grand didn't know how to handle the situation, and like the rest of us, she hoped it would get better. She hoped for a normal life with a daughter who would care for her own children. I know that Grand should've done more to take us away, but she was just as caught up in the horror of it all as the rest of us.

The wind is just starting to chill me when I feel a blanket being put around my shoulders. I turn, it's Matthew.

"You okay, Mom?" he says, and I start to cry.

Matthew pulls me into a hug and then we sit together with the blanket over our shoulders.

"It's all over now Ma, she's gone."

"Physically, anyway," I say, and he gives me a funny look. "The memories here are hard."

He nods.

"Do you think about Dad when you're here?" I can hear the hopeful tone in his voice.

"Yes, a lot actually." I tell him the truth.

"It's funny picturing you two here. I mean I can kinda' see it when I look around here, the two of you as kids, running around the lake and stuff."

I laugh and shake my head.

"So.." I say, " Marie…"

"Yeahhhh.." he puts his head down and grins, and I feel my chest flux.

"She was in my Intro to Physics class and she was the only one in there who beat my scores. We kinda' started competing. Then one day, I asked her if she wanted to study with me. We didn't study, we just talked and she's just so cool and so smart and God, she's gorgeous."

I laugh out loud and he does too. I am feeling so many things at this moment I am not sure I can identify any single one. I am happy and excited, but also scared and a little overly sensitive. I feel as if I will flinch if he talks about her again.

"I like her." I say.

"I was hoping you would." He smiles at me. There is relief and happiness in his face.

For a while, we sit and watch the lake in silence.

Soon, I can feel Matthew's head bobbing and I tell him it's time to go inside. He settles back in to his blankets and I go to the kitchen where I turn the kettle on and rummage in the refrigerator for something sweet. Grand has not let me down and there is a bounty left over from lunch. I heap a slab of apple cake and several nut brownies on a plate and settle in at the kitchen table.

The brownies seem to be just the ticket and I am stuffing half of one into my mouth as I hear Rob stirring in the living room. He staggers into the room and silently gets another cup from the cupboard and sits down across from me. We eat quietly for a while, gathering more brownies from the fridge and dipping into the cookie jar as well.

Suddenly, right in the middle of a perfectly good oatmeal cookie, Rob's chin begins to quiver. He hangs his head and begins to sob. For a moment, I am riveted and I don't know what to do. But I move at last, and sit beside him and cradle him into my arms.

"Damn it!" he says into the collar of my robe. "Damn her."

I rock him back and forth as best I can and I pat his back.

"I don't want to feel anything," he says after a few wet minutes and he wipes his nose on his sleeve.

"I know."

"It just isn't fair," he says, and his chin quivers again and he sniffs hard and shakes it off with a snap of his head.

"I know that, too."

"Hey," he says, smiling "Remember 'Rock Theater' ?"

I laugh out loud and nod my head with my mouth too full of brownie to speak.

It had been our only outlet. About half a mile down from the house there was a bank of large, gray slate rocks at the edge of the lake. One of the rocks stuck out above the rest, just at the top like the presidium of a stage. A flat piece at the bottom completed the picture and it was a natural spot for our therapeutic performances. We would entitle them cleverly. My favorite was 'Camille's Comeuppance', in which Mother died and met St. Peter at the gates of heaven, and when St. Peter refused to allow her admittance, she would rage and try to rip his wings off. St. Peter would of course report this to Christ who would sentence her to hell, where he sent her in an elevator shaped like a giant slotted spoon.

Satan would greet her with the words, "Camille Suffolk!! I love your work!"

She would spend eternity chaperoning proms in hell, having to watch all the teenagers making out with duct tape over her mouth. Rob did a grand impression of mother apoplectic over a couple going at it in a janitor's closet and unable to grunt out a word!

We laugh quietly at the kitchen table and eat more brownies and cake and drink tea until my stomach is stuffed and I am feeling drowsy. Rob kisses me on the side of my head and brushes the crumbs off his shirt as he heads back to the recliner and curls up under Grand's quilt again. I head back into Grand's room but instead of crawling back into bed I sit in the rocking chair by the window and watch them sleep. I know that Matt is light years from marriage right now, but I am struck with a "generational" feeling as I look at Grand and Marie sleeping, a feeling of continuum. It comforts me just a little.

The whole night passes and I do not sleep. At six I get up from the rocker and put coffee on. I watch from the kitchen window as the sun rises over the lake. It's such a perfect and beautiful sight. Orange sherbet rays begin to dance in over the blue of the water. Yellow and red follow and it mixes with blue sky into shade after unmatched shade. I know that I must've seen it hundreds of times in my childhood, but I feel that I have never before seen it like this. There is a newness about it, a true dawning, an age of peace if I can only find it.

At eight I call Charlie and tell him when the funeral is going to be. He tells me he will be up later tonight and I am so relieved I could cry.

At eight-thirty I call Emmett.

"Hey!" I say "Any progress?"

"The grant money is stalled," he says, and I feel my heart sink. "And, our man Franken is pulling out some interesting tricks. He's claiming that the agent who took the complaint on Hannah searched the house without a warrant."

"God, please tell me he didn't."

"Opened a dresser drawer to get Hannah a sweater."

"Goddammit!" I say, knowing what Franken will do with that information.

I had called my friend at the jobs board before dinner the night before and it doesn't look good but I decide not to share that information with poor Emmett just at this moment.

"On the grant, anything we can do?" I ask.

"Got 800 bucks you can spare?"

I laugh out loud. Emmett is offering to split it with me. It is almost a cardinal rule that we who are involved in the system never use personal funds to help out a case, because the cases never end. There could be three more in just as deep need tomorrow.

"Absolutely," I chirp, and Emmett laughs.

"Rules?" he says, "What rules?"

"I'll call Michelle and have her wire it over. Emmett, you're fantastic."

"No, I'm a sucker stuck on a lawyer with too little sense."

I feel a stab of ice in my chest.

"What did you say?"

"Ahhh nuthin'," he says, and then there is too much silence.

"Emmett. . ."

"Talk to you later, Susannah." The phone goes dead.

There is absolutely no room in my head for this. I cannot conceive of Emmett having feelings for me on top of everything else that seems to be trying to eat me alive. Emmett is kind and a hard worker. I like Emmett. Emmett is my friend. Emmett and I have shared more aggravation and more successes and failures than—

My own head stops the thought: than anyone else in my life.

These thoughts repeat themselves over and over in my head as I shower and get dressed. My mind cannot seem to get past them until I pick up the scent of pancakes.

Grand has prepared an epic breakfast and we all sit down to eat. The pancakes are perfect, fluffy and light and I drown them in syrup and take huge bites. I hold them on my tongue and all thought is relieved. There is nothing but the world that fills my mouth; the world that fills my stomach. I fill my plate again with more bacon, more pancakes. I am overstuffed but I keep eating.

The taste is remarkable. It's as if I have never eaten them before. I notice Matthew watching me eat and raising his eyebrow now and then. I notice that Marie looks at me once and then keeps her head down. I don't care. There are warm pancakes and syrup. They are on my plate and they will not be taken away. They will not be cold and hours old before I eat them. I will not have to smell them and then go hungry. I eat more and more. I have shut out the table entirely. I know they are talking, but I don't know what they are saying and I don't care. I am inside the plate, inside the pancakes. I am as light as they are, as sweet as the syrup, as gentle as the butter that melts on top.

Finally I look up and they have all gone. Grand is washing up the pans and glancing over her shoulder at me.

"Did you sleep?" she says, when I raise my head up and take a gulp of milk.

"No." I say and swallow it down. The cold milk eases the feeling of fullness in my belly. I feel my face flush.

"Susannah—" she says.

I stop, the fork crammed into my mouth, and look up at her. I have no idea how much I have just eaten. My stomach feels so full that I may be sick.

I hand her my plate and try to chew down the mass I already have in my mouth. It is such a big bite that I am struggling. I gulp more milk.

"Honey, you're hurting. Maybe we should talk," she says.

"We're all hurting." I say to her, bristling. I don't like the implication that somehow I am more affected by Mother's death than the rest of them.

"Grand. I'm fine." I kiss her on her cheek and give her my milk glass.

Back in the bedroom I have to lie down a minute before I can get dressed. My stomach is killing me. I am so full, I truly feel that moving will make me ill.

There is a knock on the door.

"Mom, ready to go?"

Rob and Jenna have headed to the funeral home. Grand is phoning up the Women's Church Association, and Matthew and Marie and I are to head out to the craft store to pick up silk flowers for Mother's pall. I have no idea what to make, or how to begin it. Every other time I'd made pall flowers, I had an image in my head of what would be appropriate. It was a reflection of the person, of what they meant to me, of how I had loved them.

"I just need a few minutes, ok Honey?" I call back.

"Ok," he says, and I hear it in his voice, the worry.

I take off my jeans and put on sweats. They are much kinder on my stomach and I pull an oversized t-shirt over them. This will work and I can almost move freely. I emerge from the bedroom and Matthew looks me up and down but doesn't say anything. Marie smiles at me weakly. I feel as if I should say something, make some explanation for my wolfing breakfast, but I don't. Instead I put my hand on Matthew's shoulder and smile at him. We head for the door and no one says a word.

At the craft store, I send Marie and Matthew down other aisles to collect up wire and floral tape and base material, felt and ribbon, and I begin to look through the flowers. I pass by the roses, too passionate in red, too innocent in white. I pass by the daisies and sunflowers and freesia, all far too happy. I turn up my nose at the cheerful carnations, and even the lillies are too dignified. I am completely lost. I stare blankly at a wall of various colors of eucalyptus and wait for inspiration, which seems to have abandoned me.

Finally, desperate, I begin thinking that if only this were for someone else, I would not be so paralyzed. I try to imagine what I would make if the arrangement were for say, Charlie's mother, a very nice woman who sends me home baked cookies every Christmas and never misses my birthday. A lady who came to my house and made me dinner when I'd had foot surgery two years ago, the lady who had given me one of the best gifts of my entire life; my Charlie. Now this is inspiration! I head straight back for the white roses, the lillies and even add a few bright yellow daisies and some freesia. I choose a mint green eucalyptus and some ivy vines and ferns. The kids come back to me with their arms loaded and we make our way back to the check out with a full cart. This will work, and I am feeling very smug until I spot a woman heading straight for me.

It is Mrs. Naysmith, one of Mother's church friends, and she has obviously heard the news. Her nose is red and her eyes are puffy from crying. She will be looking for grief. She has it to share.

"Oh, Susannah, Dear!" she gushes, hugging me briskly and tearing up over her half glasses. "I was just stunned when I got the news this morning, just stunned! That poor dear woman! Are you alright?"

"Yes, Ma'am," I say feeling myself shrink to age 10 in her presence. My stomach gurgles loudly and I feel myself blush.

"Well, you know the Association called and of course I'm going to bring my cucumber salad tomorrow and I thought I'd make a pineapple cake…" she says, her voice trailing away to tears and shaking her head, dabbing at her red nose with a monogrammed handkerchief.

It strikes me suddenly that she lives for this sort of thing, for the opportunity to trot out her best recipes and to sit in the church social hall and shake her head and dab tears away and talk with the mourning families. She'll love to have the "inside word" and pass it along to all the others. It makes me smile, and I thank her very sincerely. Mother's passing is giving these sweet and well intentioned little ladies such a nice jolt. She blankly hugs me again and wanders off, undoubtedly wondering what I was looking so happy about.

We drive back to the old house where there is still so much to be done. Jenna and Rob will be meeting us when they have finished. The kitchen, now empty save for the table and chairs, will be my workshop and I spread out my supplies as Matthew and Marie carry up box after box from the basement.

I begin snipping the wires and wrapping the stems, a rather mindless job, and as I do, I can hear the lake outside. It makes the hair on the back of my neck stand up just a little. There is too much quiet in this place today, and I can hear that lake too well. I can remember in our very first home together, Angel begging me to turn off the stereo for just a minute or two. Back then I couldn't enjoy a quiet room in any house.

Even on our wedding night I insisted that the radio be on. We danced and drank champagne and I was so exhausted that on our first night together, we fell asleep. It was the most blissful sleep I had ever had. I was safe and warm in Angel's arms and no one could ever take it away from me now.

In the morning, I woke to the sound of Angel in the shower. It seemed like the perfect way to start our new life together and so I slipped out of my "wedding night penoir", that Charlie had bought for me, and snuck into the bathroom.

The hotel room shower was beautiful, in gray marble and shining silver fixtures. I pulled back the curtain and he was just rinsing the soap from his face when he saw me.

"Well, well…" he said smiling at me and pulling me into the tub. He held me close to him, the blissful warm shower beating down on us. We kissed slowly and ran our hands all over each other.

My head began to race. As much as I knew I should be concentrating on my new husband and the wonderful way he made my body feel, I couldn't help but think of all the ways in which the act we were about to commit was going to change me. I'd heard it my whole life, how having sex diminished a woman, how it made her nothing more than used goods, how no one wanted to marry a non-virgin. The problem with all this so-called godliness was that I couldn't see how sex wasn't going to soil me now. I suddenly felt as if I were about to allow something awful to happen to myself. I pulled out of Angel's arms abruptly and jumped out of the shower. I didn't want to cry, so I held my breath to keep from it. I pulled the towel around me as tightly as I could and sat rocking myself on the bed as a damp and bewildered Angel appeared in the doorway with a very healthy erection.

"Oh God!' I yelped and buried my face in the pillow to cry at last. Gasping so hard that I was sucking the pillowcase into my mouth, I pushed my face into the pillow harder and harder, hoping it would crush the feeling out of me.

Angel threw on his robe and came to the bed to hold me. He laid the sheet over my back and scooped me up, wrapped in it, practically swaddled. He held me to his chest while I sobbed.

"I'm sorry," he said.

"You didn't do anything wrong," I told him, feeling my face blush deep red. I felt more like a preadolescent girl than a married woman. I couldn't believe that I had ruined the consummation of my marriage by dissolving into tears.

"I should have told you to wait," he said.

"NO!" I shouted at him. I wasn't going to have him taking blame for something that I knew in my heart was Mother's fault.

"Hey, how about some breakfast?" he said, smiling at me.

I was speechless. At first, I was incredibly angry! He was cutting off what was obviously a very important conversation.

"Angel!" was all I could manage.

"Let's get some breakfast," he said and he kissed me on the forehead and then disappeared into the bathroom.

I was immediately panicked. Had I ruined it? Was he so angry that he didn't even want to talk to me?

I dressed with tears streaming down my face. Our marriage was doomed. The scars that Mother had inflicted upon me were going to mar every good thing in my life. There would be no good things in my life.

Angel emerged from the bathroom, dressed, looking so handsome it made my heart hurt. I looked up at him from where I sat on the edge of the bed, holding my shoe in my hand, somehow unable to manage putting it on.

He took the shoe from my hand and kneeled on the floor in front of me. He lifted my foot and kissed the tip of my big toe before he slipped it on my foot.

This was such a "Cinderella" moment, my head began to swim.

"Listen," he said, holding my hands and staring up at me, a lock of his hair falling over one eye, "we have our whole lives together. We don't have to rush anything. This is a big deal for you—-for us. I'm going to predict that it will happen for us when it's time for it to happen and that we shouldn't worry about it."

I began to think he wasn't real. How many men would handle this with such kindness? How many men would not be angry and sullen, having expected a sex filled wedding night?

I pulled him into my arms and told him how much I did not deserve him.

Looking back, I suppose it was only one of many things that made me feel that Angel was better than me. It was a theme that began to permeate my thoughts about him.

Soon our life together began in earnest. I was in law school, and Angel was working with his father. I can picture the living room of our flat in every detail, right down to the shelf where I kept Angel's beach glass under a tiny spotlight I had found in a book store.

Life with me wasn't easy. I knew it then as I know it now, but I couldn't seem to control it. I would become unreasonably nervous. Anxiety consumed me almost daily. Angel would be five minutes late getting home and I was a wreck. Disaster had marred almost every moment of my life so far, why would I expect it to be any different now? Eventually my anxiety worsened to the point where I felt that to keep safe meant to keep to myself.

It was a devastating the first time that Angel's arms could not cure my anxiety. He'd gotten stuck in a traffic jam coming home from a build site one day. I remember it as clear as if it were yesterday, pacing the floor, phoning the foreman at the build and begging him to look for Angel on the site. After my third call, they stopped answering the phone. He had been due home at 4 and it was 5:10 and still no Angel. I walked the porch, I walked the block. By 5:30, I had begun weeping and couldn't stop.

The neighbors who lived in the flat above us came down to see what was wrong. I was lucky they were such kind people, a couple in their forties, they stayed with me and made me tea and tried to settle me. I was hysterical by the time I heard Angel's car in the drive. I burst from the door before anyone could stop me and nearly knocked him down. I had him pinned to the car, sobbing, swearing, pounding on his chest with my fists. My neighbors rushed out after me and tried to hold onto me while Angel got his footing.

"How could you do this to me?!" I kept shouting. Angel blurted his explanation as best he could between my outbursts. The freeway had been closed down due to an accident. Traffic had been at a total stand-still.

When I actually collapsed to my knees in the yard, I was loaded into the car and taken to the emergency room. The emergency room Dr. gave me a shot of something that put me out, and Angel spent the night sitting at my bedside. I was released the next day with a bottle of pills and the phone number of a therapist, which I threw away. I had spent the better part of my life keeping silence in the details of my life, I wasn't about to start talking about it.

When I felt there was something wrong, there was no comforting me, and when Matthew was born, I had a very hard time. The pills helped, but only so much, and after a while we couldn't find a Dr. who would prescribe them until I would agree to therapy. Angel would bring Matthew to me, wet and wriggling after a bath, smelling like everything baby, and it should've made maternal feelings well over in me, but I felt dead. It was as if someone had flipped a switch off inside me. I couldn't nurse him, though my breasts were gorged with milk and overflowing. It felt awkward and painful and I would give up after just a minute and dissolve in tears and Angel would have to take him and give him a bottle.

Finally, exhausted and terrified, Angel called the Dr. He gave me a prescription and told Angel to set the baby in my lap and leave the house. He told him to leave for a full day, 24 hours and do not come back and do not call. At least that was what I was told. I was told that Angel would be at his parent's house all night, a good hour's drive away. In reality, Angel was staying over night upstairs. That way if the baby cried for hours, or I had one of my "spells" he'd be right there to intervene.

I remember sitting there, stunned, staring down at this little being in my lap wondering why I was supposed to take care of it.

Matthew lay quietly for a while, staring up at the patterns of light from the window. He kicked his tiny feet once or twice and curled and uncurled his fingers. I eyed him suspiciously. Just what did he want from me? How was I supposed to be a mother? I had no idea what the word meant! How was I supposed to know what he wanted? How was I supposed to nurture him and care for him when he was hurt or upset? I was clearly the wrong person for this job. The thought came to me dispassionately, as if I were deciding whether to get a hard top or a convertible and then, Matthew began to cry. I looked down at him and considered the situation. So what? He was crying. Big deal, babies cry.

I waited a few minutes. He kept crying. The sound didn't even seem to bother me. Even as it got louder and louder, I just sat there and looked at him laying across my knees in the bed. I slid out from beneath him and stood beside the bed just watching. He seemed to be flailing a little, as if he thought he was about to fall.

The crying went on, and I just stood there. I had turned to walk to the kitchen to get a glass of water when I heard it. It was not a crying sound.

It was a choking sound!~!!

I flung my body around and in two mammoth steps I was back to the bed and had him in my arms and over my shoulder patting his back.

"Omigod! Are you okay!??!" I kept repeating as if he were about to say, "Why yes, Mother thank you so kindly, I'm very well…"

The choking sound stopped on my shoulder and I whipped his tiny body around in front of my eyes and looked at him. He had resumed crying instead, and the relief that flooded over me began to mingle with some other vague, untapped feeling.

I rested his tiny forehead against mine and I smelled him as he cried. I felt the heat from his tiny mouth and suddenly, as if a gasket had blown, I knew I was his mother. I knew he was my child, and I knew that he needed me. Me, only me, and no one else could fill this need. We cried together then, and I took him back to the bed and propped a pillow in my lap and I kissed him on his wide-open crying mouth and on the top of his head and I began to nurse him. The sore nipple didn't matter, it didn't exist. The only thing that mattered was that my baby was hungry and he needed me.

Angel came in worried the next morning, to find Matthew asleep on my bare chest under the sheets. I woke to find Angel laying next to me, his arm around us both, tears on his cheeks, even the dimpled one.

I am startled by pricking myself accidentally with an errant wire, and I look up just in time to see Rob and Jenna coming dutifully back through the door with arms full of papers and faces that have just been to a funeral home.

Jenna sets a paper carrier full of coffees on the table and Matthew and Marie wander in to take one.

They all circle the table around me, surveying my progress. I have all the stems wrapped and all the flowers laying in straight lines, good soldiers lined up in battle formation. There is something about flowers that brings home the stone cold reality that there has been a death. No other flowers look like funeral flowers, at once beautiful and sad.

They stand a long time around the table and say nothing. I pick up the first stem to put into the arrangement. As it pops into the styro-foam base with a hollow crunch, they trail off one by one, back to the business of cleaning out the house of the dead.

As I add more flowers I am having a harder and harder time making them look the way I want them to. They seem to be coming out too perfectly, a thing that would ordinarily make me happy.

I pull out a stem and put it back exactly where it had been before. I pull out another and do the same. I wish I had a picture of Charlie's mother with me as a reference. I close my eyes and try to picture her; her brown eyes, her blondish hair, the little turtlenecks and sweaters she wears, her glasses.

It helps me for a few minutes and I add a few more stems before I become entirely stifled again. A wave of exhaustion comes over me. I have not slept in over twenty four hours now and it has begun to catch up with me. I know that if I am not arranging flowers, I should be carrying out boxes or packing up the attic or, worse, cleaning out my old room. I am too tired and too emotionally boggled to even contemplate pitching in. I decide instead to take a walk, and maybe it will refresh me.

I lift a coffee out of the paper tray, slip on my coat and head outside. The sun is shining across the lake, silvery and blinding, and the leaves are a symphony of sight. This place is so beautiful in every way. The air smells clean, the sound of the lake and leaves is soothing to the senses, or at least it should be. It is the oddest mixture of appreciation and anxiety that floods me as I walk along. So much about this place is unchanged. I reach up and play at my necklace, pulling it over my lips and feeling the smooth pendant on my cheek.

I sip my coffee and stare into the lake and I realize that I am just at the spot where Angel had produced my glass from the sand. How I always treasured that beach glass. I was devastated the day it disappeared.

I was dusting, and the place where it had always sat, under it's own tiny spotlight was suddenly empty. I had been cleaning rather absently that day, my mind wandering and I was certain that I must've just knocked it down behind the shelf or under some other knick knack.

I searched for an hour, moving every piece of furniture, dumping out the vacuum cleaner bag, pulling the cushions off the sofa. Angel came home that afternoon to find the place a shambles and me at the center of it sobbing.

He had helped me put it all back together and held me as I cried. He told me that it didn't matter if the glass was with us or not as long as we had each other, that our love was stronger and deeper than any physical thing. I said that I understood, and that of course, he was right, but it left this odd lingering feeling of doom in my chest. It was as if its disappearance meant that our life and love was somehow endangered.

That feeling would come back to me constantly. If Angel was late, if I couldn't account for a particular check he had written, if he forgot to call me during the day at work, I went immediately to doom. I kept the little spotlight on even though the glass was missing. I looked at it every day, and turned it off every night with a clawing sadness in my chest.

It was on our first anniversary, some months later that I realized just how unreasonable my anxiety was.

We'd planned a quiet evening together. I had a gift for him that I was more excited about than any I had ever given him. I had found a company that made Geodesic Dome houses. I had gotten them to send me some information and I had ordered from them the plans, the actual blue prints for our dream dome house.

We ate dinner by candlelight and drank wine and then excitedly we sat on our little love seat and exchanged our gifts. I made him open his first and he was duly awestruck. He spread them out on the floor immediately and we were about to start pouring over them together, when he remembered that I had not yet opened mine.

He held both my hands in his and looked into my eyes.

"I have to tell you something," he said so gravely that my heart came up into my throat.

"I've lied to you," he said, "not an out and out lie, but the kind of lie where I didn't tell you something that I could have, but for a good reason. I hope you will forgive me."

I held my breath, overcome by fear.

With that, he kissed my hand and I opened a black velvet box to reveal my beach glass mounted onto a white gold pendant and hanging from a chain. I have to this day, never in my life received a gift that meant so much to me.

"Yes," I said, "I forgive you…"

I rub the glass between my fingers and hold it in my clenched fist. I still wear it every day without thought.

I knew I had become more and more withdrawn from him as the years had gone on. It was as if I were watching myself do it, but was unable to stop. I threw myself into work, into Matthew and for a time, into alcohol for comfort. The law was draining. The early cases I had were of the tragic type, nothing but personal injury and malpractice. I hated it, but it was the partnership track and I was determined to be on it. Independence had become all important. Deep down inside I became convinced that the only way to survive was to be certain that I did not need anyone, that my life could be entirely self contained. Only then, I reasoned, was one safe from injury. Depend upon no one and no one can hurt me.

I spent long hours at the office, and every minute at home with Matthew. Angel would wait up for me, he'd stay up until 2am just to see me when he had to get up by 5 for construction work. I would reward him by passing out on the sofa before we'd had more than just a few minutes conversation. It was the effect of two or three martinis after Matthew's bed time stories.

The lake washes loudly before me and I am suddenly aware of how much he has been on my mind. Standing here, I can almost see him down by the oak, smiling at me, the wind in his hair, that look in his eyes; warm, calm, welcoming. My memories of Angel were borne in this place and they come alive here. I only wish that I could.

The sound of voices behind me, and I turn to see Matthew and Marie. They have evidently not seen me and they are standing still and talking softly to each other. I stand still as well and watch them.

He touches her cheek and brushes an errant piece of hair from her eyes. He kisses her. This is not an innocent kiss, not the kiss of a child. She wraps her arms around his neck, she drops one of her gloves. One of his arms wraps around her waist and I turn away, my heart thumping, alarmed.

My son is a man.

He is one of them, those creatures that Mother warned me about. I am distinctly unsettled by this. A baby boy, a little boy, a young boy, a teenage boy, a young man, these are all distinctions that bring a being just short of the actual pronouncement, of the actual embodiment of one of them. I am boggled by how this transformation can have happened in three quick seconds. A girl in his arms, some physical contact and "bang" there it is. This is more than the lingering feelings I'd had yesterday when he arrived with Marie, or when he stood up to Rob's bristling.

My son is a man.

There is a girl who sits and wonders what he feels for her, who marvels at the feel of his hands on her body, who thinks about a life with him, who wonders if he is thinking of her and how.

I walk away quickly, around to the other side of the house by the road. I stand there staring at nothing and looking out across the fields. The impact of the men in my life has been staggering, either by their absence or presence, or even by their reputations they have molded me in ways that Mother never dreamed. It's funny how being warned repeatedly about them only made them more fascinating to me. I have had wonder and trauma from them all, and now there would be one more.

He who limps is still walking.
--Stanislaw J. Lec

Chapter 6

Back inside, my arrangement sits on the table looking sad and sparse and incomplete. I am hoping that if I blink my eyes a few times, ala' I Dream of Jeanie it will suddenly be whole and I will be done with this wretched act of deception.

I hear Jenna fussing loudly in Rob's old room and I hesitate, "Do I really want to know?"

I turn the corner to see she and Rob and Grand all sitting on Rob's old bed, amidst the shambles that was once his bedroom. They have a photo album and they are smiling and laughing and flipping pages. I am suddenly without the ability to move. I do not want to see her. I don't ever want to have to look at her face again. It will be bad enough trying to ignore it at the funeral.

I turn to flee, but am discovered.

"Susannah! Come and look!" Jenna says.

I take gummy steps toward them and Rob holds up the page for me to see. It is a photo of Angel and I circa 1980, dressed for the prom. I have on a cream colored dress that Grand had bought for me. It was floor length and made of a beautiful silky material with a patterned sheen to it. It was sleeveless and the top was smocked slightly. A lace vest went over the thin shoulder straps. My hair is curled at the sides like Farrah Fawcett's famous poster, and I have a corsage on my wrist of red and cream colored roses with a cream silk ribbon.

Angel is wearing a tuxedo that his uncle Tony rented for him. He looked so handsome that night that I thought I was dreaming. I had escaped the prison tower in the House of Camille and Angel was my prince. He carried me off to the palace and we danced all night long. We had avoided the nights ruination by arranging to meet at Grand's, I was living there pretty much full time at that point anyway. It was after I'd packed all my things and retreated there. Mother never even knew it was prom night.

It is a heartening memory. I laugh dutifully at our dated appearance, and take the opportunity to leave the room, clutching the memory to my chest, twirling my beach glass between my fingers and my heart.

The cell phone rings, it is Emmett.

"Okay, she's met with the manager of the apartments and she's actually moving her stuff this afternoon."

"Oh God, Emmett that is fabulous!" my heart leaps, it's good news, one tiny piece at last.

"Yeah but Franken is on it. He's had news cameras over at the boyfriends place."

At this sudden reversal, my head swims.

I lower myself to the floor of the kitchen and pull my knees into my chest.

"Tell me." My head begins to throb.

"He was over there showing the building, complete with hookers on the corner, the run down apartment, and get this: Drug paraphernalia on the kitchen table."

"How the hell did he get inside the apartment?"

"Land lord got to be on T.V.!" Emmett says and I start to cry. I hold my hand over the phone and sob.

"Don't lose it now, Susannah."

"Emmett—" I manage and I come completely unhinged. I am helpless. I am on the floor of the kitchen and Mother is coming at me with the slotted spoon. I am fending off her blows with my forearm, feeling the metal cut into my skin. She is there, swing after swing, cut after cut. I sob again, try to draw in a breath.

I press the disconnect button and turn the phone off so he can't call me back. I am consumed with the same feeling I'd always had when the teachers at school would examine my injuries and still send me home at the end of the day. It's that feeling that all of the edifices of safety in the world are really nothing more than a sham. Policemen, doctors, teachers, principals and counselors; none are more powerful than the mother who abuses. None have any ability to soothe or save, and there is no use depending upon anyone.

In the fifth grade, Mother had decided that we should wear uniforms to school. We did not attend a Catholic school as Mother could not afford it, but she decided that we were becoming far too "worldly" in our dress as she put it, and had placed catalog orders for uniforms which she made us wear. My teacher that year was a kind man named Larry Lanford. Mr. Lanford was the best teacher I'd ever had. I adored him. If I could've chosen a father, Mr. L would have been the one.

One summer day, I showed up with bruises down both my legs. There was no way for me to hide them in the skirt and long socks that went with the uniform. Mr. L had taken one look at me that morning and, as soon as he had the rest of the class reading an assignment, he'd called in one of the teaching assistants to take over. He tapped me on the shoulder and took me into the hallway.

"Do you mind if we talk a little while?" he said.

Because I trusted him implicitly, I told him I didn't mind at all and he took my hand and led me to the playground where we sat side by side on the swings.

"Susie, how's everything at home?"

My antennae went up. I knew that question. He was not the first teacher to approach me with it.

"Fine." I said.

"Well, that's good." He kind of swung a little back and forth.

"It's just that, you know Susie, sometimes grown ups need help."

I was silent. I stopped swinging and held myself still.

"Grown ups get overwhelmed sometimes. Do you know that word, overwhelmed?" he said.

I nodded.

"Does your mother get overwhelmed sometimes?" he asked, and my heart swelled with wanting to tell him.

He looked at me. His eyes were warm brown, the color of milk chocolate and he tipped his head to the side. Oh, I wanted to tell him everything. I wanted to cry and dive into his arms and let him protect me. For a moment I envisioned him taking Rob and me home. I pictured a life where Mr. L was my father, where we laughed and played games and had meals together and cleaned up the dishes singing songs afterward. I had never before trusted any adult other than Grand. I knew Mr. L would do everything he could for me, but I also knew that Mother was powerful. In my head, Mother and God were so close, they were one.

The dream of Mr. L as Papa washed out of my head like soap in a dirty mouth.

I pushed the tears off my cheeks and swallowed hard.

"I'm fine."

"Susie, how did you get those bruises on your legs?" he asked, stern now, which frightened me. He was rarely stern and had never been that way with me.

"I was swimming in the lake and hit the rocks." It was a tried and true summertime excuse. It was hard to argue with, even when some of the bruises mocked the shape of a slotted spoon like a fingerprint.

"Oh, Susie." He pulled me from the swing into his chest.

I felt myself beginning to let it go. I felt the tears stinging my eyes, felt my chest begin to fill with panic.

He rocked me back and forth and began to whisper words that I would not let myself hear. He said he could find a way to get me out of that house if I would tell him the truth. He said there were agencies that took care of kids with this problem. And at that, I sealed my mouth shut. An agency was not Mr. L as father. An agency was what Mother had warned me about over and over again.

I let myself listen to his heartbeat for a moment. I let myself feel the expanse of his chest, the strength of his arms and I felt protected. It was an image I would conjure for myself for years to come.

Finally I pulled myself away.

"I hit the rocks." I said to him, and he looked at me with such sad eyes that I almost gave in again.

He walked me back inside with his hand on my back, and took me to the nurses office. I spent the rest of the afternoon there, eating suckers and having ice applied to the bruises and welts on my legs.

Walking home after school that day, I let myself relive the fantasy of a life with Mr. L as my father. It made my chest hurt so hard that I had to stop walking and catch my breath. Mr. L had kids of his own. He spoke of them often and I was always awash with jealousy. But later that night, I buried my face in my pillow and wrapped my arms around it, imagining the embrace of the man who would be Daddy, and thinking what a wonder it would be to have those arms to run to whenever I was hurt or sad.

I take a few long breaths and am able to stop myself from crying. I remind myself that I learned about strength at a very young age, how I learned to be tough without anyone knowing, that I learned to say no, even when I wanted something so much I didn't think I could live without it. I think of Hannah, and how I need to be here for her now.

I call Emmett back and speak before he can even say hello.

"Call the TV station and give an interview, Em."

"What?—oh hell no, Susannah… what if I say something wrong for the case, I'm not a fuckin' attorney!"

"No, Emmett you are the face of Child Protective Services, an underpaid, under appreciated public servant who is, by merit of Franken's media blitz, being attacked and called a liar! You are likeable Emmett, and that is the best defense against Franken, because as much as people listen to that barracuda, they don't like him."

"Well you got that part right." he says, and I can hear him start to grumble in his throat.

"I know you hate it, Emmett, but look, you know everything about this case. Obviously, you can't go saying all the protected details, but what you can do is place doubt. You can be vague… you know what I'm talking about. It's like when a relative calls about one of the kids and wants to talk to you about a case and you can't talk to them. You just give those responses that say nothing in specific but tell everything. And the things you CAN say are that Aunt Amy had no idea that her boyfriend was into drugs, that she had not been to the apartment in days since she had been staying with Hannah at the center and that as soon as she heard of the boyfriend's arrest she made new living arrangements. That is the truth and you can say that!"

"Oh, crap! Alright," Emmett says.

"You're fantastic, Emmett, have I told you that?" I say it and realize just as quickly that maybe I shouldn't have.

"Yup, I'm a prince," he says. "Be watching at 5."

I drag myself up off the floor and try to steady myself against the kitchen counter. I pick up a flower and crunch it into the Stryrofoam. It's a start. I put in one more and one more, until it begins to look like an arrangement. Mother won't win on this one. I can do this, dammit. . . I can.

At about ten to five I turn on the news. I know which station CPS prefers to deal with so I flip the remote until I find it. Rob wanders over and gives me a quizzical look. I try to explain as quickly as I can. I'm not in the mood to rehash details. I'm beginning to feel very tired. My arms are aching and I'm getting the shakes. Rob sits beside me on the sofa and I flop my head against his shoulder.

I close my eyes. It's been such a long day already. I keep wishing there was some kind of fast forward button I could push. I want this over so much. I resent being trapped here with my life and my career and Hannah's future all hanging in the balance. It feels so stifling. It's Mother controlling me all over again.

I begin to drift a little. It's nice to lean against Rob and close my eyes. I feel as if I might even sleep.

A few minutes later, I feel a jolt to my arm. It's Rob, shaking me awake to catch Emmett's interview.

I open my eyes to Emmett's wrinkled brow. He is squinting against the camera light, wearing a rumpled white shirt and suspenders. He looks the perfect picture of an underpaid social worker.

"Can you tell us exactly what the allegations are against the parents?"

"Well at this time, the details are protected by court order, but the charges are 8 counts of abuse and neglect."

I nod along with Emmett as if he can see me through the set.

"Is it possible for you to comment on the death of the Michael Williams, Hannah's brother?"

"The details of that are sealed as well, but I can tell you that the file came to CPS immediately and the investigation into it has been re-opened in light of these new charges."

Emmett smooths his hair, he straightens his suspenders and looks more uncomfortable than I've ever seen him look. It's perfect, so perfect that I feel a giggle sneak up my throat. Take that Franken, you swine!

"Mr Cooper, can you tell us then, about the Aunt who is trying to get custody? Does she have a drug problem?"

"No, those rumors come from some inflated reports that gave out and out falsehoods. Amy is no longer living with the boyfriend who was arrested on drug charges. She had no idea that he was into anything like that and she has new living arrangements in an entirely different part of town."

Great, Emmett, great. . . I keep thinking words of encouragement. I lean forward toward the TV.

"And what about the reports that the Aunt is a stripper?"

I flinch.

"Also, untrue. She did work for a time in an establishment that had adult entertainment, but she worked as a waitress."

"Mr. Cooper, who is the attorney for Hannah Williams?"

I watch Emmett's face go blank. He does not know whether to answer the question or not. My name will appear on the court documents, which will be a matter of public record, but as of now, there hasn't been enough time for them to have been released.

"Uhhh—" Emmett says and I resist the urge to whack the TV with my palm.

Don't, Emmett… please, don't…

"I'd really rather not say at this time. She is attending. . .she needs some time to—

Emmett looks at the camera as if he has just been startled. He stops speaking and inhales deeply.

"She is attending to some personal family matters at this time and cannot be disturbed. She plans to be in court on Tuesday."

I let out the breath I wasn't aware I was holding and press my hand to my forehead.

"What is your general feeling about this case, Mr. Cooper?"

Emmett looks at his hands for a moment. He sets his jaw and steels his eyes into the camera.

"My feeling is the same as it is with every case that comes across my desk. My feeling is that no child should have injuries over eighty percent of her body. My feeling is that a child with broken bones and blackened eyes needs to be protected. And my feeling is that parents who think they are above the law, need not only to have their children taken away from them, but that they need to be exposed for what they are, child-beaters. My feeling is that no one has the right to beat up a child no matter how much money or power or position they have. They shouldn't be allowed to harm another human being and that it is the obligation of what is supposed to be a civilized society to make certain that our children are safe, especially in their very own homes."

The interviewer allows Emmett's words to hang in the air a moment for dramatic effect.

"Mitchell Forth, channel four news, Detroit."

I leap up from the sofa and literally cheer out loud. I rush into the kitchen with my cell phone to call Emmett. He's done wonderfully, and I'm filled with new hope for the case and for Hannah. I get Emmett's machine.

"You were A-MAZING!" I say and hear myself laugh. "Emmett, you could have a whole new career! TV news, game shows, imagine the possibilities!! I'm so proud of you!" I catch myself. I am gushing. I pause a second and gather myself.

"Thank you so much Em, you were perfect." I press the disconnect with a satisfying beep and am about to take a deep breath when Jenna comes into the kitchen and stands over the sink. She looks strange, pale.. almost... green.

Jenna leans over the sink and wretches.

I rush to her and put my arm around her shoulders.

"Jenna, what is it?"

She wretches again as Matthew comes up from the basement with a box. Matthew's face is almost as pale as Jenna's.

"What's wrong?" I say, supporting Jenna as best I can.

Matthew shakes his head and heads out the back door with the box.

Marie comes in from where she had been washing down the windows in Mother's bedroom. She takes my place at Jenna's side and Rob and I follow Matthew outside.

He has set the box on the ground about ten feet from the house. He is standing with his hand over his mouth and his arm wrapped around his chest.

My heart leaps into mine.

"Matthew, for God's sake, what is it?"

He reaches into the box and pulls out a large manila envelope. Rob pulls out the papers and we let our eyes focus on the words. It is a hospital record, dated 1969, the year my father left. The name at the top is Mother's. Symptoms are noted, cramping and bleeding. And then I reach the ending: Miscarriage.

My heart sinks.

I look up at Matthew who has begun to cry. He is wiping his eyes.

"She had a miscarriage." I say to Matthew. I can't comprehend his reaction to this, or Jenna's. I feel panic beginning to well in my chest. What the hell is going on?!

He shakes his head yes and points to the box. Rob steps forward to reach in for whatever else is inside, and Matthew moves in front of me, holding me a step back.

Rob bends over to examine the box and then stands up. His face is pale and his eyes have gone dull.

"Let her see." he says to Matthew, who steps aside.

Rob pushes the box flaps open so I can see. There in the box, nestled into a bed of silk material, a rosary wrapped around it, is a mason canning jar. The contents are brown and murky. All at once I understand and my stomach turns.

Mother had saved the dead fetus, enshrined it with the rosary and stored it in the basement on the same shelf she had kept the pickles and carrots she canned every summer.

I lower myself into the grass and try to stop my head from swimming again. Matthew's tears are recognition. Now he knows how sick she really was; now we all know.

Rob lifts the box and carries it to the edge of the property. He folds the box flaps closed and walks back. I notice his hands are shaking.

I hug Matthew and tell him how sorry I am that he had to see it.

"It's just," he says "I mean, I knew it was bad. I saw her get—you know, get nuts sometimes. But this—I just, I didn't know it was like this."

He takes a deep breath and I feel him square his shoulders.

"I'm fine," he says, and I feel something tear inside my chest. After all my efforts to spare him, there it was. "I'm fine." just like I always said it.

Exactly like I always said it.

I fight down a flare of anger toward her that could've had me tearing the house down.

"I never wanted to tell you everything," I say to him, hoping he understands. "It didn't seem necessary. It was all so hurtful. I wanted to protect you from it."

He sits beside me on the grass, his arms resting on his knees, his head hung down.

"I know."

Jenna and Marie come out to the yard and we all sit in the grass a few minutes. Marie goes immediately to Matthew's side and wraps her arms around him. Rob and Jenna sit on either side of me. There is a sudden new emotion among us. None of us want to go back inside the house.

Mother has chased us all out into the yard once again.

I am overwhelmed with a sudden weariness. My joints begin to ache, my head hurts. I lay myself back in the grass. The trees overhead form a canopy of light and pattern. I stare at them. Soon we are all lying side by side staring up at the trees. They seem to wave and nod as if to comfort us. The lake rushes in and out, pulling the shock from our bones.

"You know they have moving companies that will come out and pack up houses," Marie says.

None of us seem to be able to find words. Marie has no idea how carefully the inside of this house has been guarded, how closed the doors have been to anyone from outside the family. I want to tell her how sometimes secrets become a part of a person's soul. That letting strangers into this house and allowing them to pack up its contents would be like suddenly climbing to the rooftop to shout every atrocity that Mother had ever committed against us.

My stomach and heart feel sick. I didn't think that anything about Mother could shock me any more. I didn't think that she'd have any new way to hurt me. It only reinforces the feeling I've carried in my chest since I was a child. It is a feeling that comes from the knowledge that it's never really over. She may stop screaming for a few hours or let us sleep through the night. We may have made it out of the house before the hot

soup actually hit our skin, we may have managed
doors locked for a full three hours before she sta
screw driver, but it was always only a short repri
end, it was never over, and it was best to never l
might be, because it was always worse if she caug
all should have been better prepared for whatever we might find.

    Still, knowing about Mother's miscarriage does shed a little light on why my Father left just when he did. I can't imagine what she must've been like with him after that. She would have blamed him, of course. It might have been that proverbial last straw before she broke completely and before he decided he could not handle her any more.

    Marie rolls closer to Matthew, she lays her arm over his chest and rests her head on his shoulder. He wraps his arm around her.

    I take Jenna's hand on my right and Robs on my left. Jenna reaches for Matthew's free hand.

    We form a chain, a wall I keep thinking.

    "It's really over now," Rob says.

    I know that Rob needs to believe it, so I keep my mouth shut and swallow down the lump in my throat.

    After about half an hour, we've regained our ability to speak. We are chattering, hungry, ready for a break, ready to enjoy each other a while. It's an odd feeling, the weird giddy relief after something bad happens. It's uneasy, but we decide to head back over to Grand's for lunch.

    I am happy to be leaving the flowers behind. I don't want to look at them any more.

    As we drive along the twisting road to Grand's, I am feeling just slightly dizzy. The effects of an entirely sleepless night are becoming quite interesting. It's a combination of a three martini lunch and a good hour and a half at the gym. My muscles ache and I'm dopey and light headed.

    I rest my head against the window and close my eyes. Matthew is driving and he and Marie are talking pleasantly in the front seat. The sound of their voices begins to trail off distantly and in my head I see images of the lake and Mother and Angel, and a big slotted spoon trying to scoop up lake water that rushes through the holes. It's in my hand, the big silvery slotted spoon, and I am the one scooping up lake water. I'm standing in the lake up to my ankles, it's cold and there are rocks digging into the soles of my feet. I bend over and try to scoop the water into the spoon. I push it deep into the water and then hurriedly rush it to my lips where I sip at it desperately. I am overcome with thirst. I bend over again and again, frantically trying to get some water to my lips. The best I can do is suck off a few droplets that have beaded up on the smooth surface of the spoon. It is cold and tastes metallic on my tongue.

    I go for another scoop only to realize that the water has risen and is now up to my knees. The waves are hitting me harder now, and I am having trouble standing against them. Over and over again, with a great swooping gesture, I dip the spoon into the water and put it to my mouth. I begin to cry in frustration. I look down to see that the water has risen to my thighs and is dampening the hem of my red dress.

    I cry out in anger and desperation and utter frustration and stifling thirst. I feel crazed and without a hint of control and I begin flailing the spoon in the air and slapping it against the surface of the waves which continue to rise higher and higher and icy cold.

    Soon, the water has reached my waist, my shoulders and finally my neck. I bob impotently upright in the water, still parched with thirst and clutching the spoon in my hand. The sky has grown dark above me and ominous with storm clouds and I stop fighting. I feel my arms go limp, I feel my legs lifted, the red dress floats up to my chest, leaving me naked beneath the water. Just as I am about to go under, something begins to float past me. I blink water out of my eyes just enough to make out the form of Hannah Williams' dead body. Her eyes are blue and puffy, her lips the brightest purple I've ever seen. I feel as if I should be startled, but instead, I tip my head back and allow the water to lift me and carry me off, and I watch as the spoon is tossed away from me on the water along side Hannah's body, and as a wave rises above me I open my mouth to let the water in…

    "Mom!!", I am startled awake by Matthew who is standing outside the car door, hesitating at the handle for fear I will topple out, as I am curled entirely against it. I mumble an apology and stand on shaking legs. Marie comes beside me and slips her arm around my back as we walk inside.

    Grand has made huge sandwiches for lunch and I am starved. I sit down at the table. Matthew and Marie mull about me, Rob settles in next to me and Jenna pops a diet pill. I tear into a sandwich. It's dark brown bread and ham and cheese and lettuce and tomato and it tastes like nothing I've ever eaten in my life. I take a bite that clears a quarter of the sandwich away and I close my eyes and chew it, and swallow before it is really small enough. Another bite and another and a gulp of soda and then I see that Grand has put out potato salad and corn chips and pickles and olives and I heap my plate with all of it. I don't notice Rob looking at me sideways, or at least I tell myself that I don't notice it. I don't care. I am empty inside and the food is filling me. It is food made with loving hands by someone who wants to nourish me. Food that will not be thrown at me, or taken from me before my stomach can even contain a full bite. It's food that exists only to nourish and nurture me. It's like being with an old friend.

The sandwich is gone and I am scooping great spoonfuls of potato salad into my mouth. My cheeks are bulging out with the burden and chewing is almost impossible. I gag just a little, quietly and reach for my soda when I realize that Rob has turned around in his seat entirely and is openly gaping at me.

A wave of heat takes my body. I manage to swallow the mass down and I look into Rob's eyes for a moment. There is such silence in the room I imagine that I can hear the sounds of my own stomach struggling to digest the barrage I have just thrown at it.

"What are you doing?!" Rob says, finally.

"I'm eating lunch." I say, smiling feebly.

"Are you okay?" he asks me, his eyes steely with fear.

I nod and speak a little too quickly and a little too faintly. I tell him that I am fine, but that I think I would like to take the rest of my lunch with me to Grand's room and be alone for a little while.

I heap the plate again, with another sandwich, with three brownies and two oatmeal raisin cookies and a slice of apple cake. I take a huge glass of milk with me and I close and lock the door behind me.

Grand's room is quiet, soothing, and calm. I set my bounty on the bed table and collapse into the bed. My head is swirling and my stomach feels constricted. I am already full, but I am not done eating.

I switch on the TV and hunt for one of my sit-com reruns. Serendipity smiles on me and I actually find one. I keep the sound just high enough to barely make out the dialogue and the laughter. I like the sound of the laughter. I cross my legs on the bed and finish off the second sandwich and then I start on my dessert, dipping the deep, dark brownies into the milk until they are sodden and soft and then filling my mouth with them. I hold each bite on my tongue a minute, feeling the doughy brownie and the cool milk and all the sweetness. Life should be like brownies; perhaps a little dark on the outside but rich and sweet within. The cookies disappear next, chewy and perfect and finally the apple cake.

I lay back on the bed and loosen my sweats. My stomach feels like an over inflated beach toy, ready to pop at any second. But for just these few minutes, my head has been clear and serene. There have been no thoughts of mother or tortured memories, just a quiet sweetness filled with piped in laughter.

I lay there until there is a knock on the door.

It's Grand and she wants to know if I'm ok. I tell her I'm fine and she takes my dishes and tells me she will get me some tea and then closes the door behind her again.

I wish I could sleep. I turn on my belly and draw a knee up toward my chest in my favorite sleeping position and try to shut down. Again, my "off button" seems to be malfunctioning. At least I am comfortable and I love Grand's quiet shaded room. Outside, I hear Jenna. She is weeping again and Rob is comforting her. I want to smack Jenna and tell her that this is not about her for once and tell her to shut up! I pull a pillow over my head until I hear the tea kettle screaming away without attention. Where is Grand?

I get up and walk to the kitchen where I turn off the kettle and get down the mugs. Curiosity gets the best of me and I go looking for Grand. I find her in the basement, crying softly and holding a tiny embroidered blanket and a tattered stuffed rabbit.

"Grand?" I say and she startles a little.

"Oh, Sweetie, the tea!" she says and heads for the stairs, but I stop her.

"She was your baby once," I say, and I think of Camille for the first time in my life as a tiny, helpless, mewling infant cradled in Grand's arms. It consumes me with jealousy. This beast of a woman had my Grand as her mother. And I got her. It isn't the least bit fair. It isn't fair for Grand either. Her baby is dead.

Grand shakes her head yes and clutches the blanket and toy to her and cries hard. I hug her and tell her it's okay for her to cry and I ask her why she is hiding in the basement to do it.

"Well you all just don't feel the same way…" she says, and I am suddenly ashamed at my selfishness.

"I'm so sorry, Grand. We should've thought that you'd need-" I begin and she stops me.

"Susannah, it shouldn't be your job to take care of everyone. I'm fine. I just need to do this," she says and hugs me tight and keeps crying.

"Can I help?" I ask.

"No," she says smiling sadly at me and sorting through more baby things in the trunk, "I need to do this by myself."

I nod and I bring her down a box of kleenex and I go back upstairs and pour tea and take her that, and then I leave her alone. When I glance back at her, she is holding a yellow checked dress and tiny patent leather shoes.

I feel like we've all been ignoring Grand's needs terribly. She's never once cracked in front of us. She's still so strong. I hate that she feels she can't share her grief with us. We are grieving, aren't we? It's all of us in our own way. I want to go to her, but I know I have to respect what she's asked of me. I will sit with her later and talk. I will apologize again.

I wander out to the porch with my tea and think over what's left to be done. The house has been emptied save for the sofa in the living room and the bed in Rob's room and the entire contents of my old room. Rob has offered to clean it out at least three times, but I cannot face it, and I will not allow anyone else to discover what she did with my memory after I was gone. The devastation will be sickening. Rob's room had looked ransacked. Every drawer was opened and it's contents tossed about the room. The shelves were overturned, the closet emptied onto the floor. Rob had long ago taken anything important to him, but still, to see what she had done was heartbreaking. I could see it in his face when we opened the door. But he had pressed on, and now the task was done.

Personally, I prefer to postpone my misery so that I may swallow it in smaller, bite-sized pieces.

Evening is falling and I know that tomorrow there will be a funeral. I am weary at the thought of all the smiling and handshaking and social kissing I will have to do. Yuck. At least Charlie will be here soon and he will bolster me against the barrage of well meaning people that will be irritating me like a shoe full of sand.

I sit on the porch wrapped in Grand's quilt and drink tea. I rock myself slowly. There have been so many moments like this in my life, so many times when I suddenly found myself rocking, my own arms wrapped around me, looking for a comfort that I was not to find. Other arms were so much more adept.

Comfort was so easy in Angel's arms. In my early years at the firm, when Matthew would come down with some awful flu the night before an important case and we'd be up until 4 am bringing him ice chips and holding him while he vomited and bathing his head with a cool towel, Angel would always know that moment right before I was about to lose it. He'd take the thermometer from my hand and set it down and gather me into those arms that seemed able to encircle the world. I would fizzle away inside them, sobbing into his collar. He'd rock me and hold me and tell me that I was a good mother and a good lawyer and that I was going to be alright. And I always was. I'd be exhausted and I'd have a coffee the size of a wading pool in court with me, but I was always ok. It seemed that because Angel had said it, it was so.

      He'd get angry when the office kept me away from home too much. And it was too much. He'd wait up for me and he'd be mad and pacing and swearing in Italian when I came through the door.

      "Jesus, Susannah!" he'd say when he caught sight of me wearily dropping my briefcase in the hallway and taking off my shoes, "You've got a child here!"

      "I've got two children here…" I grumbled at him one night.

      "Well, maybe Miss Grown Up, but we are supposed to be a family and we can't be one if you are never here.", he'd said and pulled my angry little countenance into his arms. It was a constant pleasure and a constant aggravation that Angel had such a way of draining off my anger at him. I suppose it wasn't honest that I never let it well back up, that I never let him see it.

      I'd apologize and go shower while Angel thawed me manicotti from his mother's recipe. He'd feed it to me by the spoonful as we sat wrapped together in the blankets, watching Johnny Carson and hearing the laughter from the crowd.

      Many of those nights Matthew would get up and join us in the warmth of the blankets, the three of us curled together serenely, nothing but love surrounding us and the peace and quiet of the night. I'd lay awake and look at them both sleeping. It was so wonderful to see Matthew with his tiny mouth curled to a soft snore and Angel sawing away next to him. Matthew's pink fingers always curled around the tanned, work thickened skin of Angel's thumb. They were so beautiful together.

      Angel was a wonderful father. He played and ran and painted and changed diapers and gave baths and made dinners and packed lunches. He exacted a bit too much perfection at times, but if this was to be his only fatherly fault, I could easily accept it. I, on the other hand, always felt less than a perfect parent.

      It never occurred to me that I was already parent-weary from having to manage an adult toddler all my life. I just knew that sometimes I had no patience at all, and no desire to be the center of someone's existence. If Matthew insisted that I play with him I would manage to do it for a little while and then a feeling of strangulation would come over me. I would re-direct him in the game so that he was playing it independently, with me watching from a safer distance. I could hold him in my lap a little while, but then he'd have to sit beside me on the sofa, and I'd put my arm around him. It was confusing to love someone so completely and yet be afraid of that love at the same time. I was unable to trust my own loving instincts. I was unable to trust much of anything.

The shadows of late afternoon have begun to fall. I stare across the lake at the charcoal outlines, the trees casting shadow against the brilliance of the fading day. I look into the glassy surface of the lake aglow with sunlight and it appears unreal, as if painted in or placed in by some special effect; too bright, too perfect to be real.

Rob places a hand on my shoulder, ushering me into the car. We are heading back over to the house, Rob and I and the kids. Jenna and Grand are both staying behind this time.

The attic is still half full, and Rob has ventured into the back basement and found a virtual garbage heap. It all has to go, as the house will be sold and we will never have to see it again. It is this thought that spurs me on as I carry a dusty box down from the attic and set it on the kitchen table beside the flowers.

I know it has to be opened and the contents examined. I am paralyzed at the thought. What wretched memory would be unearthed this time? Which demon invited out to play? I pull back the flaps, noticing that my own hands are shaking, and let my eyes focus on the contents.

A pipe, a letter opener, a pen and pencil set, a blotter, a calendar. I pull the items out one by one, puzzled. Mother never had such things. They were old, and well used, but preserved perfectly, some of them even wrapped in tissue paper. I set each of them on the table and at the very bottom I find a beautifully framed picture of Mother. She is young in the picture and beautiful, and I stare at it a minute before I set it down as well. The last item is a small wooden box. I recognize it as a man's jewelry valise, and in this moment I realize that these are my father's things. He must've abandoned them as well.

I am mystified and excited despite myself. I know so little about this man, though I spent so many nights wondering who he was and what he might be like. We were never allowed to ask Mother any questions about him.

I open the valise. Inside, nestled into a deep blue velvet interior is a gold wedding band, a watch and chain, a tie pin with a diamond cluster at the center, and oddly, an oval shaped women's locket on a gold chain.

I lift the locket and open it to reveal two tiny photographs on either side; one is of a young man, undoubtedly my father. He smiles broadly and his blue eyes twinkle. They are much like Matthew's. The other is of two young children. It's me and Rob, sitting properly posed on a white blanket with the turquoise sky background of department store photography. We are smiling and watching something distantly, perhaps some photographer's puppetry aimed at eliciting delighted reactions in youngsters such as ourselves. I stare at the pictures and at the locket and I am rocked by the implications of finding it in this box, with these things. She had not just removed his picture and placed it in the box or thrown it away. She had tossed Rob and I into the box with him and closed it up tight and packed it away in the attic. But we were still here, constant reminders of his betrayal, the grating memory of what she had lost, embodied in two children that she had to see every day.

She had exacted her revenge each day of our lives to follow. We were the dolls into which she stuck her pins, hoping that by some magic, he would feel the pain.

I am suddenly enraged and I lift the calendar book and throw it hard at the window. It flaps against it like a bird mistaking glass for sky and falls open into the sink.

What on earth had been wrong with these two people? Why could they so easily put their own desires in front of the needs of their children? Why were we so unimportant? As much as I blame Mother for the miseries of my youth, there is a part of me that knows that a person cannot help having a disease. I know that she should have gotten the help she needed for our sakes, but it was the disease that kept her from that as well. My father, on the other hand, had no excuse. He chose his own self-preservation over the protection and care of his children. He ran away to wellness and left us in the mire of Mother's disease. I despise him. While some part of me, some genetic connection claims to have a deep seated attachment to this man, with the rest of my being I despise him and I hope that his life without us has been a miserable guilt ridden thing. I wish for him endless sleepless nights, a life without peace, for that is what he wished upon me, and that is what I have had.

I put the items back into the box. All except the locket, which, for some reason, I want to keep. Maybe it held the long lost time when my family was real and my mother was still human and Rob and I were cherished enough to be worn around her neck. I slip the locket into my change purse, wrapped in tissue and I call Rob to show him the rest of what I have found. Matthew follows into the room and he watches us carefully as we examine the items over and over again. An archaeological find right here in the kitchen, we are fascinated at what light these items shed upon who our mythical father was. Rob asks if I mind if he takes the watch and chain and the wedding ring. I don't mind, and he offers the diamond tie pin to Matthew who smiles and accepts it, holding it in his hand as if it might explode and carrying it of to show it to Marie.

    I watch Rob's face. Being a bit older when our father left, Rob actually remembers him. I remember asking Rob to tell me about him in our moments alone. He told me what he remembered. Our father was not tall, he was balding, and he wore glasses. He had a high pitched laugh and he would tell long stories over glasses of beer. I have a fuzzy image of him, but nothing much more. I suppose if I thought hard, I'd remember details but I don't really want to.

    It's hard not to want things you can see clearly.

    Rob looks suddenly sad, and suddenly aged. He holds the watch a moment and stares at it. He pushes it into the pocket of his jeans and I see his face break for the briefest moment before he walks away.

    The rest of the things we box back up and carry out to the trash heap that has grown to wall-like proportions in the yard.

    The night rolls on and we carry out box after box. We find baby clothes and toys and more photo albums and boxes of old paid bills and junk mail that Mother could never seem to throw away.

    I keep looking at the flowers on the kitchen counter. They are beautiful. I hate them. I keep reciting a strange mantra in my head: Mrs. Franses' flowers, Mrs. Franses' flowers, Mrs. Franses' flowers. It has begun to lose effectiveness. I wish Charlie was here. He'd have me laughing about something. He'd have my mind busy with some story of the antics of his co-workers or the details of his conversation with Richard. Where is he? He's even later than he said he would be.

    I am getting the shakes from not having slept. I feel as if I could fall down. The only thing keeping me moving is the knowledge that once this is done, I will not ever have to see this house or any of these things ever again.

    Rob carries another box in and sets it on the table. Inside we find piles of our old schoolwork. We grin at each other and pull out construction paper art-work, lined newsprint with our attempts at lettering, ditto sheets with answers scribbled in. It seemed as if Mother was reluctant to let anything go. Since we knew she had no sentimental attachment we couldn't help but wonder why she kept it all.

Mother didn't believe in praising our schoolwork. Once, when I was 10 I'd brought home an art project that I'd gotten an A on. It was a large poster board covered in glitter and dried macaroni noodles. It was my rendering of the lake, and I was terribly proud of it. I had attached it to the refrigerator with magnets. Mother had found it later that afternoon and I discovered it in shreds on the kitchen table, her Bible rested on top of the pile, opened to a highlighted passage about the evils of vanity.

It is 11:00 by the time Matthew and Marie return with fast food hamburgers and sodas and we all sit at the table and eat around the pall flowers. I am more tired than I have ever been in my life. I feel that if I do not lay down, I am indeed going to fall down. A few large bites of the hamburger and a few sips of soda and I excuse myself to the sofa in the living room.

I can hear every word they say as they whisper about me at the table. I must appear to be asleep, but I am not.

"She's kind of freaking out…" Matthew says to Rob.

"I know, I could tell at lunch today. She needs to sleep. Christ, I hope she stays asleep all night. She's going to be a wreck tomorrow if she doesn't."

"Maybe we should just stay here, let her sleep." Matthew says and Marie speaks her agreement.

"We can take some of those blankets out of the boxes and lay them on the floor in your Grandmother's room." she says, and I know she means that she and Matthew will sleep there together. I feel the hair at my neck prickle a little, but I say nothing.

"I can sleep on my old bed." Rob says, and it has been decided.

A little while later, I feel blankets being put over me, and I smell the powdery scent of Marie's perfume. I understand completely why he cares for her. Her heart encompasses the room.

Finally, the light in the kitchen is switched off, and after a quiet call to Grand, the house falls silent. My nerves sit me bolt upright. Quiet in this house is not a happy thing. I shake myself and lay back on the sofa pillow. It's different now, I remind myself. She's gone.

The lake is whispering outside and the wind is playing the leaves. I close my eyes and try to imagine that the sounds I hear are coming from an entirely different place. I picture a quiet beach, calm and moonlit, the leaves I hear are palm fronds swaying happily in the warm, welcoming breeze. I like this picture and I can feel myself drifting a little, like I would on the waves of the ocean, like I did on the blow up raft on the lake.

It was a mid-summer Sunday after church, a few months after Mother had found out about Angel and me, and she was making dinner. Angel was over and he and I were helping to set the table. Rob was out fishing on the lake. Music was playing on the radio and the sun was shining through the windows and for a few minutes, I had let the air come entirely into my chest and I had begun to breathe in that relaxed way that usually meant that Mother was no where around.

She was trying to reach her serving dishes, the big ones on the top shelf and she was having a hard time. Angel offered to help and he stepped up onto the stool in front of her. Just as he had reached the first dish and held it in both his hands Mother turned.

I could always tell by Mother's eyes when something was about to happen. It was like watching her disappear from behind them and something cold taking her place.

"Mother..?" I said aloud and she smiled at me. It was a slow, seeping kind of thing that made the blood in my veins turn to ice.

She turned slowly toward Angel who was standing on his tip-toes on the ladder with the dish just in his fingertips. I swallowed a ball of lead; Angel was a sitting duck.

I called out his name just as she reached for him. He whipped his head around to look at me and then down at Mother. I saw it all as if it were some kind of slow motion re-play. I watched her hands raise up toward him, saw her glaring at him, her head tipping just slightly to the side. I watched him look back at her, his face quizzical, a lock of his hair falling over one of his eyes.

Mother's hands moved methodically. She took hold of the belt loops on each of Angel's hips, she looped her forefinger through each one and then shut her thumbs against them like a mouse trap. I even saw the muscles in her forearms flex as she pulled downward, a sweeping motion like a wave against the shore, and Angel stood on the stool in his underwear, his pants down around his ankles.

"Mother!"

I shouted at her again but it only seemed to push her on. She turned her head to look at me and she smiled again. I started to move toward her but not before she could yank again at the band of his white underwear and suddenly, there he was, standing on a stool in the kitchen, a bright yellow serving platter in both hands above his head, mother cocking her head to the side and looking at his naked penis.

"Well, here it is Susannah!!" she said as if she were a college professor showing the class some new discovery, "Here's what you want so badly! This …this disgusting little worm." she said.

And then it all went to water again, Mother's hand moving through waves, me unable to make my feet move fast enough, my body stuck in the muddy air, Angel's shocked expression, his feet toppling as her hand made contact. I watched each of her fingers wrap around Angel's penis and scrotum as if she were snatching a fly out of the air, a quick snap and she held him fast. Angel yelped aloud and Mother's knuckles went white, squeezing as hard as she could.

"Mother NO!" I shrieked, finally making my feet work, running to push her away from him. The force knocked her backward. Angel dropped the serving dish, which exploded against the edge of the sink and sent shards of porcelain into our skin. He fell backward onto the floor, pulling his clothing back on even in mid air. I stood dumbly staring down at him, Mother clinging to the edge of the counter and panting, Angel staring up at me, his hands still on the waistband of his pants.

The air had once again been sucked from the room. All hung suspended for that moment of "What now?" that follows a full system shock.

Mother moved suddenly toward a pot hanging on the rack, and it seemed to bring us back to life. Angel leapt to his feet, took me by the hand and pulled me out the door. We ran without stopping 'til we reached the edge of the lake, down by the rock theater where we kept the blue blow up raft tied to a sapling.

We stood for a minute once we got there, panting and staring into each other's disbelieving eyes. We didn't speak. There were no words for my shame, no words for his humiliation. We climbed onto the raft and let the lake carry us out farther than we ever had before, so far out that the house looked like it was sitting on a Monopoly board, nothing more than a plastic toy place, bought and sold with pink and yellow money.

We lay next to each other and held hands, the sun baking us, the waves rocking us motheringly, comforting and lending its rhythm to our hearts so that they finally slowed to normal again.

I have not thought of that day in years. I suppose it is one of many experiences so painful that I choose to leave them in the darkness of concealed thought.

I am furious with it now. It was bad enough that she humiliated us both so horribly, that she obliterated another day of my life, that she robbed me of all joy, but the worst, the absolute worst of that day occurs to me for the first time at this moment; she touched my Angel. She had stolen that from me too. There was no privacy that I was allowed, nothing of my life that was my own. She ruined it all, pushed in her will, the force of her body, the pain she could inflict with her hands. Even my boyfriend's body was not mine alone.

I leap from the sofa and charge into the kitchen. The pall flowers glow serenely on the table, a shaft of moonlight turning them into a picture of pristine beauty.

"You don't deserve these!!" I hiss, my teeth clenched. I cannot remember ever feeling such rage in my life.

I attack the arrangement, yanking great handfuls of the flowers from its base and mutilating them between my hands, bent wire and white silk petals falling in a crumpled mass on the floor.

"For once" I shout, "for once, you are going to get what you deserve!!"

I push the door open and fall down the back steps into the yard. I feel the concrete dig into my knees but I don't care. At the side of the steps are Mother's rose bushes. For some reason, they were the only thing she ever seemed to love. She doted on them, and had even once hired a gardener to tend them for an entire season.

They are barren now and full of hard, full grown thorns. I grab at the branches by the half dozen and yank them with all my might from the ground. Clumps of dirt and moss cling to the bottom roots, showering me with earth, the thorns tearing into my skin. I get both hands full and take them back into the kitchen where I shove them into the arrangement. I push with all my might, hearing the sharp sound of the styrofoam as it snaps and breaks. The stalks protrude a foot above the silk flowers, spiking out from all sides. This satisfies me immensely and I rip out even more flowers and rush out the door again. This time the branches do not yield so easily to my pulling and I find that I am sobbing and jerking as hard as I can, thorns cutting pieces from my hands this time, blood dampening my sleeves and spotting my shirt. I don't care, I don't care about anything right now but this one mission. It is time. It is my time now. I brace my feet at the root base of one of the biggest plants and use my entire body to pull.

"To hell with you Camille Suffolk! To hell with you, and I hope you are already there!!"

I am screaming these words, my feet braced against the edge of the garden, my whole body straining with the pull on the rose bush, when I feel hands come down on my arms from behind me. I know who they belong to the minute they contact my skin. Thank God, OH Thank God, he is here, he is finally here. Warm male arms encircle me and I wonder what has taken him so long. I expected him long before now. He shushes me and pulls me to his chest where I sob and scream in pain. Physical, mental, emotional devastation overtake me and I go weak with it, my body buckling. He guides me back to the porch and sits with me, lowering me gently and rocking me back and forth and stroking my hair.

"She doesn't deserve it…" I cry, "she doesn't…" it comes in waves upon me over and over again and I cry harder with each one, almost unable to breathe. I hear Matthew and Rob at the door, wondering what is going on, I hear him tell them that he's got it under control. I feel as if I am listening from another room, though he is holding me close.

I can't stop sobbing, can't stop the burning hatred in my chest. The pain in my hands feels like want; like a craving for physical harm. My chest wants to hurt her, it wants to kill a woman who is already dead. I sob until it feels as if I won't breathe again.

I turn to him. I push my face into his collar, into his neck. His skin sticks to my cheek, feeling as if it may be the only thing keeping me in contact with the planet. His arms get tighter as I cry harder. He strokes my arm and I begin to take a few deep breaths. Slowly, slowly, the red begins to disappear from before my closed eyes. I draw more breath, I smell the lake, the scent of upturned dirt. I smell him.

Finally, I sit up on my own strength. He keeps his arm around me and he leans back to examine my face in the porch light.

His thumb swipes tears from my cheeks, and he pushes a lock of hair from my eyes.

"Hello there.." he says, smiling at me tenderly, and looking at me with eyes full of worry.

I take the deepest of deep breaths.

"Angel," I say, "what are you doing here?"

Suddenly, as rare things will, it vanished.
  --Elizabeth Barrett Browning

Chapter 7

Angel takes me into the bathroom and as we pass Matthew in the kitchen he gives me a sheepish look and I know now how Angel has come to be here, and why Matthew had asked me those strange questions on the phone before he arrived.

Angel closes the bathroom door and runs cool water. He pulls my reluctant hands into the stream.

"Geeze, Susannah…" he says examining a particularly deep thorn wound, "you really did it…"

I can't seem to find the right words to respond. I stand dumbly and stare at the bright pink blood-water swirling into the drain. Angel pumps some soap into his hands and makes a lather. He takes first my right hand and then my left and soaps each gently under the faucet. They sting with the soap and I wince, wishing suddenly that I had been able to control my rage.

"Hell of an arrangement you made there," he says, smirking sideways at me, that damned dimple pressing into his cheek, "Mother Suffolk would've loved it." He shakes his head and continues to bathe my wounds under the water.

My eyes are still bleary with tears, but I look up at him, and really take him in. I haven't actually seen him in a several years. Age has been good to him. Fine lines have deepened the character in his face, a few well placed premature gray hairs feather at his temples. There is a wisdom in his eyes.

"Angel," I say, "what are you doing here?"

"Matthew called me. Don't be ridiculous, Susannah, your mother, the grandmother of my son has died. Where else would I be? I would've been here sooner but I was in Detroit. We're bidding on a city contract, the library renovation. It should be a big job and I'd really like to get it. I just didn't think I should send Artie this time. But I left before the final word was in. I just felt like I needed to get here." He dries my hands gently and calls out to Matthew to ask which box has the contents of the bathroom. He is looking for bandages.

I am at once soothed and very upset by his presence. Deep down I had been wondering why he hadn't come, and I feared that there was more bad blood between us than I realized. I have been hating myself for my own weakness about it, but I have been too tired to close my mental gates. And now that he is here, I know the gates have flung open and I am terrified at the heartache that will consume me should he decide to walk through them.

A few awkward minutes later, my hands have been bandaged. Rob and the kids have gone to get us some tea or coffee or something from somewhere and suddenly I am alone with Angel.

We sit across the table from each other and I look woefully at the arrangement I have so badly mangled.

The silks that are left are bent and the white blooms covered in dirt, blood and muck. The rose branches protrude high into the air on all sides, bloody and brown, bent and broken and ragged. As I look at it now, it seems just perfect.

"It was beautiful before…" I say, biting my lip and twisting the chain on my beach glass around my index finger.

"I can definitely see vestiges of that," he says and smiles at me, and then takes the deformed arrangement out the door. I hear the metal on metal scrape of the garbage can lid and then he is back.

"We'll call Ben over at Rosenman's Florist in the morning. They'll put something together for us, I'm sure."

For "us", I think.

"How is Grand doing?" he asks, sitting across from me again, and I notice for the first time how he smells. It is the same scent he always wore, spicy with anise and warm with musk.

"Holding up. Trying to be brave for all of us. We've been awful, though. None of us are grieving and we just haven't been sensitive to the fact that she is. She won't even cry in front of us. She's embarrassed." I rub the palm of my left hand just a little, it stings.

"You're not grieving?!" He raises his eyebrows at me, "What did I just witness out there? Gardening by moonlight?"

"Don't be a smart ass, Angel." In spite of myself, I feel how I am catching his smirk and bearing it on my own face.

"You're all just doing it in your own way, and you know that Grand understands that."

I nod, and I am suddenly very uncomfortable. With the flowers gone he seems too close, the room seems too small, and my defenses seem too low.

"Did you bring your girlfriend?" I ask him, willing steel into my eyes.

He tips his chin up and looks at the ceiling for a minute.

"No, Susannah, I'm not seeing anyone." He says this and crosses his arms in front of himself.

I nod and try to look anywhere in the room but at his eyes.

"How's the law?" he asks, and I know that he is shooting back.

"It's great, it never let's me down."

He stares at me cooly for a minute, anger boiling behind icy eyes. Our shared wound still wide open, we sit in silence a moment, trying to gain footing.

I don't know why I was so surprised when I came home and found the neighbor there that afternoon all those years ago. I knew she was a stay at home mother and that she looked after Matthew every now and then when Angel couldn't get home by 3:30. I knew that she and Angel went to school functions and field trips. I knew her name was Felecia. What I didn't know was that she was sleeping with my husband.

The day I found them I'd been sick for weeks. I had sneezed repeatedly in the face of a new client that day and had been ordered home by my senior partner, with instructions not to come back until I was well. I was angry. What was I supposed to do? Lay in bed for five days? Ridiculous, a person did not make partner by lying in bed sick.

I slammed into the flat that day and flung my briefcase into the corner. I tripped over a pair of women's shoes that weren't even mine and didn't notice. I was too busy storming into the kitchen to pour myself a drink. I had untucked my blouse and threw my suit jacket onto the sofa when Angel appeared in the doorway wrapped in a sheet. He stood gaping at me, a look of terror in his eyes.

"What are you doing ho--?" I started and then felt the answer in the air. I set my glass down in silence and pushed past him into the bedroom where she was frantically trying to dress herself.

The oddest thing struck me in that moment; how much she looked like me. She was my height, my weight. She had a hair cut like mine. Her make-up was like mine, well, what was left of it anyway. Even the perfume that hung in the air was very much like mine.

She clutched her dress in front of her when she saw me, her eyes filled with tears, hands shaking with panic.

"Men, Susannah Suffolk, are only after one thing!!" Mother's voice suddenly echoed in my ears.

"Felecia, isn't it?" I said …."One THING!!!"

"Susannah, I-I'm so sorry…" she said, sobbing and turning away from me to put her dress over her head.

"Oh, don't rush on my account." I walked up behind her and snatched the dress away. This woman was not leaving my home with any dignity if I had anything to say about it.

"One thing, Susannah, ONE THING!!!"

"Susannah!" Angel's voice boomed from behind me.

"Don't come near me Angelo." I was purposely injuring him with the use of his full name.

He stopped and stood like a statue.

"Get out, whore," I said, "now."

She snatched a towel from the chair and wrapped it around herself, weeping as she ran out the door and across the lawn. I could hear a faint cat call from one of the neighbors down the street. Good, the harlot had been publicly chastised.

"I trusted you." I seethed at him.

"No, no you didn't!" he said. shaking his head and lowering himself onto the bed, "You made sure that you couldn't trust me. You took yourself away from me so that you didn't have to worry about whether you had to trust me or not. You made sure that I couldn't hurt you by locking me out of your life!"

"Well, you don't seem to have suffered much loneliness over it, Angelo!" I wiped angrily at my eyes. I would not let him see me cry.

"Yes I have. For months I have waited for you Susannah, really more like years. You changed yourself. You set up some kind of agenda and left me behind you with it. I was your escape from Camille and once you had that you were finished with me!!" He shouted this at me. Angel never shouted.

"That is not true, Angel. I loved you and you know that. Maybe I have been distracted and maybe I have changed, but you certainly could've found a better way to cope!!" I shouted back, feeling as if my chest were caving in upon my heart.

"Oh, like you do?! By crawling into the bottom of a martini glass?"

I threw something then. I don't remember what it was now. Something off the top of the dresser, something glass. It hit him, and broke, shattering across his shoulder.

"Get out!" I cried.

He stood and stared at me. He looked around him at the shattered glass, he looked back at me with something else in my hand, ready to throw it.

"Ok, Camille, I'm leaving."

He picked up his clothes.

And then, he actually did it.

He left.

As the door shut I caught a glimpse of myself in the mirror. My hair disheveled, my nose red, fists clenched, a weapon in my hand.

He was right, I was her. The world had crushed in on me from every side. There was no escape, there never was. Stupid, stupid, silly me. Of course, there was no escape from her.

In a matter of five minutes my two worst fears in the world had been realized. I had lost Angel, and I was becoming crazy, just like my mother.

I turned full to the mirror and shouted, "Men are only after ONE THING SUSANNAH!!!" I shrilled it at the top of my lungs, and threw my weapon at the mirror. I fell to my knees and ducked as it shattered, along with my life into a thousand tiny pieces.

I take a deep breath and look at him. My heart hurts.

I can't think of anything worse than hearing the dead honest truth about oneself. Angel had given it to me that day. The only truth he'd missed was the fact that I was still in love with him that day. That if I could've found the courage at that moment, what I would've done is pulled him into my arms and showed him how much the neighbor lady could not do for him. Instead, I let him walk out, and then I locked the door and my heart, behind him.

The leaves rustle in the wind, breaking the silence in the room and I wonder what it would've been like if we had stayed together. It is a thought I have only rarely allowed myself. In fact, thoughts of Angel do not come to me often at all. I turn them away, for they are far too painful.

"Matthew is doing very well." Angel says, bringing up the one subject we know we will have no trouble agreeing on.

"He is. Marie is wonderful."

"I can't get over it," he says, shaking his head, "They're older than we were, but just seeing him with a girl like that…its…"

"I know what you mean, I keep thinking that I'm supposed to be doing something, saying something, offering some kind of advice. The truth is, I don't think they need any."

He nods and we are joyful over our son for a moment.

I notice his hands. He is rubbing them together the way he always did when he was nervous, passing one over the top of the other and then running the palms together. I have always loved Angel's hands. They're shaped well, with long, slender, articulate fingers and despite working construction all day, they always felt soft and warm. Even better, they seemed always to know just how and where I wanted to be touched. Even tonight his touch had been perfect; gentle and kind, caring and supportive—and as always, strong.

"Um…" I start, "thank you, for…you know, before… I'm just having a hard time I guess. I'm just really angry at …her, and I don't really know how I am going to stand this funeral tomorrow…" my voice trails away without me somewhere and I can't find it again.

"You're welcome," he says," I'm just sorry it took me so long to get here. I have been worried about you. I knew this would be awful."

He reaches across the table and pulls my injured and throbbing hands into his. He holds them gently, stroking my knuckles with his thumbs.

"It's gonna' be ok, Susannah." he says and looks into my eyes. I believe him. It seems implausible but as ever, I believe him.

Because Angel has said it, I believe it will be so.

I despise my own apparent weakness at this moment. I am not the cowed, fearful, dumped upon girl that he had left all those years ago. I have convinced myself that am not the same person. I want desperately for that to be true.

I had embarked upon my single life with a vengeance. Not a vengeance toward Angel, more toward life itself. It had controlled me, enticed me, dangled happiness inches before my face and then, without so much as an "excuse me, Ma'am" took it all blithely away from me. From now on, I would become my own fate. I marched into court rooms with the courage of a woman with an army behind her. It was my revenge, my rightful place, getting what was due me.

I gained a reputation in court, the Judges dubbing me "Little Monster" for my diminutive height and vicious propensity for battle.

Two years and I made partner, the fastest of anyone before me in the firm and I set my feet down hard and wielded my power. I hand picked my clients, cases and staff and I made more money than the firm had ever seen. And then, one day, it didn't matter to me any more.

It was the strangest thing to wake up that morning and just not go to the office. I'd called my assistant and told her I'd be out for the day, and I just went walking.

It was summer, and the sun was shining and it occurred to me that I hadn't seen the sun shine on my own skin in years. Surely it had been there, but had I seen it? Had I noticed? And if I hadn't noticed, why hadn't I? The answer came to me with a full on bang. It was because I was too busy proving to myself that I was good enough. Well, good enough was suddenly enough. That very day, I called Matthew's teacher and told her to pack up his homework for the next two weeks. We flew to California that night and for 12 perfect days, I rested on the sand and watched the sun play in the blonde on my son's beautiful head. I swam and splashed with him in the water, and we laughed more than I can ever remember laughing in my life. It was 12 days where we ate ice cream twice a day and petted dolphins at night and ordered pizza at midnight watching movies.

    I realized how close I'd come to missing my life again, and when we got back, I resigned from the firm and opened my own practice, where I work when I want and how I want, still the purveyor of my own fate.

    I reluctantly pull my hands away from Angel, propriety beating out my open ache for comfort. I'm independent now, I remind myself. Independent.

    Angel obediently places his hands in his lap and stares down at them. It is strange to be looking at him, dreamlike to be sitting in this kitchen with him, staring across this table at him. Though the room seems stiflingly small, the distance between us spans the world. Distance is something we never tolerated well.

    I can see him in my mind waving at me the day I left for college. I was crushed at the sight of him there in the street, trying so hard not to cry until I got out of sight. The taxi barreled on, but I wanted it to stop. I pounded on the window quietly with my fist. Why was I leaving him? Why was I doing this ridiculously painful thing? Nothing mattered at that moment but having the car turned back in his direction and feeling his arms circle me and knowing that I would not sleep in a strange bed alone that night.

    I arrived in Ann Arbor feeling completely lost. I registered in tears. I moved into my dorm room in tears. I met my room mates in tears. I went to dinner in tears. I went to bed in tears.

    This stunning entrance earned me the name "Happy" with my schoolmates and for the rest of my time there, that is who I was.

    I called Angel every night from school, or he called me. I was such a square peg, and I felt alienated and more alone than I ever had in my life. It was Charlie who had saved me from total emotional devastation by being my friend and soul mate, always at the ready to lift my spirits and take me out dancing or over to Farrell's for a giant ice cream sundae made with 8 scoops and 4 toppings served in a "Pig's Trough" which we split and then took the bus home holding our swollen bellies.

Angel and I wrote letters to each other during those years, wonderful, intimate, often sexual letters that sustained me by their reading over and over again. Angel would talk of holding me in his arms all night long and waking with me there. He spoke of our earliest teenage times together, reliving them on the paper for me, telling me what he felt and saw and remembered most. I wrote him back in kind and sometimes he would read my letters back to me over the phone after dark. We'd lie in bed and pretend that we were there together, a pillow in both of our embraces, a hand giving us the intimate touch that we wished to be giving each other.

He'd come and visit some weekends and the girls were kind enough to stay over across the hall so that we could be alone. We held each other like people about to die, plummeting to earth in a doomed airplane, the imminent crash weighing above our heads, braced for impact, braced for death, nothing at all left to us but these few passionate, tender moments.

I was always wrecked when he left, weeping for hours and inconsolable, a mouth full of M&M's, choking on them with every sob.

I look at him now and wonder how he remembers those times. It is on the tip of my tongue to ask him, when the door is opened and Rob walks in followed by Matthew and Marie. They have been to the all night market and they carry in bags of snacks and hot steaming cups of water for tea or instant coffee.

I steep a tea bag in one of the cups and pop cookie after cookie into my mouth from an open bag at the center of the table. The rest of the group does the same, but I am beating them at least two to one. It's 1a.m. and there is a knock on the door.

I rush to Charlie's arms before he is entirely inside and nearly knock him backwards out the door.

"Miss me, Sweetness?!" he says, laughing and regaining his footage.

"Apparently!" I stand back to look at his face. He looks like a dream, like something you want in a store window so much that you dream about it and then suddenly you open a box on your birthday and there it is.

There are hello's all around and then he turns to face Angel. Charlie narrows his eyes a bit and then holds out a reluctant handshake.

"Angel," he says, "good of you to come." He stares into Angel's eyes a minute in the most male posturing thing I have ever seen him do. Angel has hurt me, and Charlie wants him to know it. They have not spoken to each other since the divorce.

"Well, it's my family I had to be here." Angel says, squaring off himself.

"It used to be." Charlie returns this hotly, and Rob steps between them, hugging Charlie and turning him away from Angel's glare.

Angel excuses himself and walks outside, Matthew follows and the rest of us return to the tea and cookies.

"You look awful, Mistress." Charlie says to me, "you've got a kind of Lon Chaney thing going here. A little Princess of The Undead, look. What's happening?"

"Can't seem to sleep." I say this around a mouthful of cookie.

"Well, we're going to have to do something about that." he says, grabbing a cup and pouring in decaffeinated instant.

" And what's with the Cassius Clay hand wrap?"

"A little gardening…" I say, and Charlie looks to Rob who shakes his head.

"I'll fill you in later."

Angel and Matthew return and Angel pops Charlie good-naturedly on the back.

"Thanks for always looking out for her, Charlie," he says, "knowing that always helps me get to sleep at night."

Charlie nods.

"A labor of love," he replies simply, and for the moment they reach détente.

Matthew fills Charlie and Angel in on all the details of the funeral. The more he talks, the more I seem to want to put something in my mouth. I tear open a bag of potato chips and eat them by the handful. Others join in. I have finished the bag by the time Marie has begun pulling more blankets from boxes.

Charlie beds down on the floor in the living room beside where I will be on the sofa, Angel and Rob and Matthew take the floor in Mother's room and Marie is forced to take Rob's old bed, much against her will.

The house falls quiet once again, but every nerve in my body is alive. I take deep breaths. Charlie reaches up and strokes my hair from the floor.

"You need to sleep, Boo-Boo," he whispers.

I try to un-focus my head. My shoulders are tight and uncomfortable and I shift position so that my ankles rest on the arm of the sofa, the nubby fabric scraping at my heels, knees slightly bent, my head and shoulders laying flat on the cushion. I lay there for a few moments and must move again. I turn and twist and flop and finally, I sit up. Hours have passed. Charlie snores softly on the floor, his hand still resting upward against the side of the sofa, reaching out to me even in his sleep.

I step over him and pull my sweater free from the cushions. I slip into my shoes and head outside into the coolness of the night.

There is a cold wind that blows in off the lake. Even on the hottest days you can sometimes get a shot of it. I stand by the oak and feel it full in my face. It moves the leaves above me, and the long grass at my feet, and my hair drifts back from my face. I breathe in deeply the smell of the lake and the damp green odor of the bank.

I have come so many miles from this place in my life. I have done so much to be away from here. I have become a person that Mother would scarcely recognize; strong, confident, my own boss, running my own business, living on my own. And yet here I am, once again trapped here against my will, in service to Mother, ever beneath her thumb.

In a creeping awareness, I begin to feel smothered, as if I cannot draw air into my lungs. The wind seems to be taking it past me and moving it all away. Suffocation wells in my chest and I lean down and put my hand into the water. It is still startlingly warm with the recent passing of summer, much warmer than the air. I catch a little breath and sigh it out again.

I drop my sweater to the ground and take off my shoes and socks. The grass is cold beneath my feet, the ground damp and muddy. I feel gooseflesh take my body. It is the most refreshing thing I've felt in days. I take off my jeans and panties, my sweatshirt and my bra and I toss them all up away from the bank.

At first I just wade a little, the water steeping the tension from my spine, bringing my nipples to a point. In a little further, the water is touching my thighs, the waves tickling between my legs.

Finally I dive in, all the way in, and I float and swim and spin. There is asylum in this water, liberation on the waves. I paddle my feet and feel the feathery touch of seaweed reaching up to welcome me as I pass. Being out on the lake was really the only place that Mother could not come get me. I remember once drawing out a plan for a boat on which I could live. If I'd have been able to build it, I might've just sailed away from this place for good.

     Time always suspends in water, and I imagine that I am the daughter of no one, that I have no idea who my parents are. I make them up in my mind. For my mother, I choose a combination of Grand and June Cleaver and one of the women I used to work with at the firm. She was determined and quick and independent. I would've liked to have seen how that was done when I was young enough to absorb it.

     When I was about 12, I found it in Mary Tyler Moore, and I secretly wished for my very own Mary-dom. I loved that show and I couldn't wait for it to come on every week. It was one of the few that Mother allowed. In creating my hybrid mother, a dash of Mary is a must. As I float along, I add more to my new mother. She loves me dearly and dotes and cleans the house and never throws things. She goes off to work each day and studies law journals and brings home her own paycheck which she puts into her own bank account. She takes my new Daddy to dinner every Friday night on her money. They are crazy for each other and I often catch them kissing passionately in the kitchen when they think I am outside.

     I twirl over and over in the water as I contemplate who my father would be. He is less specific, more a vague idea, something in the range of Mike Brady but bigger, stronger, manlier. He works hard and dotes on me as well, and he takes me to Daddy Daughter Dinner Dances and he calls me Kitten, and he interrogates my dates when I am a teenager. He gives me away tearfully at my wedding and he calls me every Sunday morning while he drinks his coffee and smokes his pipe.

     I like these people, I name them Kate and Dan and I decide that from now on, these are my parents and they are my family and that I will have lived with them until I met Angel and went to college. They live states away from me, in Boston, and so I do not get to see them often, but we are always together for holidays. At Christmas, they shower me with gifts and we all sit around a big brick fireplace while Dan reads us "Twas the Night Before Christmas" with a bad British accent.

     I laugh out loud at the joy of this picture and I swim and flip in the water. I float on my back, showing Camille my breasts as they bob up out of the water, and my bottom as it does the same. I summer salt beneath the water, taking my legs all the way over my head, feeling my hair gathering sand as it sweeps the bottom.

     "I will not be yours, Camille, I will not be yours."

I sing this to myself as I swim far out into the lake. It is even warmer at a distance, and I am blissful in my nakedness. I run my hands over myself. My breasts are full, my belly is rounded, my thighs are ample and womanly. I am not thin, but not burdened with Mother's weight either. I am just as I would like to be.

Mother warned often about "thin girls" and "fat girls" and the implications of being either in the sexual world. Thin girls were sluts, the ones that men chased after, the one's who let themselves be caught. Fat girls got pregnant and got fatter, and got abandoned. I would be neither. I would be nothing that she said I would be. When I got too close to one extreme or the other, I would change it. I would eat or I would stop eating.

Away at college, I suddenly found that my size 10 jeans came nowhere near fitting. I ate nothing for three weeks and passed out in my history class. The nurse gave me a book on nutrition and a referral to a counselor. I left both in the trash can outside the door of her office. I would control my body and no one and nothing else. My jeans fit again and that was all that mattered to me.

I will not be yours!

I sing it over and over again, sometimes getting a mouthful of lake water as I do. It doesn't matter. Nothing matters, for at this moment I know that she is gone and that she cannot come and find me and ruin it, that I will not be punished for my crime of naked swimming, for touching my own body, for being a normal girl, for being a girl in the first place.

My body has been so wracked with tension that it seems only in my best interests as I reach down and touch between my legs. The water runs over my fingers warm and then cool. Combined with the sensation of the waves it is delicious, and I find myself falling easily into my own rhythm. A sudden image of Angel's mouth springs into my head and I feel a wave of pleasure move down my spine into my stomach. I think of his hands, those lovely long fingers of his, how he always stroked my breasts as we kissed, how he ran his hands down my belly. I hear myself make a sound in my throat at the thought of it.

I picture the two of us in the kitchen, and instead of Angel taking the flowers out to the garbage can, he stands and shoves them to the floor and pulls me up onto the table. I lay flat and open my legs to wrap them around him, let them fall so far to the sides that my hips ache. He pulls off my jeans and undoes his shirt. When he lowers himself close enough to me I open my mouth as if he might dive into it completely. I pull him as close as I can, run my hands over the dark hair on his chest. Having noticed the gray at his temples I wonder if any of it has gone gray on his chest and the thought creates a chill of pleasure between my legs. I picture myself kissing his neck, down the center of his breastbone, all the way to his navel before he pulls me back up. I unbuckle his pant and he springs out. Angel's penis is lovely. It's wide with a perfect curve that finds the perfect spot inside me. He pushes into me, and I sigh and arc my back into the water.

My head goes completely under the waves at the thought of him working his hips back and forth. His eyes staring into mine, he whispers his love and kisses my neck. He tells me how his life has been nothing without me, how he can't bear the thought of taking another woman to his bed. He pushes harder until the table is wobbling and I have raised my legs into the air. Rubbing faster between my legs I can clearly conjure the memory of the sound of Angel coming. An absolute shriek leaves my throat, and I feel the total release of a rattling orgasm that leaves me gasping in the water. I let it wash over me completely, tension seeping away from me with every sigh and an exhale. It is a grand act, to pleasure myself in front of the moon, so close to where Angel is sleeping, and best of all, right in front of Camille's ghost.

I swim a long time, letting even more tension drop away, until I begin to feel a fatigue in my muscles and I reluctantly start back toward shore. I take my time about it, paddling with my feet as I float on my back and stare up at the moon. It glows warmly down at me and the stars wave and wink. I wish that I could stay here for the next 48 hours. That I could miss Mother's funeral due to swimming and just go home when I was done.

I flip over on my belly and swim in earnest the last few yards. I hit the shallow spot a little hard with my shoulder; a sandy scrape. Resting on my knees a minute, I rub the sand off and catch my breath a moment before I stand to creep up the bank. Soon I am shivering with the chill of the air and wishing I had brought out a blanket.

Suddenly, I make out a figure in the semi-darkness, I hear myself scream and jump behind the oak.

"What the hell--?!"

"I heard you get up and go out. I was worried," Angel says, holding a towel around the side of the tree where I snatch it from his hand and wrap it around me.

"This was private!!" I snap, embarrassment burning in my cheeks.

"I'm sorry."

I emerge from behind the oak, wrapped up neatly in the towel like an egg roll.

I stare at him a moment and pull my clothes from his arms and gather them to my chest, walking past him toward the house, my cheeks stinging.

"Hey," he calls to my back, "it's not safe to be out there swimming alone at night, you know. I was just making sure that you were ok."

"That's not really your job any more, now is it Angel?" I ask him, angry that my self-soothing was suddenly a public spectacle.

"Who says it's not my job?!" he calls back, angrily.

"The judge did!" I cock my hip, and drop my clothes to the grass.

"The judge doesn't live inside my chest. The judge doesn't see the mother of my child in pain and have to stand by and watch and do nothing. The judge wasn't there when we were in love." He says this, and at the realization of the conversation we are about to have, I nervously reach for my beach glass at my throat.

My fingers come up empty.

I gasp aloud and put both hands to my neck.

"What is it?" Angel asks, alarmed.

"My necklace! My beach glass!! It's gone!!" I shriek this more frantically than I would like to, but I can't help it. I had forgotten to take it off. I feel ridiculously all around my neck with my hands, my fingers desperate for the chain. I gasp in the realization.

The lake has reclaimed its treasure.

My knees buckle me to the ground and I sob openly.

It is my final undoing.

Angel is beside me the instant I fall. He sits and pulls me full into his lap. I wrap my arms around his neck, rest my head against his chest and I weep. I cannot stop. I cannot stop crying and I cannot stop myself from burrowing into his shirt, from grabbing great handfuls of it and sliding my arms around to his back to do the same.

He rocks me and kisses the top of my head.

He looks down at me, and I see in his eyes the same gentle adoration that I saw every time we made love. The years begin to blur around me. The world suddenly goes uneven. Where the hell am I and where have I been? I am cold and hot and devastatingly happy, and cruelly sad and I am so hungry that I consider taking this shirt cloth into my mouth. Angel is staring at me, looking into my eyes, he's back, he's back, thank God and I didn't ruin it and Camille didn't run him off and we can get married and after college we'll move in together, but I've been to college and I've had a baby, Angel's baby, a boy and now he's grown and I'm not with Angel any more. Camille has run him off-"BANG-BANG-BANG" with the pot, and I have to get Hannah away from her Mother, but I can't because my thighs are stinging, they've been hit with a slotted spoon. One of them is bleeding, I'm sure of it and there are bandages on my hands, wet bandages and my necklace, my beach glass, the treasure that marked the one pure, perfect moment of my life is missing. I feel for it over and over again and it's gone, it's gone, it's GONE!!! I can't feel my head, I can't breathe, I can't see right. Everything is uneven, everything is moving. Everything has turned around a hundred times and I can't find where the start is any more.

His face is moving closer and closer to mine, and it is the easiest thing to do, to just tip my head and let him kiss me. To feel his lips again, to feel his passion for me again, to be loved by Angel again, and maybe it will stop the spinning and the world can right itself again, and Angel will brace me against it. He's close now, so close and I can taste his breath. What do I care for anything else? Angel, my Angel is here. The sky, the moon blurs, the sound of lake rises. I hear the waves, I hear them louder and louder. Angel's face. . . Angel's mouth. . .

"HEY!"

We jump, both of us, startled, just millimeters from our mission. Charlie runs across the yard and lifts me from Angel's lap. I think it is Charlie… Is Charlie here?

"What the hell is going on?! Are you really going to take advantage of the state she's in? You son of a bitch, get away from her!" He fires the words at Angel, bullets of accusation.

Angel stands and silently gathers my clothes up from the grass as Charlie carries me inside and takes me into the bathroom where I sob and sob. He rocks me a minute, sitting on the closed toilet and when I finally am able to stop he leans to look into my face.

"What are you doing, Susie-Q?" he says so softly that I can barely make out the words.

"I don't know." I am unable to keep my hand from feeling dumbly at my neck.

"Sweetie, you were about to kiss him!"

'My beach glass is gone."

"What?" he says and wrinkles his brow at me.

"I went swimming, and I lost it in the water. Mother took it from me because I was sinning. I touched myself in the water and Mother took my beach glass away."

I hear the words come from my mouth but I can't seem to stop them even though they don't make sense.

"No, Sweetness, your mother is dead, and if your necklace is lost it's just because you forgot to take it off in the water, that's all."

"Oh, God, Charlie, it's gone, it's really gone. I lost it. I lose everything!" I say and Charlie looks more worried than I think I've ever seen him look.

He sits me up straight in his lap and pulls a towel off the rack to wipe my face with it.

"Susannah!" he says so loudly and so sternly that I am startled. I stare at him.

"Susannah, where are you right now?" he says.

I stare at him, unable to make my mouth speak the words.

"Susannah, I'm not fucking kidding! Where are you right now?"

I take a deep breath. I know he wants me to speak to him but all I can do is stare. I don't want words. I don't want to answer.

He shakes me a little, a kind of "out with it" snap, and I steady myself with one hand on the edge of the tub and one behind Charlie on the back of the commode.

"I'm at Mother's house." I blurt, and Charlie takes a deep breath so hard that his chest pushes against me.

"Why are you here?"

"Because she is dead and we are having the funeral tomorrow." I feel robotic, as if my answers to his questions were somehow pre-programmed.

"What the hell happened out there?"

"I couldn't sleep, I went for a swim. Angel was there when I got out and we started to argue, and then I realized that my beach glass was gone and I just. . ."

I shake my head and feel at my neck again.

"Lost it." Charlie finishes for me.

I feel my teeth begin to chatter.

"Geezus H, Qsie, you're freezing. Get in a hot shower and get the sand and muck off you and then, by God, if I have to sit on you, you are going to get some sleep!"

I nod as Charlie stands me up and starts the shower. He closes the door behind him and I step into the tub. I'll shower away the sand

and lake water and the feel of Angel's arms around me. It's just there is this loss, this horrible horrible loss, that I won't ever recover from. Mother told me he would do it. Mother said he would. Mother said that this is what men do. And he did, he did what Mother said, and maybe it means that she was right, that she wasn't crazy just that I was bad, rotten, sinful to the bone and my glass, my necklace, my gift, Angel's love…it's gone, gone forever. I've ruined it all. I've lost everything. It's all my fault.

     The water is running cold and I don't care. I can't feel my toes, I can't feel the tips of my fingers. My hands are almost immovable and I am shivering and I don't care. I've sat in plenty of cold. I've waited on the porch for hours in a sweater in 30 degree temperatures. I've hidden in snow banks and under bushes. I can stay here in the cold. . .perhaps, I will die here. It wouldn't be so bad to die here, in the shower. It wouldn't be messy or painful. I'd just cease to exist here. No thought, no pain, no problems, no life dangling before me, the eternal carrot just beyond my reach, tantalizing, making me think that I will have it, only to jump away again and again and leave me weak and hungry and tripping over my own fucking feet.

    I sit down in the tub and let the shower run over my head. And now, nothing exists but this tub. I sit and stare at water droplets as they form into tiny rivers on the shower doors and run off down the glass into the tub. I think how like these droplets my life has been, served to me only drip by drip, one tiny piece of happiness at a time, too small to take, too weak to resist being rushed off by the torrents that take them away from me each and every time.

    I think of Hannah, of how she will undoubtedly be returned to her mother. I think of how she will be beaten for "telling." I wonder if Hannah's mother has a slotted metal spoon. I wonder if Hannah knows that if you turn your face to the wall and pull your arms and legs in tight, she can only hit your back, and the back of your head, but because it's cushioned by your hair it doesn't bleed and your shirt covers your back, so there's no bare skin. I must tell her the next time I see her, before her mother takes her back. I should tell her that and I should tell her how to hide under the stairs in the basement. I should tell her how small a space it is and how it's so hard to be found there since it doesn't seem like you'd fit, but if you get in with one leg first you can. You can cram a pillow in the corner and take a blanket too and then shut the little panel door and she never knows. Mother doesn't look under the basement stairs, she just yells louder and louder 'cause she can't find you. But you don't get hit, at least until you have to come out to pee. But you can pee a little in your pants and stay there a few hours any way. No one knows but you. You can wash your clothes and the blanket when she goes to sleep. No one has to know, it's okay when you're hiding even when you're 10 years old, 'cause you can't get out until she stops banging the pot. And the clothes wash clean. The clothes wash clean. I have to remember to tell Hannah about the clothes.

There is a knock on the door and I ignore it. Someone calls my name and I pretend that I am not that person. A few minutes pass. The water is icy now and I am shivering so hard that I have bitten my lip between my chattering teeth twice. I taste the salt of my own blood on my tongue. I barely notice the taste. I've swallowed lots of blood. Mother doesn't like for us to bleed on things. We mustn't leave bloody tissues in the trash. I've swallowed more blood than this, much more than this. I suck hard at the wound and swallow. No, I won't bleed on the towels, Mother. I'm sorry, Mother, I know they are white. I won't soil the white towels. I won't soil the towels.

There is a knock on the door again, louder and more insistent this time. I plug the tub and slide down into the water so it covers my head, so I don't hear the knocking. The knocking turns to pounding and shouting. Don't shout Mother, I'm so sleepy. Oh, sleep…for the first time in days…sleep, wonderful sleep. I feel the sting of water in my nose, deep in my sinuses and I swallow. It pulls the water into my throat and I open my mouth. More water comes in. It is so quiet here. So quiet in the lake. I love the lake water, I love the lake. . .

There is darkness, and I release everything for sleep. Sleep now, sleep. . . now.

I come awake with a sudden choking gasp and the feeling that my skin is encased in ice. Voices fly above my head and I hear them but only comprehend a few words.

"…Christ!!"

"…not getting any AIR!!"

"..is she breathing?! Is she?!!"

"Get a blanket!! BLANKET!!! …blanket…blanket.." it echoes in my ears and I think how a blanket would be lovely. It's so very cold in here and why doesn't someone turn up the heat for God's sake…?

"…ambulance…?!!!

I am panicked suddenly, is everyone all right? Who needs an ambulance?!

"..Matthew…"

I open my eyes and try to sit up, but hands stop me.

"Where, where's Matthew?!!!" I shout. At least I think I am shouting.

"Shhhhh, lay still! Jesus Kitten, what in hell are you trying to do?!" Charlie's voice says this to me from a blurry place at the right, he is leaning over me. His mouth has been on mine, I can taste him, and droplets of water are falling from his face back onto mine.

"Don't move, Baby…just stay there.." Angel's voice says to me from a blurry place on the left.

"Mom?!" It is Matthew's voice, clear and bright as a crystalline sunrise, and I see him clearly at the center, his ocean blue eyes dilated with worry.

Blanketed, I reach out for him and he rushes to me. I pull his head to mine and I close my eyes and weep, my teeth chattering and gasping for air. Thank God, thank God and I am taken suddenly by a spasm of coughing. Water pours from my mouth, from my stomach, from my lungs. I wretch hard, over and over again. The remnants of everything I have eaten all day come up hard. Matthew stands back as they tip me on my side and Marie rushes in with towels to contain the mess.

A few hours later, I am at Grands, wearing two flannel night gowns, a huge terry cloth robe, socks and slippers and a sweater over my shoulders, covered in a half dozen blankets, a heating pad on my back as my spine seems unwilling to warm, and a hot water bottle on my feet. Rob sits on one side of me and Matthew on the other, ostensibly for warmth, honestly for security.

Dr. Millicken has been to see me, (the house call, a vestige of years past still alive in this rural place) he has given me a sedative, a shot in the ass, a firm talking to and a bottle of pills which Charlie has taken under his control. I am prescribed rest and warmth and food and most of all sleep. With scant hours before Mother's funeral, I hardly see how it is possible, but I am assured by the population that it will be so.

I learn that Charlie had called my name, checking on me, and when I didn't answer, Angel called, and then they both called and pounded on the door demanding that I open it. I had locked it upon Charlie's exit, ensuring my privacy. After a few more minutes, and after the pounding continuously went unanswered, Charlie and Angel had stood side by side and kicked the door in, only to find me under the water, blue and still, the tub running over.

They had pulled me out together and Charlie had given me mouth to mouth. Amazing.

I kiss my guardians on the cheeks as Charlie enters and they slip off from their posts and Charlie slides in on the left. He puts both arms around me and pulls my head onto his chest.

"Your lips are still blue," he says, "and it's not a good look for you. If you're going to go with it, you'll have to change the blush…"

I giggle and cough, and his arms tighten around me.

"Don't you ever do that to me, Susannah." The words catch in his throat, "Don't you ever make me say goodbye to you." He sobs a little, a small manly, held back kind of sob and he squeezes me tighter and tighter.

"I'm sorry…" I say, and I am.

If he were to ask me at this moment if I intended to kill myself, the answer would be no. For a moment, I just stopped trying not to die. I was just tired of the fight.

"Look, nobody wants to ask you for fear of making it worse, but what the hell is going on with you?" I hear fear and anger in his voice.

"I'm not sure." It is the most honest answer I can manage.

"You know if you are grieving your mother that is normal—"

I cut him off.

"It's not THAT."

"Then WHAT?" he mimics me.

"Why are you acting so angry?" I say, and pull away from him.

"Because you are behaving like someone I don't even know. I come in to find out you've torn up your own hands trying to yank out your mother's rose bushes, you've not slept in what? Two days? Then I wake up and you're not there, and I walk outside to find you naked in the arms of your ex, about to be washed away on a wave of passion! Next thing I know, you're effing dead in the goddamed shower!"

"I'm a feeling a little pressured and confused, Charlie, you don't get that?" I say, feeling my face flush.

"No, I get that. Everyone here is feeling that. You, on the other hand are the only one so far found dead in the bathtub!" He looks at me with the face of someone who is completely terrified.

"I'm so sorry that I scared you Charlie." I am horrified as he drops his head and starts to cry.

"Charlie…." I say and pull him close to me. He pushes back and then shakes his head.

"It was this same time last year that William died." He is sobbing, and now I know the full extent of what I have done to him. Charlie spent a year sitting bedside with our friend William, who died of AIDS this time last year.

"God, Charlie…" is all I can manage and then I am crying too.

We hold each other and I apologize again and again. Suddenly, I feel his fear in my own chest. It comes to me with an almost stabbing pain that not only did I nearly lose my life, but I nearly harmed everyone I love in the worst possible way. I feel like the most selfish person who ever walked the face of the earth.

"I've been going through some really bad—" I start and Charlie interrupts me.

"I can only imagine how this has been for you. I know its the worst, and with your case and now Angel being here, I am amazed you haven't run home screaming your head off and hidden under your bed." He stops a moment and we both grin a little at the image. "But you have to get both your feet in the here and now, Kitten. She is gone, the monster is gone and this will all be over soon, unless you let it make you sick. I want no more sick friends, do you hear me? And dear God, no more dead friends."

I wrap my arms around him and kiss the side of his head. We sit holding each other a long while, and I am about to try to say something else to explain my behavior, when Charlie talks over me.

"Are you sleepy yet?" I must admit that the sedative is getting the better of me.

"Will you stay here?" I ask him, a little girl's voice coming from my throat.

"Just try to stop me…" He flings the covers back and gets all the way under them with me and wraps me in his arms, my head resting on his chest, listening to the lullaby of his heart beat, letting my breath fall into it's rhythm. Oh, safe, safe in Charlie's embrace, I finally feel the blissful release of my consciousness, only vaguely aware that Grand has tip-toed in and turned out the lights…

Heroism…is endurance for one moment more.
   --George Kennan

Chapter 8

    I open my eyes to bright serrated beams of sunlight that smatter across the bed through the stitching in the blinds. I feel so different than I have for the last two days that I almost forget this is the day I have been dreading. This would be the day that I go into that church, the one I swore I would never set foot in again, and tolerate hearing what a lovely and faithful woman my mother was. This is the day that I will have to tolerate the weeping and well wishing, the sorrowful friends and onlookers. I lay back and relish the feeling of the bed, the pillows warm with my body heat and smooth beneath my cheek. The blankets are satiny soft with wear and they smell of a strange but satisfying combination of Grand and Charlie. I close my eyes and doze through another hour before my bladder forces my feet to the floor.

    Mother's funeral has been postponed a few hours. I learn this upon my rising, finally at 10 am, an hour after it should have begun. For a moment, as I look at the clock, I let myself believe that I have missed it, the tragedy of the night before leaving me too weakened to attend. My fantasy is soon shattered as the family cautiously fills me in. They tell me it will be at noon instead and that everyone is fine with it. They tell me Angel has checked into a hotel, and that he is fine, and that he has already called three times.

    In remembering the events of the evening before I am sickened. I have made an emotional fool of myself, skinny dipping like a teenager, letting Angel cradle me in his arms, sucking water into my lungs. I don't know how I will face my family, let alone Angel.

    I sit at the table and Grand sets steaming coffee before me, with a plate of pancakes and bacon and orange juice. The pancakes are perfect, fluffy and buttery and I coat them heavily with maple syrup. I hold them on my tongue, each bite a symphony, my rattled anticipatory nervousness ebbing away with each pass of the fork. Grand is an artist with bacon as well, and I eat 5 slices, the salty chewy meat the perfect antidote for the sweetness of the pancakes. I eat every bit, and only resist refilling the plate for fear of becoming a spectacle again.

    And now it is time to shower and dress for mother's funeral. I soap and rinse and get out of the shower quickly, a creepy prickly feeling coming over me at the sight of the tub. I sit in front of the mirror in

Grand's room and methodically put on my make up. I put a beige shadow on my eyelids, watching as the brush strokes the color back into my pale and sickly face. I line my eyes with my every day black liner, I put a brown shadow into the crease—it is as if I am standing behind myself, watching me as I perform this "count down" to the blast.

My cell phone rings and I stare at it. I am not certain I can even physically lift it from the dresser. It rings six times and then stops. I feel my muscles release involuntary tension. Please, no more. Not now.

It rings again and I snatch it up and press the button in a spasm of nerves.

"Hello?"

"Susannah Suffolk?" a voice says. It is a deep voice, full of timbre and it echoes into my ear.

"Yes." I say, still startled.

"This is Frank Millsner, Channel 7 news, what can you tell us about Hannah Williams?"

I am dumfounded. I have been discovered.

"I have no statement to make at this time." I say, too fast, and disconnect.

My heart is pounding. All the implications of this call begin whirling inside my head. There could actually be reporters waiting at Mother's funeral. I rest my head on the dresser a moment. My stomach seems willing to offer back my breakfast but I fight it down.

The phone rings again. I let it ring until it stops. It rings again.

I snatch it up from the table.

"Listen!" I shout, "I am attending my MOTHER'S FUNERAL!"

"Ms. Suffolk, I'm very sorry to hear that," the voice says. It is a different voice this time. This time it is Jefferey Franken.

"I wanted to let you know that my office has faxed over the paperwork for Tuesday's hearing. I understood you were out of town and I wanted to make certain that you were up to speed."

This is one of those moments when, as a lawyer, it is necessary to think on one's feet. This is a chess game moment, and though my head recognizes it, my heart just will not get on board, and neither, it seems will my vocal chords.

"Ms. Suffolk?" I am awash with an image of an iceberg. He is cool and blue, he is Antarctica.

"I'm here," I say.

"I hope that is satisfactory. If there is somewhere else you'd rather I fax the papers—"

"NO," I say too loudly, "it's fine."

"I caught the news last night," he says.

"Are you looking for some kind of deal?" I reply, a bit harsh, but cutting through the game.

"My client loves her daughter and does not want to lose her." He says.

"Your client loves her status and her money and does not want to go to jail." I say.

"My goodness, aren't you making some lovely assumptions. One could almost say you were showing a kind of prejudice. Whatsa' matter Ms Suffolk, you had a poor childhood, so the rich must suffer?"

My throat begins to boil with the words that I am barely holding back.

"No, Mr. Franken," I say, " I had an ABUSIVE childhood, and I know what Hannah is suffering, so let me tell you something; I don't give a damn how high profile you want to make this case. I don't care how many times you show your smarmy face on the news. I don't care how many little seedy tricks you pull, you are NOT going to intimidate me. I know what it's like to stand up to a bully Mr. Franken, and after what I have been through, trust me, you don't scare me one goddamned bit." I feel a flood of relief as the words pour out of me. I feel as if they are words I've been holding inside me for a hundred years. "So fax your paperwork and get on with it. And don't bother me again today, as I said, I am attending my Mother's funeral."

"There's no need to become adversarial, Ms. Suffolk."

"Yes there is Mr. Franken, there is every need to become adversarial because I am just that, your adversary and Mrs. Williams' adversary because I am on Hannah's side. Your client is guilty. She killed her son and she had a near miss with her daughter, and I promise you that as long as there is breath in my lungs, that little girl will not be released into the hands of my Mother!"

I hear the words too late. I said it, I actually said "my" Mother.

Before Franken can respond I press the disconnect button.

As I hold my head in my hands I can feel him smiling. I can see his horse-like face, the way he always leers into the TV cameras. I see his three thousand dollar suit, his silk tie, his Gucci shoes.

I cannot breathe. My chest is compressing inward. I am suffocating. I bend my head down and push against my stomach trying to force some air. Finally, I stumble to the bed and lay down. My heart is racing so fast that it feels as if it will roll out of my chest.

Not only did I just entirely lose it with the opposing attorney, I practically handed him my weaknesses on a platter. My head swims. I take slow deep breaths and hope against hope that it's just too soon for them all to find out where Mother's funeral will be. Knowing Franken, he'll send the reporters over himself if he gets a chance.

Finally able to stand again, I rifle through my suitcase for my underwear and bra, and I cannot find my slip. I take out everything piece by piece; still no slip. I pull my garment bag from the closet and unzip it, still searching. Nothing, no slip. I sigh and resign myself, pulling out my suit and trying to put it on.

I find I am struggling with it. I reach around and pull at the waistband which seems to be stuck on something. The button absolutely will not reach the hole. It is now that I look in the mirror and realize that what the skirt it stuck on is my stomach. My on again, off again romance with an extra ten pounds is apparently, on again. I curse loudly and zip the zipper as high as it will go, a full inch below the waistband.

The hem of the skirt itches me as I walk across the room. The hem is stitched in a heavy thread that rubs against my legs and sends me into fits of scratching. I am damning myself for forgetting my slip when a thought occurs to me. I slip the skirt back off and toss it on the bed and dash back to the garment bag where I produce my beautiful red dress. Form fitting when I am at my smallest, it will definitely make a passable slip today. I put it on and admire how it hugs me in the mirror. The beads are just below the bust and at the hem, they will not interfere with my suit at all. I beam at myself in the mirror and put on my sleeveless black mock turtleneck and the jacket over top. Perfect, no one will ever know and the hem is no longer itching.

I sit down again and dry my hair. I put it up into a neat twist in the back, curling it around my fingers and tucking it away at the back of my head with bobby pins. Just as I put on my lipstick there is a rap on the door.

Rob comes in sheepishly and sits on the bed, watching quietly as I spray my hair and tuck in a few frizzy ends. He does not speak as I put on my earrings. I turn and look at him finally, ready to go.

He stares back at me and in his eyes I can read a thousand things. He is marveling over our freedom. He is dumbfounded by sadness, by grief. The grief is for our suffering and not for her passing, and by this he is also consumed with guilt. I know what he feels because I feel it all myself. I move beside him on the bed and we lean against each other the way we have so many times in the days when we would be reeling in the aftermath of Camille the Horrible. We would sit on my bed, shoulder to shoulder and not speak, staring out ahead of us at the grim spectre of our young lives, grateful for a moments reprieve.

Jenna bursts the door open suddenly and we both jump, the vision of Mother's ghost just an inch before her in the doorway.

"Well, for God's sake what on earth are you doing?!" she says, frantic as usual, "We are all waiting, we have to go!! My God, aren't you ready? Well look at you of course you are, now let's go! We should go, shouldn't we?!"

My hand reaches for my missing beach glass and I grit my teeth. My neck feels empty, naked, even with the turtleneck in place. We head for the cars and, settled into the back seat beside Matthew and Marie, I hunt in my purse for Mother's locket. Matthew helps me with the clasp, and while it is not as satisfying to my fingers as my beach glass, it is at least it is something for them to play at.

We travel to the church and I feel my stomach knotting. I will have to see her, to look at her face, I will be watched and people will be expecting me to cry. Perhaps out of frustration I will be able to accommodate them.

St. David's is a beautiful sight even to my prejudiced eyes. Scrolling stonework adorns three towers and a spire that lifts an ornate gold cross victoriously into the air. There are dozens of stained glass windows depicting the saints and each one glints with light as we round the building to park in back beside a long, shining, black hearse.

We file out of the cars and into the church in silence. Even Jenna is uncharacteristically quiet. I can hear the soft scritching and crunching of our shoes overtaking the gravel in the parking lot. We are soldiers off to the final battle of the war of Camille: loss and victory all at once.

Rob pulls open the big double doors and we enter behind him, Father Satine is there waiting to greet us, all sympathy and "God be with you." at the door. He holds Grand's trembling hand in both of his for a moment. I watch her and my heart hurts. What she must be feeling. Anticipating the sight of one's child in a casket; I cannot imagine the agony.

In the great hall of the church, at the end of all the pews, beneath the protection of the mountainous vaulted ceiling, red draperies flow liquid and bloody in the distance. The stained glass is a contrast in purple and blue, the light of twenty candles glints off the ornate appointments of the golden cross standing at center. The organ is silent and waiting at the right, the emblems of the body and blood of Christ are laid out on the alter at the left and in the center sits Mother's coffin draped in white satin. Even from this distance, I can make out white and red roses and the banner ribbon that reads Beloved Daughter and another that reads Beloved Mother. I hate these flowers instantly, but I hate them less than the arrangement I had made deceptively with my own hands the day before. I reach to hold my beach glass and find the unfamiliar contours of Mother's locket, the ill-fitting pacifier to my nervous fingers. I fumble with it a moment and then let it drop, choosing instead to gnaw at the skin on the edge of my thumbnail.

We approach her slowly. Grand in front, leading the charge, Jenna close behind, Matthew at my elbow and Rob and Marie behind us.

Each step seems to pull the casket farther in to the distance. I watch as the aisle way grows to hundreds of feet before me, the longest walk I have ever made, unsure my legs are up to the task. Time begins to echo in my ears, it is a millisecond and a decade before the casket it just a foot away.

Grand steps up first, supported by Jenna. I watch her closely, keeping my eyes riveted away from the lifeless face in the coffin. Grand tips her head to the side and she smiles the most weary and heart-rending smile I have ever seen. Her eyes well with tears and she reaches down and touches the blur in the casket. From the movement of her upper arm, I can see that she must be putting her palm to a cheek. It is an overwhelmingly mothering gesture, and she keeps smiling even with tears on her cheeks, just smiling down at her baby in the casket. I wonder what she must be thinking. Perhaps that the suffering is over, perhaps that now her baby and the rest of us will have peace. If this is what the smiling is for, I think I can understand it, for there certainly is no other joy in this moment.

Jenna weeps loudly and calls "Camille, Camille" over and over again. She braces herself on the casket, her skin-tight black dress clinging to her bony hips, she drops her head down, a picture of catlike tension, claws on the edge, shoulder blades pushed up high in the back, knees slightly bent as if she were about to pounce. She trembles from head to toe and finally she retreats to a pew, holding Grand and sobbing into a designer handkerchief.

It is supposed to be my turn now, but I am still. I reach behind me and Rob takes my hand. I pull him around me and give him a nudge to go first.

I'm not ready. I may never be.

He steps up and stands with the straight back of an angry man, his hands clasped in controlled fists behind him. He stares ahead for a moment, at the curtains, at the organ. He looks up at the ceiling and out at the stained glass image of Christ that looms behind the altar.

And then he looks down. He looks at her, he actually looks! I want to rush to him and pull him away, yell to him not to do it, not to look at her, it's a trick, just a trick, and she will sit up and start banging a pot on the edge of the coffin and shout obscenities at him.

I squeeze Matthew's arm and back away further down the aisle. He takes ahold of my wrist but I break away from him entirely and walk halfway back to the doorway. I stand lost and floundering, waiving Matthew and Marie ahead of me. Matthew follows me back and tries to comfort me. He puts his arms around me to hug me but all I can do is stare over his shoulder. I watch in abject horror as Rob continues to stare down at Mother. He stands so still that I fear he has died in his shoes. I see no breath, no movement, nothing, just his eyes looking down in to that casket, standing so close to it that the satiny edge of the upholstery is brushing the leg of his black wool pants. It's like watching a man on the edge of a subway platform, knowing he is about to step out in front of the train. I clutch Matthew's shoulder with my arm and try to take deep breaths.

Rob's hand moves suddenly and I gasp, startled. He reaches it ever so slowly, ever so steadily toward the casket. My God, is he going to touch her?! My heart sits steadily in my throat, pounding so hard that I am unable to swallow. I brace myself against the side of one of the rows of pews. I follow his hand as if life depended upon it's reaching out. I follow it up from his back, out from his shoulder, away, away from his body and further and further toward her. He reaches and reaches, it seems to take an hour. I am going to be sick.

Finally, more quickly, it moves sharply to the side. He touches the edge of a white rose, runs his fingers over the velvety petals, he cups a red one in his hand and leans in to smell it, and as he does, he reaches fluidly with his other hand, down into the arrangement. When he steps away, the banner reading "Beloved Mother" goes with him. I watch him turn it around and around in his fingers, until it is curled neatly into a roll and he tucks it into his pocket. He walks away, back up the aisle and past me, stopping to kiss me on the cheek as he heads out into the foyer, his back still plumb-wire straight, hands clasped neatly behind his back, the color now returned to his fingers.

I back further and further away, push myself out of Matthew's embrace, and finally I turn and fully walk away, back into the safety of the foyer, where Charlie holds his arms out to me and I run to them, terror taking my voice, shaking so hard that I feel as if I am about to shatter.

"Shh-shhhh", Charlie whispers in my ear, "It's okay. You need to do this, Kitten. You need to see her." I shake my head "no" and cling to him until he extracts me from his arms and looks into my eyes. "You're all grown up now, Susannah. She can't hurt you anymore, she hasn't been able to for years but you don't seem to see that!" he says to me, an edge to his voice that brings tears stinging in my eyes and heat to my cheeks. I yank my arms free of him and step back, injured, fuming.

"You need to do this," he repeats, taking me firm by my shoulders, staring into my eyes, searching for recognition.

I nod at him, angry, speechless, knowing he is right, hating it, and loving him for it all at the same time. He hooks his arm resolutely through mine and we begin the march up the aisle once again. This time I count the steps as I go. I do it to keep me centered, to keep me here in this time, in this place, in my adulthood.

We are in front of the casket and Charlie puts his hand on the small of my back as we stand there. I am seeing her already but I can't quite take in the picture. Her dark hair is pinned neatly away from her face and the back is laid out in pretty curls on the pillow. Her eyes are closed, their dark burning extinguished. Her lips are slightly pursed, just as when she was asleep. She wears her favorite blue dress, her hands crossed in front of her, a blue beaded rosary draped around one of her wrists and placed under her palm. It is a picture I cannot quite understand.

Here, embodied in the hateful visage of Camille Suffolk is a woman with wrinkles on her face, a woman with beautiful dark curls cascading down the sides of a satin pillow, a woman sitting as still as a porcelain doll, clasping her religion in a hand that will never again count it's beads or clutch it to a chest while prayers fly about it in the air. I see an empty, drained pot, the fury smothered like a stove top fire, the pan lid resolutely clasped upon it. I lean in a little closer and I can see that just inside, her lips have been stitched together. A black thread holds them closed, never again to open and destroy me with judgment and accusation.

I feel my hand moving as if it is not a part of my body. I am fascinated by the ebony curls on the pillow. I don't remember ever having touched Mother's hair in my whole life. It would have been far too affectionate a gesture, far too personal, and it would've put me way to close to harms reach.

 I touch each curl first with the palm of my hand, the edges of the bandages making a prickling feeling, my fingertips outstretched and tracing the spirals down to the bottom and then by mingling my fingers in to them just a little, the way an infant held over the shoulder does upon discovering the hair of it's mother's head.

 Charlie's hand strokes me and I am summoned back to my inner cautions. I take my hand abruptly away and Charlie leads me to a pew where I sit and stare and stare at her. I am in wonder at being in the room with her and not being afraid. I am in awe that I can sit back in this chair, cross my legs, take a deep breath and let it out again and feel the air actually coming in to my body. That I can rest my head on Charlie's shoulder in the pew and not fear being poked hard in the ribs and told to sit up, that I can pop a mint into my mouth without the paper being snatched from me and opened before me, demanding that the mint be instantly deposited. Had she only done these things in my childhood it would have been one thing, that she did them well into my twenties, until I stopped coming here entirely, was another.

 Charlie leans over and kisses the side of my head and tells me how beautiful I look and that he is proud of me. I feel proud of myself and I decide that I am going to approach the rest of this day as the "lawyer me", the face of the independent woman that I show the world. The one who rages into court and takes on my cases like a bull dog. The one who looks the judges square in the eye, and can have a jury wrapped around my pinkie finger in a matter of seconds. I will not be bulldozed by this situation, and now that I have had a little sleep, and faced the grand horror of Mother's corpse, I think I may just be able to pull it off.

 I catch a movement out of the corner of my eye and see that a few more people have entered the church. They stand in a clump, whispering to each other. One of them points to me and I nudge Charlie and he turns to look at them. It's two men and a woman. One of them carries a large case which I recognize. I know it contains a camera.

 Charlie is immediately on his feet.

 "Absolutely not," he says, walking up to them. Rob and Matthew follow closely behind him.

 They whisper, but I can still make out random words.

 "… a few questions."

 "If we could just have a moment…"

Matthew steps in front of Charlie suddenly and takes hold of one of the men by the lapels of his jacket.

"This is my Grandmother's funeral and if you are not out of here in ten seconds, you are going to regret it," he says. His voice is very steady, his words very deliberate. He is so loud that I am startled to my feet and Father Satine races toward them.

The reporter raises his arms and I feel my mouth fall open as Matthew adeptly flips the man's arm behind his back and pulls up on it so hard that the man's hand rests high between his own shoulder blades. The man yelps in pain and Marie begins to run past me. I catch her by the arm.

"Too late!" Matthew says, between clenched teeth and he walks the man toward the exit.

Father Satine follows after as fast as he can, and Charlie and Rob escort the other two reporters out the door, albeit much more gently.

Grand comes over to put her arm around me and I keep hold of Marie who feels as if she is surging. Every few seconds her body moves forward and I have to pull her back.

"He can handle it," I say to her, finally and she stares at me, her eyes frightened. Obviously, she had never seen Matthew physically confront someone either. I hear a strange rustling sound and turn to see Jenna digging in her purse. She produces a make-up mirror and starts dabbing her cheeks with the frantic motion of someone trying to tamp out a fire. Of course, the reporters, their cameras. . . I can't help but smirk just a little.

After a few long minutes and some raised voices, I hear Rob in the corridor on his cell to the police.

Marie and Grand and I walk together out of the sanctuary. I look back at Jenna, so absorbed in her lipstick that she doesn't seem to even notice us leaving.

Father Satine is at the door with Charlie, pulling the dead bolt across. A jumble of voices are converging outside. Matthew has removed his suit coat and is leaning against the wall, sweating. Marie darts for him.

One of the sisters rushes in from the rectory office. She takes hold of Father Satine's arm and whispers a bit too loudly. "Father, there is a Jeffrey Franken on the telephone asking for Ms. Suffolk."

I feel a mix of disgust and nausea. Franken was making a point, posturing again, trying to show me that he was powerful beyond powerful. What an ego this jackass has. I take a step toward the sister when Father Satine holds up his hand.

"March back in there and hang it up—hard! Then take it off the hook," he says, and winks at me as he pushes down with a bit too much gusto on the dead bolt.

Charlie slaps a hand across his mouth to keep from laughing.

I smile at him, almost against my will. Perhaps I was being looked after just a little bit by some higher power. Or maybe it wasn't higher power at all. Maybe it was just the power of people who love each other. Perhaps that *is* the higher power of which people speak.

Father Satine makes a beeline for Grand.

I follow after Marie to see about Matthew.

"That was something," I say to him, and he shakes his head.

"Sorry, that guy just pissed me off—" he flinches, remembering we are in the church, "er, made me really angry. They have no right to be here, Mom."

My son is a man. Not just a man, a good man.

The words echo in my head over and over again. He's a man. A man, better than the grandfather he came from, a man a lot like his father.

"I understand, Sweetheart," I say, and I smile at him. He grins and hugs Marie close to his chest.

In the distance I hear a siren and then the police are knocking at the door. Father Satine opens it carefully and two uniformed officers step in. Just at this moment, Jenna emerges from the sanctuary and lets out a startled yelp. She clutches her chest as four more officers outside begin directing the reporters to stay back. There are maybe 15 people in total but it feels like a circus. All at once it's my sixth grade graduation all over again.

By the time I was 12, Mother rarely left the house. When she did, it was for church or once in a while, the grocery store.

The day of my sixth grade graduation, I was shocked, when suddenly in the middle of the ceremony, the doors of the gymnasium had burst open and Mother stood there in the center, scanning the stage for me as if she were delivering me from kidnappers.

"Where is my daughter?" she shouted, just as the music had started for the choir.

A few of my classmates turned to look at me. My chest went cold. Tears sprung to my eyes. I was alone with Mother in public. Rob was in junior high school already and Grand had wanted to be there but had twisted her ankle in the garden and wound up nursing a sprain. We had tried to keep it from Mother, but I knew she'd overheard at least part of the last conversation I'd had with Grand on the phone. It had evidently been enough to get her here, though she obviously had no idea why.

The principal had rushed to her to reassure her and found himself the victim of her full fury. At first he spoke in a hushed tone that we couldn't really hear over the piano, but then as Mother shouted louder, his voice rose as well.

"Mrs. Suffolk, your daughter is fine, she is in the graduating class!"

"Her class room is empty, what have you done with her? Where is she? What have you done to her? You pig, disgusting pig, I know what you did! I know where she is, I know what you did!"

When she raised her purse above her head to swing it at him I stepped out in front of the class.

"MOTHER!" I shouted as loudly as I could from the stage.

I remember hearing the squeaky p.a. system echo the word into the air of the gymnasium. It seemed to bounce off the rafters and disappear.

Somehow, though it seemed horribly loud to me, she didn't hear it over the music. The choir had begun to sing, but I could still hear her.

"You touched her! You touched her! You pig, you dirty disgusting pig you touched my daughter!"

"MOTHER!" I shouted again, my feet riveted to the stage by fear and embarrassment.

Two teachers ran to help Principal Kendall, but they were too late. Mother had begun to swing her purse and had made a direct hit. The principal went down. Suddenly, the crowd was on its feet. Suddenly, the music stopped. Suddenly, the nightmare was complete, and I was wide awake.

Mother kept swinging and yelling.

"You touched her, didn't you? You ruined her! You ruined my daughter you pig, I wont let you have her! Pig, pig, dirty pig!!" she shouted over and over again; the class, now in full hysterical guffaw, the teachers running to assist, the parents standing with their jaws gaping.

Finally the police came in. They restrained Mother and called EMS. She was bleeding and so was Principal Kendall. She'd hit him square in the face with her purse. His nose was gushing.

They brought me down off the stage and over to where she had finally been seated. The paramedic held an ice pack to her cheek and she stared at me dumbly.

"Mother?" I said.

"Where's my daughter?" she asked me, "Do you know my daughter?"

My cheeks burned as the policemen stared at me.

I didn't know what to say. I had never before felt that kind of complete humiliation. Sure, she'd embarrassed me daily, but never like this, never in front of the whole school which was my whole world, all at once.

I stared at her a moment and then answered.

"No."

Again, the word echoed up into the rafters. But this time it wasn't because of the P.A. system. This time, my utter anguish had given the word its wings.

I walked away; out of the auditorium, out of the school and all the way to Grand's house, a full four miles from the school.

I take a deep breath and try to shake the memory from my head as the two officers inside the church explain to us that they will keep guard at the door if Father Satine and Charlie will help them identify who is to be allowed to enter and who is not.

I feel sick. Once again, Mother has me pinned to a public humiliation, and worse, it is my fault that the rest of the family is dragged into it this time.

"Grand" I say, rushing to find her "I'm so sorry about all this. It's my fault."

She gives me a tight smile and turns away. I feel my heart fall into my stomach. She is angry. Grand does not show her anger often. She turns to me and the look on her face is so stern, I barely recognize her.

"You never come here," she says.

"Grand?"

"You never come, Susannah. You call me once a week and tell me all about your life and all you have going in the city and you never ever come here. How many times in the last two years have you been out here to see me?"

I don't know what to say. She's right, of course, I had stopped coming to this place many years ago. I have invited Grand on every occasion, had Matthew pick her up and bring her down for holidays and other events, but she was right, I did not come to this place and very deliberately so.

"Now, when you finally manage to come here, you bring this!" she gestures toward the door. "And in the church, Susannah, the CHURCH!" she is shouting now, and Father Satine begins a kind of shushing sound as he pats her shoulder.

"I-I'm sorry, Grand, it's not my fault, I didn't tell them where I was going to b--"

She cuts me off, shouting over me.

"This was your home, Susannah. This place was your home. I was your home, and you never come here. This could be my funeral! Don't you see that? This could be my funeral and would you even be here if it was? If it was Camille that was still alive and me in that casket, would you even be here?"

I knew what she was saying was irrational. I also knew what she meant. I'd let my fear and hatred of Mother keep me away from her.

"When you left home, you left me and you forgot where I was. I didn't exist here anymore for you Susannah, and I'm ashamed of the way you gave up on me!"

This hurts more than nearly anything she could have said to me, but what rears up inside me is not shame or even pain, it's anger. My mouth opens and the words pour out.

"You're ashamed of me?!" I shout at her. "How dare you say that? You know something, I have held you on a pedestal all my life and do you know why? Because you weren't cruel to me like my mother was, because you were the only adult I could count on in any way in my life while I was growing up. But you know as well as I do, that the reason you are really so upset right now is because you didn't do what you should have done and now it's too late! And seeing all those reporters outside that door only makes you think about being exposed! You were too afraid to take us away from her when you knew you should have! You let her bully you as hard and as bad as she bullied us and you let your own fear and insecurity push you into doing the wrong thing! You did the wrong thing, Grand!"

I pause and try to draw breath inside me. My own posture surprises me; my body cocked forward, my finger pointing hard at Grand. She gapes at me, her eyes look overly wide, like a victim about to be murdered in a horror movie.

"You were all we had, Grand and you should have made sure that she couldn't hurt us ever again. You should have had her locked up and you didn't! You failed us, and that's the truth! And those reporters and my being here only make you know that even more, and my fight for

Hannah only makes you feel that even harder! Well, I can't protect you from the truth any more than I can protect Hannah right now, but I'll tell you something, at least I'm trying and that is more than I can say for you."

Grand crumples like a wet sheet released from a clothes line. Her legs fold under and Father Satine is barely able to catch her before she goes down. She clasps her hands over her face and the only way I can describe the sound she makes is by saying that it is a howl. She howls in pain and grief and sobs so hard I can't tell if she's choking or crying or about to throw up.

"Mom!" Matthew's voice booms behind me.

I look into his angry face, and am filled with such panic and grief that I can only run past him into the sanctuary. I run as hard as I can toward Camille's casket. I slam the lid as hard as I can, but my hands are still not satisfied. I am burning inside.

This is all her fault. All of it. Everything this family has gone through; my craziness, Grand's pain, Matthew's pain, the loss of my marriage, everything, all of it! My hands ache with wanting to hurt her. I pound the coffin lid and my bandages begin to leak, leaving stripes of my blood on the beige wood.

"You did this!" I shout, pounding harder. I know I shouldn't, I feel caution coming down on me, but I am beyond anything like control.

I push all the flowers off their stands. Each bouquet toppling over feels like one more secret being revealed, one more truth being set free. The church begins to blur, the cross above me looks menacing, as if it is about to fall and trap me beneath it. The flames on the candles seem to flare up to a dangerous height. The organ is too close to the edge of the platform, as if it will roll off. I see the entire sanctuary turning to rubble, the ceiling caving downward, the candles igniting the drapes, the carpet, the walls. I look up into the image of Christ. His eyes are glassy and dead. I see the windows shatter, the pews begin to buckle upward.

It is the apocalypse at last.

I turn toward the side exit and run smack into Charlie's chest. He wraps his arms around me as I struggle against him, and he holds me tight.

"Stop it, Susannah… shhhhh… stop, stop, stop…" he whispers, his voice barely audible over my own breath panting in and out of my lungs.

"Kitten, you can't go out there. Geezus H, I'm giving you a pill!"

And it hits me in this moment, I am indeed trapped inside the church! My fury and destruction fantasy dries up before my eyes like celluloid film too long in front of a bulb. If I go out the exit, I'll be swamped with reporters. It's as if I can feel my pupils closing up. My lungs seem to be following suit.

Charlie sits me in a pew and Marie comes in with a glass of water. I drink it and swallow the pill that Charlie produces from his pocket.

"Is Grand ok?" I say, crying, barely able to ask.

"She's fine. She needed to hear it, Q. I mean, she attacked you first, you just struck back. Now shut up for a little while and let that pill kick in. You are seriously a heartbeat from being taken to the emergency room."

This is a sobering pronouncement. Charlie sits beside me with his arm around my shoulders.

"I should go see about Grand." I say, hearing my own voice shake. I glance at the mass of toppled flowers and then back at Charlie. "Oh, God.... I was horrible to her. I was horrible...!"

"Shut up, and I'm not kidding. Sit still," he says.

A few minutes pass while I catch my breath. I can feel the pulse in Charlie's wrist where it rests on my shoulder. He's angry and upset.

No, he's afraid.

I rest my head on his shoulder and feel him take a deep breath. I want to comfort him but can't. I want to tell him that I'm really fine and I'm really in here—all of me, the regular me whose mental baggage usually remains in some kind of control.

Charlie's hand begins a rhythmic patting on my shoulder. I take a deep breath and shift my eyes to the side, hoping to catch a glimpse of Grand. Every time I lean forward to try to see, Charlie pushes me back.

I hate my own mouth for speaking the words that have hurt her so badly. I hate myself in this moment more than I think I ever have. The façade of our family has been knocked down forever. The funeral is in ruins. All appearances have been lost.

Father Satine appears and approaches us from the middle aisleway. He stops only briefly to look in shock at the flowers I've demolished all around the casket.

"We were thinking it might be best if the family stepped into one of the side rooms for a few moments while the other attendees begin to enter. And, we'll take care of, uh. . .this," he says, looking back over his shoulder at the mess around the altar.

One of the sisters appears in the doorway and leads us off to a small room with soft chairs and a coffee maker.

Inside the room, Rob sits holding his forehead in his hands. Marie paces in a small circle by the door, and Jenna is in full cry. She moans and cries out and wails into a handkerchief while Matthew stands beside her looking tired, patting her shoulder.

Grand is nowhere to be seen.

"She's resting in the rectory." Rob says, watching me frantic, looking side to side as if she would suddenly appear. I nod. I am not sure if this is a good sign or a bad one. Charlie and I sit side by side, and he keeps his arm around me.

The room falls silent. Even Jenna stops squawking and sits still.

I see our thoughts as if they were materializing in the air above us.

"It's almost over."

We are worn out. We are gutted and in pain, but at least it's almost over.

We begin to hear the sounds of people entering the sanctuary: sniffling noses, murmuring, foot steps.

Then the organ begins to play. It's as if I can physically feel the music in my joints as it plays. Each raised note makes me ache. It's all I can do not to rush out and push the sister away from the keys.

Finally we all hear Grand's voice. We hear it at the same time and Rob and I look at each other. He nods toward the door and we all file in. By now, Jenna has settled and is in the perfect state of runny eye make up to encounter the waiting mourners.

It's a small group at first, only six or seven ladies all around Grand in a clump. Each of them hug her in turn and they stand talking quietly. I catch her eye from time to time, and I watch closely as Rob walks over and hugs her. Her face has resumed it's usual look; calm and oddly happy in this situation.

I can't stop staring at her. I want to go over and hold her, tell her how sorry I am and how wrong I was. It's not true, I wasn't wrong, but I want to be. I know Grand did the best she could.

It just wasn't enough.

In the middle of a conversation with a small woman in a blue print jumper, Grand suddenly looks up and into my eyes from across the sanctuary. She smiles a sad little smile and blows me a kiss. I feel my eyes tear up and blow her one back. I take a deep breath and feel what must be the effects of Charlie's pill for the first time. We'll be okay.

More people begin to filter into the church, well-wishing and weeping and resting themselves in the pews to dab at eyes and blow noses. They hug Grand and they comfort her. It's good for her. I am glad they are here for her, but I really want them to leave me alone.

I have underestimated the draw of Camille's long lost, city dwelling daughter. The one who went off to Sodom and left her husband and lives all alone (can you imagine?) in some apartment above a shop on the street! They come to me and introduce themselves, they remember me when I was just a baby, they knew Mother since she was a teenager, they have been friends of Grand's since high school, and the worst, they knew my father. I nod and smile and hug and shake hands and thank people for coming. I really think I may throw up.

Flowers have continued to arrive since the morning. The place is full of them, every conceivable type, size, color. I am stupefied at this outpouring. Most of the flowers that I toppled have been propped back up and the damage minimized. The casket has been re-opened in our absence, I can only assume my blood has been washed from the lid, and yet, a part of me feels it would be more appropriate to leave it smeared there.

As Father Satine sets up yet another arrangement of serene red roses, I can't help but wonder who they are really for? They can't be for Mother, for she never engendered such feelings in any of these people. Perhaps they are for Grand, or perhaps for Rob and me. Those poor, poor children...how often I heard those words as a child.

I was 13 years old and in the grocery store. There was only one in town at the time and so the entire population could be seen there on a weekly basis. Mother was in the midst of a heated discussion with the butcher over his having placed, she was certain, an inferior cut of meat into the white wrapping paper, instead of the one she had chosen. It was loud and I began backing away from the scene, hoping to distance myself enough so that the onlookers would not associate me with her.

I ducked down an aisle full of cereal boxes, listening as her voice rose higher and higher and pretending that I did not know her at all. I began browsing along the boxes, looking into the eyes of athletes and child stars and cartoon characters who all seemed to be living in some world different than mine. I was staring at a box of chocolate flavored puffs when I heard a woman's voice directly behind me.

"Ellen!," she called to her friend, "it's Camille Suffolk..."

I looked up at them, and I recognized them as the mothers of two of the girls in my class at school. They huddled close to each other to talk, their carts full of eggs and milk and bread, the metal sides scraping against each other as they stood on tip toes to peer over the racks at the commotion.

"My God!" the second lady said, "That woman is just totally insane!"

"You don't know the half of it. My Jennifer told me that her daughter comes to class with food all over her clothing. Apparently, Camille throws it at them….", the first woman said in a low whisper, her eyes shooting sideways as if she were imparting some kind of CIA secret to her fellow agent.

"It's a shame…", her friend returned, "Gregory knows the boy. He says he's not allowed to play any kind of sports. She thinks it's a sin…and she hits them, those kids of hers, and not just a spanking either….Gregory says the boy told him so."

"OH!" the first lady said, grasping her chest for drama, "Can you just imagine what those children will be like when they grow up…!?"

"Murderers and deviants," the second lady said.

"Oh, those poor children," the first said, shaking her head "Those poor children."

The pity in their voices rings in my ears as I hear it again in the voices of the attendees of this fiasco. I have been trying to keep my venom seated in my chest, to not let it come up in my throat and vent itself in my eyes and in my voice, but I am beginning to lose the battle. Charlie's pill is making my head feel a little woozy. I survey this room and I see all of these people, shaking their heads, consumed with grief and I wonder where all of this community feeling was when they knew that my brother and I were being abused on a daily basis? Where were all these "good hearted" people then?

I despise these people. They all stood by, my whole "village" as Hillary Clinton would say, and let it happen. Adults, big and strong, stood by while children took the pain, and they did it because it was too "uncomfortable" to get involved in "private" matters of the family. It simply "wasn't done." I feel the floor take a dip beneath me and decide that I should get some air. I look for Charlie, but he is engrossed in conversation across the room and I just don't have it in me to walk over to him.

I excuse myself and take a walk into the rectory behind the sanctuary. My skin has begun to feel overly hot even though the temperature in the church is very cool. I stare out the small window on the door that leads into the back garden. My eyelids feel heavy as I look at it, longing making my chest hurt.

The gardens at St. David's are a community project. The parishoners grow vegetables and take them to the homeless shelter in Pontiac, and they feed underprivileged families in other areas. They grow flowers to take to the senior centers and to make arrangements for funerals that do not receive the response that Camille's has so inexplicably prompted.

As much as I have always hated the church, I remember always loving the garden. I want so badly to walk out into it that I find myself tearing up again. Trapped with Camille again. I sigh. How many times did I resign myself? How many more times do I have to? I press my forehead to the glass. The room is dancing beneath my feet.

From behind I suddenly feel a cloth slipping over my shoulders. I turn to see a small sister, her skin almost translucent on her very time-lined face. She is draping me in one of the sister's overcoats. It's rather like a cape with a hood, and without speaking, I understand that she has found a way for me to take my walk in the garden. I pull the hood over my head, and smile at her, tears pouring onto my cheeks. She pats me gently on the back. "The love of Christ is always with you, Child," she whispers. I cannot respond, except to nod as I slip out the door.

I find the garden a bit barren at this time of year, but the changing leaves, and the sun still make it beautiful. The mums are in full bloom and as I round the path to them, they take my breath away. In the distance, near the front of the church, I can see the reporters still milling around, coming menacingly close to the mourners as they arrive. I shudder and continue my walk.

Mother always allowed me to walk in the garden as she socialized after church. It was a quiet place, somewhere I knew she would not come to get me, a place she approved of and therefore I was safe here. I came to this garden in all seasons, enduring the extreme and stifling humidity of the summer and the deep bone cold of the winter for just a few moments freedom from Camille.

I sit on the wooden bench overlooking the little pond where water lillies grace the surface in spring and summer, and where my stillness would produce the sight of all sorts of little creatures; frogs and lizards, little rabbits, squirrels and darting chipmunks, even an occasional snake. Apparently forgiven for their previous affiliations, they too were welcome in the church garden.

I take a slow, deep breath. It is sunny and the temperature is mild. A breeze smelling of autumn and the damp green of Walloon rushes by me, stirring the trees and whipping the leaves into tiny wind devils that whirl at my feet and then disappear just as quickly as they had formed, tossing the leaves off gently to rest on the ground again.

The ceremony will be starting soon and I know it. I should go back in, but just don't want to. Charlie's pill has kicked in full force now and I feel sleepy. The church bell begins to chime and I know that it has begun. I cannot make myself move. I have no desire to. I have no need honor her by taking communion and singing hymns. I feel no obligation to do so, nor do I feel that God, whomever they, he, she, it, is—would disapprove. I look at the sky, a thousand questions brimming in my heart and in my eyes.

"Why did you let this happen?" I say aloud.

It is the great unanswered question of my life. What had I done to 'God' in order to deserve the life that had been given me, and why, when there are others who have endured so much more and healed, am I sitting here, still weeping and still asking the question?

I had decided at a very early age that somehow, I did not matter to God; that if all that Mother and the church had said were true, I was somehow "reaping what I had sown" and that I somehow deserved everything that happened to me.

I was fascinated by the account of Job. Here was a man, faithful in every way to God, following every command, a true lover of what was good and holy and true and for sport, the devil decided to play a game with him. He challenged God to roulette with Job's life. Would he remain faithful or would he not? And go ahead and take everything from him, was what God had said. Kill his children and take his wealth for which he had worked so hard, ruin his marriage and make him sick. Take his friends, and the cruelest of all perhaps, was that the one thing the Devil was not allowed to do! He was not allowed to kill the man, not allowed to end his suffering, only to deliver and prolong it.

I never understood this story. I tried and tried, and I read it over and over again, and asked the Priest for guidance. I bought theology books, and I looked up the corresponding stories in all the other cultures and religions that I could find it; in Buddhism and in Judaeism, East and West and every which way I could find it. I talked to youth counselors and Baptist Ministers and Jehovah's Witnesses who knocked at our door, and I still could not understand it.

God's point, they all said, was proven by the fact that Job would not let go of his faith even though it seemed that God had abandoned him, and for his faith, he was rewarded as God replaced his wealth and gave him more sons and daughters, even more than before. Yet, I always wondered, what of the ones that were killed? Were they not still gone? Had he not still been punished for his faithfulness? Why didn't God just smite the devil right then and there and tell him to remember his place and let that be that? To this day, I still do not understand.

As a child, hearing this story, and all the others, I did my best to be what I thought God wanted me to be. In fact, I tried to be perfect. It didn't matter. It turns out that either God knew better anyway, or he wasn't paying attention. Either that, I began to reason, or the devil was asking him questions again. I didn't want to be in the story book. I knew I could never do it anyway. I had no real faith of my own.

All I had was fear.

Mother had made it clear that she and God were my judge and jury and should they decide that I was not worthy, which of course, they had, then that was all there was for it. There was no redemption for me, none for my family, and I should simply prepare my horrible, sinful self to burn forever.

But how could I fear the final accounting at death when I was already having my hell?

I hear them singing the second hymn. It comes to me on the breeze, distant as if in a dream. In the pond, a deep green frog lumbers out of the water and sits inflating its throat on a gray stone at the edge of the grass. It half closes its eyes as the ecstasy of the sun-heated rock comes over it. I watch the glistening of its yellow-green throat ballooning out and then falling back into place perfectly over and over, again and again. I envy its contentment, such an uncomplicated life; sleep, eat, procreate and then die, never even aware of one's own existence. It's the joy of life without sentience; existence as bliss.

I hear Father Satine talking. His voice is muffled and I can't make out the words. I am happy that I can't, I couldn't bare to hear them. Next is the voice of Mother's church friend, Mrs. Allison. It is the eulogy. A shiver runs down my back and I wrap my arms around myself, and pull the cloak tighter around me. I am so tired and the narcotic in my system is trying very hard to make me sleep.

A movement catches my eye at the back of the church. A figure walking solemnly, head down, shoulders hunched, headed for the door. It's Angel, coming in late so as not to upset me before the service. I watch him open the door and after a brief discussion with the officer and a flash of his drivers license, I see him step inside. I wonder what he will think when he does not see me there.

I sigh one of those deep, long, soul rending sighs. The kind that you release hoping it will change the way you feel.

Why? Why again, I am asking. Why did you let it happen? Only this time I am not talking about Camille.

It was a good four months into our marriage before Angel and I actually made love for the first time. We'd gone out to the park for the afternoon and taken a slow walk. It was fall, just about this time of year and the trees were brilliant with color. We had moved downstate immediately after the wedding and Angel missed the woods, so we spent a lot of time in the parks. Today we were in Heinz Park, on the bank of the river. It wasn't like Walloon, but it was beautiful in its own way.

It was quiet and the river made a beautiful trickling sound. Angel was holding my hand and the next thing I knew we were kissing. The sun had begun to set and all at once there wasn't a thing in the world except what Angel was making me feel. We spread a blanket on the bank and sat close. Angel's hand slid under my blouse and stroked my nipples as we kissed.

I felt my entire body become liquid. Angel rested himself on top of me and he began to move his hips. I pushed mine against him and without any thought to where we were or what we were actually doing, I had opened his pants and he had opened mine and we'd tossed them aside. The sun kept slipping lower and lower, the air getting cooler against us, but we didn't' care. It was too delicious.

We were starving for each other, starved for the normalcy of husband and wife making love, of a time when we could let our life start, separate from Camille and her damage. We didn't know it would never go away, and for that moment, we felt liberated. We had left her hundreds of miles away and, at long last had found our escape.

I opened my legs around Angel and he wet his finger-tips before he touched them to me. I rocked my hips against him as he tickled at me, kissing me harder and harder, his other hand on my breast, still under my shirt.

I pulled my face away from Angel and took a deep breath. I stared into his face, stroked his cheek and nodded at him.

"Really?" he said, trying not to let his shock ruin the moment.

"Really."

He kissed me again and again and finally I felt the head of his erection dipping gently at me. I spread my legs as far apart as I could get them, I felt my knees fall to the side and it seemed as if every muscle in my body relaxed.

Angel pushed inside me. He whispered his love in my ear. He kissed my neck. It was the oddest feeling, wanting him inside me, wanting to feel him more and more but feeling as if something were in the way. Then all at once, Angel pushed and it was as if something gave way. It was a small pinch of pain and then Angel and I were together.

His body rocked and mine rocked with him. He fell back onto his knees and held on to my legs. I watched him. It was like watching from outside myself. I wanted to remember every moment of this, wanted to see his face when it happened, wanted to know that I'd made him feel everything.

I watched Angel's arms flexing, watched his stomach muscles straining against me.

I lifted my legs against him, raised myself up by putting my hands under my own bottom. He laughed. It was glorious. Suddenly I understood. This was what play felt like! This was the wonder of being with someone you loved! This was why sex was so powerful, and this was what Mother feared my having. It was joy.

Mother never wanted me to have joy.

I arched up against Angel as hard as I could. I rocked my hips and pushed and bounced against his body. The wind played in his hair, he tossed his head back and laughed again and then I could tell it was about to happen.

His brow wrinkled, his breath was reduced to a pant, he pushed his hips harder against me. Finally, he grabbed my hips and pushed hard. Three, four, five times and then he lost his breath. I watched his face as it happened. It was that immediate blank expression, his eyes closed, his mouth dropped open. I felt that pumping sensation, only inside me this time. He let the sound come from his throat. It startled me at first, something like a growl, something like a gasp.

We laughed together then as he fell forward against me. He rested on top of me, the full weight of his body on mine. It pressed the breath from my chest, but I wouldn't move. We were finally complete, finally one the way we'd always wanted. I remember thinking in that moment that Mother would have hated how I felt, that she'd have pushed us both into the river like unwanted puppies and drowned us without saying a word. I had to keep my eyes open and stare at Angel to keep the image out of my head.

I am hearing the last hymn of the funeral, and I wonder if Grand is alright. More than reluctantly, I leave my pew in the garden, disturbing the Father on the rock as I pass by. I hear to the soft fluttering of the water as he baptizes himself again, undoubtedly sullied by my presence at his service.

I creep into the church just in time to slide in beside Grand as the family makes its way down to the church social hall, to stand at the doorway as all the well-wishers come by again, sniffling and weeping and making my stomach turn.

Charlie hugs me tight and asks if I am ok in my ear. I tell him yes and he winks at me as he passes by and gathers Matthew into his arms. I endure the seemingly endless line of weepy and sniffling ladies, the "tsk-ers and the shakers" heads going, tongue's clicking away, and patting me comfortingly on the forearm. My head is swimming. I wish I hadn't taken that pill. All I want is to lay down somewhere and sleep.

There are many people I don't recognize, including a man who only nods at us all as he and a young woman pass by the line. He looks strange, somehow embarrassed, and as I watch the pair slink off to a corner of the social hall, I think to myself that this man seems to be the only one in the room who feels the sham of this event as severely as I do.

Last of all is Angel. He hugs Grand warmly, and shakes Rob's hand and he stands in front of me, eyes full of apology and fear and something that reads like regret.

I let him hug me, and I put a perfunctory arm around his neck, but I do not embrace him. He nods at me, and looks at the floor and bear hugs Matthew, who wipes tears on the back of his hand. As I watch them I wonder if Matthew's tears are for his Grandmother, or for his foolish and ridiculous parents, and a lump wells in my own throat. I turn toward him and Matthew gathers me into the hug, one arm around Angel and one around me.

My stomach pulls itself in so tightly that I cannot breathe, tears spring into my eyes and I am sobbing so hard that I am making no noise whatsoever. Here we are, the three of us, incomplete for so many years, finally triangulated again, finally joined, arms about each other, union and bliss and agony all in such a heady and overwhelming mixture that I am dizzy. Matthew cries. Angel cries. Our tears fall together for the loss, the loss of Matthew's grandmother, the loss of our love, the loss of our little family, just us three. We share a pain that only we understand, that only we will ever know. The wound we bare is unique, it is as big as the world, a space living and growing within our hearts and it has the shape of those missing in our lives, the triangle broken.

I want to blurt out apologies. To tell Angel everything; how much I loved him, what an incredible father he is. How there will be things about me that only he understands, and that only he ever will. I want to tell Matthew how he was conceived in such love, how there was a time when his parents loved each other so much that they couldn't bare to be apart for more than a few hours without feeling pain. I wanted to take the blame for it all, then climb into the casket with mother and claim my punishment.

It was my fault, all of it. I left. I did the damage. It was me, all me and they were not to blame.

Matthew finally breaks away and walks with his arm around Marie out into the garden. Angel and I are left standing there, wiping our faces and feeling ashamed. Our son had left in tears, we are still unable to spare him this pain.

I have never felt so much like a failure as I do at this moment. I walk away from Angel, to the far side of the room where I wipe my face with a napkin and pour myself a cup of steaming coffee from the same voluminous stainless steel pot I've been seeing at these gatherings since childhood. If I don't do something, I will not be able to stay awake.

I sit at a small table as far from the crowd as possible and sip at the coffee. It's strong, heavenly, and I find that I am looking to it as the key to restoring my very being. Shaking, I watch the crowd. They are interesting, if nothing else.

Rob stands with his arm around a lovely blonde woman, undoubtedly Karen whom he said was coming. She beams at Grand who stands beside her beaming back. Rob is studying her face as she talks, and I can see something in his eyes that is making my heart feel something warm seep in. Maybe, just maybe…

At the table to my left, two of the church ladies are going on about Mother.

"…Sainted woman, I mean she never missed a Mass…."

"—and volunteered at the rummage sales whenever she was feeling up to it. You know she suffered sick…"

"Oh, and always a contribution for the orphanage at Christmas…"

Bile comes up in my throat as I listen to them. I will myself not to hear it and turn to the right of me instead. On this side, a weeper, Mrs.

Miller, a friend of Mother's since childhood who has lost several friends in the last few months, a story I received moistly earlier today. She sobs into a paper towel and two other white-haired little ladies sit on either side of her patting her back and urging her to take a drink of water.

I look over at Grand again. She's still hugging and talking. She looks a bit better, the color has come back to her cheeks.

Mrs. Miller starts talking about what a "good Christian" mother was and I leap up from my chair and head for a spot further away, at the other side of the room, where there seems to be less activity. The flock has lined up for the buffet now, and I watch as they shift from one foot to the other, standing in line and looking over each other's shoulders at the food. A bevy of little women with gray hair and flocked aprons flurry around the table adding spoons and wiping spills, and pouring cups of punch. In their glory, they are, and adorable, their pale cheeks shining rosy, brilliant red-lipsticked lips pursed with concentration around their "good teeth". I have a fleeting fantasy of taking them all home with me and letting them care for me. I can see them all in my tiny apartment sized kitchen arguing over the proper amount of salt in my home made stew, or the proper temperature at which to bake my fresh bread or chocolate chip cookies.

I picture them ironing my sheets and guest towels and filling my closets with mothballs. I feel myself smile and I look down into my coffee.

"My goodness, that's a smile…"

I look up into the utterly pleased face of Angel.

"I still do it every now and then," I say, feeling my eyes crinkle at the edges.

"Once a month whether you need it or not, right?" he says, and lowers himself into the chair next to me.

"Right…"

"You seem better today," he says, cautiously.

"Finally got some sleep," I am willing myself not to feel embarrassed.

"Susie, I'm really sorry if my being here has made things worse." He twists the empty sweetener packet from my saucer in his fingers over and over again.

"Yeh, you bring out the best in me, dontcha'?" I feel myself smile again.

Angel seems thrown and I have to laugh.

"It's not your fault," I feel myself getting grounded at last. "This is just such a .... situation..."

Three little ladies settle in at the table next to us and two little men. They spread out their plates and plastic ware and they fuss around their coffees and iced teas and finally set about eating. They begin to talk about Camille. They talk just like the ladies at the other table, Camille the Good Lady, Camille The Faithful, Camille The Saint.

I sneer and Angel motions with his head toward the buffet, "Come on, let's get something to eat."

We are almost to the table when the embarrassed looking man and the young woman step toward us.

"You must be Susannah," he says to me.

"Yes" I say and I look into his eyes. My heart begins to flutter a bit. There is recognition, and I realize …

"My God, you're so beautiful…" he says, and I realize that the eyes I'm staring into are Rob's…they're Matthew's….they're…my father's ! My God…!

I am speechless. The more I stare at him, the more I can see it. The picture sitting at my throat, nestled inside Camille's locket. It's him, it is definitely him.

The young woman steps up.

"I'm Kimberly," she says, and I look at her, and I see the same eyes again, and another dawning, I am looking at my half-sister.

"I wasn't sure I should come," he is saying, "I mean, I didn't know how you and Robert would …well, what you'd think. It's just I thought I should come…you know, for you and Robert…to be here for…" his voice seems to melt away into nothingness.

Is he really standing here? Is he really standing here trying to tell me that he came to be here for Rob and me? Now?! Now that the danger has passed, now that it's all over?! Now?! Now?!! Can he possibly ?!? How many times had I longed for this moment? How many nights did I spend praying to God to send my Father to come rescue us, for surely he was only working to make us a home, get his affairs in order and then he was going to come and take us away; away from flying dishes and Bibles that left a mark across the cheek, and the constant banging of a pot on the counter. He would stride into the house, kicking down the door and demanding his children be saved! He would show up in a limo full of toys and clothes and warm dinner, and he would take us far away from the sound of the lake, from the sound of Camille's voice, to a place where my Stepmother would tuck me in with a kiss on the nose and my

Daddy would read me a story, and promise me that no one would ever hurt me again. To a place where there was a family and a home and where I would be hugged and kissed on the cheek. Where I would be made to stay in bed and brought chicken soup and crackers on a tray when I was sick. Where the TV would be rolled into my room when I had the chicken pox, and Daddy would bring me home ice cream bars and call me "Punkin" and "Kitten" and "Princess", and I waited and waited and I wanted it so bad that sometimes I swore I heard him pulling up in the driveway! I 'd run to the window to look, and I'd wait by the window and stare out and listen and hope…and Now…and NOW he comes, here like this?!!!

    My hand reaches out and slaps his face before I can stop it.

    "Daddy!!" Kimberly screams and takes him by the shoulders, "Daddy, are you ok?!"

    Had he slapped me back, it could not have hurt me more.

    "Daddy" she was saying, "Daddy". A word I don't ever remember addressing any one by in my entire life, a word whose meaning completely escapes me, and mocks me at the same time.

    "Do you want to get out of here?" Angel's voice is saying in my ear.

    "Yes."

*In the day time you have options,
but in the dark, the night decides.*
—Robert G. Taylor

Chapter 9

5 minutes later I am standing on the front step of the Church and a throng of reporters are shining lights in my face. Angel tosses his arm around me protectively and my every instinct is telling me to run away.

My father, my God, my father has just stood in front of my very eyes, now when everything is all over and it's too late. It's too late, too late for me, for Rob for Grand and even Angel and poor Matthew. But it occurs to me suddenly, as if something has hit me in the head, that it is not too late for Hannah.

I stop, and though Angel tries to pull me away, I resist.

"Susannah, you are not in the right frame of mind!" he says.

"I'm in the perfect frame of mind," I say. I wipe my face and hold up my hands to ask for quiet.

The tiny red on-light on a news camera blinks at me. It's a kind of quiet fade in and out, an almost distant-looking light, and it reminds me of the way light always shined from the houses across the lake. I could sit for hours and wonder what the families were doing inside all those houses. They always looked so warm and inviting. Some nights I could smell the scent of wood burning in fire places. I could see the happy smoke coming from all those chimneys. I could sit out in the cold waiting for Mother to stop banging her pot and think about what it would be like to be warm in front of one of those fires.

My life is still so cold, I think, and a chill runs up me and makes me cry.

I steady myself against Angel.

I open my mouth to speak. For a moment, nothing comes out and I feel Angel try to push me forward, to take me off the steps and away. I resist.

"I'm Susannah Suffolk," I say and it feels as if I am standing in front of some kind of support group meeting.

" I have just attended my mother's funeral, so please keep your questions to a minimum."

"Ms. Suffolk, what can you tell us about Hannah Williams?"

Again it takes me longer to make my voice work than it should, but I clear my throat and speak.

"I can tell you that she is currently staying safely with her Aunt in an undisclosed place."

I smell it now, the wood burning in some hearth somewhere…

"Are you prepared to make a statement about the allegations that the charges against Mrs. Williams are a personal vendetta?"

Franken has spoken to the press. My heart hesitates.

"Yes," I say, and I wipe my face again. I smell it, I truly do, someone is sitting by a fire, I just know it. I can picture the hearth, the iron gate in front of it, a soft pillow on the floor, a flannel blanket…

"I find this very personal. I take it personally when any child is harmed in any way. I fully intend to try this case as if it were extremely personal." I feel myself slurring words.

"Shouldn't you remove yourself from this case, for the sake of the child, Ms. Suffolk? Isn't it true that you yourself were abused as a child?"

My ears hear the question repeated ten times. The roof has been peeled off the house on Walloon Lake. Our secrets are bleeding into the water.

"That's crossing the line!" Angel says.

I catch my breath. I let the tears fall on my cheeks because I know I won't be able to stop them.

"Yes," I say, and I feel as if my chest has cracked open."Yes, I was."

I can picture the flames so easily. They are not the threatening kind of flames that make a person jump away from a fire. They glow and dance. I smell spice cake baking. I smell the wood burning.

The reporter shoves his microphone closer to me. "Shouldn't you excuse yourself from this case?"

"As-ss a matter of fact," I say " I think that I am more qualified to try this case than most. I know what it's like to love someone and have them torture me. I know what it's like to have bruises and cuts and burns and to have every humiliation you can imagine. So, you know something. . .?"

I pause and look into their eyes. In the middle of every pupil I see the hearth fire. Suddenly the reporters don't look so menacing, they don't frighten me, they don't even seem to be real.

"This is just easy for me, even this, all of you here right now when I am barely able to speak to you for my own tears. This is just easy, because I spent my childhood learning how to do it. And since I did that, I can do this." I hear my own voice. I sound way too calm.

Tears fall off my cheeks and onto my chest. I feel them hit. Everything seems in some kind of slow motion. The fire still burns in all their eyes.

I feel myself starting to laugh. It's a strange laugh, the kind that happens when you cry too hard and suddenly you start hitching in that funny way.

Angel puts his hand on the small of my back. He wants me to stop but I can't. I feel drunk suddenly, as if humiliation were alcohol. I stare into the eyes of a blonde woman who stands with three microphones hooked together in a kind of gray brace with a television station insignia on it. Her hands are trembling.

I open my mouth again.

"The mess you are all staring at right now is the product of abuse. It's my job, see, to make sure that Hannah and any other child that faces this kind of monster does not turn out like me. You got that? You got every word of that in your little notebooks and on your recorders and on your film?" I stop talking now and sob. Angel tries to push me forward.

I am getting angry now, the kind of anger that wells up and makes me do things before I think.

I laugh again, louder this time, and Angel is whispering in my ear. I don't hear him.

"I got a message for all of you and for Jeffrey Franken and for Mrs. Williams, and even for my own damned father, are you ready?" I pause, and really look at all of them, I feel dizzy as if I might fall down the steps of the church. "The message is, that you won't win. You won't win because as much as I'm fighting for Hannah, I'm fighting for myself. So it's my life on the line now, you got that?" I am shouting now, and flashes start going off in my face. I know I should stop but I can't. It's too late, it's all over and I'm past the point of reason. I have at last embraced my own insanity.

I shout again.

"And I'm not a scared little nine year old any more! Do you hear that? Do you see me? I'm not going to roll over and let you all beat the hell out of me! I'm done! Do you hear me, done!!"

Angel is starting to talk out loud now. He is saying we should go. He is pushing me hard and I whip around and slap his hand off my back!

I turn back to the stunned reporters " My monster is dead!" I shout.

The woman in the front row has all but dropped her microphones. She looks as if she is about to cry. I catch myself in her eyes and my anger melts away again. I start to dissolve.

"The only regret I have," I say, and I hear my voice become so steady that I'm not sure it's mine. "is that I didn't kill her myself."

At that Angel wraps his arm around my waist and shouts.

"No more questions!" he says, so loudly that two reporters in the front row actually jump back in fear. Angel shoves me off the church porch, supporting me with his arm around my waist. He is practically carrying me as he rushes me to his car, the reporters trailing along behind us like ducklings, shouting questions, begging for more, calling my name.

Soon I am sitting in a car beside Angel, sobbing into a handful of napkins and fuming. I can barely recall what I have just said. In my mind, I see my father and a sea of reporters. I see a girl named Kimberly who calls him Daddy. That word keeps echoing in my ears. It begins to make a mocking sound, like little children singing some kind of taunting song.

"Da--ddy."

"Da--ddy."

"Da--ddy"

I take a deep slow breath and try to stop crying. It begins to dawn on me that I have just admitted every secret I've ever kept held in the darkest places of my heart. I've told them to the entire world, and I've done it sounding like a complete crazy woman.

I can't even begin to order my thoughts. I pull a handful of tissues from the box in Angel's car and blow my nose. My chest won't stop that horrible hiccupping that follows an uncontrolled burst of emotion, I try more slow breathing.

"You sure said a mouthful back there," he says. His face is drawn tight. He looks worried. It makes my chest hitch even harder.

"I had to say something." I say.

"You could've left it at "no comment."

"No, I mean I had to. I had to speak, Angel. I am so barely holding on to—"

I stop myself. I am not about to tell Angel how bad off I am. So what if he already knows, I'll be damned if I'll admit it to him.

He shakes his head.

"Is there someone you should call and give the heads up to about this?" he says and I realize that he's absolutely right.

I pull my cell out of my purse and ignore the blinking light that tells me I have no less than 25 new messages. My voice mail will not hold any more than that.

I dial Emmett and hate myself for what I am about to tell him.

"Em." I say when he answers the phone and my own voice sounds so grim that I flinch.

"What is it?"

"I ran into a bunch of reporters at my mother's funeral. I should have kept my mouth shut, Em. I'm so sorry. I don't even remember what I said."

"How bad is it? I mean did you compromise the case, give away details, what?" he says, and he sounds at once angry and empathetic.

"I don't think I did. I mean I don't think I gave away any details. Just,…. just you might want to watch the news tonight. It's … I … I got out there and it was right after the funeral and I'm not feeling well, Em… and I…" I lose it again. I'm crying.

"Hey, hey… Susannah." Emmett says and I realize that I should not be crying into his ear this way.

Angel's face screws up and I feel him bristling.

"Susannah… shhhhh, it's going to be okay." Emmett says " Do you want me to come out there?"

My heart leaps and sinks and does some kind of spin that makes me feel nauseous.

"NO." I say, too quick and too loud.

Silence. In the car and on the phone. All I can hear is my own damned sobbing.

Angel's hand takes the phone from me.

"Hello?" I hear him say "This is Angelo Manotti, I'm Susannah's ex-husband."

My ears don't want to take in the rest of what he says, but I hear it in spite of myself. I have told the world that I am an adult from an abusive home and that because I endured the pain of that childhood I am the perfect person to fight for Hannah. Only I did it sounding like more like Courtney Love than a seasoned attorney.

". . . yeah, I mean she didn't give out any details. . . Right… right. .." Angel is saying and I tip the seat back just a little. I'm so tired. My stomach growls and I realize that it is 5pm and I've had nothing to eat since breakfast. This thought makes me want to weep. It makes me want to cry so hard that I know if I do I will throw up the nothing that is so painful in my stomach.

I open Angel's glove box and rummage. He was always a creature of habit and I find what I am searching for: a snack sized packet of cheese crackers. In fact, I find four. I pull out two of them and tear them both open.

Angel looks at me sideways and grins.

"She's . . .uh… she's going to be fine," he says, and I know now that Emmett has expressed his worries.

Suddenly, I want my phone back.

I hold out my hand but he pulls away.

I dump half the first bag into my hand and cram them into my mouth. They are the best thing I've tasted in days. In this moment I could say, maybe ever.

Finally Angel pushes the disconnect on my phone.

"He's a nice guy. How long have you been dating?" Angel says, and I nearly choke on a cheese cracker.

"We're not dating. Not that it's any of your business, and please can we not have this conversation right now?"

"Absolutely."

I look over at him. He's grown a mustache and it suits him. It frames his mouth perfectly. Angel's mouth is beautiful. I used to lay in bed beside him while he slept and run the tips of my fingers over his lips. He has the kind of upper lip that displays emotion in and of itself. It points, it curves, it flattens. Right now it is tight with anxiety, slightly drawn and even so, it is all I can do not to reach over and touch it.

"Where are we going?" I say, wiping mascara and eye liner from my face and flipping down the visor to check the damage. I have cracker crumbs on my cheek and I brush them off.

He turns his head and looks at me. His lip jumps a little as he smiles.

"I want to show you something," he says.

I nod and settle in for a silent ride. The air prickles between us, but we do not speak. There is too much and too little to say.

I cannot think about what has just happened. My mind is simply too full to take it in. My long anticipated father-daughter reunion consisted of a slap and a dash. I will have to push it down, push it away and pull it out later, when my head and heart can comprehend. But I keep hearing that awful word echoing over and over again. When I reach into the bag of crackers, it is empty.

I pour the other one into my hand and begin munching them absently. I glance over at Angel's hands on the steering wheel.

There has always been something about riding in a car when a man is driving. At least there is with a man that I find attractive, especially if the car is a stick shift, as Angel's is. There is a force to his movements, the push and pull on the stick, the tightening of his thighs as he works the pedals, the fruit of his work propelling us down the road. It's about control, about being taken, and Angel is definitely taking me now. He speeds along the freeway with a mounting speed and am I reading…excitement? The lip curls to a smile on one side as I scrutinize him.

"You never were very good at waiting for a surprise," he says without looking at me, and I smile again. How he knows me.

The whole car smells like his cologne. I think this is a vestige of previous animal-like tendencies, that a man must pour aftershave into his hands in order to splash it on his face, thus effectively leaving his scent on everything he touches thereafter. The air bristles more intensely.

Suddenly, I wish I didn't smell like cheese crackers.

I am beginning to recognize where we are. We are heading around the lake, to the big cabin on the other side where the rich neighbors used to live. Oh, no…was he taking me there for some kind of sexually stirring memory on the hopes it would rekindle…oh, no.

I eye him suspiciously and the lip curls even more and is matched by the lower one.

He stops the car about half a mile from the cabin and pulls over to the side of the road. We get out.

"I want you to cover your eyes," he says

"Oh come on?!"

"I want you to cover your eyes…just for a few minutes..and walk with me."

"Angel, if you are up to something creepy, I swear, I will let Charlie at you!!" I say, clenching my teeth. I am in no mood for games.

"I'll be good," he says, "I promise…" and he gives me a smile so charming, that I actually feel my insides going liquid.

I roll my eyes and cover my face with my hands as he leads me along the rocky and pitted dirt road.

We have walked about 5 minutes and I am ready to tell him I've had enough, especially since the feeling of his hand on my arm is starting to bother me and the narcotic in my system has me in no physical mood for a hike.

"Okay," he says, turning me around "Open your eyes"

I take my hands away and blink against the sun for a moment when a shape on comes into view.

It's curved, it's huge! It's....

"Oh ANGEL!!" I say, clutching my hands to my chest, "You did it!!!"

I am staring at Angel's dream. The dome house, exactly as he had described it to me all those years ago, in every detail.

My mouth will not stop hanging open. I am emitting something between laughter and a sob and I look at him in wonder.

He is smiling like I have not seen in years and years, that boyish smile, free of any kind of pretense or cover, full of unbridled, unmitigated joy.

He takes my hand and we run together to the top of the hill, to the door of the dome, to the beautiful stained glass double doors that we had drawn together as teenagers. The glass depicts a sunrise over the lake in shades of yellow and blue. It is dawn on the doorstep.

He unlocks the door and takes my hand again as we step inside. The door opens to the great room, the comforting curve of the ceiling towering above us, bright with sky lights. The room is done in shades of gray and black and white, Angel's artistic tastes so close to mine. And then, there it is, a full fireplace at the far wall with a sofa and love seat positioned around it, a cushion on the floor in front of it.

I well up with tears again.

The kitchen opens to the great room with a bar counter and stools, the appliances all inset and hidden, the tiles gleaming red and black, the colors I had chosen all those years ago.

There are two bedrooms on the first floor, one an obvious guest room, the other a library with a desk positioned under a triangular window, the sun beaming in, inviting me to sit down.

We head up the stairs next, to the master bedroom. It makes my mouth drop open again. The bed sits below a beautiful sky light, just opposite another fire place. A chair and chaise are set artfully to the sides. The master bath is all gray stone and glass block, a jacuzzi tub, one of my particular requests, sits gleaming with chrome fixtures and a basket of bath items on the side. A row of triangular windows follows the side of the tub with an expansive view of the lake. I cover my mouth with my hand.

"Oh, Angel…" I keep saying over and over again. It is all I can manage. My whole body is vibrating with excitement.

There are two more rooms upstairs, an office, where Angel's computer sits whirring away, one of his computer graphic creations showing on the screen.

"Oh, Angel, you did it! You have your dream!" I say turning to him and placing my hand on his chest.

He hesitates at the door of the next room.

"Well, I have part of it," he says and opens the door.

My breath catches in my throat.

I had always dreamed of a room of my very own. A little space with a window seat covered in pillows, where I could sit and read and look out at the world and have quiet and perspective. I'd have so many pillows that I'd barely fit there myself. I'd have a blanket, a little table on which to set my cup of tea, some shelves to hold my books, a desk at which to work if I desired, a stereo on which to play soothing music. I'd have an escape room, a place truly my own, and here it is in every single detail.

Joy and disappointment crash over me all at once. My life had been created without me. I had lost it, let it be ruined and now it had left me behind.

"This place," Angel says softly, "as much as the structure was always in my head, this home, this was about you and me. It was always about you Susannah, don't you know that? I know I never said this and I know it sounds like a cheap excuse even now, but if I had been able to reach you…" he stops a minute and bites his lip, I see tears in his eyes.

"I only went to her because I was so desperately lonely for you. When I was with her, I was imagining you, I was wanting you. I loved you—you Susannah and you were all I wanted. She reminded me of you. I even bought her some perfume…it was the one you always used, so she'd smell like you and when I closed my eyes…"

I wince at the image of him being with her and wrap my arms around myself for comfort.

He stops talking and sits on the window seat wiping at his eyes and hanging his head. I am compelled to sit beside him. He puts his arm around me and we are silent. We were so young when it all happened. We were trying to find our way when the maps had not yet even been written. I want to hold him. I want to pull his head to my chest and shout out that I forgive him, that nothing he could ever do would make me stop loving him, that I never had. That I never will. But fear sets paws on my chest and I cannot speak. To have lost my life once was bad enough, to get it back and lose again would be more than I could bear.

We sit together for a long time. I can see the sun beginning to set from the window. It is a lovely picture and the window seat is the perfect place to be taking it in. My chest aches. This should be my home. I should be here having this life, fulfilled with a husband and son instead of hiding away in the city waiting for a man who could make me feel like Angel did.

And I was still waiting.

It isn't that there have been no other men. Relationships have come and gone and I have even taken some of them to bed. It took me a long time to be able to kiss a man or be kissed by a man and not be actively comparing him to Angel the entire time. In fact, it took me a long time to even start dating again. It had taken Charlie's intervention.

Two years after the divorce I had still not had a single date. I had been asked, I had not accepted. Charlie had been after me for a full year, offering to fix me up, to take me out, to find me someone. I had refused with "maybe next week" or "not yet". It was a cold winter night when Charlie had come to my apartment with a bottle of tequila and a box of limes and sat me down on the sofa and demanded to know what in hell was wrong with me.

After a few drinks I began to talk, and what came out of my mouth surprised me as much as it did Charlie. It wasn't just about still being in love with Angel. It was about me, about my sexual experience or rather my lack thereof. I had not been allowed to date, to find out who I was as a woman in relation to a man. My education had consisted of Mother's horrid and lurid attitudes and finally my experiences with Angel. I had never even held another boy's hand before Angel, had never kissed a boy, had never spent time with one. I was afraid. Were all men like Angel? Did their bodies look like his? Did they function like his? Did every penis look the same? Did every man move the same, come the same? What was in store for me that I did not know? How was I supposed to embark upon adult relationships when I had no idea what to expect?

I had blurted out question after question and watched as the look in Charlie's eyes had changed from one of interest to something else. Was is pity? Was it sadness? His eyes still shone with his usual affection, but there was also something different than I had ever seen.

We had a few more drinks then, a few shots and we laughed and played music and danced, and after a while, Charlie disappeared into the bathroom.

I was dancing all alone in the living room and laughing at the last thing he had said when I heard him calling my name.

"What?!" I yelled from outside the door.

"Come here a minute!" he said.

"No Way!!" I laughed, certain he was kidding again and about to say something outrageous.

"I'm serious Susannah, come here," he said and I put down my drink and pushed open the door to the bathroom.

The room was filled with steam, swirling in the air, so much so that I couldn't see an inch in front of me.
The shower was running.

"Charlie?" I called, "What are you doing?"

A moment later I felt his hand grab hold of my wrist and pull me forward. The open door had disbursed some of the steam and now I could see. Charlie was standing inside the shower. He was wet. He was naked.

"Oh, my God, Charlie, what the hell--?" I said, and tried to back away, but his hold on my wrist was firm.

"Come on, Kitten" he said, smiling at me with that huge white smile of his, "let's go to school…"

Charlie had been with women. It had been a realization in his senior year at high school that had started his life with an honesty to his sexuality. Charlie loved women, he loved their bodies, their softness he had told me, but they just didn't do the same for him that a man's body did. Perhaps, he had said to me, he was just a little more gay than straight.

Reluctantly, and with my heart pounding I stepped into the shower, fully dressed. Charlie was a beautiful specimen of a man. I had many times seen him nearly naked, running around the pool in a speedo that left little to the imagination, but I had to admit, it was nothing compared to the full picture. His body was covered in a deep red fur at all the right places and he took pains to keep himself in shape. He took the shower gel off the shelf and made a lather over his chest to which he put my hands.

We didn't speak, we didn't have to. I trusted Charlie more than nearly anyone in my whole life and I felt safe with him. School was indeed in session. Charlie ran my hands over his chest, over his ribs and I could feel each one and the muscles that supported them, his pecks, the bones at his hips, his bottom.

I looked into his eyes for reassurance and found it as he placed my hand on his penis. He was erect, something I took with surprise. Charlie was big, bigger than Angel, longer and he was shaped differently. Angel's erection had had a more forward shape, Charlie's ran straight up his belly. I took it in my soapy hand and I explored it. I looked, really looked at it in my hand, and Charlie looked too. It was almost as if it were a separate entity, a thing we were observing from a distance, and yet it was the most intimate of moments between us.

My clothes were soaked, my white t-shirt showing the lace of my bra and my nipples. I began to move my hand up and down, sliding with the soap and Charlie moaned. It was a sound I had never heard from him and I was fascinated by it, I wanted to hear it again. I moved my hand faster and squeezed a little tighter.

"Unnnnghhhh, Kitten..." Charlie said, and he stopped me long enough to pull my t-shirt over my head and unbutton my jeans.

The water was warm and soothing and Charlie's voice was the same. I stepped out of my jeans with Charlie's help and I watched this time as he put his hands on my shoulders, and then ran them down to my breasts. My bra, lacey and wet was the next thing to go and Charlie held my breasts in his hands and then included them in the suds of the shower gel. Charlie's touch was different than Angel's. It was more staccato, more even and measured. It was not different in a bad way, nor could I say one was better than the other, it was just...different.

I put my hand back to his erection, still soapy and warm. I moved my hand and swirled it around as I went up and down, seeing that he liked this movement more than that one, this pressure more than the last.

Charlie was more vocal than Angel. He called my name, called me "Susie" and "Kitten" and "Baby" and he leaned over and pushed my panties down, his soapy and slippery hand finding its way between my legs, and inside me. He was gentle and rhythmic and he seemed to know what I wanted before I did.

It had been so long since I had been touched, so long since I had been close to a man, I found myself lost in it. Lost in my love for Charlie, different than for any other man I would ever have in my life, more constant, more sure and enduring, lost in what he was making me feel, in what I was able to make him feel. The world had gone away in the excitement of such an unexpected moment and the passion of our friendship, the hours we had spent being close and sharing our innermost secrets serving as years of foreplay to this moment.

Charlie came with a growl, a sound in his throat and chest that made me laugh and catch gulps of excitement in my throat. He pulled me close to him as he did and he turned my head up and kissed me, really kissed me, tangling his tongue in my mouth, moaning into it, making me feel as if I were in his body, experiencing his orgasm, sharing it with him.

After a few long lingering kisses, he reached behind me and turned off the shower, he pulled a towel off the rack and dried every inch of me, kissing my breasts, my belly, my thighs as he made his way down with the towel. He dried himself quickly and led me to the bedroom. We slid beneath the covers together, giggling like children.

Charlie kissed me again and then he disappeared for a minute and came back with the tequila and some slices of lime.

He poured us each a shot and held the lime to my lips for me to bite it before he did. I looked at him sitting there completely naked, outside the covers, so comfortable in his own skin, so perfectly at ease. I longed to feel that way, me with the sheet tucked up under my armpits.

Charlie grabbed hold of the sheet and pulled it off me, until it rested just above my knees. I felt so exposed in that moment that I started to object.

The stereo was playing Peter Gabriel. The song was "In Your Eyes" and he looked at me and smiled and I rested myself back down on the pillow and gave my trust to Charlie.

He ran his hands over my belly and kissed my navel. I closed my eyes, our lesson was not over. He kissed my hips, each one slowly in an arch toward my inner thighs. I shifted a little, the feel of it was making me want to be less the student.

Suddenly there was a cold sensation and I jumped and opened my eyes to see Charlie pouring tequila into my navel. We laughed out loud together and then I held as still as I could while Charlie lapped it up and then bit the lime that he trailed down between my legs.

I opened to him. Charlie's mouth was a symphony. His tongue danced, spun, twirled and tickled at me and now it was my turn to make sounds that Charlie had never heard. He brought me close over and over again, stopping just short each time until I heard the sound of something tearing and I opened my eyes to see him putting on a condom, his erection once more pointing an arrow toward his navel.

Panic welled in my chest.

"Charlie…I don't know…." I said and he kissed me again and lowered his body onto mine.

"You need this, Kitten…" he whispered in my ear and bit when he was through, "…to tell you the truth, I need it too. Let me be the one…please?" he said, and I pulled him to me and kissed him.

He reached down and pulled my knees up around him with surprising force and certainty and in just another moment he was inside me. It was so odd, to feel him there. Slightly different than it had ever been, the shape of him matching mine in just a slightly different way, meeting his rhythm with a different rocking than Angel's. I felt myself begin to be encompassed by the feeling. Charlie's hands, Charlie's eyes, Charlie's lips, Charlie's shoulders and back and Charlie's scent, and the feel of his hair on my neck and my cheek and my breasts, and I began to understand that each man is his own work of art, that this biology, though basically the same was a different story for each and every one. The wonder of it swept me away.

Knowing each other as well as we did, this song we made together was very harmonious. I had been so close to orgasm when we began that it had not taken long for me to get there again.

"Ohhhh, Susie , ….you are so beautiful…" he was saying, and I looked in to his eyes, into that wondrous dopey, taken expression and he smiled at me, his million dollar smile and he winked, and I was there. That a man could be making love with me and still be flirting was just so delicious that I was overtaken.

I found that since Charlie had a lot to say, I did too. I opened my mouth and "Oh Charlie…" came out, in a way that I will never be able to say it again.

I wrapped my legs around him and he seemed to know exactly what to do to prolong it for me. Small movements held and then changed.

By the end I was panting and laughing and crying and Charlie was too. I pulled myself away from him and he laid on his back.

I climbed onto him instantly, my turn to drive.

I lowered myself back onto him and began to rock my hips. He put his hands on them as if to guide me and I pinned them above his head.

"Whoa…" he said and smiled, and let me.

I rose and fell, braced with my knees resting on the bed on either side of him, released his hands and put them on my breasts which he held and caressed. I sensed his tension and when he was almost there I stopped and leaned into him and kissed his chest and ran my tongue down the center of it. I was drunk with my own knowledge. I did know how to please him, I had the elusive instinct that I so feared would escape me. I tossed my hair back and sat up straight and rocked and charged up and down and I gave Charlie all I could give to make him feel all he could feel, my Charlie, my teacher, one of the sexiest men I'd ever met in my life and best of all, my dearest and closest friend.

It started as a low growl again and he rocked his hips forward, raising me up into the air, my knees off the bed, his knees bent and his feet braced beneath him. It went from a growl to a shout to a growl again and I watched him with complete fascination. His face, his body everything about him was a picture of concentration, each corpuscle focused on the intensity of this one brilliant moment.

"Susannah…..", he called and "God…God Susannah.." again and I watched his face, his eyes shut tight, the loss of expression entirely, the slight curl of a smile, his chest out, back arched, his hands grasping great handfuls of the blankets and then releasing and closing again.

At the end, he pulled me to his chest, still joined and stroked my hair and caught his breath as I caught mine. I felt so liberated in that moment. It was as if some kind of imprisonment had finally come to an end and I was emancipated and seeing the outside for the first time in years and years, perhaps a lifetime.

It wasn't until that moment that I heard Mother in my head. Charlie had chased her away entirely until then.

"Whore!"

I closed my eyes and listened hard for Charlie's heartbeat. It was still fast and I let myself count the beats over Mother's voice.

"Don't you know what happens to girls who have sex outside of marriage? Don't you know that God has sent AIDS to the earth to punish the sexual deviants?"

I shook my head.

"Are you ok?" Charlie said and lifted his head to look at me, alarmed.

"Mmmm-hmmmm" I answered and kissed his neck. He took hold of my chin and lifted it to look into my eyes.

"Don't listen to her, Kitten," he said.

I welled up and tried to speak but Charlie put his finger to my lips.

"Q. Don't. Don't talk about her now. Just make her go away."

From that moment, I began to talk back to her words inside my head. I just kept repeating, "Charlie says go away."

It would come back to me later, but for that one incredible moment, Mother all but vanished.

We lay together a long time and then each took a turn in the bathroom. When he came back to the bed I was wearing my robe and he pulled it off me.

"Just for tonight, let's not hide," he said, and pulled me to him beneath the covers, his warm skin to mine, holding me in his arms and he turned out the light. I slept so soundly with him that night, never more than inches away and re-gathered to him any time I wandered too far. He had held me, stroked my hair and my shoulders, spooned with me all night long, a protective hand on my belly as we slept.

In the morning, I woke before he did and watched him sleeping for a long while. I pondered the fate of our friendship, I pondered the notion of Charlie and I being more than friends, of the two of us having a romance and even a marriage. It was funny, but as sure as I was of our friendship and as much as I loved him, I knew that this was not who he was. Those other pictures, as much as they made me feel a kind of longing, they just didn't fit.

I kissed him on the forehead gently and slid out from beneath the covers so as not to wake him. I took a long hot shower while the coffee brewed and I dressed in my sweats. I felt as if I had been changed over night. The knot of stress that I had been carrying in my chest for weeks and weeks, maybe years, seemed to be entirely unraveled and I felt so serene that I actually wondered if I weren't still under the influence of the tequila.

I heard him start the shower himself while the eggs were cooking and I turned on the stereo. It was the same CD as the night before, the Peter Gabriel and I danced slowly about the kitchen as I set the table and poured the juice and popped bread into the toaster.

Charlie wrapped his arms around me from behind as I stood at the stove and kissed me on the cheek.

"And how are we feeling this morning, Mistress?" he said leaning around me to look at my smiling face.

"At long last freedom!" I said raising the spatula triumphantly into the air, and he laughed and poured himself some coffee and sat at the table.

I set the plates down and settled in and we started eating.

"Charlie," I said, "why did you do that last night?"

He looked at me and dangled his fork above his plate between his thumb and forefinger. He waved it back and forth a minute, collecting his thoughts.

"I just wanted it to be with someone who loves you," he said simply.

"My very next first experience?" I smiled into my coffee cup.

"It could've been with some guy who was just looking for a night, a lay, and Kitten, that would devastate you. Besides, I was being a little selfish," he said, and looked sheepishly at me, setting the fork down and running his finger at the rim of his coffee cup.

"Selfish?"

"The more I thought about it all evening, I wanted it to be me. I wanted to be there to experience it with you, the wonder of it all. It's been a long time since I experienced anything close to 'first-time wonder', but I did last night, and it was with you, which made it all that much better."

And then he reached across the table and gathered my fingers into his.

"Thank you," he said, "for letting me." and we looked into each other's eyes for a long time before returning to our breakfasts. I was awed by him, by his capacity for love and generosity, that he would be thanking me for something that was so obviously his gift to me.

We decided that our shared intimacy was not going to change things for us, but the ensuing weeks were a little strained. I suppose we both kept looking for expectations in each other. For all the things that Charlie and I can talk about, the one thing we are lousy at is discussing our own relationship. We had learned this early on, when a disagreement over what time to leave for a movie had left us unable to speak to each other for a week in college. But, eventually, we made our way back to each other, and we added the experience to the world's longest list of shared affinities, one more seal on the warm, encompassing envelope of our love.

After that, there had been John, a man I met in court. He was an expert witness in a case I was trying, a pediatrician testifying in medical malpractice. He had dark hair with a few well placed streaks of gray and kind sparkling blue eyes. It was his smile that drew me in that day. It was beautiful and white, but there was a single tooth just slightly out of place. Something about the way his lip brushed over that tooth when he smiled made my stomach flip.

He had approached me after hours of exchanging glances across the court room and asked me to dinner. I accepted and flew home to call Charlie for dressing advice. Charlie had arrived a full 3 hours before the date and picked out everything from the scent of my shower gel to the shade of my panty hose. I'm not sure which of us was more nervous.

He answered the door bell and let John in, introducing himself with, "Hello, I'm Charlie, the gay best friend! We're still dressing, we'll be out in just a scosh!"

"Wear the good bra," he said rushing into the bedroom, "he's adorable!"

John, ten years older than me, was kind and sweet and accommodating. He took me to dinner and for long walks and we talked about our families and children and our own childhoods. John's divorce had happened early in his marriage, after only two years. It was nice to talk with someone who shared that experience. John was easy to talk to, and he made me feel young and feminine, always saying what an "old man" he was with me. It was true that we didn't go repelling or roller skating together, but I was never really into those things anyway. I was much happier with John's version of a big night: Dinner at Andiamo in Rochester followed by drinks, and a slow dance or two.

The first time we made love I was nervous and hoping he couldn't tell, but of course he could and he asked me what the matter was. It was then that I told him of my inexperience and he was intrigued and assuring at the same time.

I suppose that I was thinking that an older man would have the kind of experience that would make him an empathetic lover. It wasn't that John didn't try hard to take my feelings into consideration, and he was gentle and loving, it was just that he seemed to be so focused on all of his parts, he wasn't always aware of mine.

Still, it wasn't bad, it just wasn't Angel.

We had been seeing each other for six months when I decided that I could never feel for him what I had felt for Angel. And though somewhere in my heart I knew the comparison was unfair, I was unable to feel it any other way. The unfortunate men who came after Angel would all be held up to him for scrutiny.

Angel stands and pulls me to my feet. It's been two hours since we left the funeral and I am feeling so tired that I can't stop staring at the bed in the next room. I rub my temples and look into the strain on his face.

"Is it really just impossible for you to forgive me?" he says, and I feel myself sink inside.

"Do you really know what it did to me, Angel?" I say and I know now, that it's all going to come out. I am too tired to stop it. "Mother had said that all men would do it. She had chanted it, screamed it and pounded it into my head from the time I was old enough to understand words. When I met you and we fell in love, I thought that I finally had proof that she was wrong, and crazy and that my own perceptions of the world were right and not hers, and then…then you proved her right. You, Angel, the one person I thought would never ever hurt me. It just brought my whole world to pieces. And I know it's not your fault that my mother made your mistake worse. I do forgive you Angel, and I should ask you to forgive me as well, I made mistakes too." I say it, and watch as he smiles sadly, "I forgave you a long time ago. Mother ruined me and then she ruined us, before we even had a chance to make any mistakes."

"But if we can forgive each other—" he starts.

"Being able to forgive each other is one thing," I tell him, "Being able to be together is another Angel, you know that."

He nods and shakes his head. He looks tired.

"Do you want to get something to eat?" he says at last, and we make one last tour of the house before we head back to the car.

On the way to town, I ask him all the details of the building process and how long it took, and who he got to do which parts of the dome. He comes to life with the telling, and seeing his enthusiasm comforts me. The conversation we just had was ten years in the making and I am still recovering. I am reeling from seeing the house, from seeing the embodiment of what my life was supposed to be rising like a great ghost from the bank of the lake.

We follow the road into town and Angel talks on. I know the Embers will be busy tonight, there will be a live band and dancing, people celebrating special occasions and romantic evenings. It will be difficult for me not to envy them. Glancing at my watch, I realize that I never told anyone where I was going when Angel and I disappeared from the funeral. I pull out my cell phone and call Grand's.

"Susannah?" a voice answers the phone and I know how badly I have worried them.

"It's me, I'm so sorry…"

"Where in hell have you been, Q?" It's Charlie and he is fuming, he must have seen me leave with Angel.

"I'm sorry, Charlie, I just had to get out of there. That man, the one in the blue suit, that was my father."

"Geezus, Mary and Joseph…!" is his stunned reply.

"Angel took me for a ride. I'm fine—and we're going up to Embers for dinner."

"Do you need me to come up there?"

"No, I'll be fine." I say, less sure than I would like to be.

"Keep your head, Susannah," he says "You remember this is the man who broke your heart and slept with your stubby neighbor!"

I laugh and assure him that I will be fine, and promise to call if I need him.

"Susannah, we saw the news," he says.

My heart sinks into the car seat.

"How bad was it?" I will myself not to start crying again. I'm just too tired.

"Actually, Q, the reporter on channel 4 was all on about how you'd been attacked by Franken before your mother's funeral and I mean, nobody likes that asshole already, you know?"

"So it came off like he attacked the poor unstable woman, or what?"

"No, no... well, not exactly, I mean you didn't seem crazy Suze, just overwhelmed and really emotional. Honestly, it was pretty moving! Very Marlee Matlin in Children of A Lesser God, only without the sign language."

I laugh and let just a touch of relief fill my veins. Charlie is notorious for "the positive spin" but right now, I'll take it.

"There aren't any reporters hanging around out there are there?" I ask, hoping to God that they will give us a break. They had attempted to follow us to the dome house but the police had intervened, pulling their cars neatly in front of the exit as we sped off.

"Oh well, there were a couple of stragglers but we called the Mounties and they came out and russled 'em off."

"Thanks, Charlie. I'm so sorry about everything." I say, and I am reconsidering whether I want him to meet us at Embers.

"Stop being so sorry and just be ok," he says "Call if you need me."

I hang up and hold the phone to my chest.

"He really loves you." Angel says, trying to be generous about Charlie's obvious grudge and mistrust.

"Yes he does, and he has been there for me always." I say to him and put my phone away.

We fall silent and try to let the ride soothe our nerves.

I am lost in the sad trees of my youth
                                    -- M.L. Liebler

Chapter 10

The Embers is jumping just as I suspected it would be. We step inside and I am struck by how festive and romantic the whole place looks. Tiny white lights, the kind used on Christmas trees, are pinned in row after row on the ceiling above the dance floor. The band is playing and couples sway back and forth while groups at tables sit sipping champagne and drinking coffee. There is a warm, happy spirit in the room, people eating companionably and staring off into the fireplace and watching others on the dance floor.

The Maitre'd calls Angel by name and seats us at a table near the dance floor.

"Will you order me some coffee?" I ask him and excuse myself to the rest room.

I stare at myself in the mirror. It has been the most desperate of days. I am weary, and worn out, and every emotion I've ever had has exploded inside me in the last 48 hours. I watch a woman next to me fussing with her hair and make up. She is obviously excited, obviously on a date and she shares her enthusiasm with me.

"Don't you just hate the lighting in here?" she says, dabbing at her glossy lips with a wand.

"I swear, I can't tell if I have dark circles under my eyes or if there is just a shadow on my face! I'm so nervous. I really like this guy and it's our second date!" she gushes.

"That's nice…" I try to push a smile onto my face.

"You two seem to know each other pretty well," she says, "I saw you when you came in—you know how you can just tell? Well, I could tell about you two. He's really cute, have you been seeing each other a long time?"

I am flustered at her perception of our entrance.

"Um…a little while," I say weakly and suddenly I am excruciatingly aware of how I look.

I look haggard and my make up has faded and or smeared off completely. My hair is pinned up like a school-marm, with scraggly bits sticking out on all sides and my suit is wrinkled. Good Lord, this was how I looked on the news!!

"Would you excuse me?" I say and duck into the stall, where I pull up my skirt and discover the hem of my red dress beneath. I catch my breath. I had completely forgotten.

Before I can stop myself, before I can make myself think reasonably, before I can hear Mother in my head or Charlie, I am taking off my jacket and pulling my sweater over my head and stepping out of my skirt. I gather it all up and return to the counter. The woman is gone, thank God, and I step in front of the mirror.

I begin pulling the pins out of my hair. The twisting has left it in ringlets as it falls to my shoulders. I take out the last pin, which lets a lock fall almost entirely hiding my left eye. I push the right side behind my ear and pull the ringlets out fully with my fingers. I reline my eyes and refresh my blush and shadow, covering the dark areas under my eyes and putting some color back into my face.

I don't know why I am doing it, or at least I will not let myself know why. I don't want to think about it, I just want to do it, I just need to do it. I line my lips and put on my best red lipstick, packed in my purse for the trip.

A bad habit I picked up from Grand has me tearing out perfume samples from magazines in waiting rooms and cramming them in my purse. I use one now on my wrist and can't help but feel completely smug.

I step back from the mirror and spin a little, checking the back of my beloved red dress, seeing how it hugs the contours of my bottom, how it lets just a touch of the top of my breasts show at the front, how it follows me in at the middle and how the beads catch the light. I am infinitely pleased and I toss my suit over my arm and emerge from the bathroom transformed.

As I approach, Angel glances up and then looks away, obviously this is not the woman he is expecting back at the table. And then he looks again slowly, recognition and disbelief coming over his face. I stop a few feet from the table and cock my head to the side and smile at him, peeking around the lock of hair that obscures my eye.

"Oh, My God!" he says, standing and smiling at me, his eyes betraying shock and total appreciation.

"Just a little something I threw on…" I say in my best smart ass.

"I don't even know what to say," he says, his mouth his fully hanging open until he kisses my hand as I sit beside him.

The waiter returns and asks if we need a third place setting for the lady who went to the rest room and we laugh.

"No thank you," I tell him, "she won't be joining us this evening."

"Where exactly were you hiding that outfit?" Angel asks, pouring me a glass of the wine that he has ordered in my absence.

"Under my suit. I always thought I'd wear a red party dress to Camille's funeral." I say and he raises a single eyebrow at me.

"I forgot my slip and this worked just fine."

"Still is," he says, and I feel heat in my cheeks and thank him.

He raises his glass.

"To old friends and round houses," he says.

It is the perfect toast and I laugh and agree and we touch our glasses together with a resounding clink, the deep red wine swirling happily in the glasses, catching light from the dance floor and shining rosy as we tip them to our lips.

I take a deep drink of the wine and feel it's warmth follow into my body. It's over, I keep thinking. Camille, the funeral, it's over. And here I am—with Angel.

Angel orders us dinner. I let him, as he has always been so good at it, his tastes impeccable and his manners even more so. As I stare into his eyes across the table it occurs to me that most women would give a kidney to be sitting across from this man, commanding his attention the way I am right now. Most women would've pulled him into bed under that skylight in the dome half an hour ago, and shown him just exactly how they had forgiven him.

What is wrong with me?

I take such small spoonfuls of life, pieces small enough to quickly swallow whole, and not big enough to choke on. Joy has always crept uneasily upon me. I can never claim it for long and never fully enjoy it while it is there. I wait constantly for the proverbial other shoe, which always came in the form of Mother.

She had come into town once when I was dating John. It was a completely unexpected visit and I can remember with photographic clarity the look in her eye when I opened the door to my apartment and found her standing there.

It was a Sunday morning and John had spent the night. We had made love until early morning and then slept in late. I was in the kitchen listening to my favorite CD, feeling calm and happy, and satisfied. The man I cared for was in the shower, about to have coffee and bagels with me and sit with me on the sofa in his robe and read the paper. We'd fight over who got the lifestyle section first and then we'd compromise by reading it together, him with his arms around me on either side. It was a glorious plan for the day.

    He was still in the shower when she arrived and I had dropped a full cup of steaming hot coffee on the beige carpet of my living room when I opened the door.

    "Mother!" I exclaimed in disbelief, wondering briefly if I wasn't some how hallucinating.

    "Susannah.", she said coldly and then stepped around me into the apartment. She strode in as if she were the owner of the place and everything in it.

    "Mother what are you doing here?" I said, panic welling up in my throat, making me feel as if my insides were about to leap from my mouth.

    Her attorney had summoned her to a meeting. Something about zoning on the lake and the size of the house and taxes. Mother had never, to my knowledge, left Walloon without one of us at her side. Either she was getting better or she was getting worse, and I had no way of telling which. She came in and seated herself on the sofa. I kept just standing in the doorway and gaping until she turned her eyes to me and said,

    "Perhaps you have some tea, Susannah?"

    "Uh, oh, sure Mother, just a minute." I fluttered, forgetting about John entirely until he entered the living room a few minutes later wearing nothing but a towel.

    Mother had just set her purse on the coffee table and I was in the kitchen turning the tea water on and wondering what I was going to do with her when John strolled in, drying his hair with a towel and talking to me about staying at his place next weekend.

    "Uh, JOHN!" I said, a little too loudly.

    He pulled the towel from his head and looked at me standing stick still in the kitchen cocking my head to the side and widening my eyes to saucers.

    "I'd like you to meet my mother, Camille." I said and held my hand out in her direction.

    "Hello." Mother said, in the most controlled voice I have ever heard in my life.

    "Mother, this is John Gabel my boyfriend."

    "It's nice to meet you, would you excuse me a moment, please?" John stammered.

Mother's face turned red, she began to shake and John apologetically dashed into the bedroom and threw his pants on.

Mother had already begun to percolate by the time he returned, red faced and wearing his pants and a shirt buttoned half way.

"I didn't know we were expecting your mother today, Susie." he said and gave me a pained and sorry look.

"Neither did I." I said, mentally adding, "EVER"

Mother drank a cup of tea in stony silence, staring across the room at John and giving me the evilest of sideways glances.

"I didn't realize you were living in sin, Susannah." she said finally, and I actually sighed with relief, at least the horrible wait was over, it was about to begin.

"Mother, we are not living together." I said flatly while John shifted in his chair.

"Oh, I see, not even that much decency eh? Just a little lay for the road John?" she said, raising her voice.

"Mother!!" I shouted at her " Stop it this instant!"

"OH, and I see you've ruined her! How many men have you spread your legs for Susannah?! Is there a long wait, John or were you able to just get right in?!"

"Mother that's enough!" I shouted again.

She stood now and made a dash for the kitchen. I could not believe my eyes when she reached into my cupboard and pulled out a stainless steel pot. She rose it in the air above her head, above my counter in my kitchen. I became paralyzed with the sight of it. Here it was, come to find me in my very own home, so far away from Walloon. I'd finally found my own place to be, my own world and now the misery had tracked me down and was about to consume me again. It was never over. I should have known better, I should have never relaxed, not even for a second.

I backed into the far wall in horror as she started banging the pot and screaming, "Whore, whore, whore!!!" and talking incomprehensibly to herself.

I crumpled to the floor, pulling a sofa pillow to my chest and feeling my breath begin to leave me. I pulled at it hard, gasped it into my chest. She was here to kill me at last.

John had sprung to his feet and dashed out the door. As I watched the door close behind him, it was as if a coffin lid had closed over my head. So there it was, I would never be able to have a quiet life with a man, I would have to eternally fear Mother's sudden appearance,

Mother's sudden ruination of every shred of happiness I was able to eek out for myself in this wretched life.

I watched her bang the pot over and over again and just sat still. She banged it on the counter and then on my table and then she smashed my coffee maker onto the floor and threw my toaster into the sink. I thought that perhaps I could set it on the counter again and fill the sink with water, hoping she would repeat the act. She was headed for the vase of tulips that John had brought me the night before when a vision appeared. It looked like John came back through the door carrying a small black bag with a handle on it. He set it on the table and produced a syringe which he filled from a small medicine bottle. I watched in silence, unable to move, unable to comprehend what I was seeing. Did he really walk back through that door on purpose? Why? Why would he do that? Why would anyone come back into a room where Camille was having one of her rages?

He approached Mother with the syringe held down facing the floor.

"Mrs. Suffolk, can I just take your hand a minute?" he said to her in the calmest, most soothing voice I have ever heard in my entire life. She stopped reaching for my vase and turned to him, her eyes blazing, breath coming heavy in and out of her chest.

"Can I take your hand a minute, Mrs. Suffolk?" he said again, and she stood still and looked at him.

There was no air in the room. It was suspended, along with all sound and all time as she just stood there staring at him. I wanted to warn him to run for his life, her stillness meant that she was about to attack.

But instead, against all odds, against every thing I ever expected to happen, ever so slowly, she reached her hand out to him.

"Thank you, Mrs. Suffolk, thank you," he said. "That's just great, really."

In the fastest movement ever made before my eyes, he took hold of her wrist firmly in one hand and put the needle in gently with the other, and pushed the plunger.

Mother screamed bloody murder and then, just a few seconds later, she stopped, and I watched as John led her back to the sofa where first she sat and then, he helped her to lie down. After a minute, she closed her eyes and fell into a very peaceful sleep.

John came for me next and helped me off the floor. I couldn't believe what I had just seen. A man with a single small implement in his hand had just put the monster to sleep. How could it be possible, how could it be real?

He pulled me into his arms me as I sobbed and told me he had no idea that she was still so bad. I had told him of Mother's fits, even in some detail, but I had not wanted to linger over the subject. The truth was that I was afraid that if I told anyone what my life had really been like, they'd know I wasn't who I said I was. They'd know how damaged I really was, how worthless. It hadn't changed a bit from when I was a child. Silence was always our greatest protection.

I had completely forgotten that John was a doctor when the hysterics began.

"What did you give her?" I asked finally.

"A sedative" he said, and he rattled off a name I didn't recognize. "She needs help Susannah, medication, maybe even hospitalization."

I told him of Mother's diagnosis years ago and her refusal of treatment.

"You can sign papers, Susannah, you can have her put away. I mean if you and your brother both signed…"

I shook my head no and backed away from him.

"Hey, hey…don't go away." he'd said and put his arms around me again,

"I understand."

We called Rob to come and take her back home and he came before the sedative wore off completely. When we'd gotten her into the car, John gave her a booster shot just to ensure Rob a peaceful trip.

He had helped me to clean up the kitchen and had turned up the following afternoon with a new coffee maker and a pound of Sumatra from Starbucks, my normalcy restored, and yet I knew I could never really set both feet down again. I had gotten too complacent, had allowed myself to think that life was going to let me in, that for the first time ever, I was going to just drift away from Walloon and it was going to become my past. I had forgotten that I was not allowed a past, only a present in which I never knew at what point the peace would be shattered, like the broken bits of my coffee pot, swept into the dust pan and thrown in the bin.

The food arrives and Angel and I eat well. I do not feel so desperate with my meal tonight, though my stomach is emptier than it has been in days. We linger over the courses and we talk. It has been so many years since Angel and I have just talked with each other, just talk that didn't involve attorneys or visitation. We talk about work, about friends and family and Matthew and even about old times.

"Do you remember that picnic by the lake?" he says to me over a mouthful of prime rib.

"Of course I do." I say.

"What a night." he returns and shakes his head at me and smiles, openly reveling in the memory of our intimacy that night.

"I don't know how we didn't do it that night." he says sipping his wine.

"Mmmmm," I say, "iron will."

The wine is making me feel a little fuzzy and too relaxed and I am flirting with him, not really a wise thing to do, but I don't care. God, he is beautiful. Wiping his face on the napkin, cramming in a forkful of uncooperative salad, he is just beautiful. His eyes shine with affection and expressive lines have deepened at the corners of them. Now and again his tongue flicks up at his mustache and I feel my insides take a dip.

Finally we are drinking coffee and sharing a plate of cheese cake. He serves me the first bite off his fork and I do not object. I take it and he smiles at me.

We finish it off, forks scraping against each other, fighting over the last strawberry and finally splitting it in détente'.

The band begins to play What's New, and he looks at me.

"Dance?" he say,s and smirks, his lip twitching.

I take his hand and we head out to the dance floor.

Angel's arms encircle me and the whole world runs liquid into the night and disappears. It leaves me in a timeless, limitless place where there are no broken hearts or broken promises or broken dishes on the floor. We come together like puzzle pieces, made to fit, made to match, and incomplete apart.

I know his world has also departed as I look into his face, nearly expressionless, staring into mine and then gathering me closer to him. The music rises around us in waves and takes us farther and farther from the wreckage of our lives. His hand travels slowly down my back and rests at the small, just above my bottom. He dances me slowly, finding the sweetest time to the song and holding me there. There is nothing in my life that feels like this—this completeness, this home coming, this place of perfection. I love this man, I do, and I feel it in every cell of my body as he holds me. There will never be another man who can make me feel the way he does. This comes to me like a flash of fire. This part of my life is done and over and it will never come again. Angel and I share something unfound on this earth, and even though it is so close that we can feel it beating in our chests, we cannot have it.

Knowing this, I decide that I will at least have this moment. This night will be ours, Angel's and mine, one last night of completeness together. He rests his cheek to mine and he whispers in my ear.

"I've missed you so badly."

"I've missed you too," I say and though I know I shouldn't I add, "so much."

His arms tighten about me and now I can feel his heartbeat against my chest. How I love the feel of it. I can smell him, taste his cologne on my tongue. I can feel the heat from his body, the scent of his breath, warm on my cheek, my neck, my ear. I can feel the muscles in his thighs flexing with the beat of the music, my legs nearly entangled in his.

I sigh and let every ounce of tension in my body escape with it. I am safe here in this place, in these arms and I rest my head on his shoulder and allow my entire body to contact his.

We move together to the music and I cannot think of anything but how perfect it feels and how terrifying that perfection is to me. Nothing this good can last, I remind myself, there can only be more heartbreak ahead. My wound is not healed, and may never be. Forgiveness is just so much easier than forgetting.

The song ends and we still sway on the dance floor, waiting for the next to begin. I don't look to him to see that he wants to wait as well, I just know he does.

The band plays The Way You Look Tonight and we settle into the rhythm of it, perfectly matching each other again. Union and blessed comfort and soothing come over me.

Angel leans over and whispers in my ear.

"Come home with me, Susannah. Come home…" he whispers.

I am startled from my place of dream and perfection and I pull back and look into his face. Those words come from reality. And the glass starts crashing around me inside my head.

"Angel, no!" I say, and step away from him completely.

"Why not?!" he demands, his eyes slitting with anger.

"You know why not!" I say, stunned that he thinks dinner and dancing means we are reconciled.

"No, no I don't know!" he says, chasing me as I rush back to the table.

"Because we can't do it, Angel. We tried it, remember, and it didn't work?!"

"It didn't work because we were young and stupid and made mistakes. It didn't work because we had too much pride and too little sense. Those things have changed, Susannah!" he says looking at me as if I am insane.

"You're taking a giant leap here!" I say a little too loudly and look from side to side as people turn their heads.

"I don't think so." he says.

"Just because I had dinner with you and danced with you doesn't mean I'm ready to jump back into a marriage with you! In spite of what you've seen this weekend, Angel, I have changed! I'm not the same terrified, small, world-fearing girl that you gave her first kiss to on the lake all those years ago. I take care of myself, and I'm damned good at it!" I say, angrier than I should be.

Angel snatches me into his arms so hard that my fist thumps against his chest.

"You need me." He says it slowly, deliberately, enunciating each word.

I take a minute and catch my breath. I look away from his face, away from his eyes, aflame with the fire of knowing in his heart that he is right.

I look back up, take his eyes, "I always did, didn't I ?" I say, and he nods. His arms are so tight around me that I feel the breath being pressed too hard out of my chest.

"But Angel, did you ever need me?"

"What?!" he says, taken aback by the question so much that he lets go of me and jumps back. I nearly fall down with his release.

"See, Angel, you think that our problem was some single mistake or some single set of mistakes that we made. You're wrong. Our problem was that our relationship was never balanced. It was always you in the lead with me following along behind. It was never equal, and I never felt good enough. I never felt like I had anything to give you, Angel! It made me feel like I had to find something to give you. I had nothing inside me, nothing! Hell, I could barely find it in me to be a mother! So, I went out to find something to fill myself up with and while I was doing that, you found something else to fill yourself up with. Partly out of loneliness and missing me, I don't doubt that, but you have to admit to yourself that the truth is that you saw me growing, and you saw me filling up on the inside and you were afraid! If I didn't need you desperately, then maybe I didn't love you and just maybe, I would leave you, Angel, and that's why you found some other ridiculous, needy woman to take to bed with you!"

Angel sits down at the table and up-ends his wine glass. He takes out his wallet and lays money on top of the check. He moves methodically, almost mechanically. He helps me on with my suit jacket. I know I should say something. I know I've gone too far but I don't know how to fix it now. I don't know how to unsay what I have just said. I also know that what I have just said is the truth.

I follow him out to the car. I wish now that I had kept my mouth shut. I should've just said, "I'm not ready for that, Angel," and kept dancing. I know that there are things to be said between us still, things that neither of us want to hear. Obviously, he was not ready to hear this one.

We drive in silence, the entire twenty minutes back to Grand's house. He pulls into the drive and opens my door for me. He offers his hand as I step out of the car and as I turn to walk away, he catches my arm.

"You will never know how much I needed you," he says.

"Did you know, Angel?" I say, "Or did you find out later, like I did?"

He smiles sadly at me and he kisses me on the cheek before he gets back into the car. I watch him round the hills in the distance, and disappear.

I step up on to Grand's porch and can't make myself go inside. There is a light in the kitchen and someone's still up, though I imagine that most of them are asleep, as exhausted as we all are.

I sit in the rocker and hold my jacket tight around me. The feel of Angel's arms seeps over me again. How could I have ever let him walk out of my life? Worse, I've just done it again.

I see the lights of his car on the other side of the hill, heading up the ramp to the freeway. Why did I let him go?

I stare off across the lake and it's as if everything I've ever lost in my life is somewhere beneath the water with my beach glass.

I remember breaking up with John. It had been only a few weeks after Mother's visit. I had been unable to relax. For a week I woke every night from nightmares. I had insisted that John install a chain on the door. I called apartment security and gave them a description of mother and asked them to call me immediately should she arrive on the premises.

It was another Sunday morning and John had stopped me from pacing in the living room and sat me on the sofa. He kneeled down in front of me and took both my hands in his.

"I want you to listen to me." He said and his voice sounded strange in my ears. "You know that I care about you very much, don't you?"

"Yes." I said. I'd heard these speeches before. It had been a long time, but I had heard them. It was usually in school, a teacher who caught on to what was happening, a guidance counselor, one of the sisters in the rectory.

"You need to see a counselor, Susannah," he said, and he looked so desperate, that for the first time in my whole life, I considered saying yes.

"I'm fine," I said.

"No, you are not fine. You grew up being horribly abused by a very very sick woman. You are so terrified now that you can't even live in your own home! Susannah, you are a prisoner here and you're making yourself sicker by the minute!"

"I am NOT sick!" I said and pushed his hands away from me. That kind of sickness was Mother, it was not me.

"Susannah, please," he said and so sadly and so sincerely that I felt a lump coming up in my throat.

"John, do you really think you are the first person to tell me that you think I need to see a shrink?" I said, my voice sounding dull. I knew what I was about to do. I'd let him get too close. I'd let someone in too far. He'd seen Mother in action, he'd seen my past. He had to go.

"I'm sure I'm not," he said and stood to walk to the other side of the room.

"Of course not," I said and stood myself.

"John, I don't think we should see each other any more." My eyes darted to the newspaper sitting on the table waiting for us to read it together. I started to cry.

"Hey, hey!" he said, rushing to me. "Let's not make leaps here! Just because I suggested that you need to get some help with your anxiety—"

"It's not that, John. The reason I've been so restless is that this hasn't been working out for me. I mean it's just not…" I stared at the paper. How I loved the feel of sitting with him on the sofa, feeling his arms around me as we read that damned paper.

He tried to put his arms around me then. His face was so stricken, he looked as if he'd just been slapped.

"Please, Susannah, you're just upset. Let's just not talk about this any more today."

"Stop it," I said, and pushed him away.

He stood and stared at me with his mouth gaping. He reached for me again and again, I pushed him back.

"Please, just go," I turned away from him. I couldn't stand to watch it happen. I couldn't stand to see another door close behind a man that I loved.

John began to cry. I hadn't expected that. I heard him, he was sobbing and I wanted to tell him that I didn't really mean it. I wanted to turn and pull him close and tell him that I'd go to a therapist, that I'd do anything he wanted. I wanted to tell him that I would never hurt him.

Mother's voice rang in my ears.

"You'll never find a decent man to want you, Susannah. You're a whore, you know. You're a whore." It was her "matter of fact" voice. In some ways, it worse than when she shouted.

I was doing the only decent thing, letting John go. He had a chance to find a woman worthy of him if I did.

"Get out!" I said, never turning back.

The door slammed hard behind me and I dissolved to the floor. I'd done it again, another man gone. Another love ruined.

It took me weeks to recover. I wept for days. John called a few times but I never picked up the phone.

His last message to me still rings in my ears.

"I love you, Susannah. It doesn't have to end."

But he didn't know, he hadn't lived it. Happy things always come to an end. Happy things do not last.

Suddenly I am blinded by the glare of car lights. Reporters. It's all I can think as I dash for the front door.

"Susannah."

But it isn't a reporter, it's Angel. He's come back.

I watch him march toward me across the yard and my heart is leaping and sinking all at once.

"I've made this way too easy for you," he says and I push my back against the door. "Yeah, you already know that, don't you?" He rests a foot on the step. "I walked out when you told me to. I took no for an answer, even when I knew it was the wrong answer!"

He steps too close to me, his arm above my shoulder, his hand pressed into the door.

"What are you saying, Angel you should have forced me to stay with you?" I sputter, already knowing what he means. I am stalling for time, searching for a good answer to the question I know he is about to ask me. His face is so close, his words are so tender, it's all I can do not to pull him into my arms. He stares at me in what is the longest pulling silence I have ever felt.

"What will it take for you to trust me again?"

And there it is. The unanswerable question.

"It's not that simple, Angel, it's just not!" I say this and I allow myself to push past him. My body brushes against his as I do and the feeling is all but unbearable. I sit down, willing my legs to get me all the way there.

"I think you've lived so long feeling like everything in life has to be complicated that you don't recognize when something is simple."

"I'm not an idiot, Angel, don't treat me like one," I am getting angry now. This was Angel assuming he knew more than I did, treating me like a child again.

"You're not an idiot and you're not handicapped either," he says.

"Handicapped?"

"You seem to think that because your mother abused you, you have some kind of handicap that means that you can't have a relationship!"

I'm on my feet now, my legs are miraculously steady.

"How dare you?! You don't know about my relationships! You don't know much about me at all these days, but you seem to think that because you knew me when I was 16, you know me now! Don't you get that that's part of the problem?!"

"No, I don't," he says and shakes his head, "In fact, I don't see how there is a problem."

"You've lost your mind!" I say, and turn my head toward the lake. Clearly, Mother's death has him in some sort of situational denial.

Before I can object, before I can tell him that he has blinded himself into thinking that all we have to do is say that we want it, before I can bring an ounce of sense into my head, Angel has caught me by the arm. He turns my body easily, as if I am made of paper. There is not a second's hesitation before he kisses me.

His lips press close into mine and I feel my whole body turning to clay, to porcelain, ready to shatter.

Angel's mouth is as sweet as I remember it, no, it's sweeter. It's the best thing I've ever tasted.

It is the answer to the unanswerable question.

I try to resist but only lamely so. The surrender is far too perfect to fight it. I wrap my arms around his neck, I open my mouth and take his tongue, push my entire body against him. I feel as if I am drowning. The lake has covered our heads and there is no air. We are sinking, and the sand and seaweed of the lake bed is no where to be found.

Angel has just tipped his head and pushed his tongue into my mouth again when I hear it: My cell phone.

The ringing is the slam-bang impact of reality whacking us both in the backs of our heads. I dive for my purse and answer without taking the time to check the number. I'm too rattled to think.

"Hello?"

"Susannah, are you alright?" Emmett's voice makes my face flush and I turn abruptly away from Angel and walk to the end of the porch.

"Uh, I-I… I'm fine, what's .. what's going on?" I say and I hear the creek of one of the porch chairs behind me as Angel sits down.

"I saw the news," he says, and I steady myself against the railing. I can't find words to reply. I can't think of the right question to ask. I can't think at all.

"Susannah, I think it might be… Susannah…"

My heard thumps so hard I think it will burst from my chest. Suddenly my head is working again.

"You want me to drop the case!!" I blurt, and feel my chest getting ready to hitch.

Emmett sighs. It's a long, hard sigh into the phone, and I lower myself onto the porch and lean against the wall.

"I've got a lead on an attorney who says he's willing to take over pro-bono." He says this, and it's as if I can feel my life draining down the way sand runs out of an hourglass.

"Emmett, I know that I didn't look good in front of those reporters, but this case is important to me."

My head speeds with the reasons. It is important for Hannah, and I know I can fight for her harder than some lawyer that doesn't even know her, that doesn't know what she's been through. It is important so that I don't gain a public reputation for emotional melt down and lastly, it is important so that Mother does not ruin Hannah's life the way she has ruined mine. I'd never forgive myself if someone else took over and lost the case.

"I know, Susannah but I've had a couple department heads on the phone since the news was on. They aren't happy. We could lose funding."

"You know better than anyone that I am the right person for this case. Em—this is my life. You can't take this away from me, not now."

There is a long silence.

"I've talked 'em into 24 hours for damage control. I don't know what the hell we are going to do. We don't have a job for Aunt Jenna, Franken is breathing down our necks and taking every interview he can get his slimy hands on to talk about your apparent instability, and honestly, changing lawyers, would buy us more time if nothing else!"

"I've never known you to be disloyal, Emmett." I say and I know it isn't fair.

"This isn't about loyalty!" I hear his voice rising. "It isn't even about you or me or anything but Hannah and all the future kids we wind up having to fight for!"

"That's very self-less of you, of course," I say "But it's also about covering your own ass and you know it. What will it say about you if you vouch for the crazy lady?"

Emmett lets out a snort of contempt.

"You gotta' be kidding me. No one has fought harder for you than me. Do you think this is the first time that you've done something overly emotional that I've had to answer for?" he says, and now I realize that my stumbling attempt at a news conference was not my first and only offense. It was the capper to many offenses, of which I had never let myself be aware.

I am emotional in court. I know I cross lines. I know that judges all but hate to see me on their rosters. But this work is about my heart and soul. This work is the only thing that makes me feel as if I am defending myself. This work is the emotional equivalent of hiding under the stairs and I know I don't dare come out.

"Emmett, we have 24 hours, right?" I say.

"Yap." He sounds so tired that I am awash with guilt for making his already almost impossible job even worse.

"I will think of something. I will fix it." I say.

"I hope so, 'cause if you can't—"

I cut him off. " I know, Em. I know, and I'm sorry that I put you through this."

There is another silence.

"Susannah, you know I care about you, don't you?" His voice is so tender, it brings the lump up fully in my throat.

"I care about you too, Em." My heart hurts, knowing the other conversation we will have to have.

I disconnect the phone and rest it against my forehead a moment.

"Why won't you tell me that you've been seeing him." Angel's voice says, interrupting my recovery.

An impulse shoots through my arm and forces the cell phone at Angel. It hits him in the arm and he is startled.

"I'm not going to let you scare me away with that again," he says, charging toward me, lifting me to my feet. "And I'm not going to let you become your mother every time you are angry at me. I know better. You are not her. You never will be. You never could be. She was sick, and you never accepted that. She was wrong about everything, Susannah, about you about Rob, about sex, about men, about God, about the world, everything. She was wrong, do you get it?!" he says, and I have the same feeling I get every time I watch the Wizard of Oz. It's that bizarre surreality that makes me feel slightly giddy and frightened all at the same time.

"Can we please sit down and just talk?" My head is spinning with everything I should be focusing on, but can't. He nods and we settle into the chairs, side by side on the porch.

Angel's hand reaches out and takes hold of mine.

"I have a better idea. How about we just sit here a while and we don't talk."

I rest my head on the back of the chair. The night is cool and clear and when I open my eyes I can see stars through the slats on the awning. Lake Charlevoix sweeps in and out, the rhythm at once maddening and comforting. If nothing else, it could always be counted on.

The waves never stop coming back to the shore, and the shore is always there when they do.

Half the future and half the past, they're waiting inside your eyes.
--James Taylor

Chapter 11

The sun rises over the lake and I am still rocking in the chair on Grand's porch and watching it.

It's over.

I can't believe my eyes as I watch the yellow ball rising higher and higher into the pale blue of the morning sky, the only thought in my head; it's over.

I breathe in the cool wet smell of the lake as the wind carries it past me, and I poke my nose into my coffee cup and close my eyes as I swallow and breathe deeply again. Grand's quilt around me, I feel as if there is nothing that can permeate its protective barrier. I feel almost relaxed, and so eagerly looking forward to going home. I want so much to reclaim my life, to see my clients, to wake up in my own bed with a cat standing on my swollen bladder, to walk the street in front of my apartment and stop in at Starbucks, and linger over my latte' with a good book.

It's so close now, I can taste it, I can hear the city in my head as I close my eyes tighter and imagine every last detail of my living room, right down to the little tufts of fur that Chipmunk leaves on the corners of the sofa.

My heart flutters with a pang of missing her, and then suddenly I am flush with the feeling of having been in Angel's arms last night.

He'd stayed and sat with me for hours, and just as he promised, we didn't speak. But we'd held hands the entire time, and when he left, quietly at about 3am, he kissed me on the cheek and we had smiled at each other. It certainly wasn't peace, but it wasn't war anymore either. In this moment, I find myself very willing to settle for that.

There are only a few things left to be done here. The house has been emptied of everything but the contents of my old room. It is the last task before I can leave this place and even its grim anticipation can't keep me from feeling liberated.

And I am thinking about Angel.

I sigh, and Grand comes out and sits next to me in the giant rocker. She slides her arm around me and I pull the blanket over her.

I rest my head on her shoulder and we rock in silence for a while, just staring out across the shining waves of the lake, the gulls swirling in the sky and diving at the surface for breakfast, calling to each other across the distance.

"You're still in love with him," she says.

I turn my head to the side and look her straight in the face. "What?!"

"Angel, you're still in love with him, Dear," she says, and I can't hide the truth from her.

"I don't know," I sigh, "he is Matthew's father after all, but I don't think I can feel…"

"That's your problem, it always has been," she interrupts.

"What's that?" I say, feeling the hairs on my neck bristle a bit.

"You think too much. You were always such a serious little child. I know that your mother's illness put a lot of pressure on you, Susannah. It made you grow up too fast, and I always regretted that. I always regretted that I was too afraid to take you and Robbie away from her. I wanted to, you do know that don't you? But with your Grandpa's death and all, I just didn't think I had the strength to defend myself against her. I should've, I should've done it anyway…" A tear rolls down her beautiful, soft, crepey cheek.

I dab it away with the edge of the blanket and rest my head back on her shoulder.

"Do you forgive me?" she says.

"Of course I do." I say into her neck, "You were always there when I needed you Grand. I love you, and I'm sorry for what I said at the funeral. I was just so upset with everything. And I am sorry that I let her keep me from visiting you."

"Don't be sorry. You were right. It's never easy to hear the truth, but it was the truth. I was weak. But you don't have to be."

I feel her words hit me as if they were materializing and dropping down onto my chest; heavy, like wet cloth.

"Let yourself be happy, child, the worst is over."

We rock together for a long time.

"Grand, I might get fired," I say, and she wrinkles her forehead.

"I've been thinking about that," she says. "maybe it's a good time for you to take a break. You can always come and stay with me a while."

My heart sinks. Even Grand has lost faith in me.

"Susannah, you better get in here!" Rob's voice calls suddenly through the screen door.

"What is it?" I say.

"There's a news conference."

I leap off the rocker, sending Grand into a spasm of rather choppy back and forth and dash into the house.

Grand is close behind me.

A local news reporter is standing in front of the familiar steps of the church, the scene of the previous days meltdown. My heart skips, there is a banner stretched across the doorway, it reads: ASoCA: Adult Survivors of Childhood Abuse.

As the camera pans the crowd, I begin to recognize the faces.

I know these people. My heart beats so fast I think might faint. Rob pulls me onto the sofa and I cover my face, remembering.

It had been on one of my very few trips home for the holidays, after Mother had devastated us all that year by actually setting the gifts on fire in the yard, that I had found myself so shattered, I was unable to drive home.

No matter what I did, I couldn't get my hands to stop shaking and it seemed that my concentration had been completely ruined. I had phoned Dr. Millicken hoping for some kind of nerve pill to swallow and instead he'd given me the phone number of the group leader and told me that if it did not help to call him back and we'd see about the tranquilizers.

I hated the idea, but I knew I wasn't getting home any other way. Grand had dropped me off at the church that very evening. The meeting was held in a small recreation room at the back and I had walked the hallway thinking I was about to walk into a roomful of cowed, trembling messes.

Their laughter met me about halfway there and I began thinking I'd been dropped at the wrong meeting. I rounded the corner and took in the sight of about 8 perfectly normal and strikingly happy looking people. I stood in the doorway taking it in. These people couldn't possibly have been abused like I was. They all looked too normal, too whole.

It was then that I was discovered and a tall, smiling woman with bright red hair came toward me and held out her hand.

"I'm Ginny." She said.

"Hi, I'm Susannah."

I shook her hand and as she looked into my eyes, I felt something inside me starting to give. She tipped her head to the side and then immediately dropped my hand to gather me into a hug.

I couldn't believe my own actions. I never let anyone in, never opened my doors to allow someone to see the reality of what was inside me, and in one ten second look, this woman had stepped right smack dab into the center of my pain.

She held me as I sobbed and I could hear her saying things to the others.

"I think it's her first meeting," she said and suddenly, there was a circle of people around me.

I pulled out of Ginny's arms and pushed back. The crowd was too much, my heart was racing and all in the world I wanted was to hide.

Ginny caught me by the arm and another woman put her hand on the small of my back and they lead me to a chair.

A man with small round glasses and kind eyes gave me a cup of coffee and they started the meeting without saying another word.

I sipped the coffee, feeling Ginny's arm at the back of my chair the whole time. Oddly, it felt comforting and I allowed myself to settle back and listen.

A small blonde woman with fragile features began to speak.

"I'm Crystal and I am an adult survivor of childhood abuse."

As Crystal spoke, I began thinking once again that I was in the wrong place. The way she talked about the struggles she had with feeling as if she would fail, how her father's constant criticism of her had made her believe that she was unable to accomplish anything of value. "Blah Blah blah" I kept thinking. And I kept thinking that now I understood why they all looked so normal. They were not really abused. So her father was critical, at least she had one, at least he didn't—

And it was then that Crystal changed. Her somewhat animated face screwed into a painful sob and she started talking again, saying how she'd started a new job and was on her very first day when she'd had a flash back to the first time her father had stripped off her clothes in front of his friends.

She said he always had a group of five or six men over for poker night and her mother would go out with her girlfriends, leaving the children asleep. Only, her father didn't let her sleep. He made her get up and put on her mother's make up and one of her dresses. And when the poker game was at full swing and the men were half drunk and the house had filled with cigar smoke, he called her into the den and put music on.

That first time, she hadn't understood what he wanted her to do. She was only 11. He'd gotten angry and shouted at her to dance and the men all howled and laughed and slapped each other on the backs. She could remember their faces and the feeling of poker chips pressing into her hips as her father lifted her onto the table and pulled off her panties.

I found myself suspended in her. I sobbed into my hands so hard I thought I wouldn't be able to breathe. These people did know. These people, as normal and happy as they all looked, these people were like me.

At the end of Crystal's time, Ginny and two other women stood to hug her and the woman sitting beside her kept a reassuring arm around her shoulder. Mike, the group leader spoke next.

"Crystal, you are so brave. Do you see how much strength and power you have to be able to tell that story and trust in yourself and in the safety of this group? Your father's actions were beyond abusive, but it's good that you remember that it was his illness, and not something in you that made it happen. This was not your fault in any way. You were a child. And now, you are able and capable of any success in life, and the fact that you have come here to share your experience shows just how strong you are, and just how capable you are. Crystal, thank you so much."

And I watched as Crystal's face took back its shine, and she smiled and wiped her nose and sat up straighter in her chair.

When it was my turn I wasn't sure what to say.

"Um I'm Susannah and I was abused by my mother." I said, and with those words a flood was released.

I told the story of my Christmas, and the story of my father's abandonment and Mother's constant rages. It was more than could be told in one twenty minute outburst. By the end I was sobbing and asking why it had to happen, and why I couldn't just get away from her and stay away from her.

Ginny kept her hand in the middle of my back the whole time (a gesture that would be explained to me later as their method of constant support, a gentle hand on the center of the back to keep the person grounded in the present while they explored the horrors of the past) and when I was done, she and another woman came to hug me.

"Susannah, you've been carrying this with you for so long." Mike said, "Don't you see that part of the problem is that you've had no one to talk to about it? I'll bet you and your brother don't even speak of it. That's how it usually is, no one wants to talk about it. But you're brave for coming here, Susannah and strong. You're an adult now and you don't have to allow her to hurt you any more."

It was funny, but I never believed those words. As much as it helped me to get home that year, and as often as I sent them referrals, I still didn't believe those words. How do you not allow the all-powerful to hurt you? Still, these were wonderful people and they knew just what I needed. Apparently, they knew it better than I did.

I look back to the television and I recognize the female reporter from the night before. She gives a small, sad smile and I know she is hoping for something good.

It is Ginny who steps forward toward the microphones.

"Last night Susannah Suffolk spoke to you after leaving her Mother's funeral. As you now know, she is an adult survivor of childhood abuse. Some have suggested that she should not try the Hannah Williams case as she would not be able to do so without her own issues interfering on the taxpayer's dime. We are here to add our voices to Susannah's and to tell you that a person who has experienced the kind of abuse that Hannah Williams is being defended against is uniquely qualified to try this case. Last night, you all saw a person feeling very profoundly, the death of her abuser and I can't say that it doesn't affect such a person on a day to day basis. But I can tell you from my own experience as an adult survivor, that we are strong and passionate people and that in my own life, I've had to fight for many things that I believed in. This fight may have been more fraught with emotional difficulties for me, but I did it, and I fought harder for it than most of my peers. In a few minutes, I will tell you more about my past, but right now I'd like to introduce you to Michael Becker, the group leader of the Charlevoix Chapter of ASoCA who has a few things to tell you about being an adult survivor."

My hands are shaking as Michael steps forward.

As Michael speaks I watch the faces of the reporters and I know that the damage is indeed under control. Michael rattles off statistics, he tells of the thousands of adult survivors who hold jobs of great delicacy and importance. Surgeons, airline pilots, nuclear physicists by the score are adult survivors. He tells of how important it is that we as a society recognize that it is an epidemic, and that most survivors never seek help and never work toward the eradication of the problem. He says that I am, and I have and that instead of there being a backlash against me, it should be against a society that allows this to happen, and it should be against any lawyer or organization that would stand in the way of justice being served upon any man or woman who would harm a child.

Michael is cool and calm, and so professional that I feel as if I am getting taller just watching him.

As he reaches the end of his speech, the other members of the group begin a slow gathering process. They come together behind him and he introduces them one by one. There must be twenty of them in total and each gives their name and at what age they first experienced abuse and what they do for a living now. One is a teacher, one is an investment banker, another is the owner of a chain of shopping malls, another runs a bakery. Each face is a miracle, each voice is a victory.

I feel tears welling in my eyes. It's like watching the end of a war. It's armistice day.

The news switches back to a shot of the local reporter as the group takes questions from the crowd.

"Important information here, and perhaps new light shed on what is so often a problem hidden away from public knowledge and reaction. Here's hoping for better. Phil Morton, channel 7 news, Charlevoix."

A cheer rises from the living room and I am startled. I turn to look at them all. Charlie has snatched Grand up into a hug and spun her off her feet. Matthew and Rob are high-fiving, Jenna is squealing and jumping up and down next to Marie who can't help but laugh, and each face is filled with joy. Everything inside me spills out. I am laughing and crying and I cannot find words to describe the sight of my family--my entire family--looking so happy.

As soon as we recover, and Grand and Marie are rattling pots and pans in the kitchen, I dash for my cell phone and call Emmett.

"Did you see it?!" I say, when he answers.

"Who do you think arranged it?" he says, and I am stunned.

"Oh. . . Em. . ." I don't remember ever remember feeling the cliché of being speechless before, but at this moment, I am.

"You're welcome," he says.

"Oh, Em… thank you. Thank you, so much. You are such a good friend."

"Yeah, well we're not out of trouble yet, Susannah. Aunt Amy is still unemployed and my resources on that one are drying up."

"Can't we enjoy this little victory for just a few minutes," I reply, so unwilling to give up the first feelings of real joy I've had in so long that my head hurts trying to remember when I may have ever experienced it before.

Emmett laughs softly into the phone and I join him.

"Yeah, I guess you're right. It was pretty great wasn't it?"

"You're a freaking Genius!"

Suddenly I hear telephones ringing.

"Here it comes," he says.

"You're getting pretty comfortable talking to reporters, Sir. A week ago, you'd have been hiding under your desk!"

"Let's have a drink when you get back."

My heart falls. How I do not want to hurt him.

"Sounds great." The joy is too good to ruin now.

Soon, Grand has made another epic breakfast, and we are all sitting around her big table eating. For once, I am not so absorbed by my food that I am unaware of what is going on around me.

All of a sudden, the chatter at the table goes quiet. I look from face to face and they are all smirking

"WHAT?!" I say, finally, unable to handle another second.

"I heard a noise on the porch last night and I looked out the window and, uh, caught an interesting sight," Rob says.

Matthew and Charlie crack up.

"Oh, what is this, Jr. High?!" I say, and I realize in that seeing me kiss Angel has made them all giddy.

"Look, I don't want anyone getting their hopes up, okay?" Charlie tips his head and gives me an almost menacing look. Charlie was going along with the joke, but he was still skeptical of Angel.

"We know, Mom," Matthew says, "but I still think it's funny that you guys were making out on the porch last night."

"Oh my God! It's fabulous, isn't it? I mean of course it is. I just think… well you know Angel is delicious! You know that don't you? Well of course you do. Don't you have anything to say about it? Well I suppose you said it all last night on the porch!" Jenna blurts, and I am amazed to see her actually putting a bite of pancake into her mouth.

They all laugh again and I roll my eyes. The laughter, though, it feels so good. It seems to find its way right into the pleasure center of my brain. I close my eyes and pull it in. I need all the good feeling I can get right now.

"Yes, yes… well Angel and I are talking. We're talking, okay?"

"Kinda' hard to talk with somebody's tongue in your mouth isn't it?" Rob says and they all dissolve again. This time, I join them, throwing a torn off piece of pancake at Rob, and feeling so happy I think my heart may break.

Too soon, we are in the car heading back over to the old house. There is just one more room to be emptied. Rob and Charlie come with me. The rest stay behind to help Grand clean up.

As we pull up to the house, it seems to be growing taller and higher the closer we get. My heart is thumping so hard I think it may just leap out of my chest and run across the road to safety.

Charlie puts his arm around me and walks me through the door. He starts to take me to the door of my old room and I stop him. I am braced for the devastation, for decapitated dolls and shredded bed clothes and upturned dressers and gutted closet. I am ready.

"I can do it." I tell him and he smiles at me and sits down across from Rob at the table, the last remaining item to be carried off.

I walk to the door and place my hand on the knob. It feels cool under my sweating palm and I take a deep breath and remind myself that I am strong. I am a lawyer, this door is the jury room, behind it is the courtroom, behind it sits the judge. I conjure the image of Ginny and Crystal and Michael all standing behind me.

I breathe in, and push the door open.

The shades are drawn and the room is dark. It takes my eyes a moment to adjust but when they do, it is more than I was ready for. More than I ever could imagine. I gasp aloud and Charlie and Rob are beside me in an instant.

The room is perfect. Each item is exactly as I had left it all those years ago. The ruffles of my pink bedspread are perfect, even and ironed. The curtains hang with each section meticulously arranged. My worn bunny-rabbit and monkey, my two favorites, sit pristinely on the pillows, they have been washed and restored.

On my dresser sits two bottles of dried up Sweet Honesty perfume, and a pink handled brush and two barrettes, exactly where I had always kept them.

The clothes are missing from the closet as I had taken most of them with me, stuffed into garbage bags the day I left. But there are remnants, a pair of old tennis shoes, a dress I had out-grown, a couple of t-shirts that had missed my desperate grasp. They are washed and on hangers.

My stereo is still set up, the dial still set to my favorite radio station, the antenna still slightly to the left, the only way it would come in properly.

On the bed-stand sits my white lamp, and a glass of water. I always kept a glass of water on the bed stand. I hated having to get up and walk across the cold kitchen floor. I hated the idea that I might wake Mother.

Charlie lets out a long slow whistle and Rob shakes his head and begins taking out the chairs from the kitchen. I know this has hurt him.

I lower myself onto the bed and look up at Charlie, wide-eyed. I run my hands over the edges of the bedspread, over the corners of the bed stand. I open the drawer. Inside I find my treasure box. I can't believe that I left it here all these years. I can't believe that Mother left it here all these years.

When I was 6, before all the madness had begun, I'd found an old jewelry box that mother was about to throw away. She'd said I could have it and I had begun saving my "treasures" in it. It was green and crusted with fake jewels. A metal hook held it closed.

At first, it held gum ball machine rings and cereal box prizes, shiny stones and sticks from the lake, some of which are still inside. I lift them out and hold them, the stones smooth and cool and the sticks so dried up that they would drift away on no more than a breath. I spread them on the bed and I tell Charlie where I had found them and when. He smiles and takes them into his palm and rolls them about with his fingers.

There is a ring, a small gold ring that Grand had given me when I was 8. I remember how proud I had been of it, and how heartbroken I was the day it would no longer fit me. There is a sugar packet and a matchbook, both souvenirs from dates with Angel. The sugar packet is from the prom. There is my baby spoon, one of my baby teeth, and one of Rob's. It's the one I knocked out with a sofa pillow in the living room when we were play fighting. Rob and I had laughed for hours once the bleeding had stopped and he had taken to calling me "slugger" for a few weeks. I relate this story to Charlie as well, and he laughs and watches me as I pull the last item from the box. It's odd, a plastic tip, the kind that goes onto tubes of frosting, the type that people write on cakes with. A dab of ancient blue frosting still clings to the inside.

I hold it up and show it to Charlie who frowns.

"What's that from?" he asks, twitching his nose.

"I don't know…" I hold it in my palm and stare at it. "I don't remember."

I am troubled by this. That something would be important enough to be included in my treasure box, but not important enough for me to remember seems impossible.

I hear Rob in the kitchen lifting another chair into his arms.

"Angel's out there," he calls "he's walking the edge of the lake. He's about half a mile down."

I look at Charlie who pushes my hair behind my ear while I play with the plastic tip.

"I don't know what to make of this room," I say, sitting up and looking across at my hope chest, still sitting empty in the corner. I had never come here to take anything else with me. I had never dared to ask. I had never opened the door to this room. All the times I came back from college and tried to be here for holidays, I never wanted to see this room. I stayed at Grand's at night and only came here when I had to.

"It's hard to say," he says looking around at the perfection of it, "I mean, there isn't even any dust, Susie. Either she kept it up herself or she had someone do it."

He asks me if I want him to start putting things in boxes and I say no, I would rather do it myself.

"I don't understand..." I feel a different kind of pain in my chest. It is a different kind of tears that come to me now, the kind of tears that come from having missed something. Regret fills me to the bone and I lift my monkey into my arms and hold it and cry.

"I should've done it, Charlie...I should've had her committed...she might have gotten well..." I say.

"Or she might have died sooner. She hated doctors, she hated hospitals, Suze, she would've been really bitter."

But there was something here wasn't there? Didn't this say something about her feelings for me? Or was this just another manifestation of her illness?

I watch as a tear soaks into the worn fluff of the monkey's head.

"There is no way to know, and you'll only torture yourself by wondering., Kitten." He puts the monkey back onto the pillow.

"Why don't you let Rob and I take care of this?" he says trying to usher me out of the room.

"No...she kept this. I need to do it."

I put my treasures back into their box. I take the box, the rabbit and monkey and place them on the kitchen counter. I never thought I'd want anything from this house, but these things are going home with me.

Charlie wanders off after kissing me on the head. He has gone to see about helping Rob. I drag a box into the room, my chest still aching, a lump heavy and imposing in my throat.

I load in the lamps and take down the curtains and the hangers from the closet. I take the bed-clothes off and fold them neatly and set the box aside for taping. Another box and then another, I feel robotic, lifting items from the drawers and putting them in box after box. An hour passes, and I have not felt it go by. Time seems to flow over me like waves on the lake, liquid and moving, suddenly slippery and fast and getting away from me. There is nothing worse, I think, than regret. I will have to live with my inactions forever.

The rational, thinking part of my brain knows that each situation holds its own sadness, its own miseries. But the emotional part, the part that is crushing my chest and making my teeth hurt with clenching, whispers, "should've done…should've done…" over and over again.

As the contents of the room disappear, I am more startled and baffled than ever. Charlie had been right, there was not a speck of dust anywhere, not behind the shelves, or under the bed or in the corners of the closet. It was as if she expected me to come home at any moment, as if she had been waiting for me. After all, I could see her illness and she was not so far gone that she did not know that…at least, I think so now.

When everything else has been packed, Rob and Charlie take out the dresser and the shelves and finally the bed. I sit on the floor in the empty room and open my treasure box again. The frosting tip glows at me, and I lift it out and stick it on the tip of my index finger. I wave it around and point with it, I run it over my lip and into the palm of my other hand.

The lake sounds peaceful in the distance, its usual threatening tone cowed by the relieved quiet of the old house. It's gone. The malevolent spirit of my past has departed, taped up and carried out with all the boxes, wrapped in paper and taken out bit by bit, memory by memory with all the contents. There is nothing left now but a shell, just like the one I had seen in the casket.

I close my eyes and sigh, and I can feel my shoulders release a jolt of tension. And it is now, sitting so still on this floor with my eyes closed, that I remember why I saved the treasure I hold on my finger. The memory comes to me at first in small familiar flashes. I see snow and ice, a bowl on the kitchen table, I hear the whirr of the electric mixer…

I was six years old, three years before my father left, and it had been a brutal winter. The lake had iced over early, in October, and a bitter wind had blown lake effect snow for days. There were several feet on the ground by mid December and not a lot of relief in sight. About the first week of December I had come down with a nasty cold. Not the kind that has you in bed with a fever, but the kind that just keeps a head so stuffed up it's difficult to hold it upright, the kind that lingers for three weeks and outlasts box after box of tissue.

I'd had to stay home from school for a week and I was so bored, I thought I might just start drawing murals on the living room walls just to shake up the routine.

Mother had come home from shopping and knocked the snow off her boots. I feel a shock in my chest as I can see exactly what she looked like that day. She was smiling at me, calling me Baby and knocking clumps of snow off of her brown knee high boots, the one's with the little brass buckles at the sides. She had on a heavy brown coat with tufts of white fur at the wrists and on the hood which framed her face. She was not as big as she had been when I was a teenager. She was still ample, but with bright apple cheeks and rounded shoulders and voluptuous hips. She took off the coat and her hair fell down her back, dark and wavy and she pushed it away from her face and excitedly started pulling things from the grocery bags.

"I've got a surprise for you!" she said, "It's something we can do together."

I danced around the table as she pulled item after item out of the bags. Flour, powdered sugar, eggs, butter, milk and a package of little fluted papers, and most exciting of all, three tubes of ready made, colored frosting. She pulled muffin tins from the cupboard and a mixing bowl and spatula and the mixer. She set it all on the table and then she helped me on my knees in the chair and tied an apron around me under my arm pits.

We made cupcakes. She stood with her arms on either side of me and helped me to break eggs and measure flour and milk, sugar and vanilla into a bowl. She helped me turn on the mixer and guided my hand with the spatula in between the twirling mixing tines.

The radio was on. It played "Mrs. Robinson" and we sang, "hey, hey, hey…" along with the Simon and Garfunkel, and danced about the kitchen, pouring batter into the fluted papers nestled inside the muffin tins, and then set the timer for the long 25 minute wait.

As the cupcakes were baking, we cleared away the batter mess and set up for the very best part; the decorating. It seemed an interminable wait, the baking and then the cooling, and finally it was time.

Mother had tied the apron around me again and this time she sat across from me with a cup of coffee. There was a big bowl full of fluffy white butter cream frosting, and she gave me a spatula to smooth it on with. I did all the cup cakes with this first, lingering over each one, making sure every millimeter was covered entirely with frosting.

We talked, and I remember telling her how when I grew up I was going to make cup cakes every day and feed them to my children.

When each had been covered in the butter cream, Mother snipped the ends on the tubes of frosting and showed me how the tips screwed on to each one and how each tip made a different design. I spent hours decorating, swirling and dipping and making letters and numbers and drawing pictures on each one. I used blue for the boy's cup cakes and pink for mine and Mother's and green for the extras. When I was done, Mother had arranged them on her good china tiered plate, the one she only got out at Christmas time, and that night when she presented them at dinner, Mother clapped and Rob clapped and I know my father must've clapped too if he was there.

It is a beautiful memory, every detail is sweet and happy and perfect—and it is the result of this room, of Mother's preserving it for me. I don't know that I ever would've had it otherwise.

I weep now, with joy and with grief. I have had the first happy childhood memory that I can ever as an adult, remember having. I did have a mother once. She loved me and she made cup cakes with me and she called me Baby and tried to make me happy when I was sick, and she was gone. She had been gone for years now, years and years and years, but I had not ever been able to grieve her, not until this moment.

There is relief in this weeping. There is something being released from my chest, a burning feeling that I have carried with me every day of my life that seems to be ebbing as I cry. I focus hard on each and every detail I can remember and let them intensify my aching chest. My mother is gone, she is gone and she is never, ever coming back. My Mommy is gone. I shrink back into the skin of the six year old and I cry for her, for the mother I had then, the one that wanted me to be happy.

The mother that I loved.

Charlie comes in and finds me on the floor, the frosting tip clutched to my chest, crying so hard that I cannot even tell him why. He sits with his arm around me for a while until I can find my voice again, and I tell him. I tell him about the boots and her hair and her soft hands tying the apron strings at my back and guiding the eggs in two and the bowls and the little paper flutes and the frosting. I tell him about my mother, the person she was then, and as I am speaking, a flood of other memories come to me; the way she would dance in the living room when the radio was on, the scent of her hair spray as she bent to tie my shoe laces, the coral nail polish she wore impeccably every day, the sound of her laughter echoing from the kitchen after I was in bed and she and my father were cleaning up the dinner dishes.

My God, there had been another life! She had wanted me to have it, to remember it. She remembered it, and it was her gift to me that she had preserved my room and my memory so that I could do the same.

I am stunned and shaken and filled with agony and relief, the whirring emotions fluttering in my chest and my stomach, making me feel light headed and giddy and sick all at once.

"I had a mother, Charlie." I say to him, and he wipes at his own eyes and kisses me on the top of my head.

"I know you did." he says, "I could see it in her eyes sometimes, Susannah. She'd be looking at you and this expression would come over her face, something so different from the way she always looked and I just…Well, I suppose I hoped that I was seeing how she had loved you back when she still could."

I smile at him and flood over again, filled with joy and sorrow and the bitterest grief; the best feeling I've had in days.

A little while later, Rob and I walk a slow circle around the house. There is already a buyer showing interest, and the price of lake front property at Walloon is nothing to be sneezed at. Mother will have left us something substantial.

We are awed at the spectacle; the house, empty and helpless, muted—impotent. This place of such dread and fear now nothing more than a structure of wood and brick and nails, it suddenly appears old and fragile. The realtor has already posted a sign out front, and the truck has come from the Salvation Army to take away the boxes and the beds.

Rob and Charlie help the workmen lift the dresser into the truck as a blue car pulls into the driveway. The blonde woman from the funeral gets out. My half sister, Kimberly is walking toward me across the yard.

I steel myself. What does she want? Why on earth would she come here?

"Hi," she says as she approaches, and I lower my defenses a little.

"Hi," I return and wrap my arms around myself.

"I'm sorry about yesterday," she says and her face crumbles, "I told Daddy that he should've called you first. I mean the shock on top of everything else, it had to be just terrible." She bites her lower lip, "I tried to tell him, but he wouldn't listen to me…"

"It's not your fault," I say, and then as much to myself as to her, "We don't have any control over what our parents do."

"Or don't do," she counters. She blows her very red nose into a wad of tissue.

I smile and she smiles back at me. It's a strange connectivity I feel, standing here and looking at her. Odd to be seeing someone who looks like my brother, who looks vaguely like my son.

"Did you know that I'm an only child?" she says and I laugh aloud at the irony.

"I mean, I don't have any full brothers or sisters," she says, blushing.

"No, I didn't know anything about you at all until yesterday."

I see her eyes well up.

"Daddy talked about you all the time." I motion toward the lake, and we walk together.

"He used to talk about how you had little natural curls on the back of your head when you were only 3 months old and how you were talking at only 6 months and how, when you were 2, you'd tried to drive the car and nearly run it into the lake by taking it out of park." She laughs nervously.

"Wow." I laugh too.

"He'd say, 'your sister used to sit just like that' or 'your brother used to run that way'," she says, "and I always wondered why I wasn't allowed to be with you and my brother. I wondered what was wrong with me."

Her hands are trembling as she gestures.

"Why did I have to grow up alone?" She shrugs, and clasps the shaking hands together and forces them down. We stop walking and she looks at me.

"I know that what our father did was terrible. I mean, I know it now. I never knew when I was a kid, I had no idea…" she looks away from me and at the dirt, bearing the shame of our father's cowardice, the shame of having been the one that he raised instead of the one he abandoned. This was a scene I had never imagined in all my hoping for my My Father the Prince to come rescue me.

"Go ahead," I say, and I even reach out and squeeze her shaking arm a little.

"I'd really like to know you," she says, "and Robert if I could."

I don't know what to say for a moment. I only just discovered her yesterday in a haze of emotion so daunting that I had all but forgotten her until the moment she stepped out of the car. Seeing my father had been so overwhelming, she was kind of like the last cinder after a fire storm, part of the action but not the thing that keeps you riveted to the scene.

"I don't want to hurt your feelings," I say after finding my voice again, "but I need a little time to …get used to the idea of you."

She hangs her head and I reach for her arm again.

"Just a little time," I say, "and then I would like to know you too."

She looks at me and smiles.

"Could I hug you?" I feel a need from her so desperate that I hear myself saying yes.

Her arms come around me and I feel the strange familiarity of genetics as I hug her back tightly, and in this moment I realize that she too has been a victim of the war of the Suffolks.

I give her my phone number and she gives me hers and she leaves me, wiping tears from her high cheek bones and laughing and smiling and waving from the little blue car as she drives away.

I stand under the shade of a tree, feeling the wind on my face and waving goodbye to "my sister." How very, very strange. I say the phrase over and over in my head, "my sister", "my sister"….my sister.

Rob wanders over. He puts his arm around me.

"Guess we've got a baby sister, eh?" We both shake our heads in wonder and laugh.

"Did you talk to our father at the funeral after I left?"

"Nah, he left right after you. I mean, he shook my hand and stuff in the reception line but I didn't know who he was." Rob says, and I see a crease of pain run across his face.

"Are you going to get in touch with him?" I say, half hoping he says yes, and half hoping he doesn't.

"I dunno." Rob squeezes me. His eyes are distant, and I know exactly what he is thinking. How would he even begin to forgive that man?

"I love you, Lumpy," I say to him.

"I love you too, Stinky," he says and we laugh.

Soon we are standing very still as if we are both waiting for something else to happen. It seems completely inconceivable that it's really all over now. The sun casts itself through the windows of the house and it becomes an image I will never forget. It glows like a freshly washed face.

Matthew and Marie pull up into the driveway and they get out for good-byes.

"Hey, Mom," he says "can I talk to you a sec?"

We walk together to the side of the house and my heart flutters as the sun hits his hair and the wind gives it a tousle. He is so handsome, so grown up.

"Are you gonna' be okay?" he asks, and my chest sinks. I've been so selfish the last few days, my thoughts have been so internal. He must be worried sick.

"I'm going to be fine, Matthew!" I say and I take hold of his hand.

"Mom, you're really not." He says this, and I step back just as quickly. "You're not okay, Mom. I mean, now that I've seen all this—", he pauses and drops his head, searching for words. My heart hurts. What I have put him through this weekend.

" Grandmother was really really sick. And you, your reaction all weekend--Mom, you're not okay."

"But it's over now," I say to him, and hear how small my voice sounds.

"You know better than that," he says.

Suddenly, I realize that my very own son is giving me "the you need therapy talk". I am unable to do anything but stare at him dumbly.

"You know you need help. You know you do."

I still can't speak.

"Look, I'm not going to push it okay, but I just want you to know that. . . well, that I know. And I am asking you to get help."

He hugs me tight and I feel tears pouring down my cheeks. How in the world can this be my child? How could he have developed such insight so very young.

I haven't recovered entirely when he pulls back and speaks again.

"One other thing," he says and I brace myself.

"Are you still in love with Dad?"

Suddenly, it's as if the lake has swallowed the atmosphere, I can't draw a breath.

I stare at him again. I feel like a complete idiot. I have no idea what to say.

"Mom?" he says and tips his head to the side. His eyes are impossible to fight.

I can't help but laugh.

"You don't have to say anything, and don't worry, I won't tell him," he says, but he is smiling so brilliantly that I can't help but think of how happy he'd be if only—and I can't allow myself to finish the thought.

Soon Marie wanders over and hugs me and they head back to college, young and happy and secure in themselves, and I feel abject pride welling in my chest as they drive off. What a nice young man, what a beautiful, kind young lady…what beautiful grand children they would make! I laugh aloud and shake the thought from my head. I am still too young for that, but somehow the promise of it seems so hopeful. It calls to the future, Matthew's future and it is therefore happy and bright, I think, and it might even include me.

I am still waving at Matthew and smiling when Angel comes into view. He is walking in the edge of the water of the lake, slowly making his way along. He doesn't see me as I watch him, the sun glinting off his hair, the wind pressing his shirt to his chest.

He catches sight of me then and waves. I wave back and I can't stop myself from smiling at him. He is about a quarter of a city block away, but I can still make out the dimple in his cheek.

Rob calls me to say goodbye to Karen, having stopped by on her way from the motel, and I hug her and tell her how nice it was to meet her and watch as he kisses her and she gets into her car and pulls away. Just a little while, just a few hours and I will be getting into my own car and driving home.

"Susannah!!" Angel calls to me, and I turn to see him just beneath the oak tree.

I walk across the grass to where he is and my heart stops.

Squatted down, toad-like in the water, just at the shallow place beneath the shelter of the guardian oak, he looks up at me, a glowing boyish expression in his face, deepening into the creases at the corners of his eyes. He holds up his hand and shows me my beach glass, still in its mount, glinting in the sun amidst the gritty sandy debris in his palm ….

. . . you compare what you see to the pictures.
It's like filling in some big crossword puzzle.
—*Jim Daniels*

Chapter 12

Back at Grand's place, I am putting my things into my car and feeling so excited and so exhausted at the same time that I'm not sure I'll actually be able to make the drive. Jenna's exit had been tearful and full of wailing only moments before with promises to call and write 'every single day, don't you think?' and all of us hugging her tight. I can still smell some kind of coconut scent on my shoulder from where she'd wept for a full five minutes.

Rob carries my suitcase out and shuts the trunk and soon we are standing, all three of us in the yard, just me, Rob and Grand, the original three soldiers of this battle. We stare at each other in silence. Lollie snorts and rolls over on the porch and we all three take a step toward each other.

This time we are crying because it's over. I don't think any of us ever thought we'd see this day. We rest our heads together, a triangulated prayer, relieved, liberated, and so sad that we are leaving each other.

"I'll be back in two weeks!" I tell Grand and she beams and wipes her cheeks.

"I'm comin' up next weekend with Karen," Rob says, and we are stunned into a momentary silence.

"I love you kids," Grand says, and Rob and I both giggle like kids.

We give each other one last lingering smile and then Rob and I get into our cars and start the trip home.

I watch Grand in the rearview, waving and blowing kisses and trying not to dab her eyes. I have the thought, not for the first time that soon I will need to talk her into leaving that house so far away from me and moving closer so that I can take care of her when she needs it. It is my turn to take care of her, and I will not let that responsibility fall out of my hands. I hate regret, I've felt so much of it this weekend and I never want to feel it this way again.

Just as the road begins to stretch into yawning straights of pine trees and multicolored leaves my cell phone rings.

It's Emmett. God, the last few hours have been so full of good things that I had actually let Hannah slip my mind. Our time had now dried up, and there was still no job for Aunt Amy, which meant that our battle in court tomorrow was anything but an ensured victory.

"Good evening, Sunshine." Emmet says and I suddenly think I'm speaking to someone else.

"Feeling optimistic, are we?" I say, and can't help but laugh.

"Very. How are you doing?" he asks, with way too much tenderness in his voice and I feel sick.

"I'm doing much better, Em, thanks," I leave everything else to hang in the air.

"The ASoCA chapter called. They got over a hundred calls of people inquiring about meetings after their news conference," he says. I can feel him smiling.

"Oh my God, that is fantastic!"

"Sometimes everything actually works!" he says and now I am completely baffled as to his total optimism.

"Any ideas on how we approach things tomorrow in court?" I ask, and there is a long silence.

"What do you mean?" he says, sounding as if I am being absurd.

"Well, I mean we have to have an angle, a prospect, something that makes it look good for Amy."

"I think that should all be covered, don't you? I mean what else do we need?"

"Emmett, are you forgetting? Aunt Amy is jobless!" I say, getting frustrated, feeling as if he is playing with me.

Suddenly, Emmett laughs. As I listen, I think how infrequent it is that I actually hear him laugh.

"You don't know, do you?" he says.

"For God's sake, Emmett, what?" I say, going from slightly lost to almost angry.

"Oh My God." Emmett says, "He's going after you, isn't he?"

"What?! EMMETT!" I shout.

"Aunt Amy has been hired as a receptionist," he says.

"Oh my God that's fantastic!" I feel my heart do something like a dance, "Where?"

"Manotti Construction. Apparently their field office at Woodward and 11 Mile Road was in great need of more help."

My chest goes cold. Angel has once again swept in and made everything right. I can't even think now. My heart is swelling up and cutting off the oxygen to my head.

"He's going after you." Emmett says.

"He helped us both," I say, and nearly hit a construction cone on the freeway.

"I suppose." Emmett replies, and in the long silence that follows, I realize that I will not have to have a conversation with Emmett about his feelings for me. Angel has inadvertently taken care of that as well.

"Guess I'll see you in court tomorrow, then." Emmett says and my heart aches, hearing all the joy seeped out of his voice.

"Emmett, we've saved Hannah." I say. "We're giving her a chance at a happy life."

"Yeah," he sighs, "a happy life."

The phone disconnects and I am not sure if my cell has dropped the call or if Emmett has hung up.

I'm not sure it matters then as the road stretches out, slowly but surely taking me home.

Not knowing when the dawn will come, I open every door.
　　　　　　　　　　　　　　　　--Emily Dickinson

Epilogue

This chair is never comfortable. I think this to myself as I shift in it again, and try to arrange my legs into some semblance of a good position.

He looks at me over the tops of his glasses and smiles.

"How is the packing going?" he asks, and flips up the sheet on his note pad.

"Slow." I rearrange my legs again.

I let my eyes wander to the window where spring is melting away the ice and snow of a Michigan winter. A sparrow sits on a wire just outside. It swings a bit with the wind and puffs out it's feathers against the chill. The sun brings out its colors, as it turns a sleek beige beak inward and tucks it under a velvety brown wing.

"How have the dreams been?" he asks, as I knew he would.

"I'm still having them. Last night I dreamed of my fourth birthday. My father was there, and Mother and Rob, and Kimberly was there too, only she was little like me, exactly my age."

"Have you spoken to her lately?"

"A couple of days ago. We talked for about an hour, I think." I feel myself smiling and I put my hand over my mouth.

"You don't have to do that." He shakes his head.

Sometimes I wish he had to wear a blindfold and just listen to me talk.

"Yes, I do." I look at my hands and fiddle with my beach glass.

"You're enjoying getting to know her, Susannah, that's a good thing." he says, and tries to get me to let him look into my eyes. I take them away from him and give them back to the sparrow. I still have not gotten used to the notion of happiness, of good things happening to me, of the possibility of more good things to come.

"It won't always be easy for the two of you, you'll have conflicts," he says and this makes me feel somewhat more comfortable, "Sisters always do."

And with the last phrase I am squirming in this horrible chair again.

"What did you do after you hung up the phone?" he asks me, his voice soft and intimate, this is one of the tough questions.

"You mean did I get upset and eat something?" I say, cutting to the chase.
He looks at me, waiting for me to answer my own question. I stare at my hands a moment, and suddenly I am in confession.

"Susannah, it's okay to talk about it, this is a safe place." he says, and I want him to say it again. There have been so few truly safe places in my life.

"A safe place…?" I ask, and he understands that I do need to hear it again.

"Yes, this is a safe place, Susannah. You are safe here. I'm not going to judge you or scold you. I'm here to help. I'm one of the good guys, remember?" I look up at him and watch him smile. I like his smile, it comforts me.

"I…ah…mmmm, it was cookies."

"How many cookies?" His voice is softer still.

"A lot of cookies…" I say, "I honestly don't know, I lost count after four."

"You lost count or you stopped counting because you didn't want to know?" he says, and I swear there is no padding whatsoever in this chair.

"I'm not sure."

"Ok, that's fair. Why didn't you call me instead?"

"That's not an easy thing to do." I rearrange my legs again.

"What makes it so hard?"

"…asking.." I say, and feel the lake welling up in my throat.

"It's hard to ask for help." he says. I pull tissues angrily from a box beside me on the table. I hate it when I sit here and cry, it's just such a perfect stereotypical picture.

"Susannah, do you know why it's hard for you to ask for help?"

I do know. I know it because it has been with me since I was old enough to understand it. I can't ask for help because when I needed help so desperately and completely that it was consuming my entire existence, when I was too young and too small to know how to help myself, or to be able to do it even if I knew how—there was no help for me. Not from teachers who saw bruises and did nothing, not from my absent father, not from the neighbors who heard the dishes breaking and saw my brother and I fleeing for our lives, not from the police, not from God. There was to be no help for me, and looking back on it, it was somehow easier to never have asked for it.

"No one helped us." I hold the tissue over my face and sob into it. I can feel him watching me. I wish he would say something. I wish he would hug me. I begin to feel some kind of pressure letting off my chest.

Suddenly, I can sense that he is closer to me and I take the tissue away and look at him, squinting away tears as I see that he has moved his chair to within a foot of mine.

"Susannah, I am here to help you. I want to, and I consider it an honor and a sacred trust that you would allow me to do it." He says the words and I am amazed that I believe him.

"Will you call me next time and let me help you to talk about how you feel instead of hurting yourself. I know it hurts you when the food gets out of control, and I don't want you to be hurt."

I look into his face and I believe him, I truly do. I tell him that I will call him next time, he makes me promise and I do.

He gives me a moment to recover.

"What's left of the packing?" he asks me, knowing I have been procrastinating about my weekend.

"Oh, just my clothes.. and my toiletries... and, basically, everything."

"Why do you think you're waiting 'til the last minute?"

"I don't know." I say, leafing through the files in my head for an answer that sounds like it might be the right one.

"It just makes me feel...better..."

"Better how?" he asks, and I want to throw something at him.

"Safer."

"From what?"

"What?"

"Well, people don't usually need to feel safe unless they perceive some kind of danger. What is the danger?" he asks, sounding patient and softening his voice.

"Everything is the danger. This life is the danger." I say feeling myself start to panic, "What if it all falls apart again? What if ...what if I lose it again, Sam, then what?"

"Then you will find a way to survive, Susannah, just like you did the first time, just like you always have."

He plays absently with a bright yellow highlighter, turning it over in his fingers, flipping it and pressing the end into his knee and flipping it again to do the same at the other end.

"Tell me" he says, "do you believe that people can be happy?"

I think of Matthew.

"Yes." I say, a little quicker than I would've liked. This room seems always to be filled with truth serum, his eyes filled with some sort of hypnotic rays.

"Then you have to believe that you can be happy too. You are no different than any other person walking around on the planet. You have the same capacity for happiness as anyone else. It's in you, you just have to find it."

I like this prognosis and I smile again and put my hand over my mouth again.

"You don't have to do that," he says, and he laughs aloud with me.

A moment passes quietly between us and then he asks me about Mother.

"You were telling me last time about what it was like when you were 15." he says, "Why don't you tell me more about that."

I take a deep breath and I start talking again, about Mother and Walloon and Rob, and the life that is to become my past. I rub my beach glass hard with my thumb as I talk. I twist the chain around my fingers and even rest the smooth glass against my cheek from time to time.

Half an hour later I am driving along, anticipating the door of my apartment. When I finally get there, I open the door and Chipmunk presses herself against my legs, purring madly, and I lift her and kiss her on her fuzzy nose. I sit on the sofa and kick my shoes across the room.

Charlie emerges suddenly from my bedroom startling the daylights out of me, "How was Sam today?" he says, smiling his "gotcha" smile and putting his hands on his hips.

"Wonderful and maddening all at the same time---WHAT are you doing here?"

"A certain Miss Someone is supposed to be going away for the weekend and I came by to make sure that a certain Miss Someone packed properly. Imagine my surprise to discover that Miss Someone has not packed at ALL!"

I laugh and he disappears and returns carrying a suitcase into the living room and sets it atop the coffee table.

"Don't put it here!" I say, whining, feeling uprooted and scared.

Charlie sets the suitcase on the floor and grabs me by the hand. He pulls me to my feet.

"It's just a weekend, just a date. You are going to go and see how it is. You'll never forgive yourself if you don't." He rests his forehead against mine. "Besides, it might just be fun—remember fun??!"

He whacks me on the bottom and I give him my best offended glare.

"Hey, a weekend away with a handsome, sexy man! How can this be bad??" he says.

"Wellllll—" I start and he interrupts me by pushing me toward the bathroom.

"Now, get your little fanny into the shower and start makin' pretty! I am going to pack your good undies and your jeans and that great red dress, and then you are going to put your make up on and your perkiest bra and you are going to end this latest round of celibacy!! –oh and I brought you some condoms.."

"Charlie!!" I say, and can't help but laugh.

"SCOOT!"

Two hours later, I am packed and smelling like vanilla body wash. I have perfected my hair and make up under Charlie's unflinching supervision and he has left me alone only scant minutes before there is a knock on my apartment door.

I open it and there he is, Angel holding a single perfect rose and smiling at me with the same joy as he did the last time I saw him, looking up at me, his palm full of sand and water, having recovered the greatest treasure of my life.

It is at this moment that I have a sudden realization;

I was 41 when I fell in love again on the soft leafy bank of Walloon Lake.

-- The End --

Cheri L. R. Taylor
Biographical Notes:

Cheri L. R. Taylor holds a Masters of Fine Arts in Writing from Vermont College and is currently a writing instructor at Macomb College in Warren, Michigan. She has facilitated writing workshops with the Arts in the Spirit Program at Oakwood Hospital and as a Writer in Residence with the Inside Out Literary Arts Project conducting writing workshops in the Detroit Public Schools. She has four chapbooks of poetry and has been published in *Ellipsis, Awakenings Review, The Café Review, Reintigration Today, Clean Sheets, Current Magazine, Rattle, Third Wednesday, Strange Michigan, Jezebel, Love Notes, An Antholgy* and others. Her book, *Wolf Maiden Moon, A Tale in Thirteen Poems,* was released from Pudding House Press in 2010.

Cheri is the recipient of a 2007 RARE Foundation Everyday Heroes Award for her work in dedication to the healing potential of expressive writing community settings and was awarded a 2009 Ragdale Foundation Artist's Residency.

Director of Blushing Sky Writers, an organization dedicated to all things creative, she established the Projection of Soul Poetry Workshop Program for Boysville in Clinton Twp. Michigan and was the founder and Director of the Blushing Sky Poetry Performance Troupe.

Cheri has presented writing and/or performance workshops for The Washtenaw County Intermediate School District, University of Detroit Mercy College, The Vermont College Masters of Fine Arts in Writing program, Young Chicago Authors, The Neighborhood Writing Alliance, The Detroit Public Library, and many others.

Cheri also works as a writing coach, editor, and technical and copy writer. You can contact her at Cheri@blushingskywrite.com